Introducing a crusty old codger with a twisted sense of humour, as displayed in the twenty-odd books written by him: some for children; also hysterically historical tales, others spooky, a few of them gruesome, but usually offbeat. He is a fit eighty-three-year-old with a beautiful wife, four adult children, twelve grandchildren and three great grandchildren. He loves sport and has played cricket, rugby, tennis, hockey, football, squash, golf, table tennis, is keen on fishing and did car-rallying for many years. But now he's getting too stiff to tie his shoelaces and finds pleasure in pounding the story-telling keyboard.

Orca's Revenge

Lance Cerff

Orca's Revenge

Vanguard Press

VANGUARD PAPERBACK

© Copyright 2023
Lance Cerff

A CIP catalogue record for this title is
available from the British Library.

ISBN 978 1 83794 034 9

*Vanguard Press is an imprint of
Pegasus Elliot Mackenzie Publishers Ltd.*
www.pegasuspublishers.com

First Published in 2023

**Vanguard Press
Sheraton House Castle Park
Cambridge England**

Printed & Bound in Great Britain

My grateful thanks to my beautiful wife, Peta-Ann, or Pet to those who know and love her, who puts up with my tantrums when my limited computer skills let me down. She patiently puts up with my grumpiness while editing my manuscripts and giving me straight advice when I need it most. She's my special angel.

Acknowledgements

Thank you to my wife, Peta-Ann, or Pet to those who know and love her, and who puts up with my tantrums when my limited computer knowledge lets me down and patiently edits my manuscripts. Thank you to my daughter, Bronwen, who owns a computer shop and freely gives her technical advice and repairs to my machinery when I do strange things to it. My son-in-law, Mike, has spent many hours trying to sort out the computer tangles I get myself into, mostly successfully; And now my daughter, Megan Markotter, has taken over the tedious business of getting my numerous manuscripts published, bless her. This is proving to be the hardest challenge of all, but she is one determined lady. And some thanks to the rest of my family and friends who reluctantly read my literary efforts in case they may have to get involved. But I still love you all.

Chapter One

Jason Malvy stood nursing a beer at the bar counter of Sandy's Pub and Dance in San Diego. He was anything but happy. He was bored stiff. If this was the civilian life he was returning to after a five-year stretch with the Navy SEALs, he'd forgotten how dull it could get. They didn't stand about much in the SEALs. Anybody seen resting or goofing off by an officer was usually sent away to do a dirty job to keep him busy and out of mischief.

There were times when they took a break, of course, but that was normally because it was badly needed. And if there was any free time, there was poker or bridge or some other game, instead of regurgitating the same old trash that everyone had heard a hundred times before. They also discussed or argued about warfare and future careers and various sports.

Of course, the subject of women was a huge topic of conversation, but most of them had a regular girlfriend or wife at home and nobody was allowed to be loose-mouthed about their special girl. There were also a few far-fetched stories doing the rounds. The only difference was that more bullshit was added to spice up the story every time it was retold. Come to think of it, there was not a lot of difference in the crap they were dishing up today.

Jason stifled a yawn out of sheer boredom. This was not really his scene. Danny Foulkes, the guy he'd given a lift home to, was his buddy mainly because they came from the same area. They were very different in nature, which was why they hadn't really become mates during their time spent training together.

Other than boozing and women and diving, more or less in that order, Danny had no real aim in life. Now he had snapped out of his travelling daze and wanted to introduce his driver to his barfly buddies as soon as they hit the main drag, and Jason nudged him awake.

'It's like a club inside the bar. The same crowd gathers there regularly. Newcomers get to know the rest of the crowd, and sometimes we have outings together, or the occasional barbecue or house party. We've become good mates, and there are always plenty of girls who hang around the men.'

He turned towards Jason and said: 'They're not all that sexy, but they make up for it by giving it to us when we want it.' He grinned at his thoughts. 'In fact, we've become such good mates that we share them out with the less attractive guys, whether the girls like it or not. And one of them squeals like a dolphin when any guy really works her up to a pitch.'

Jason had been happy to go along with Danny, having lost contact with his own circle of friends, but now he was sorry that he'd agreed to come. What a bunch of pricks they were. All they could talk about was drinking large quantities of booze and what girls they had slept with lately.

If I had to match this group of punks with the men at the base, they'd be eaten for breakfast, he thought to himself. He took another sip of his already warm beer. The heat of the afternoon was already melting the place away. His stiff shirt collar was scratching away at his neck, making him more uncomfortable than ever.

Jason couldn't wait to get into a pair of shorts and a casual shirt. He had worn his uniform to keep it neat for the next time that he needed it, but now he was paying for his conservative approach.

The bartender was a friendly sort. Jason and he had discussed the merits and disadvantages of picking up girls in a bar. Now he gave a little nod and a jerk of the head as he wiped the countertop. Jason looked over his shoulder to see a really cute girl heading in his direction. Already standing on the outside of his group, he made room for the new arrival, sending her a clear message that there was a place for one more, right at the spot where he was positioned.

She took the hint and came up to the elbow room he had made for her. Jason had learned that he who hesitates misses out.

He nodded to the young woman with a welcoming smile. 'The name's Jason — Jason Malvy. I hope your name's as pretty as you are. Could I get you something to drink?'

Her smile seemed to lighten up the room. She offered her slim hand, and he took it carefully in his large grasp. He wasn't all that tall, but tall enough. Even then, he had a build like a pocket Hercules that usually impressed the fair sex, and he'd learned not to be a finger crusher when being introduced to attractive and dainty women, especially when they had delicate fingers like this one.

'I'm Tilly Markchester, and a cold beer would go down well, thank you.'

His companions were engrossed in an involved tale about a camping trip they'd been on recently. It was a raucous story that they all wanted to add their piece to, about how one of them had staggered out of his tent in the middle of the night to throw up and have a pee.

In the dark, he had forgotten that they were camped not far from the edge of a cliff and had grabbed at a bush at the last moment, before sliding into what seemed to be a bottomless pit. His drunken friends had woken up to his screams as he clung on to the bush in abject fear. His rescue had become the one major event in the group's current, and even recent, past activities.

Jason's meeting up with Tilly was barely noticed by the barflies. Seeing this, he quietly suggested that they sit at a table, because they could hardly hear themselves speak above the racket that the group was making.

'That's a good idea,' agreed Tilly. 'Your friends are certainly a noisy bunch, aren't they?'

He laughed. 'You're so right, but don't blame them on me. They are Danny's pals, and I've only just met them myself. But I'm really glad that he dragged me along to this important conference,' — he waved his hand in the direction of the noise — 'otherwise I would never have been lucky enough to have met you.'

The young diver glanced at her fingers while he was talking. She was wearing no rings, which made him feel even happier.

'That's really a sweet thing for you to say. If you must know, you've also turned my blue day into a blossom day. It's been truly grim until now. So please give my thanks to your loud-mouthed friends, but only after I've left.'

Suddenly, a morbid afternoon of time wasting had developed into this special meeting up with Tilly. She had a sweet-sounding voice that sent delicious tremors up his back. Jason was quietly thankful that the anticipated drag of wasting an afternoon with a bunch of losers had ended up in time spent with a pretty girl who had brains to match her good looks.

They had so much to discuss that the time flew. The only negative factor was the heat that seemed to build up as the day wore on. But neither of them seemed to want to bring an end to their first meeting. The couple ordered hotdogs with wedges and more cold beer, but the food and drink only served to build up the heat inside their bodies.

'Have I forgotten how hot it can get in San Diego?' Jason complained.

'You're right, and today has turned out to be a real peach,' she agreed. 'I'd love to splash along a quiet little beach at the water's edge right now,' she added, a wistful look on her heart-shaped face.

Jason grinned at her. 'That's the best idea I've heard all day! Why don't we get out of this place and do it?'

She shook her head sadly. 'I'd really love to, but there's only one problem,' she sighed. 'I haven't got my swimsuit with me.'

Jason raised an eyebrow. 'That shouldn't be a great problem in San Diego. Without my trying to be too personal, you have a perfectly trim figure, and you could use a pair of my gym shorts and keep your bra on. Then you could dive into the surf if you got the urge, and get wet all over.'

She looked at him with some doubt, and then her face cleared. ' All right, as long as you don't get the idea that I'm quite happy to jump into any pair of shorts belonging to a good-looking guy!'

He smiled cheekily. 'Actually, I'm quite fussy about what kind of girl I invite into my shorts — on the beach or anywhere else. In your case, I have no problem, because you'd look cuter in them than I ever would.' He finished his beer and stood up, holding out his hand. 'Come with me to my car, and I'll give you the shorts. But first let me speak to Danny, the guy I gave a lift to, and get him to collect his duffle bag from my car. I'm sure one of his mates will give him a lift home. They all live around here, somewhere.'

***

There was a thick mist rolling in when the three young people approached Jason's car in the bar's parking lot. Danny didn't mind being dumped by Jason. He gave an approving nod and wink to his friend behind Tilly's back, particularly after he'd had an appreciative eyeful of her.

After Jason had unpacked his bag and handed his shorts over to the young woman, both men paid attention to her hips swinging as she walked away to the female restrooms, and there was silence for a while as they watched poetry in motion.

Then Danny wistfully broke the silence. 'That's quite a number you've got there, mate. We've been here for only a couple of hours. How did you latch onto her?'

Jason grinned. 'By keeping my eyes open while you lot were bragging about going camping and nearly falling off a cliff. Never switch off the scanner, my friend, no matter how interesting the story that's being told.'

They parted company as Tilly returned to the car, wearing Jason's shorts. He had to admit that they looked better on her than when he was wearing them. She grinned happily when he told her his thoughts.

'I suppose you'll say something like that when I take off my top on the beach,' she laughed.

'Well, with this thick fog rolling in, the beachgoers may not even notice that you're not wearing a bikini top,' he teased.

'Come on,' she grinned. 'My boobs are not that small.'

'No,' he agreed. 'I think you have a perfect figure.'

She laughed and gently cuffed him on the shoulder, but she was pleased with the compliment. Jason was a performer at heart. He grabbed his shoulder as if in pain, then pinned her hands behind her back while making bodily contact with Tilly.

She lifted her face to him. 'Right, now you've got me. I'm yours for the rest of the day,' she said, as she wriggled out of his grasp and pushed him against the car, before letting him go.

'Then get in the car and take me to your lido,' Jason growled, doing a fair imitation of a dangerous gangster in a 1930's movie.

Tilly directed Jason to her favourite secluded beach, where they parked the car before stripping off. This gave Tilly an opportunity to study his muscular build, with his well-developed pectorals, large biceps and his well-ridged six-pack. It all met with her silent approval, but her little smile told it all.

Jason found a beach towel for his new friend and was agile enough to take off his clothes, fold them neatly and put on his swimming trunks while

Tilly held a towel for him, after promising not to peer over the top of it. He did let out a yelp when Tilly playfully let the towel slip.

Taking his car keys with him and tucking them into his bather pocket, after they put their discarded clothing in the trunk, Jason dashed down to the water's edge with Tilly, clutching her hand on the way. They dropped their towels onto the sand before they dashed into the water and felt the delicious relief of the wavelets cooling off their parched bodies.

What neither of them had bargained on was that Tilly's lacy bra did little to hide her dusky-pink aureoles and nipples as it became soaked by the waves. Added to that was the tendency of Jason's shorts to slide down her thighs, being much too large for her hips to keep them up.

Finally they slid down to her knees when she was buffeted by a larger wave, and she grabbed at them too late. Jason got an appreciative eyeful before Tilly pulled them up.

'I give up,' she gasped with embarrassment. 'I'm showing far too much flesh for a first date.'

In answer, Jason spun her around and took her in his arms as they were buffeted in the breakers, pressing against her and kissing her thoroughly while she tried unsuccessfully to cling desperately to her shorts that were busily sliding down to her knees again. But now she gave up all efforts at modesty and let them go, while she returned his kiss with the passion she was feeling right then.

'Don't worry about showing too much flesh,' he whispered in her ear. 'All of you is beautiful.' He pressed against Tilly. 'Can you feel my body agreeing with me?' he whispered.

Arm in arm, they dashed ashore after Tilly rescued her shorts once more, and spread their towels on the sand, before falling down on them with their arms wrapped about each other. There was nobody else on the beach. The heavy fog had driven everybody away. Jason wanted her so badly it actually hurt. He rolled the girl gently onto her back and bent over her, kissing her deeply while he tugged at her loose shorts.

'I want you too,' she gasped, shivering with desire as he pressed his rigid body against her. 'But you must please use a rubber. I'm too young to fall pregnant when any sailor boy takes a liking to me.'

He rolled off her. 'You're right. Wait for me, just as you are. I've got one in the car. I'll go and fetch it now.'

Jason kissed Tilly one more time and then dashed off after checking that his keys were still safely in his bather pocket. He was hungry for sex with this lovely young woman. He could almost feel himself slipping inside the soft warmth of her beautiful body.

It wasn't only the fear of falling pregnant that made the young woman ask Jason to use a condom. He had told her that he had been in the Navy SEALs for some time. Tilly didn't want to make an issue out of her reticence to have unprotected sex with him, but she didn't know where he'd been, or what he'd done, during his time in the service. She was not prepared to take an unreasonable risk of picking up something from this stranger, no matter how badly she wanted him.

Jason wasn't going to even think about quibbling over using protection. Going flat out, he charged up to where the car was parked, unlocked the door and found the condom he was looking for, in the glove compartment. Closing up and locking the car again, he turned and sprinted down to the shoreline.

The fog was thicker than he had imagined it to be. He couldn't see where Tilly was lying. Jason ran down to where the waves were lapping at the shore and searched for her, but she was nowhere to be seen. Then he came upon their things, spread in disarray. Tilly's towel had been dragged to the water's edge and was half floating in the ripples. There were large red stains on it.

Jason was suddenly frantic with worry. He shouted out her name but heard nothing — or was there some splashing out there? It had to be his imagination. He called again, screaming out her name, with a sob in his throat. Was there more splashing, or was it only wave action?

He stopped calling and listened for any sort of response, but he could hear nothing but the slap of the water against the shore. He began dashing in and out of the surf, calling out her name desperately, but he could get no reply to his frantic shouts. Lovely Tilly had simply disappeared from sight.

Finally, exhausted, he returned to where the towel was half floating in the wavelets and yanked it out of the water. He returned to where his own towel was spread out. He picked it up along with Tilly's bra and blouse, shook out the sand and made for his car and his mobile phone, carrying his belongings.

He needed help, badly. After using the phone to ring the emergency numbers listed in the index, he towelled the sand off himself and dressed in some clothes out of his pack, while anxiously waiting for help to turn up.

It seemed to take an age for the emergency services to arrive, although they were probably as prompt as could be expected. By then, Jason was mad with worry and self-recriminations of all kinds.

He phoned Danny Foulkes' listed number, but his friend didn't pick up his phone. Was he still busy at the bar? Probably too plastered to even hear it ring, by now. Jason could have been there with them right at that moment, if Fate had turned the other cheek.

Tilly's purse could provide a useful lead. He opened it and looked through it, but there were no contact numbers or addresses that could prove useful. There was only a piece of paper with "Angie" scribbled on it, with an address and a phone number. Jason rang it but it was engaged. He recorded the details, just in case.

He contemplated contacting his parents or his own circle of friends, but he'd made no plans with them. In fact, his parents weren't even sure when he would put in an appearance. He had deliberately kept his options open. This wasn't the first time that he had been hijacked for drinks.

That can all come later, he thought to himself. *No use in making Mom and Dad anxious over nothing.*

There was not much that anyone could do when the rescue service and the police did arrive. The tide was coming in and had obliterated all traces of where the two young people had spread their towels on the beach.

The patrolmen marched up and down and peered around negatively for undisclosed clues, while attempting to keep their highly polished footwear out of the seawater. While kicking about in the sand, they managed to bury all traces of blood that remained.

They gave up their search after calling out the girl's name dozens of times and shining bright lights into the wall of fog, which did nothing to help them. In fact, the police officers sent away the ambulance men after a while and had one of their officers direct the confused young man to the police precinct in his own car, while they followed on closely behind.

'Sounds like a load of crap to me, Bert,' said one uniformed officer to another. 'What the hell were two youngsters doing all alone on a beach in the middle of a thick fog? And what did you think of the way they were dressed? Her in his shorts and wearing a see-through bra? Did you check out the damn thing? It was nothing more than a tiny scrap of gauze. No wonder she took it off.'

'Yeah, and that's after meeting up with that prick for the first time only a few hours before, in a bar? What did she see in him? And he admitted that they were preparing to have sex, Jimmy.'

'In a fog, on a lonely beach, of all places. Why not in his car or a hotel room or someplace a little warmer and more comfortable? I can't imagine having sand on my dick while I'm having sex. It wouldn't surprise me if he was trying to rape the girl and lost control of the situation.'

'Yeah. Maybe she managed to break loose from that young sod and tried to get away into the water, or along the beach. The poor thing may still be in the water somewhere, shivering her heart out. Or maybe she's floating about, unconscious in the shallows, with her neck broken or battling to breathe.'

'You've got a point there. Maybe the other men should have hung about a little longer, while she got up the nerve to come back to the beach, after having managed to get away from that young brute.'

'Another thing: if she's waited about until everybody's gone and then comes off the beach looking for help, there's the chance that some creep could pick her up, dressed as she is in a baggy pair of shorts and not even a top to cover her tits. If she tried to catch a lift somewhere along the road, she'd be in deep trouble. Can you imagine what would happen to her then?'

'Makes sense. I've got a daughter about that age, and she's more or less as stupid as our missing young woman, to be hanging about with some creep on a lonely beach in a thick fog. Then again, maybe I'm being a bit hard on my little girl. Maybe she's not quite as stupid as I think she is.

'I'm radioing base to report that we're going to go back to the beach, so that we can hang about a little longer. Can you imagine the kudos in store for us if we pick her up wherever she is and save her bacon by using a little initiative?'

Chapter Two

Tilly Markchester wiped the worst of the clinging wet sand off her golden tanned body and rolled over onto her stomach, while she waited for Jason to return to her side. The girl was glad that she'd been working on her tan of late. She was aware that she had a sweetly curved bottom, or so she had been told. When she stood in front of the mirror and twisted her body to look back at it, she had to agree that it looked round and perky, just the way men seemed to like it.

She remembered, with disgust, that those were the words used by her stepfather when he crashed into the bathroom without knocking, only a few months previously. That had been the last time he had cornered her. The bastard. It was not the first time that he had burst in on her privacy like that. And he was mean and strong, knowing how to use his power to hurt a girl.

She had tried to tell her mother what was going on, but the old woman would hear nothing about her husband's constant touching and leering at her daughter. Now he had gone overboard. Last time he had turned her around and backed her up against the washbasin where she had been washing herself, whipped down his sleeping shorts and grabbed her around the waist, pushing his oversized and hairy old dick deep into her, in almost no time at all.

There was no point in her crying out for help. Her mother was as drunk as a skunk, which was nothing unusual. Tilly had given up fighting the old man off, who was much too strong for her. He began beating his body against her pelvis, and she could feel the panting old sod thrusting in and out of her, not caring how much it was hurting. She gave up struggling then, and just took what was to come.

He speeded up his pounding to a crescendo until he squirted his semen into her in a series of jerks and animal moans, and finally pulled out with a satisfied grunt after his climax, which sounded like a pig rooting about in a trough.

Casually wiping himself off with her panties, he'd tossed them at her and warned her to keep quiet, or he would say she'd begged him for it. Then he'd left her alone to clean herself up and have a good cry.

Against her better judgement, she felt that she had to tell her mother what her stepfather had done to her. Unfortunately, the old lady was suffering from a king-sized hangover when Tilly managed to get her on one side, which was nothing unusual.

Her old girl had sneered at her and said, 'I don't believe a word of it. You're just trying to make trouble in this house for both of us. You know that I'm getting mine when our mattress squeaks, so that makes you randy as hell. Go and find your own man — someone in your age group — and leave mine alone, you jealous little bitch!'

Tilly had tried to make certain that she was never alone with the lecherous old bastard, but this was difficult to arrange, particularly late at night. Both parents would hit the bottle, and her mother was usually the first to drink herself into a stupor. It was then that Tilly would have to get the timing of her night-time bathroom visits right, or creep inside the house especially quietly if she'd been out with her friends.

But it had never got all that serious until the time he had raped her a while back. The trouble was that there were no locks on the doors. Tilly dreaded watching for the door handle to slowly drop when she was sitting on the loo.

While washing herself at the basin, she would keep one eye on the door, expecting Clarence to push against it at any moment. The nervous young woman was convinced that he would lie there in his bed, waiting to get his chance at her, with increasing impatience. He would be hungrily biding his time until his stepdaughter went through to the bathroom.

Tilly had tried to jam the back of a chair against the handle. That trick worked sometimes, but often the chair slid away, and then she not only had a lascivious man to deal with but also someone who made out as if he had been unfairly treated by her in not giving in to him when he needed a woman most of all.

Up to now, he had only fiddled with her, touching and handling her in a supposedly jokey way. But lately Clarence had become more demanding. After having raped her, he felt that he now had the right to do what he wished and that she also needed him, hanging about at night, wanting more of him.

That was why the young woman spent so much time in the company of men in her own age group. She had a stepsister whom she hardly knew. Angelica, or Angie, as she was called, was a couple of years older than she, and also a stepchild of Clarence's previous marriage. Tilly would have liked to get to know her better, but she had left home to stay with an aunt, only months before Tilly's mother had married the lecher and moved in with him.

She was sorry that they had never met each other. The family didn't even come to the wedding. Her mother had huffed and puffed about them, but Tilly could now begin to understand why they had kept out of Clarence's way. In fact, she wondered if Angie hadn't left home because of her own experiences with the stepfather.

Anyway, she hankered after meeting up with Angie and comparing notes with her. She had found her stepsister's address while scratching through her mother's things and kept it in her purse, meaning to follow it up soon.

Better to give herself to a virile, good-looking, young male than to be groped by a wrinkled old fool who thought that the sun shone out of his backside. Her love affairs also kept her out of the house late enough to avoid meeting up with Clarence, her stepfather and her nemesis.

But enough of her stepfather. She couldn't wait for Jason to return to her side and to cuddle with her. Not only was he handsome, but he had the manly build that she admired. He was well proportioned and muscular, without having those bulging muscles that men thought were so attractive to women. Tilly really wanted to make love to this one. He was so gentle and had good manners too. Her life was almost too good to be true at the moment.

She could hear the waves rushing in, out of the mist, the water running up the shallow gully to her right. It was quite soothing to listen to. There was a splashing nearby, and she wondered idly what had caused it. Then a shadow looming over her shoulder blotted out what little light there was. There was a scraping sound on one side of her before something huge clamped down on the unsuspecting woman's waist with terrifying force.

Tilly felt no immediate sense of pain at first, only tremendous pressure on her body where she was clamped in a vicelike grip that she would never be able to squirm out of. She gasped speechlessly at the overwhelming power crushing her hipbones together with mighty and relentless power.

There must have been terrible pain, but she was hardly aware of it. Instinctively her hands grabbed for the towel she was lying on, to hold onto some security, but her efforts were useless. Then there was a burst of agony as if she was being ripped apart by a giant mincing machine. Her squirming body was dragged into the gully from where the monster had swept ashore on a bow wave of its own making.

Her face registered the horror she felt, as she was hauled into the waves within a few seconds. The sea monster kept its grip on her body as it wriggled its unbelievable mass back to its own watery world. Then her head went underwater, and she began fighting for enough breath to survive her immediate drowning.

But there was no respite for her. The creature took its prey out further and tossed her high into the air with unbelievable power, before effortlessly catching her again. It preferred to swallow its prey headfirst, as an efficient means of subduing it.

Blood pumped out of her torn frame, as her unresisting body performed a parabola which ended up with her descending helplessly into the huge creature's maw. Her borrowed shorts had come off as she was flung about, floating away as a last evidence of her time on earth.

Then the half-conscious woman was inside the creature's jaws, her hands weakly beating at the fleshy inside of the creature's mouth, with only her legs nervelessly flailing about in the open. This was a cavern with outer rows of conical razor-sharp teeth. It was much, much larger than the mouth of a great white shark.

The bleeding victim found herself trapped inside a dark void, which allowed her only a few seconds of life until the ravening hunter began grinding and shredding her soft young flesh, ripping her apart, swallowing and digesting her with practised ease. Her face and her brain were crushed like a soft nut until a wave of welcome blackness spread over her. Then Tilly was gone forever.

Chapter Three

The police officers hadn't gone out of their way to treat Jason with kid gloves. He had the impression that nobody believed a word that he said, but they were too well trained to say it to his face. The sooner they could grind a concession out of him, or trip him up totally, the sooner they could go home to a hot meal and a drink. A drink that was well deserved by them, they felt.

He had to admit to himself that his was a shaky sounding story, when he thought back over the circumstances of Tillie's disappearance only an hour or so ago. He couldn't believe that his life could change so rapidly.

From being bored in a bar to meeting up with a very pretty girl; then losing her as their relationship was heating up. And then her disappearance, after which he was having to face pointed questions by a cynical group of disbelieving detectives. What a transition.

Now that Jason was in the police precinct, the plain-clothes officers took over the interrogation. They made no bones about the fact that they didn't believe Jason's story at all. In their eyes, something didn't ring true, and they were going to get to the bottom of it, come hell or high water.

A rotund plain-clothes cop by the name of Joe Robson, took on the job of interviewing Jason soon after he was shown into the interrogation room. The man's fat body overflowed the edges of his chair, like pie leaking out from under an overcooked crust.

The chair creaked as it took great strain in keeping him off the floor. His jaws never stopped working on whatever was in his mouth from one minute to the next, more than merely hinting to the world why he was so fat.

Robson leant back in his chair, creating more stress for it, with his trousers slightly undone in front under his overlapping big belly, and his shirt pulled out enough to show off his hairy navel. It looked like a mountain of dirty snow, with the middle exposed to reveal a hairy volcano.

'So I'm given to understand that you met this young woman, whom you only know by her name, and after an hour or so, you talked her into taking off her slacks and putting on your gym shorts, before getting her to go with you onto a deserted beach.'

Jason shook his head. 'It was her idea to go swimming, and she knew where the beach was situated. In fact, she guided me there.'

Robson put up a restraining hand. 'Wait a minute, Mr Malvy, you'll get your turn. Then you got her to take off her top and paddle about with you in the fog, nearly naked, only in her bra and your shorts, all this because it was a hot day.' The cop studied his scribbled notes. 'Then you took her out of the water, removed her bra and attempted to have sexual intercourse with her.'

'I didn't take her out of the water. We left the breakers, hand in hand. And she wanted me as much as I wanted her.'

Robson held up an admonishing finger. 'But then you broke off mating with her when you realized that you needed a condom. Were you scared that you would leave traces of sperm inside her? Maybe you didn't want to make her pregnant and have your DNA used against you at a later date. The Department of Health and Sexual Hygiene would be pleased to hear of your dedication to its plea to prevent STDs, if that was your motive.' He looked up at the young man on the other side of the table. 'Tell me, did you expect her to hang about while you fetched a rubber? Did the sight of your weapon hypnotize her? What, did she fall asleep from boredom while she was waiting for you to come back? I find that hard to believe. If I were that girl, I'd run like hell. I'd be in another part of the country by now.'

Jason didn't like the way this interview was going. 'I've explained to the patrolmen that we went swimming because it was hot. I didn't drag the woman into the sea. She was as keen on the idea as I was. In fact, she suggested it in the first place, when we were still at the bar.'

'And all she wanted to do, after going into the water for a minute or so, was to have sex with you?'

'Well, yes, our relationship developed something like that. But there was much more to it than you're intimating. Her shorts slid down. We put our arms about each other and kissed with some passion, arousing both of us, partly due to her standing pressed against me with her shorts around her knees.'

'Then why didn't she wait for you to come back with a condom if she was so hot for you? Why run away when you were getting ready to bang her, if she wanted you all that much?'

Jason shook his head in frustration. 'I keep on telling you guys, that I don't think she ran away because of any threat from me. We were becoming romantically inclined, and we were getting on well together. She saw something that made her scared and caused her to run off. That's the way I see it.'

'Maybe your equipment was larger than what she expected,' sneered Robson.

'Very funny,' returned Jason, who was getting a little peeved with this mode of interview.

Just then the door of the booth opened, and another detective entered the room. He was as scrawny as his partner was fat. To Jason, they looked like the number "10" when put together, but he didn't smile. He somehow didn't think that they would appreciate his sense of humour.

'I'm Arnold Pearson,' the newcomer announced, without attempting to offer his hand. 'How's it going with your little chat you've been having?' he asked his colleague. 'I believe that this guy and his girlfriend were having quite a beach party when things began to get a little too hot and then, suddenly, she changed her mind and she just upped and left him. I wonder why.'

Jason knew that the comment was meant for him, but he chose to ignore it. He was asked to make a list of those people he had been with prior to the disappearance of Tilly Markchester.

He was stared at with some disbelief when he couldn't provide names and addresses of those people he had mixed with at the bar. The best he could do was to furnish Tilly's surname, as well as Danny's name and address, although he wasn't even too sure of the latter, yet he could describe where the fellow lived.

To the average cop with a structured lifestyle, this seemingly casual attitude was hard to swallow. After answering many questions as to whether he was on any drugs and whether he had other girlfriends with whom he slept, the two detectives announced a coffee break. This didn't come too soon for Jason.

'How long will you people be keeping me?' he asked. His head was pounding, and he was near the end of his tether. 'Should I contact my parents and tell them what's going on? They don't normally keep tabs on me, but they would have expected me to roll up by sometime today, at the latest.'

Robson looked up from his paperwork and leered at the interviewee. 'We're not going to let you go in a hurry, Mr Malvy. This is a strange affair, with plenty of loose ends for us to tie up. We'll not let you chat up your contacts before we've had a chance to talk to them. You'll be here for a while, certainly tonight and probably over the weekend. You'll be kept in one of our holding cells, where you'll be on hand for us if there's something in your evidence that we need to verify.

'If you can get an attorney to start the spadework of releasing you sometime today, he'll probably arrange for a magistrate to take your case on Monday morning, with any luck. By then we'll have contacted most of your witnesses, and our prosecutor won't object too much if you're released against a bail bond on Monday.

'You can ring your parents from this phone, to arrange an attorney to take care of the details. Tell them to get a move on. If nothing happens pretty soon, all the legal beagles will disappear for the weekend on golf dates and other activities. They'll leave vague messages on their answering machines and not go through them until Sunday evening at the earliest. You'll still be sitting here on Monday morning with no court appearance having been arranged. So get on the phone and arrange some legal assistance, but be careful of what you say. We'll be monitoring your conversation. Any smart messages will count against you if you choose to get clever.'

***

It began to impact on Jason that he had more than lost a pretty companion, who could have become more than merely a girl to have a sexual romp with on a lonely beach. He was busy losing his liberty.

Up to now, he had been confused and surprised by Tilly's disappearance, but he had not thought that he would be suspected of being the cause of her sudden vanishing act. Yet, here he was being treated as the main culprit in a kidnapping, if not worse. He knew that he was innocent of any wrongdoing, but it seemed that he was very much in the minority at this stage.

His mother answered the phone. It was early morning, but his parents always rose early.

'This is the Malvy residence. Who's speaking, please?'

'It's me, Mom. Jason.'

'Oh. Hello, my son. It's so good to hear from you. I've missed you very much lately. I can't wait to have you back home, where I can look after you. I suppose you'll probably need a good deal of feeding up, after all that horrid government food that you've been getting. But why are you phoning so early in the morning?'

'Actually, I was planning to surprise you last night by walking through the front door, but things went a little wrong for me.'

He heard a gasp of anxiety on the other end of the line. 'You're not in any trouble, are you, Jason?'

'Well, I've done nothing wrong, if that's what you're worried about, but someone I was spending some time with disappeared yesterday evening. Now the police are asking a thousand questions to establish what's happened to her.'

'Now, why did I think that your friend was a female? All those modern young ladies that you run around with are no good for you. I think that what you need is a good, steady lady who would be willing to marry you and look after you and raise your children one day. But when will you ever listen to your mother? Perhaps I'd better get your dad on the line. These escapades of yours just get me all upset.'

'No, wait, Mom. I've done nothing wrong. It's simply that I was the last one with her before she disappeared, so the cops are asking questions to establish any connection I may have had with her.'

'Connection? Do they think you did something to her? You weren't rough with her, were you? Do you even know the girl? Could you have hurt her in any way?'

'No, Mom, of course not. I've never treated any woman roughly.'

'Then what about that woman whose nose bled after you slapped her?'

'That's something entirely different. She was drunk, and she said some disgusting things about you, even though she didn't know you from a bar of soap.'

'Yes, I understand all that, and you were protecting my good name, which I appreciate, but that gave you no right to hit her. You weren't raised to do things like that, even to young women with dirty mouths.'

'Yes, yes, I was wrong to do that, but it was a purely instinctive reaction on my part; and I only caught her with the tip of my fingernail, and there was little damage done. It was all settled amicably afterwards.'

'Only after your dad took out his chequebook and paid the woman to keep her mouth shut.'

This wasn't getting him anywhere. He suddenly remembered that the call was being monitored. He quietly cursed himself for opening up the present line of conversation. How would the police react to this information? Would they classify him as a brute who went around beating up women?

'I suppose you're right, Mom. Anyway, I've done nothing wrong. All I'm trying to do is to tell you that I'm with the police and I'll contact you as soon as I can. Give my love to Dad, and don't worry. I'm completely innocent of any wrongdoing. But I've got to go now. The cops have got a thousand questions to ask me. I hope they'll be as keen on finding the girl as I am, so I can get out of here in a reasonable space of time. I'll be in touch as soon as I can. Love you. Bye.'

No sooner had Jason put the receiver down when the detectives filed back into the interrogation room.

'I suppose you were listening in on all that,' remarked the suspect.

'Of course,' replied Joe Robson, his jowls jiggling as he chewed on the last of his meat stick. 'It wasn't as if we didn't warn you about the phone, right? And while we're on the subject of strange conversations, how about telling us a little more regarding your taking a punch at that rude girl and making her nose bleed?'

Arnold Pearson nodded. 'Yes, that didn't make you sound quite as sweet and innocent as you'd like to make out you are. Even your dear old mother seems to think that you have a penchant for getting rough and tough with the girls, when you don't get everything your own way.'

Jason shook his head. 'It was only an accident. There was no punch thrown by me. I meant to slap the bitch after she called my mother a whore, and a lot worse. Unfortunately I caught the tip of her nose, and it started bleeding.' He breathed heavily as he recalled the incident. 'Of course, that turned everyone against me, but I didn't do it on purpose. She made good capital out of it afterwards, believe me. She was well paid to keep her blabber mouth shut.'

'Yes, well, it shows that you let your temper go from time to time, not so? How do we get in touch with this dear lady with the blabber mouth? We'd like to hear her side of the story, with no money flapping in front of her this time.'

Once more, Jason didn't have the female nose-bleeder's address, another reason to make the detectives' ears prick up.

'You don't know the woman's address? She would have had you in court if your daddy hadn't paid her to shut up, but you don't know where she stays?'

'No, I don't. I had very little to do with her. Anyway, that was a good few years ago, before I joined the SEALs. This all happened in the bar, and I'd never met her before. I had no reason to know where she lived. Quite honestly, my father's attorney advised me to keep well away from her. He agreed that she was nothing more than an opportunistic tart, with a filthy mouth, who drank too much.'

The two detectives were apparently in no hurry to get on with the interview, although they would have loved to close down the questioning and go home. But they knew that now was the best time to get cooperation from the suspect, while he was tired and confused, and no doubt, worried.

In the meantime, they took it in turns to grill their victim about, inter alia, leaving his girlfriend alone on a deserted beach while fetching something from his car.

'What was it you went all that way to get? Suntan cream? Burgers?'

Jason shook his head wearily. 'I've told you before. I went to fetch a condom.'

'What, so that you wouldn't leave any traces of your sexual act?'

Jason shook his head vehemently. 'No, she asked for it.'

Joe Robson was still chewing away methodically. 'What did she ask for — the sexual act or the condom? So, then you gave it to her? Did you happen to scrape her nose by accident, or what?'

The young man glared at his accusers. 'You don't want to hear what happened out there, do you? It looks like you only want to ask me a lot of dumb questions that don't make any sense.'

'Well, then, you tell us what kind of sense we're supposed to get out of the story of a girl who just disappears while her sexual partner goes to fetch a condom.' Robson shook his head sadly.

Pearson stepped in to take over the pressure on their victim. 'By the way, what happened to that condom you went to fetch? Are you still wearing it, or what?'

Jason listened to that question with his mouth open. Then he shut it to respond, 'I don't know what you're talking about.'

'You said that you went to all the trouble to fetch a condom while your lady friend stayed alone on the beach, waiting impatiently for you to return. So what did you do with it, then?'

The young man stared at him in consternation. 'I don't know. I haven't given it a thought.'

Pearson shook his head slowly from side to side. 'I don't get it. You go to such a lot of trouble, in the heat of your passion, to go and get a condom, and then you lose it on the way back to your passion partner. You're mighty forgetful, aren't you? It doesn't make much sense to me. What do you think, Joe?'

Robson agreed with his partner. 'I'd be hanging onto such an important piece of equipment with both hands, particularly after my sex partner disappeared, but he doesn't know what happened to it.'

'Somehow I don't think that the team looking for evidence is going to return with a neatly rolled up rubber that they found on the beach.' Pearson shook his head again.

'Maybe some great white shark is swimming about while wondering what's stopping him from satisfying his lady shark.'

'Or a crab could be staggering around with the equipment stuck over his head.'

Both detectives thought this highly amusing, although Jason didn't see the funny side of it at all. He mopped his head in frustration.

The door of the interview room opened, and a uniformed officer stuck his head inside and exchanged a hurried few words with Robson. Then he left the room.

'A new development,' announced the burly cop. 'A team of searchers has been busy from first light, scouring the beach and surrounding waters for traces of the girl. The mist has cleared up, and they've got divers in the water and officers combing the beach.

'They've come up with a pair of torn shorts, covered in partially faded bloodstains, which was floating in the shallows of the bay. Although you didn't bother to mention it to us, a bloodied and wet beach towel was found in your things when a search was made through the contents of your car and your clothing. The blood groups should match up, although it would have been useful if you'd mentioned that you had a bloodied towel in your possession, that your girlfriend had been using prior to her disappearance.'

Pearson glared at the suspect. 'This doesn't look very good for you, young man. Your girlfriend didn't run away, even though she may have tried to. She didn't go for a swim in the fog, or get picked up by a lonely sailor. I can't see what a heavily bloodstained towel was doing in your car, when you had no idea what had happened to the girl. What were you doing with it? How did it get there? Whose blood was it, anyway?'

Now Jason remembered how the towel had been found in his car. 'When I ran down to where we'd been lying, she was gone, so I ran into the waves and found the towel floating in the shallows. I picked it up and looked around a short while to find Tilly, before running back to where we'd been on the sand. Then I collected everything, took it all back to the car and phoned you people.'

'Didn't you wonder why the girl's towel was full of blood? D'you think that she was shaving somewhere important and cut herself badly while she was patiently waiting for you and your valuable condom?

'No,' added Robson. 'And the poor girl never had a chance. She must have been brutally ripped apart, somewhere around where you said you left her, although there was nobody else on the beach at the time.'

The cop added dramatically, 'And don't come with that bullshit that it could have been a great white shark called Jaws 2, that came ashore by launching itself blindly out of the mist and dragging your girlfriend off the beach, while she was waiting patiently for you to poke her silly, considerately protected by your condom. 'You must have worn it over your head so as not to catch an STD when you grovelled somewhere down there, in front of her. That's why you didn't notice her being carried off right before your eyes. Maybe you got bored and fell asleep.' The cop stopped to catch his breath, winded by his efforts.

Jason Malvy stared at his accusers with a look of horror on his face. He could hardly believe what he was hearing. If this was the kind of crap that the police were putting together to paint him into a corner, then his future looked very bleak. From the initial shock he'd had, of having a pretty girl disappear like that, the cops seemed to be building up a lurid rape and murder case against him.

They didn't appear to be seriously considering any other possibilities, although he had to admit that he couldn't think of any alternatives right then. Actually, if he tried to think of the evidence from a neutral point of view, some of his statements seemed to work against him rather than for him.

It didn't appear to be likely that Tilly had disappeared into thin air, and he couldn't believe that anybody else had interfered with her. If she had screamed, Jason would have heard her clearly.

He made up his mind that he needed some help, and soon. 'I'm not getting any further involved with this witch hunt of yours without my legal adviser being present,' he announced, sitting back in his chair and staring up at the ceiling as a gesture of finality. He put up a hand and wiped the sweat from his brow.

Pearson saw the nervous gesture and filed it away for future reference. He was busily noting down various points that could be kept for later use.

Robson rolled his eyes. 'That little speech of yours sounds very important, although we were only asking a few questions, merely to clear the air a little. But calling in an attorney is your right. To be honest with you, I can't see why you really need legal assistance if you have been as lily white as you've painted yourself to be, but it's your decision to make.

'I hope you have deep pockets, or rather your daddy has, because you're now about to build up a fortune in fees while discussing your innocence with your legal shark of another sort.'

***

His mother must have been sitting at the phone, waiting for her son's call. She answered within a couple of seconds.

'Yes, yes, is that you, Jason?'

'Yes, Mom, but I don't have much time. Is Dad there? I need to talk to him urgently.'

His mother's gnarled hand started shaking as her level of panic built up. 'What's happened, son? What have they done to you? Are you hurt? Can we call you an ambulance?'

'Nothing like that, Mom. It's just that they've only given me a limited time to make my call before they cut me off.'

'Well, they can't do that! We'll protest. They won't get away with it. We won't let them.'

'Please, Mom!'

'Keep calm now, Jason. I've got your dad's attention. He's on his way. Are they treating you well?'

'Yes, Mom. As well as can be expected from boneheads who won't listen to reason and are determined to blame the nearest person they can lay their hands onto, instead of using their butts and their brains to sort out the problem on their own.'

'Well, be brave, son. If you've done nothing wrong, get down on your knees and pray about it. Perhaps you should also say a prayer for forgiveness if there is something on your conscience. It's marvellous what help one can get from above. I certainly will call on the Lord's protection. Here's your dad. Love you.'

Jason's father came on the line, and Jason could picture him with his mouth all twisted up as he was forced to find out what his errant son needed him for. Sometimes he thought that his permanently sour-faced old father would probably be better off not having a son at all.

Charles Malvy muttered and mumbled to himself as he approached the phone, at his own measured pace. Why should he hurry for that young man who appeared to go out of his way to irritate him? The boy always seemed to get himself into trouble. When would he be old and wise enough to handle his own problems? He let out a deep sigh as he took the phone from his wife.

'Hello, Jason, it's your father. I hear that you've got yourself knee-deep into trouble again. How do you manage to do it? What have you gone and done now? No more rough stuff with women, I hope.'

'Hi, Dad. I don't know what trouble you're talking about. The only mess I ever got myself into was over that silly drunken cow who foul-mouthed Mom at a bar five or six years ago.'

'I won't forget it in a hurry, son. It cost me an arm and a leg to keep you out of prison and our good name out of the papers.'

'Dad, I'll repay every penny of what you had to fork out once I get myself a reasonable job. I wish you'd tell me what I owe you, anyway. You're never willing to talk about it when I bring the subject up.'

'I paid that slut, not to smooth your way, but to save the family name from being dragged through the gutter, young man. But that's enough of that. What's gone wrong with your career at the SEALs now? I thought that you were finding your feet in the world, at last. Have you blotted your copybook there as well? What have you gone and done to spoil things, now?'

Jason rolled his eyes but let this all ride over his shoulders. His father had never expected anything but the worst from him. At least he didn't have far to fall to hit rock bottom, as far as his male parent was concerned. It was his dear mother who worried terribly about him, without constantly being of the opinion that he was one step away from being in deep trouble.

'Dad, I have no problems with the SEALs, although I cleared out of the organization because I felt that I had little future with them. I was on the way home to tell you about my decision and to find myself a job somewhere.'

'Well, you haven't exactly made it home yet, have you? Don't tell me that a bunch of your loose friends and a bar got in the way of your telling us that you had made it safely back home without incurring more trouble? You talk about paying me back for the costs I've incurred over you, but we're still waiting for the first instalment to arrive, however small it's likely to be.

You have free board and lodging wherever you go, but you can't seem to save any of it. There's no "How much do I owe you for board, Dad?" Only "How can you cover me for the latest jam that I'm in?" How come you didn't arrive home like a dutiful son would, before going on a tour of the local bars with out-of-workers and pick-up girls, during a weekday?'

***

Jason silently ground his teeth before replying. His father was like the detectives at the police precinct. Always probing and expecting the worst of one. He had a way of putting a person's back up for no good reason.

'There was nothing like that, Dad. I gave a lift to an acquaintance who stood me a few beers. I met up with this girl, and we went for a swim on the beach. You know how hot it was yesterday.'

'Do I know this girl?'

'I can assure you, Dad, you'll be hearing all about this woman pretty soon, I promise you that.'

'Now, what's that supposed to mean? And come to the point, young man. Is there more bad news on the way? Don't play games with me. Spit it out.'

It flashed through Jason's mind that it was said that one couldn't get blood out of a stone, but it would be easier to get a smile out of his father, who never displayed humour unless cracking a thin smile if someone fell on their face in front of him — and that only for a second or two.

'Dad, just listen!' exclaimed Jason, impatiently. 'I was on the beach with this girl when she disappeared. I'd gone to fetch something from my car. When I returned to our place on the beach, she was gone. We were the only people there at the time. I hunted for her, but there was a thick fog yesterday morning, and she seemed to have vanished into it. I phoned for the police, and they searched for her, but she was nowhere to be found.'

'And you maintain that you had nothing to do with her disappearance?' queried his father.

'Of course not,' Jason replied vehemently.

'How was she dressed at the time?'

Jason winced. Now they had come to the tricky part. 'Well, she didn't have a bather with her, so I lent her a pair of my shorts and she swam in her bra.'

There was a long silence while Jason waited for the explosion, with half-closed eyes. He didn't have long to wait.

There was a stony silence for a few seconds, before the next question arrived: 'How long have you known this person, Jason?'

'Oh, we'd just met at the bar this afternoon.'

Another long silence. Jason held the phone further from his ear, although his father was not known to scream or to bellow with rage.

'So, you're telling me that you lend a total stranger — and a female, at that — your shorts, and she uses it to go swimming with you, wearing nothing else but a bra? And then she disappears? Tell me, did your shorts have a tag in them, giving your name?'

'Oh, the shorts are about the only things that aren't missing. The police divers found them floating in the bay when they did another search for the girl.'

'And what condition were the shorts in, Jason?'

'They were bloodstained, Dad.'

There was a sharp intake of breath. 'Where are you phoning from right now?'

'The police precinct.'

'And I suppose they've been questioning you all this time, from yesterday afternoon?'

'Yes, that's right.'

'And obviously they have held you as a prime suspect on a murder charge? So now you need a smart attorney, I would guess.'

'That's about the picture, Dad.'

'Well, now you listen to me most carefully. It took a long time for you to get to this important point. You're normally allowed only one call. So, button up that free-flowing mouth of yours until I can get there with an attorney.

'And if you're mildly interested in my reaction to this tale of woe, you're probably quite right. I do think that you're a raving idiot, but you're already deep in the you-know-what, so it's unfortunately too late for me to disown you or divorce you or whatever they do these days.

Merely for the sake of interest, fathers used to send their sons to far, distant places in years gone by, to get them out their hair when they caused too much trouble or besmirched the family name. But these places have got wise and don't want any trouble from the same dropouts, therefore they send them back these days without giving them a visa. So I'll do what I can to minimize the damage you've caused, after which you're welcome to see if there are still some far-flung sucker outposts that will take misfits like you. Until then, please shut up and wait for our attorney to pay you a visit.'

The phone was banged down, coming close to damaging Jason's eardrum, as well as those of the amused police eavesdroppers who had been listening in and recording the conversation on an extension line.

'If I'd gone to the beach with my father and he went missing, you'd have a far better case against me than what you've got right now,' Jason grumbled, fairly certain that his listeners were still on the line. Then he heard the click as the extension was hurriedly cut off.

***

Chapter Four

Greyton Elliott was a careful dresser, to say the least. There didn't seem to be a wrinkle in his pinstriped suit, which had that expensive sheen to it that screamed out "money", with "big fees" echoing in the background.

He flicked an imaginary speck of dust off his chair, in the visitor's room, with a snowy white handkerchief while waiting to see his client's son, Jason Malvy, before pulling the item of well-battered furniture back carefully and easing his angular frame gently into it.

The defence attorney put on his studious professional pose in readiness for the interview. This was different to the one he wore when playing poker with his friends, or sneaking into girlie joints wearing the ubiquitous dark glasses and his mouth wet with drool.

There were other faces that he wore: the dutiful son-in-law; the prim father of two who sometimes beat his wife in the bedroom, with his hand over her mouth to prevent her screams filtering through to the servants' quarters. They were all facets of his chameleon-like personality.

Now he examined his nails carefully while waiting for the prisoner to be brought in to him. Malvy was well bound. The police weren't going to let him disappear the way that his girlfriend had done. Jason looked a proper misery, and his head and his lip were competing about how far down they could hang.

'Well, young man, I believe that you've got yourself into a load of trouble over a vanishing woman. I have a number of clients who would like their womenfolk to disappear — usually unwanted wives and bloodsucking girlfriends — but you say you would like yours to be found. So I must ask you to tell me, in fair detail, how you came to lose your particular one.'

Jason didn't particularly like the look of this man, who had an air of careless superiority about him as he flicked an errant lock of hair back into place. His offbeat sense of humour didn't seem to fit in with the situation, either.

But then he realized that Dad was paying and had the right to select what his son would have to put up with. That meant that Jason would not be in a position to get a second bite of the cherry. He would have to make do with what he had been given, which didn't look like a helluva lot to him.

Actually, Charles Malvy, Jason's father, also didn't have that much of an option regarding whom he'd like to select as a legal adviser for any problem facing his family. This attorney had found a way to firmly force himself into the saddle, early on in their relationship.

There had come a day when he and Greyton Elliott had crossed swords in a rather heated way, about how a certain matter needed to be handled. Charles had lost his temper, which was a fiery one at the best of times, and this was one of the uglier confrontations that wouldn't lie down and die. He told his legal man to pack up the Malvy client files in readiness for transfer to another firm of litigators.

'Do you want me to include the file on Jerrison, where you hired a strong arm to beat him up and threaten him with something even worse, should he not get out of the premises he was hiring from you? What about the on-the-side rental books we use to bypass fixed rental laws? Do you want me to keep those back for a short while, until you can trust the new man with all these secrets?' Greyton Elliott continued with a straight face. 'There are also a few factors regarding building safety regulations that should have been rectified, despite the fact that you managed to persuade the powers in control to lose the relevant report.'

He mentioned a few other undesirable deals, while Charles Malvy blanched and began to realize that certain relationships were not easily parted, where dark and dirty deeds were involved.

'Oh, I suppose you may as well carry on as usual,' Malvy Senior had growled, 'but I'm not prepared to kowtow to that bastard, even if you disagree with me. All right, then. Handle it as you like. You always do, in the end, but this is a tricky swine, so watch out for him.'

Jason's father used this legal man for all his business matters these days, without even a whimper. He was too scared to cry out aloud.

Jason soon discovered that Elliott was not a patient man who sat taking copious notes when attending to a client. He slapped down a tape recorder and had Jason tell his story once more, while he sat with eyes closed and fingers intertwined, with what he fondly imagined was the sort of pose that Sherlock Holmes would have adopted in similar circumstances.

When his young client ground to an eventual end, he yawned, switched off the recorder and stood up. 'I'll be going through this in my office in great detail, to establish whether there is other information required in your defence. In the meantime, I'll try to speed up your release from detention. The state has certain rights regarding retention of suspects, particularly when foul play is suspected.'

'How long will I have to sit here, then?'

The attorney absentmindedly picked at his thumb. This criminal procedure stuff was a bit hazy to him. Now if it had concerned property rights… 'The big thing is that a judge will have to adjudicate at a bail hearing, as soon as this can be arranged. I'll get it seen to immediately. It's Friday today. I should be able to get a bail hearing organized for Monday, if the police are still looking for your girlfriend and nothing serious has been unearthed in the meantime.

'There are still some of the judiciary who owe me a few favours. I'll see who I can speak to in order to expedite this business. After all, that's what our legal system is based on —you scratch my back, or I'll beat yours. All in all, I hope to get you out of this place on Monday, provided your daddy is prepared to wave money about. Your job is to sit tight, to stop offering unnecessary ammunition to the investigation team, and to wait until you hear from me, which will probably be early Monday morning. Don't do anything outrageously stupid until I contact you then, if that's at all possible. You've got that wild look about you, as if you're simply aching to get into some more trouble or other.'

Jason couldn't see how he could do otherwise. The police were hardly going to unlock his cell door and let him stroll around the block when he began suffering from cabin fever. They wouldn't let him strangle a warder and steal the man's weapon before making a dramatic escape. That had been tried before. His recent diving school activities were beginning to look more attractive by the hour, however boring they had seemed at the time.

The police officer, Callow Birnum, was there to take him back to his cell. Looking after prisoners must have been a boring and lonely job. To a man, they all had something they wanted to say to a prisoner in their care.

'It's not as easy to get out of here as it is on TV is it, chum? Hopefully they won't start to forget about you, or you could be here forever. Why, some time back, we forgot a prisoner in a back cell. The poor fool didn't get food or drink, or anything, for over a week, until he was discovered by accident.' He continued. 'He was one of the quiet ones who didn't like to complain about his lot. So don't sit for too long, should you end up in a back cell and things go dead still. On the other hand, if you make too much noise and whine all the time, then you'll be likely to get a visit from a couple of my mates in the middle of the night. They know how to do their job, all right. They're experts at beating up a prisoner without leaving a mark. They use rubber or plastic on certain areas of the body. Electrocution of the genital areas and beating the soles of your feet will teach you some self-control and good manners. Of course, a nice simple torture is to have the prisoner stand on his toes, with a rope around his neck. Dripping cold water on his head will make a man go dilly after a while. And those are only some of the tricks of the trade. OK, here's your cell. Now try to keep it quiet, will you? We wouldn't want these guys to pay you a friendly call one dark and lonely night, when they're feeling bored and a little mean, if you get my drift.'

'What happened to the prisoner who was forgotten in his cell then?'

'Oh, I wouldn't worry too much about him. I hear that he didn't make it in the end. Too much loss of liquid, I believe. His organs closed down one after the other, so that was that for him.'

'What happened to the warders who forgot about that guy?'

Birnum shrugged his shoulders. 'Nothing much. They got the doctor to make out a certificate that some or other organ had failed. Nobody kicked up a fuss. He had no relatives, and the guys who looked after him said that he seemed to be as guilty as hell, anyway.'

'What was he supposed to have done?'

'Oh, I don't know. Something to do with fiddling with a schoolgirl on a train late at night. Now I ask you, what was he doing on a train in the first place, at that time of night? He was probably intending to rape her when they caught him, although I don't think he managed to get that far.'

Callow Birnum was one officer who seemed to be a little more human than some of the others who shared his duties.

40

Jason had planned to keep his mouth shut regarding the stories that he'd been fed, but they began preying on his mind. 'Could things like that really happen in a modern prison cell?' he asked his favourite keeper.

The warder had a job keeping a straight face, because he loved to amuse himself at the prisoners' expense. To see the ones behind bars squirm was a great pleasure to him. But Birnum felt sorry for this young guy, who looked pretty harmless. So, he decided to give up on the tall tales he was telling. This young jerk would probably already be in for a few juicy nightmares after swallowing all this bullshit.

'Look, things have been known to happen in any prison. You only have to look at Guantanamo Bay to see how some guards get out of hand and mistreat their charges, for various reasons. But we're not all like that, and certainly not at this place. We don't normally allow butch women to come in here and beat up the prisoners and sit on their faces, out of pure spite. So, relax and enjoy your stay. I'll try to keep a weather eye out for you. If you go missing, I'll go to the trouble to try to find out where they've taken you.' He grinned and left Jason to figure things out for himself.

Chapter Five

The killer whale, or *Orcinus orca*, to give him his scientific name, had been little more than a baby when he was captured and taken to Sea Wonder World in San Diego, where he spent months in solitary captivity while he was being acclimatized to a life of daily boredom and heartbreaking routine.

His keepers were knowledgeable in managing sea creatures and training them to forget all their old ways and distant memories of things that they had experienced long, long ago in the open sea.

Their basic methods were based on reward and perseverance. Or so they said. Whenever a creature was taught a new sequence, usually as a forerunner to a heart-stopping trick, it would be rewarded with a special titbit, usually comprising fish, accompanied by an encouraging word or a pat.

If the trick was initially unsuccessful, it would be repeated ad nauseam, until the animal got the hang of it out of sheer desperation, usually encouraged by a reward of additional rations. This system usually worked in the end. Or at least this was what they liked to tell the public.

The truth of the matter was that starvation was often thrown in as a final incentive to obey and perform. It was true enough that dolphins enjoyed showing off and doing tricks to please an audience, but there were days when they didn't feel like putting on a show for a raucous and largely unappreciative crowd of paying customers. Many trainers have admitted to starving their charges to get their cooperation.

To ensure a good performance by their performing animals during show-time, handlers often keep their charges hungry while going through their routines with them. Instead of feeding them between twenty and twenty-five pounds of fish per day, which is what they normally require, their keepers hold back their meals or reduce them until they are receiving only three to five pounds of fish a day.

Eventually the poor dolphin gives in and does what is demanded of it. But there has been at least one documented case where food was withheld from a dolphin because of its unwillingness to leave its pen, after which it died, presumably of starvation. This disgraceful action was brought about by the total dependence these penned creatures have in relation to their handlers.

**

The capture of the killer whale and others of his kind had been ridiculously easily. For such a huge creature, with no known enemies apart from Man, it was not particularly aggressive. It would attack and kill anything in the sea, should it feel inclined to do so, but there had been only a few reported cases of any aggression being shown towards humans, usually for good reason.

Even then, there was precious little evidence of any physical harm being purposely done to those that the orca came across. When it was netted for purposes of capture, the orca seldom vaulted over its restraining nets, which would be relatively easy for it to do. For some reason, it remained docile even then.

At first this particular gentle giant was peaceful and cooperative. With its spectacular black and white markings and its massive bulk, it was a sure-fire pull towards the gate money that had become the centre point of modern entertainment complexes.

At first there was only cooperation between the seagoing giant and its keepers, but the tricks became more elaborate and the training rigours harsher. Loving trainers slowly morphed into frenzied tyrants when their killer whale performers either made a mistake or battled to understand what was expected of them. Or maybe their stubbornness to perform was merely their way of showing that they'd had enough of being pushed around by pint-sized humans.

One of these beautiful creatures either became bored by its confined space or gradually traumatized and stressed over a period of time. The constant noise of the crowds that gathered to view it in its holding tank or during its regular performances, and the shouting and screaming of a typical stand full of sugar-overloaded spectators, created increasing pressure on the confined animal.

Nobody seemed to notice any change in the personalities of any of the amiable creatures, until one of them savaged its keeper one shocking day. With a packed stand of shouting and cheering spectators watching the performance, a trainer blew her whistle, and the giant mammal hurled itself out of the water to accept the fish offered to it.

Normally a reward would be offered at the end of a stick that was similar to a fishing pole. But this particular minder was more progressive than that. She had trained her charge to accept her offering on a shorter and shorter extension, until it was taking its reward from the tips of her fingers.

There was tremendous cheering by the excited crowd, as three giant killer whales answered the summons of their three distinct whistles by shooting up from below and leaping mightily out of the water in unison. Two of them accepted their rewards at the ends of the pole contraptions, but the third orca had only a few fingers holding its fish to aim for.

It shot up in line with the others, but its mouth closed over the arm of its handler, neatly severing her limb somewhere between elbow and wrist. It dropped back into the water with her lower arm in its mouth, whereupon it swallowed part arm and fish, as if that was part of the act.

The young woman fell down and cried out as the blood pumped out of her shattered stump. A big "Ooh" escaped from the stunned crowd, while a few confused ones stared at their fellows, wondering if this was not a dramatic antic meant to sucker them into thinking that something gory had really happened.

The emergency medical team sprang into operation, and the blood flow was stemmed before the woman was taken away. An announcer tried to make light of the occurrence, but everybody with reasonable intelligence could see what had happened. The show staggered on but in a subdued way. Now the bloodthirsty ones who went to see drama happening, really had something to gossip about.

In the furore that developed over this incident, one party wanted to have the killer whale exterminated. Others wanted to put a stop to getting such immense creatures to perform tricks, which they said were against nature itself.

As usual, the media had a field day, not only in reporting the incident but also presenting interviews between numerous people who were mostly portrayed as being knowledgeable about orcas, the teaching of tricks and the captivity of the giants. Some of these experts knew as much about their subject as Aunty Ida down on the farm, but if the relevant channel thought that they had something to offer, they were brought into the studio or had a portable microphone shoved into their faces.

Everybody had the opportunity to air their views, but some were more radical than others. Another employee of the firm took over the care of the marine entertainment team, and the show went on in true Hollywood tradition.

Yet there were still unhappy people who were determined to have their way. One night, another orca and its mate were released by their keeper, for personal reasons which would later become clear. The two creatures were sometimes later seen cruising outside in the bay, with a baby calf by their side. This area had become their home, and they saw no reason to leave it because of their newfound freedom.

After more distressing incidents and deaths among the growing population of captive killer whales, some sensible people in authority sat down and promulgated laws and regulations governing the capture and holding of these gentle giants. But the numbers in captivity grew steadily.

In previous years, there were a number of them held by various organizations, some of these supposedly held in the name of research, but many of them were used as a drawcard to attract paying patrons to the daily shows. They were a great attraction and certainly kept the customers rolling up to the ticket kiosks.

And then the unthinkable happened. Joyriders in the bay had heard of the happy family of three killer whales that had been released from captivity, and they decided to pay them a visit. Two couples set out in search of the cruising threesome, armed with an expensive speedboat and plenty of booze. They found them and rode them down mercilessly for their own evil reasons.

The black and white baby orca was the first to succumb, mortally sliced by the powerful boat after it was forced to come to the surface for air. The mother stayed with its baby, trying to protect it with its own life, but these efforts were in vain. A high-powered rifle was taken up and emptied into the female orca, which was destined to die later of its wounds.

Alone in the sea, with its family torn from it, the male called on its knowledge and experience of mingling with the humans. This most recent torment had been too much for it to bear. In all the vastness of the sea, Man was the only creature that had proved dangerous to the killer whale; the only enemy that had caused any sort of regular distress to its kind.

At this stage, it was time for the orcas to strike back and to wreak vengeance on Killer Man by Killer Whale.

This latest motivation was the start of a dimly formed plan by one creature to even the score between the creatures of the sea and those who had crept out of it aeons past, to overpopulate the land and to poison and to befoul both it and the sea. For it was time for the human race to become accountable for its actions.

Unbeknown to both man and sea creature, this latest son of the ocean had evolved into a beautiful creation of immense size and agility, but also having a brain a lot more developed than the rest of its seagoing kind, and sharpened by years of association with the heartless creatures onshore.

Now it was ready to go to war, but first it had to assemble its troops and train them, for a great general cannot fight and win a war all on his own, without a strong fighting force to command. So the grieving orca, bigger, stronger and smarter than any other of its kind, shrugged off his grief and went out in search of reinforcements to help it fight its cause.

But first he had to eat. And what better meal could there be than an unsuspecting person lying on a lonely beach in San Diego? Samson — for that was the name its captors had given him — was ready to pull down the pillars of the human temple. He had heard the two humans cavorting in the surf and had closed in to engage his first quarry. The opening salvo in its battle against mankind was about to be fired.

But now they had left the water, although he could still hear them chattering away through the curtain of heavy mist hiding his presence. Then the male onshore left his partner at the water's edge to fetch something.

So much the better. It would be far easier to slaughter his first catch when it was on its own. And he knew, by the movement of the incoming breaking waves, that there was a gully developing to one side of his target.

This was formed by a specific pattern where the current gouged out a furrow in the beach. He could use this deeper trench to heave himself up onto the beach in a copy of the method his kind used to attack seals in other areas of the world.

Using a wavelet of the incoming tide to build up speed, Samson used the gully to force himself onto the beach, right next to the human lying on the sand. His system of echo location had identified her position as accurately as if he could see through the curtain of fog blanketing the area.

One mighty lunge and one great bite, and he had the woman in his mouth, gripping her just above the hips. It was an effort to get his huge body back into the water, but he had timed the grabbing of his prey with a precision that only he could manage.

The giant sea creature wriggled and squirmed backwards into the water, using the power of his great muscles, while his victim was gripped agonizingly between his razor-sharp, conical teeth. His tough and elastic skin was not harmed in any way while the giant porpoise heaved his way down to the waterlogged sand, and from there onwards it was increasingly easier to slide through the watery, slick surface.

It became easier to move down through his natural element. At last, he could feel the water begin flowing under him. After that he dove down to get away from the shore, surfacing a short distance away from it. He flung his catch into the air, rotating it so that he would take it headfirst into his huge mouth, as he was used to. Luckily the towel and the shorts had come loose, leaving only the thin material of the bra to be easily digested, along with the meat of his prey.

One facet of killer whales that caused frustration to their handlers was the fastidious eating habits that these huge creatures displayed. They would be tempted by one kind of food and enjoy it for a while, only to turn up their mighty snouts to it when the spirit moved them, before being attracted by something else.

It had taken the keepers some time to absorb the fact that killer whales also had their preferences. Throwing the same sort of food at their massive charges, in the sort of quantity that they required, had conditioned the handlers to believe in the lack of variety in their diet. If they only had stopped to think, the careless handlers may have realized that an orca has the abundance of the whole ocean to choose from. It can vary its diet from day to day, as it chooses to.

They had achieved a far better success rating when they began experimenting with various foods. Instead of ignoring their rations, the orcas began to show interest in their food and in life itself; until the next bout of boredom with their food set in. These keepers were not all that bright, it seemed. An orca could say that they were, in fact, slow-witted, by and large.

Meanwhile, the body of the keeper he had tossed so casually into the air came tumbling down towards him. Catching the human expertly in his mouth, he bit down on the head and face of his victim, feeling the brain burst in his maw. He swam off, crunching his catch while thinking that his first attack had gone well. Maybe the brain and the head parts were better-tasting than the rest of her body, although the heart and liver were also good.

There wasn't as much flavour in the flesh as there would have been with red whale meat or fish, but he could get used to the taste, in due course. This was not only sustenance; it was the elimination of one of his hated enemies. He could always catch seals and fish to vary his diet. He wouldn't even battle to find delicacies. There were lots of good things in the ocean to choose from.

Then there were also the humans. Every human he crushed between his mighty jaws was one more disgusting thing that would be eliminated from this beautiful planet. There was a lot of work to be done, judging by the crowds that had come to watch him perform.

How long would it take to rid the world of humans? He had no conception of how many people there were living on the planet. Oh well, he supposed that he couldn't do it all himself, but he was sure that he could train other killer whales to carry on his quest, now that he had his human "mother" safe in his belly.

He was definitely larger than any other orca he had come into contact with. Samson intuited that he was something special in his species. There should be no problem in getting others of his kind to follow him. In the meantime, he would breed wherever and whenever possible. His genes needed to be spread far and wide.

Chapter Six

Monday morning couldn't come quickly enough for the young man. Jason had spent a lonely weekend in unfamiliar territory, and he had been virtually on his own for most of the time. The prison guards had done little or nothing to lighten his fears that he was going to be abandoned by society, or even suffer a personal attack by unscrupulous warders. Some of his nightmares could be attributed to the scare stories his keepers had dished out to him.

His mother had never learned to drive, and his father was certainly not going to ferry her to the prison — a considerable distance from their home — to spend time with him. Unlike most fathers, he considered his son to be guilty of whatever crime the state wanted to pin on him, until he could prove himself innocent. And sadly, in his father's mind, that was debatable anyway.

The cold war between Jason and his father had been ongoing ever since he could remember. Maybe the old man had resented the time his mother had spent in taking care of him. Jason had been quite sickly as a baby, causing his mother to spend many hours in nursing him back to health.

Charles Malvy had, himself, had a tough upbringing by a hard-as-nails father, so maybe he felt that he deserved better than what his wife was able to offer him. On the other hand, Mathilda Malvy was a childlike figure herself, unable to stand up to her husband or, in fact, anyone she considered to be a figure of authority.

If he'd had any choice in the matter, Jason Malvy might have chosen at least one parent to give him better guidance as a young boy. But he muddled through, not knowing what it felt like to enjoy decent parenting, and not coming to too much harm, except for now, when he needed positive support most of all.

He wasn't allowed to use the phone, and his mobile had gone flat. Asking for it to be recharged was like ordering the president to make him a pot of tea. Things simply weren't done that way in prison.

But he was a resourceful young man. At least he had been allowed to keep his haversack in his cell, once the contents had been thrown onto the not-too-clean floor and examined for weapons, escape tools and other harmful items. There was a writing pad and pen that had not been confiscated, unlike a number of other items, such as bootlaces for morbid prisoners who wanted to hang themselves.

So he sat and jotted down his thoughts, or a carefully edited version of them. He wisely treated his writings as fair game for anyone who wanted to use them as a means of wringing a confession out of him. But then, he came from a military background, where even the most innocent of writings was in likelihood of being censored.

Early on Monday morning, he was aroused and hurried into showering and cleaning himself up, including wearing his tidiest clothing. Then he was transported to court to attend his bail hearing.

He was naturally apprehensive. He'd heard nothing of importance over the weekend, but Jason was certain that he would have been informed if Tilly had been traced. Come to think of it, her not being found was not a good sign at all. It meant that something bad had happened to her. She had either drowned or been murdered, and the body disposed of where it was not likely to be found.

It was hard for him to imagine that the voluptuous Tilly had been slaughtered by someone to whom she had done no harm. He couldn't honestly say that he was heartbroken. He'd only known her for a few hours. Yet he had found something special in her, which could easily have led to a more permanent relationship. At least the whole episode left him with a nagging sadness inside his heart.

Either way, fingers would be pointed at Jason. He hoped that his attorney was on the ball, but he couldn't imagine that his father would appoint any idiot as his legal man. He was pleased to see that Danny Foulkes had turned up to give him some support, but he would be required as a witness anyway, so the two men were kept apart, Jason coming up through the holding cells into the courtroom after his arrival.

He was comforted to see both his father and mother in the courtroom when he entered. His mother had been crying, which was par for the course, but his father was stony-faced as usual. Did the old bugger have any real feelings for him at all? He doubted it very much.

His mother called out his name and made as if to touch him on his entry into the courtroom, but his guard pulled him roughly away, as most uniformed guards with a sense of self-importance, or the fear of allowing a bomb to be passed, could be expected to do.

Jason's case was called out, and he was made to stand and face a stern-looking carbon copy of his father. The presiding officer was a no-nonsense type of individual who looked as if he had had any form of humour or compassion dried out of him a long while before. Aaron Jeeves was his name, but he was certainly no butler.

'Present your case,' he ordered the prosecutor, Byron Minkby.

'Your Honour, last Friday, the twenty-first of August 2015, at about five p.m., the police received a call emanating from the mobile phone acknowledged by the accused as belonging to him. He reported that Miss Tilly Markchester, his companion at the time, had gone missing, or "disappeared", as he so claimed.

'According to the accused, he had left her on the beach while he went to fetch a prophylactic device from his car, known as a "condom", which he intended to use during sexual intercourse with Ms. Markchester. When he returned to the place where he had left her, she was gone, or so he claims. He states that there was a blanket of thick mist at the time, which had rolled in from the sea, rendering a proper search difficult.' The prosecutor stopped for a few moments to study his notes. 'The police and an Emergency Services ambulance arrived at the beach, more or less simultaneously, about ten minutes later. The ambulance left after some minutes of fruitless searching for the young woman, but the police officers put in a thorough search, hampered by the density of the mist. But they did what they could before leaving the scene and taking the accused to the police precinct for further questioning.

'Because of the mysterious disappearance of the young woman, and fearing the worst, the accused was held overnight, as a more detailed search was planned for the next day. Because of the heavy fog of the previous evening, police divers were tasked to comb the area at first light the following morning.'

'And the result?' queried Jeeves.

'Only a beach towel was recovered at the shoreline, displaying some bloodstains partly washed out by action of the waves, and later a pair of men's white shorts was found further out in the bay, which were also stained with traces of blood.'

'What was your reaction to these findings?'

'We decided to hold the accused in custody until at least this hearing, Your Honour. What we discovered in the water points to a brutal attack by a crazed individual on an innocent and unattached young woman, guilty of nothing more than having sexual pranks with a young man on a deserted beach. She could not have expected to be torn apart by the savagery of somebody overcome with evil lust.'

There was a stunned silence in the court — apart from a few shocked gasps — after this evidence had been presented, only interrupted by the sobbing of two women: the missing woman's mother, and the mother of the young accused who seemed to be not far away from tears himself.

The judge studied the prosecutor balefully. 'Your dramatic words have done nothing more in this court but to upset at least two ladies. Other than that, they have not impressed me at all. Simply put, it sounds as if you intend intimidating me into detaining the accused forever and a day. We'll see if the defence has something to say in response to you. Defence?'

Greyton Elliott, looking very smart in his robes, stood up on cue. 'Your Honour, as usual, the prosecution has little evidence to present, other than what has already been mentioned. Until the relevant blood tests have been finalised, there is nothing to identify the blood as being that belonging to the missing young lady, or any other human being, for that matter.' He spread his hands dramatically in front of him. 'There could be a number of reasons for the bloodstains. Ms Markchester could have hurt herself in defending her virtue against an unknown attacker who seized his opportunity in foggy conditions while my client was busy elsewhere. The deceased may well have been attacked by some creature from the sea that appeared out of the mist and dragged her into the water, Your Honour. She may even have had some internal haemorrhage that had nothing to do with any attack at all. It seems harsh to incarcerate a young man while various tests are being carried out, and then to half-heartedly look for another scapegoat while he languishes in prison.' He pointed to Jason. 'Here is a young man who has more than done his duty to defend his country, having now been honourably discharged from its service. Can one expect him to be locked away until such time as the state decides to release him, in spite of his having an unblemished record?'

The judge peered across to the prosecution. 'How say you?'

'Your Honour, the authorities that we have approached consider that no shark, even of the great white variety bandied about in "Jaws", could have attacked and dragged away a young woman lying on the beach. At the same time, the accused's slate is not all that unblemished. It is on record that he had previously assaulted a young woman who said something that he objected to, resulting in his giving her a bloody nose. There seems to be more than a little violence buried inside this brave young hero.'

The prosecutor sat down with a satisfied smirk on his face.

Greyton Elliott jumped up, looking positively indignant. 'Your Honour, this matter has been taken out of context. My client intended giving the injured party — that the prosecution has now referred to — a light slap after she grossly insulted his mother, but his fingernail caught the side of the young woman's nose, causing it to bleed slightly.'

'How did this evidence come about?' the judge wanted to know.

'The police overheard this while they were monitoring a call made by the accused to his mother, Your Honour. Both mother and son discussed the matter quite openly.'

'Have you anything to add, regarding the motivation for my keeping the accused in prison while your investigation continues on its merry way?' the judge asked the prosecution.

'Yes, Your Honour. We are still interviewing witnesses as to character and fact, in this case. We need to hear their viewpoints before the accused has an opportunity to interfere with them.'

The judge replied: 'I hardly think that it is necessary to lock everyone up while the police take their time over interviewing people. Are there any investigating officers interviewing witnesses right now, for instance?'

'We have been told,' said the prosecutor, 'by a witness at the bar where the missing person and the accused met, that they heard them arguing about something before they drove off together.'

'And this witness can't tell you any more about what they disagreed?' queried Judge Jeeves. 'Did you take a signed statement, or was the witness unable to make one because of his, or her, condition? That all sounds desperately vague to me. I would say that young people often view their differences of opinion quite openly.'

After more items of little consequence were presented, the judge cleared his throat and pronounced his verdict:

'I understand that the accused's parents are here in court today. I hereby release him into their custody, on the proviso that they take responsibility for his appearance at the next appointed hearing.

'This pronouncement is also subject to his refraining from interfering with any witnesses who may yet be interviewed by the police, regarding this case, according to a list that they should surely have drawn up by now.

'For the sake of covering the state's costs, should the accused not comply with these conditions, I hereby impose an amount of ten thousand dollars as security, to be forfeited should these terms be disregarded.'

Arrangements were made for Jason's immediate release, but Charles Malvy was not prepared to let his son off that lightly. After Jason was released along with his possessions, father and son came face to face again, when they were both at home.

'This doesn't mean that you'll become a human parasite while the police are busy with their investigations,' he told his son. 'I expect you to pay reasonable board and lodging — the amount which I will set — and heaven help you if you leave me responsible for the loss of the ten-thousand-dollar bail money. Of course, you realize that you will need to get a job to cover your board and your personal expenses.'

Mathilda Malvy had been twittering in the background while her husband was laying down the law to their son. 'The poor boy has only now been released from jail, and you're already hounding him, Charles. Can't you merely welcome him with open arms? He is our son, after all.'

Jason let his parents do their squabbling while he packed his navy clothes away in his bedroom. At least his tough-guy father had not turned this room into a workshop or something similar. His father and he had never seen eye to eye, although he was generous enough to suspect that his father had deeper feelings for him than he would admit to having. With a wry smile, he would often speculate where the old man hid those feelings and why he didn't let them shine through occasionally.

He had learned to accept his dad for what he was. His mother had sat him down one day and explained that his father had been brought up under harsh conditions and found it difficult to relate to other people.

'The poor man is far softer than he lets on, Jason. That's why I've stayed with him for all these years. If you treat him right, he's nothing but a puddle of treacle inside all that bluster of his.'

For all her advice, his father could get under his skin, along with that of many others.

When his parents left him alone in his room, Jason thought through his position and came to two conclusions: He would get himself employed, to get his father off his back and to build up capital for himself, and he would quietly dig deeper into the disappearance of Tilly Markchester. That girl had not simply abandoned him. She had been snatched away by something brutish, and he wanted to find out what he, or it, was.

To his thinking, the creature that could drag a girl away off a beach with hardly a trace, leaving but a few bloodstains in the sand, had to have superhuman strength. He wanted to find out what on earth possessed such mighty power.

Chapter Seven

Jason believed in playing the high cards in his deck. He had two trumps to choose from. One of them was that he was an accomplished diver. The other was that he was a qualified realty agent, having registered through the agency that was owned by his father. The old man didn't believe in a son of his not bringing in an income.

Charles Malvy didn't have much to do with the agency other than using it to put through as many property deals as possible, thereby saving his firm a mint of money in fees and other spinoffs. Sometimes even he lost the plot as to what deal was going where and at what date, which was critical in itself at times.

But he left the finer points of reducing tax liability, and making bigger and better profits, to the man running the show. He had an efficient and innovative manager named Joe Caldecott, whom he left alone to row the boat his way.

Joe Caldecott, who had a sizeable stake in the property agency, was to some degree as stroppy as his senior partner. The two men had been involved in confrontations in the past, which had taught Malvy to keep his nose out of the business if he didn't have something material to add to the running of it. And that was most of the time, as far as his executive partner was concerned.

Not only did Caldecott know all about some rather doubtful business decisions that Malvy had made for beneficial tax reasons, but he had enough personal magnetism and know-how to take a large slice of the clientele away from the business, should any differences of opinion turn ugly. For all his tough mouthing, Malvy knew when to back down, no matter how humiliating the situation. Face-saving meant little or nothing to the canny old business tycoon. Money and prestige were of prime importance, definitely in that order.

Jason didn't bat an eye when he called in on his past property mentor to ask for a desk, stationery and some leads. Joe hardly twitched a muscle when Jason sat down in front of him. Both men had a lot of respect for each other. The property man felt like an elder brother to Jason. He remembered the laughs they had shared together, and the hard work they had put in to beat the competition to the punch.

Joe remembered how Jason had knocked up a seller at three in the morning, to get him to sign papers clinching the deal. The seller had needed to sell badly, being desperately short of cash at the time. He had handed the sale of the property to a number of realty agents, allowing them to squabble over the sale like dogs over a bone. The problem was that the old house was decrepit and turned prospective buyers off as soon as they saw the outside of it, never mind what they encountered when they walked in the front door.

Jason asked to be allowed to place the advert, and Joe gave him his head, sitting back with interest, to find out what his approach would be.

The ad started off: "We crept through this dirty and rundown old house, with candles in our teeth..." and continued in a similar vein. Curious readers wanted to see this place, nestling between flowery ads for "upscale accommodation in a beautiful area" and other exotica. The price was also well below average value for the area, for the property had been on the market for a while, without any interest being shown in it.

There was a rush of attention, and Jason had to arrange viewings on a ten-minute basis, with viewers meeting him on each of the four street corners to go through the old house. Luckily his firm was allowed access during the day when the owner and his wife were at work. Keys were no problem, for every realty agent worth his salt had sets of master keys covering most residences.

The young agent's ploy worked. Before long, he had a signed Offer to Purchase in his hand. The trouble was that there were now a few interested buyers floating around, ready to outbid his client. The Offer to Purchase had been signed, followed by a drinking session which Jason had difficulty in getting away from.

In the end, he had escaped just before three in the morning and gone straight to the Seller's house, knocking lustily on the front door until the old man came staggering along to open up for him.

'What the hell do you want at this time of the morning?' he moaned, wiping the sleep out of his eyes.

Jason was ready for him. 'You know how long you've been trying to sell this place,' he said. 'Well, I've worked my butt off to sell it for you, and I've even got the price you were prepared to accept. The buyer has just signed this Offer to Purchase that I've got in my hand. Let me in, sign it and your problems are over. You can sleep all day tomorrow, knowing that your bank won't foreclose on you. This, by the way, is a cash deal.'

The old man grumbled, but he let Jason in and signed the papers. The young agent handed the papers in to the seller's nominated transferring attorney the next morning and got on with his next challenge.

Some weeks later, the seller phoned the office in as angry a state as the receptionist had ever experienced.

'Where is that idiotic young man who sold my house the other day? I'd break his damned neck if I got half a chance. My friends are all laughing at me, regarding a slanderous ad that he placed in the newspaper concerning my house. I've spoken to my attorney regarding the trash your firm wrote about the property, but apparently I signed some sort of waiver which handed over control to your organization. Just tell that young punk to stay away from my family, and me, from now on. I'll murder him if I get hold of him.'

***

'So, you're making a name for yourself in the papers, young Jason. I'm not going to ask you any silly questions. But if you're asking for your old job back, I hope that you're not going to mess me around if I give it to you, as you know I will. Just keep your appointments and bring in some fresh listings. Don't tread on too many toes. Other than that, you're your own boss.'

'You're not concerned that the cloud hanging over my head will affect the business?'

'The thought did flash through my mind, but there is a good side and a bad side to it.'

'How so?'

'The bad side of it is that a few jittery females may be too nervous to have you escort them to a vacant apartment block. On the other hand, there will be plenty of sellers and viewers who will get a vicarious thrill out of being alone with you.

'There's a case in South Africa that's been bubbling away for over twenty years now. A highly skilled surgeon was used by the old apartheid government to run a department that was reputed to do hideous things to people. He was never found guilty, but the medical fraternity has been hounding him for decades, intent on taking his medical licence away from him.

'For all this time, he's had a booming heart practice, and people clamour to be treated by the man. Now if so many people are prepared to literally leave a man holding their hearts in his hands, what is the significance of an unresolved case of whatever the police are trying to pin on you?'

There were a number of reasons why the job suited Jason. Apart from the fact that he was starting on the run, as Joe was prepared to advance healthy monthly advances to successful agents, he could also move about fairly freely.

This would give him the opportunity to do a little digging into Tilly's disappearance himself. Like so many others, he didn't have an awful lot of faith in the speed and dedication of the average police detective. He was aware of the dangers of getting entangled in police investigations, but he thrived on danger, or else he would have given up diving immediately.

Other than pure mobility, he would be hard to pin down to any specific location, even from a time point of view. All he had to do, now, was to figure out how he could put his skills to good use in tracing Tilly's whereabouts. One thing he would like to do was to have a good look at the ocean floor off the beach where Tilly and he had been swimming. He didn't know what he might find, but he wanted to have a good look anyway.

He had a feeling that something was far from right, but he couldn't put his finger on what was bothering him. All he knew was that he had done nothing to the girl, and now she was gone. He didn't think that the detectives handling the case would know where to start looking for reasons for the girl's disappearance.

It seemed logical that they would keep tabs on him, in the hope that he would pull a rabbit out of a hat and solve the mystery for them. So he would make it as difficult as possible for them to follow his movements.

Jason visited a man he knew, who rented out fully equipped dive boats, with or without crew, to tourists as well as those who had some project in mind. He knew where he was likely to find his man, who had a favourite boat he used as an office when he was not at sea.

Without making a big deal out of it, Jason wandered around the boatyard, seemingly without any real purpose, until he slipped aboard the boat he was aiming for. He chuckled to himself. Anybody trying to stay on his tail would probably wonder where he'd got to.

Although the owner, Mike Creaser, was good at looking the other way and not asking unnecessary questions, he was aware that many of his clients were treasure hunters or involved in the collecting of goods that had never seen the inside of a customs house shed.

The two men ended up shaking hands on the use of the boat and crew for an initial two days, with a possible time extension built in if necessary. The contract would commence when Jason was ready to put it into operation. Jason was just as devious on leaving the boat as he'd been on his arrival. Let them figure that one out, he grinned, with boyish satisfaction.

There were still a few hours of sunlight left in the day. Jason drove to the beach where Tilly had gone missing. As he had suspected, there were no police divers searching the nearby waters, nor was anyone combing the beach for further clues. He felt as if he was carrying a large sign on his back saying "Ignore any other clues — this is the one you want to watch."

Actually he wasn't far from the truth, as a detective was parked quite a distance from him, his binoculars trained on the suspect's current movements on this strand. He couldn't make out what the young man was doing, but he would have given a lot to know. Well, on his pay, maybe a beer. A small one.

Jason had taken the trouble the previous Friday, while waiting for the police to arrive, to use his cell phone to take a few snaps of the beach where he believed the two of them had put down their towels. His guess as to where they had been was hardly scientific, but it did narrow down the possibilities a little.

There was a metal detector in the boot of the car. Another one of his myriad interests. He enjoyed the occasional wander across a deserted beach on the lookout for valuables lost by careless beachgoers. Jason told anyone who cared to ask that he could imagine distant voices calling to him: "Help! Let me out! I'm stuck down here!"

The young searcher carried the gadget down to the beach after studying a tide table and making adjustments accordingly to identify the area that he wanted to start operating the machine. Then he began systematically combing the area that his guesstimates had expected Tilly and him to have been lying on that fateful Friday afternoon.

He was looking for Tilly's belly ring and tiny chain that she had been wearing when she had vanished into foggy air. If there was blood on the towel that had been recovered, as well as on the shorts, it was possible that the ring had been torn loose in her struggle. Unfortunately, there was no way of hiding his possible intentions from any likely watching detective. Instinctively, he expected to be under surveillance at all times.

The light was fading, and Jason was ready to call it a day, when the machine gave a tiny chirp to indicate something metallic that it had encountered in the sand. He carefully pinpointed the target area before sinking to his knees and burrowing away like a demented rabbit.

With one hand on his glasses, the detective phoned in the news: 'He's been searching methodically with a metal detector, and it looks as if he's struck it lucky.'

'Then keep an eye on him. Don't let him dispose of anything in his possession. We'll send out a couple of men right away to find out what he's up to and confiscate anything he's found.'

It took some careful sifting until Jason came up with the little ring and chain, he remembered that Tilly had worn on her belly. It felt quite strange to have it in his hands. By now it was getting dark. The sooner he could get it to his car and get it home, the better.

But he was a little too late. By the time he got his booty to the car, there were headlights on the beach track, and he was boxed in by the police.

They were closing in on him. Never one to sit still and give in all that easily, Jason got the car going and sped off in the opposite direction. Sure enough, on came the flashing blue lights and the siren. He ignored them and picked up speed, but they kept on his tail.

Then he realized that he was only causing unnecessary grief for himself, so he eased up and stopped the car. He sat waiting for his followers to come to him, feeling the old adrenalin rush that the brief chase had stirred up in him.

A burly cop came clumping through the thick, sandy track to where Jason was sitting in his car, with his hands on the steering wheel.

'Get out of the vehicle, with your hands in the air,' he ordered.

'That's a physical impossibility, Ossifer,' Jason beamed. To get out of the car, I can't possibly manage without using my hands for leverage.'

'I don't care, and don't get smart with me. Get out of the car now!'

'So may I use my hands then?'

'Do what you damn well like with your hands; just get out of the car.'

'On any particular side?'

The officer didn't suffer from an overdose of humour. 'Listen, buster, if you don't get out of this car right now, you'll be sorry when I cuff you, because I'm not too gentle with those things.'

'I'm not surprised,' chirped Jason, making sure that he was obeying instructions while he spoke. 'If one gets worked up over every little thing, coordination of the hands is one of the first things that will suffer.'

The cop took out his firearm and stuck it in his prisoner's back. 'Now put your hands on the roof of your vehicle and show me your driver's licence and vehicle registration papers.'

Jason shook his head slowly from side to side, being careful not to make any rapid movements. This sucker was burning a short fuse. It was one thing to take some mickey out of him, but it wouldn't do to push him too far.

'I can't possibly get to the papers you want me to show you, with my hands on the roof of my car. Could you please tell me what you want me to do first?'

The policeman growled like a caged lion. 'Then get me your papers, but I'll be watching every move you make. One mistake, and you may get a bullet in your back. It would be my pleasure to accidentally put a hole in you, smartass!'

Jason had taken the trouble to start up the recorder on his mobile phone, in the hope that he could rub up the law the wrong way. Now the thought of replaying this conversation in front of the right audience was more than worth the indignity he was being put through.

There was nobody more disappointed than Officer Kissart when Jason handed over his papers and they were all found to be in order.

'Why did you drive away from us when we signalled for you to stop?'

Jason pointed to the headset on the passenger seat. 'I was listening to music at the time and didn't notice you behind me, at first, but I did stop eventually, and here I am, as you can see.'

'You can call yourself lucky, this time,' the patrolman mumbled. 'But there'll always be a next time. We'll be waiting for you, make no mistake.'

'Does that mean I can go?' asked Jason, hardly believing his luck.

'Yes, go, but you better watch out in future.'

The young diver didn't wait for another moment. He climbed into his car, put his papers away and sped off into the fast-approaching darkness. But he was sure they had meant to pull him in for his activities on the beach. However, he wasn't going to hang about while they made up their minds.

Sure enough, the blue light and siren came on again, and they were catching up to him again. He mentally shrugged his shoulders, not wasting any more time in pulling over and stopping.

Officer Kissart was back at his window. 'Get out of the vehicle,' he barked.

Jason made a half-hearted attempt to follow instructions. 'But Officer, don't you recall that you stopped me a little way up the track and went through my papers?'

'Just get out of the car. I've got to search you.'

'I don't know what you expect to find, but go ahead,' said Jason, as he did what he was told.

He was clumsily frisked, and the patrolman found the little chain and attached ring.

'And what's this, then?'

'I guess you know. I've only found it minutes ago, as your lookout who was watching over me probably reported.'

'You've got an answer for everything, haven't you? Just follow us to the station, and no tricks, mind you. The lieutenant wants to have a word with you.'

'How about handing over the ring and chain?'

'I'll be keeping it nice and safe until we get back to the precinct.'

***

He was ushered into the same interrogation room as on his original arrival at the precinct. Detective Joe Robson was still chewing and as fat as ever. It wasn't long before scrawny Arnold Pearson entered the room to support his colleague.

'So, you're lucky enough to be floating about the countryside on bail, so I hear,' warbled Robson, wiping a splash of spittle off his lips as he spoke. 'But instead of sitting at home like a good boy, you're belting about the town like somebody with an itchy backside. Now, where does this chain and ring here come from? You'll notice that it's all safely tucked away in an evidence bag, rather than merely floating about in your car. Tell us, now, what were you doing with it, and where did it come from?'

'I think you know very well where it came from. If your spy was awake on the job, he would have seen me dig it up from the beach, exactly where I told you we were sitting before the girl disappeared.'

Robson hooked a piece of tired chewing gum out of his mouth with a fat finger and dropped it into an ashtray on the table. 'We can't go about digging up the whole of San Diego because somebody goes missing.'

'And that's the attitude I expected you to have. That's exactly why I went to the trouble of digging it up myself, because I was sure that nobody around here would have the energy or initiative to do their own digging.'

'You were just lucky you found a little trinket like that in all the tons of sand on the beach,' chipped in Pearson.

'Maybe so. But at least I got off my backside and found Tilly's ring, by using a little effort.'

'We've been plenty busy, following up people who know you.'

'What did you have for lunch today?' Jason challenged.

'I don't see what that's got to do with you, punk,' snarled Robson.

'That's not a nice word to use, Defective — sorry — Detective. What you had for lunch is not really my business, I suppose, but I haven't had a lunch break yet. That's the difference between us. To you, it's just another case. To me, my future is hanging in the balance.'

The three men glared at one another, but somehow, the point had got across.

Robson broke the uneasy silence: "Well, how long would it have taken you to get this bit of jewellery to us?'

Jason shrugged his shoulders. 'Maybe a little quicker than your officers took to get it here. Look, this is not a competition. I'd like this whole sorry business cleared up more than you can imagine. That's why I'm doing your work for you — to speed things up a bit, before evidence like this is washed out to sea. Talking about the sea — have your divers gone on their annual holidays, or do they still intend to comb the seabed in the vicinity of the beach?'

'Don't try to teach us our jobs,' sneered Robson. 'We know exactly what we're doing. Anyway, you were expressly ordered by the judge not to interfere with our investigations.'

'But you see, you need to be shown where your duties lie. Start off by carefully reading the judgement that the man made. The judge expressly ordered that I not interfere with any witnesses. Nothing was said about my picking up evidence that you've casually left lying around on the beach or in other places.'

Robson stood up violently enough to knock his chair over. 'Go on, get the hell out of here, before I have you locked away purely for the fun of it. But mark my words: you'll trip over your own clever feet yet, or maybe it's your tongue that will get you into a whole heap of trouble, and then you'll see what power we're able to exercise over you and your smart mouth.'

Chapter Eight

Killer whales are awesomely fierce creatures, yet they seldom fight among themselves. In a pod of orcas, hierarchy is quickly established and adhered to. Even the question of choosing a mate is not a threatening factor. Although males and females tend to pair up for long periods — and sometimes even for life — there is usually no strict form of sexual exclusivity involved.

Mating between different pairs often takes place. It seems as if killer whales of the same sex are self-confident enough not to brawl with one another over something that is not all that important in their lifestyle.

Although both males and females are motivated sexually, there are times when one or other sex takes the lead in wanting to mate. As is most unusual in mammals, male and female orcas' mate in a face-to-face position. When a female is not feeling ready for sex, she has the simple remedy of rolling onto her back so that the male can't get to her sexual organs.

Of course, she can't stay in this position for too long, because her blowhole is being obstructed. The male, being as smart as he is, hangs around at times like these, waiting for the female to turn over for a breath of air. With any luck, he'll be able to take his chance and connect with her at the right time, making himself available to slide underneath her and impregnate her.

Males have even been observed waiting in small groups in these situations, hoping to turn the female and so to take their pleasure with her. Not only human males let their urges get out of hand sometimes.

Samson, however, had been differently programmed to other orcas in the wild. He had developed a slow-burning hatred of mankind in his years of incarceration, which superseded normal urges, whether sexual or otherwise. He wanted something that his fellow creatures seldom sought out: he wanted revenge, not only for being confined for so long, but mainly for the way his new and peaceful way of life, along with his family unit, had been ripped apart. Perhaps he was the next small step along the path of evolution, for he was bigger and heavier than others that had been accurately measured. Along with that development, his brain was larger and more intricately programmed than that of his peers.

He seemed to know that he was meant to lead others of his kind. Samson went out of his way to mix with those of his species, after seeking them out, and he would set out to take over the particular pod that he linked up with, forming them into a cohesive unit that took directions from him.

**

Not much was known about the killer whale, but there were tales of them operating in packs against other whales, preventing them from "sounding", and even obstructing their blowholes in efforts to suffocate them. They would tear big lumps of blubber and flesh out of their targets and even tear out the tongues and cheeks of their victims when they caught them in defensive situations.

They were revered by the traditional whalers, who were adamant that the dolphins sometimes made them aware of the presence of whales, even cornering the huge animals in a small cove or inlet for the easier capture by humans. Of course, it was hard to establish which were genuine stories or old wives' tales, but there were many seasoned whalers who would be ready to corroborate this story.

Whalers of the days when men still bravely operated out of small boats, recounted that killer whales would not interfere with humans should they happen to fall into the sea from their boats. There were even tales told of native tribes that stroked the orcas with long spears as these leviathans cruised past a headland, as a cat or a dog might enjoy being stroked by its owners, although these stories sounded a little farfetched and likely to be dredged up around a fireside while drinking down something fiercely alcoholic in nature and strength.

But it was true that little record was available of orca attacks on divers or boatmen. The giant orca was not bound by tradition, hearsay or even record. He was not interested in statistics. He had only one thing in mind: this dedicated mammal was merely set on causing mayhem amongst the people who had abused both him and his family over a terrible period of time.

This particular orca was not merely a standard-sized killer whale. The average size of its species is just under eight meters for males, with a maximum weight of a little more than ten tonnes. Samson, however, was a giant amongst his fellows, being more than ten meters in length and weighing well over thirteen tonnes. His extreme bulk and weight made it nigh impossible to measure him accurately.

The orca pods that this giant encountered seemed to respect his great size and were quite willing to accept him as their leader. Even when his intentions regarding attacking humans were made clear, they were prepared to follow him wherever he led them. The largest female of his new family also made it known that he was her new mate, staying by his side as much as possible, although his nature was such that he would always be something of a lone wolf.

What he did possess was the urge to breed. It was as if he wanted to pass on his oversized genes to as many females as possible. This meant that the other males of his increasingly enlarged pod had to make way for the mighty one, instinctively compelled as he was to increase the size of his kind. The rest of the males stood aside for Samson, with the respect that was his due.

And so, the giant orca led the way in encouraging his followers to target humans on beaches, boats or in the sea. The size, strength and mobility of certain boats made it most difficult to get to their occupants, unless they targeted dinghies and other smaller boats. But the killer whales had even more problems to contend with when it came to targeting beaches.

The slope and the tide had to be right, and beachgoers had to be positioned near the wave edge of the shore. There was also a preference for foggy surroundings if possible, otherwise the bullocking attack of a leviathan would be noticed by the majority of bathers, who could mostly take avoiding action if they were lucky enough to see the oncoming attacker.

Amazingly, the killer whale could usually keep its bulk underwater and out of sight for long enough to give little warning to bathers both on the beach and playfully frolicking in the waves.

It was found to be far simpler to hunt the prey at night when bathers went into the water for a swim in the dark, often in romantically inclined pairs. Their togetherness and bodily contact would distract many of them from a fast-moving black and white shadow in the breakers. They would then be grabbed and taken before they were even aware of a creature bearing down on them.

Even so, any unobservant person was liable to be attacked if they weren't alert to possible danger from a darkened sea. And so it was, that a couple of weeks after the disappearance of Tilly Markchester, a young rabble-rouser staggered down the beach not far from where the young woman had originally disappeared.

He was alone and very tipsy, a condition which had caused his date to get a lift home with somebody else. As he was young enough to have to face irate parents should he stagger inside the family home in a poor condition, Reuben Dickson had decided to take a quick dip to sober up a little.

Without a thought being given to any danger he could face, Reuben, a competent swimmer, staggered into the sea until he lost his balance and fell into the water, then he stood up again and managed to paddle out through the breakers until he was bowled over by a larger-than-usual wave. This was the bow wave of Samson, who claimed his second victim that night.

Grabbing the lolling young man with his numerous sharp, conical teeth, the killer whale dragged his catch back into the sea, with the upper half of its body firmly in his jaws. All the man was aware of was the interior of a black cavern, along with the burning pain around his waistline where his body was being ripped apart by the tremendous force of rows of grinding teeth.

He tried to scream for help at first, but his voice was muffled in the maw of the creature that was ripping him apart. Then his yells stopped as his lungs collapsed and were punctured by the relentless force devouring him. That was the last that anyone would see of Reuben Dickson. His car would be found on the sandy track the next day, with his clothes stacked untidily next to it.

The verdict would be that he had been mugged, as his mobile phone, watch and wallet were missing. What the indolent police detectives didn't figure out was where the man's body had been taken to.

He had been robbed, after all, but this was only when a passing tramp had helped himself to an unusual windfall in the early morning, some hours later. When his parents notified the police that their son was, in fact, missing, the detectives came to the conclusion that he had probably left home.

Reuben's car was more carefully examined, but nothing unusual was found, including blood traces or narcotics. His case was logged under "missing persons", but no further action was taken. He had simply disappeared.

Later on, people began to wonder if Reuben had simply made the decision to end his life by wandering into the sea and letting the waves take him away. But his family and friends insisted that he was not a suicidal type of person. Had some monster come out of the sea and claimed a victim? It was certainly a more acceptable outcome, if only for life assurance claim purposes.

Only a few days later, a young couple went for a midnight swim off another beach. It was just about warm enough for a swim, but they would have gone skinny-dipping even if the water temperature was a lot lower than what they encountered. What they didn't expect to face was the yawning chasm of a killer whale's mouth, as it lunged at them from out of the darkness of the ocean.

They didn't even see it coming. They both had their eyes closed and their tongues lashing against each other, as they pressed together in an ecstatic frenzy of desire. Then the girl was ripped out of the young man's arms. He staggered backwards as something rough gouged a bloody furrow out of his arm. Shocked, the man opened his eyes to see his lady friend with her mouth open, being dragged from his grasp.

The girl was immediately taken and mostly engulfed in a giant maw, without any resistance on her part. As the monster dragged itself, along with its trophy, back into the sea, her boyfriend instinctively tried to grab her out of the orca's mouth. He tried a little too hard. The killer whale's mouth closed over his arm, and he fell to his knees before being towed out to sea along with his lover, never to be seen again.

When another couple of deaths were reported, the newspapers picked up on these mysterious disappearances.

"Four young people have disappeared mysteriously within a few weeks!" read the headlines.

Pressed to provide a response, the police spokesman pushed out the usual story of working day and night to find a solution to the mystery.

'We are examining many avenues and are following up all reasonable leads right now,' was the answer that was given to the press.

Another interpretation would be that officialdom hardly knew where to start looking. In the sort of deaths that were occurring, victims being dragged into the sea didn't leave much in the way of clues as to their manner of disappearance.

The newshounds weren't going to be fobbed off that easily. 'What sorts of leads are most likely to present results?' asked a reporter.

'With all the unrest going on in the world today, it could be that these people were members of a radical group, who had flown the country to link up with an overseas organisation.'

'Are you referring to ISIS or a similar body?'

'Not necessarily, but we are busy finding out whether any of them were members of, or were affiliated to, any such groups.'

'What about merely being members of a secret society, or even a gang? How about their assimilation into a religious body, like the Seventh Day Adventists?'

The spokesman raised up a hand in protest. 'All these possibilities are purely speculation. They are mostly all under investigation at this stage. When we have anything more definite for you, we will let you know.'

'Why have so many people disappeared off a beach or from a boat? What connection is there between a secret society and a swim in the sea? This doesn't seem to make the least bit of sense,' remarked a reporter.

'All we can say at this stage is that we are exploring all possibilities. You'll have to be patient with that until we can give you more definite answers.'

But the press had the bit between their teeth and weren't prepared to let go of a potentially gripping story so easily. They went to the friends and colleagues and parents of the missing persons — some of whom hated the publicity involved, and others who hated their personal family business and private affairs being dragged across the printed pages and the newscasts.

Much of the published interviews were based on hearsay and wild accusations and statements. But the more that conservative people protested, the more publicity their comments were given. Of course, there were those who loved the notoriety of being quoted and even filmed by the media. They went to the trouble of having their hair done and putting on their finery, usually accompanied by an overdose of makeup. And some were then too tongue-tied to have much to say for themselves.

Not many of the witnesses knew Jason Malvy all that well, but almost all of them had some sort of opinion to hand out. The older neighbours were convinced that the young man was up to no good at all, like "all the young of today, with their loud music and their drugs and their floppy clothes." It didn't matter if they weren't even sure what he looked like, but that's how they felt.

The younger set who didn't know Jason — and there were quite a lot of them — looked at the snapshot the police showed them and formed an opinion from that alone. The girls and young women thought that he looked "cute", stated that they would go out on a date with him anytime and that they would trust him on a lonely beach, whether they happened to be wearing a bathing suit or not. The thought of strolling naked with this good-looking young man made a few of them catch their breath, in a sort of hungry anticipation of the event.

Although their mothers and fathers were quite shocked when they heard their daughters giving their opinions, many of them thought that it was quite romantic — and even sexy — to wear a young man's shorts on the beach if they didn't happen to have their swimsuit with them. Then they looked at their husbands' bulging midriffs and tried to wipe the mental picture from their minds.

As for a bra, many tops were a lot more revealing than even a see-through bra was. On Bondi Beach, one of Australia's prime swimming holes, some girls suntanned or swam topless. It was the modern way of girls showing their equality with men. In fact, one or two of the young maidens even paraded bottomless, feeling no shame at all in displaying themselves to the world.

The males were more noncommittal in their answers, but few of them thought that he was a danger to society. Most of those canvassed didn't see Jason as the type who would go around murdering young women. One teenager summed it up by saying that many girls that he knew would probably let the young guy have sex with her, without putting up a fight at all. In fact, she might even encourage him a little, if she were a little tipsy and in the mood.

A lot of this sensational reporting appeared in the local papers, because the reporters had jobs to do and pages to fill. Jason read some of this but was soon bored by some of the stuff they were dragging up, about what he had been like at school and whether he had been of any trouble to the teachers.

On the negative side, one not-so-young woman reported that she was sure she had heard the deceased and the accused arguing about something when she went past them to the ladies' toilets. Although asked what the disagreement had been about, she couldn't give a definite reply.

When she was pressed for an answer, from the few words the witness had picked up, it had something to do with the young man wanting to take her to a spot where they could be alone and cuddle together, whereas the victim wanted to stay at the bar with the group of young people she was with. When it was pointed out to her that Tilly Markchester hadn't had any friends at the bar when she had met up with Jason Malvy, she shrugged this off.

'I'm sure there had to be someone she knew there,' she responded, not willing to give an inch to the reporter. It seemed to be clear that she didn't like men all that much and had labelled this one as a rapist.

'They're on about you again,' his mother called out, as the daily newspaper was delivered to their door.

His father never said a word to him about what was in the papers. Jason wondered what the old man thought about it all, but not a word about it passed between the two men.

Inside his twisted, old soul, Charles Malvy harboured a burning jealousy for his only son. He had all the limelight in his business dealings, and he wanted it all at home as well. If he had been less bombastic, his wife would have had more time for him, but that was the way with people like Charles Malvy. They chased away the very people that they wanted most to look up to them.

In the meantime, the bitter old man drummed his fingers on his desktop and thought his dark thoughts.

The phone did start ringing from a variety of sources. Some of Jason's friends wanted to tease him about his sudden notoriety, and the family also phoned, mainly to share in the Malvy family's sudden rise to fame. But worst of all were the crank calls with vicious comments and vile warnings, including threats to throw a brick through their front window and to arrange a communal beating for Jason.

Even the girl whose nose Jason had caused to bleed had a lot of spite and slander to get off her chest when Jason picked up the phone.

'I always thought you were an awful little bastard. You should have been locked away years ago. You're a danger to society, and I hope that you rot in hell.'

After more of this, while Jason listened with his mouth open, she slammed down the phone in the gibbering rage she had worked herself into. He shook his head in a mixture of sorrow and amazement as he put down the instrument.

'I think that you should let me screen your calls from now on,' his mother advised, when her son told her what so many callers were saying. 'If they try that sort of thing on me, I'll simply let it fly over my head or give them some lessons in telephone technique and good manners.'

Strangely enough, Mathilda Malvy did a good job of keeping calm and not letting crank callers get under her skin. She was one of those quiet souls who do best when they have a problem that they can sink their teeth into. And she would do anything for her son, mainly because of her awareness of her husband's harsh treatment of their only child.

Gradually, most of the more toxic calls petered out, as no advance was made against her calm and impregnable defence.

It was awkward for Jason to be seen in public. Whether it was his imagination or not, everybody seemed to be putting their heads together and pointing at him when he went past. Or else they were gossiping to somebody about him.

The sooner this is over, the happier I'll be, he thought to himself. And yet, in a strange way, his sudden notoriety seemed to be good for his renewed career in the real estate business. Viewers were asking specifically to be shown around new listings with the newest agent on the block.

They were quite impressed when he appeared to be quite knowledgeable as a realtor, which was not surprising since his father had groomed him in the business from his teens, because "No child of mine is going to receive any sort of allowance from me without working for it."

Chapter Nine

It was a sunny Saturday, and Peter Melrose, together with his wife, Agnes, wanted to try out their new fishing boat for the first time. It was not actually brand new, but it had been sold to Peter in good condition. According to the previous owner, it was a really sound boat, but he never seemed to find the time to use it these days.

Peter had always wanted a boat of his own. He was mad about fishing, but catches off the side were dwindling, what with over-fishing and pollution caused by anybody who was careless enough to throw a plastic bag, or something similar, into the ocean. After seeing an ad in the local papers for the sale of an eighteen-foot boat with two 40-horsepower Yamaha engines and a tiny cabin, for a price that he could just about afford, he couldn't turn his back on it.

The boat had been standing waiting for him in his backyard after he had towed it home and sorted out all the paperwork involved, but business had suddenly given a lurch in the right direction, and his vehicle windscreen installation service depended largely on what insurance company was smiling down on him at any given time. If they pointed business his way, he was obliged to handle it.

The smile always widened when he offered the largest backhander to the insurance adjuster handing out the business. But this dubious transaction tended to sour the cream off his profits. Nevertheless, he had to do it if he wanted to do well in the trade. There were few car owners who didn't insure their wheels, these days. Few motorists would come directly to him with their damaged windscreens, so he had to keep on good terms with the insurance firms.

It wasn't easy to persuade Agnes to join him on his outing and to bring their two children with them. Sheldon, aged six, and Maureen, aged five, had clamoured to go on the trip, but his wife had an inherent fear of the sea, and although she had reluctantly agreed to go, the timid woman would have much preferred to leave the children in someone's care for the day.

But Peter needed someone to help him with his boat, and he'd left it too late to organize an experienced boat enthusiast or fisherman to crew for him. Apart from that, he didn't want to make an ass of himself in front of a guy he hardly knew, even if this was merely a male pride issue.

However, everybody seemed to have something to distract them from giving him a hand, and the kids really wanted to join them. Sheldon was mad about toy boats, anyway. He was already putting on a big defiant performance when Agnes finally gave in on condition that Peter provided lifejackets for them all. The adult ones formed part of the boat's safety equipment, but Peter had to buy two jackets to fit his young ones, the cost of which made him shudder.

There was a lot of running about to do for him to launch the boat. Agnes had no experience at all, and Peter had to do just about everything to get the boat off the trailer and into the water. The eventual retrieval of the boat was something that the new skipper put out of his mind for now.

It was one thing to reverse the trailer into position on the slipway and then to put Agnes behind the steering wheel. He would push the boat off the well-greased trailer runners and leap aboard to start the motors, while his wife found parking for their rig.

Then he would nose into the step-off point to collect his wife when she returned to the slipway. A relatively easy routine. But what about the procedure when they returned to harbour? Could Agnes reverse the trailer down the slipway, when her battles to park their car were the basis for many a family leg-pull, although she took the ragging with a fixed and slightly sour smile.

Would she be able to help him retrieve the boat? Maybe he could tie it up against the harbour wall and hop off to fetch the trailer. Then he would reverse it down the slipway, park it there for a minute or so, while he went back to the tied-up boat and drove it onto the trailer.

But he would have to get it right at the first go. It would be just his luck if somebody else wanted to use the slipway while all this was going on. At times like these, that's when something was sure to go wrong.

A bigger worry for Peter was the seaworthiness of the boat. He knew that he should have taken it out for a test run before he bought it, but he happened to be terribly busy about that time, and the private seller was pressing him to pay over the purchase price. "There's someone else who's interested," he'd said, which was the usual threat always used as a prod by canny sellers.

So, Peter gave in and handed over the money, on the assurance that the seller would take out his own mother in the boat, it was so seaworthy.

The bugger must have been talking about his mother-in-law, Peter muttered to himself, as he stood alone at the tiller. Agnes and the children were huddled in the tiny cabin, as protection from the occasional flying spray that the wind lifted off the sea.

It was not that the sea was rough that day. But there was a chop in the water which made the boat bounce about uneasily. It felt as if the cabin, probably erected as an afterthought, made the boat too top-heavy for its lightweight design. Maybe it needed a little ballast down below. *It feels as if I'm trying to keep a bucket of bolts upright, not a shipshape boat. Or should that be shitshape?*

Anyway, like most men determined to have their pleasure at all costs, he kept the nose of the boat pointed out to sea, while Agnes made their children join hands with her and say a little prayer for their safety. Then she got them to sing Christian choruses.

Actually, the boat was not quite as unseaworthy as it felt to the brand-new boat owner. If it bobbed like a cork, Peter was reminded of a friend who always had something wise to say, even if he was a fool himself: "If it bobs like a cork, be thankful — corks don't sink."

Peter gritted his teeth and kept the boat pointing away from the harbour. There weren't many boats at sea, but then it was a cold and overcast sky that was developing. His adrenalin was still pumping at a high rate of knots. What didn't help was the coastline disappearing into the distance.

Actually, he wasn't having much fun at all. His body was as tense as a board. Maybe it would get better later, as he got used to handling the bucking craft under him.

If he let the bounciness of his new boat get the better of him, his heart really plummeted when he looked out to sea. There were three huge shapes ploughing towards him with a force that generated three substantial bow waves. Behind these curling hillocks of water were three immense humps flag-masted by three tall fins.

A trio of killer whales was charging at the boat with murderous intent. He couldn't believe it. This sort of thing was not set out in any boating manual that he had ever read. And there was no hope in running for the harbour. They were too far out to sea for that to do much good.

He could only watch in horror as the terrifying shapes sped up to the boat. He was stricken into immobility, not even having the presence of mind to try to turn away from the mountainous shapes. He hung onto the wheel with his jaw set tight.

Moments before they were struck with tremendous force, Agnes happened to look out to see the three sea giants charging at their flimsy boat. She was horrified and let out a piercing shriek, pressing her children's faces to her bosom so that they could not see the hideous sight about to engulf them. It was then that the boat took a tremendous blow, the force of which knocked the helmsman overboard.

One of the terrifying orcas broke away and scooped up the kicking man in its voluminous mouth, while the other two creatures leant their weight on the side of the boat and began rocking it like a cradle. Now there was more screeching from the open cabin as Agnes, and then her children, lifted their heads to the mind-boggling sight of two giant orcas busily engaged in toppling the boat over.

Sheldon and Maureen added their shrill voices to their mother's screams, before they were swept from the cabin, landing in the water at the mercy of the marauding killer whales. They were scooped up with ease, and the orcas swam away triumphantly with their trophies, leaving the overturned boat to look after itself.

It was later found and towed back to harbour, with its engines having overheated and seized up. There was no sign of its occupants, and it was some time before the authorities could piece together who had been aboard at the time. What did puzzle everyone was the fragments of life jackets that later floated ashore. They looked as if they'd been put through a mincing machine.

How could life jackets get in that condition? Sea Rescue wondered. Man-eating sharks? Scavenger sharks? Speculation ran wild, but there was no evidence to back any of these ideas. Other than the engines having been seized up through being run dry for some time out of the water, the interior of the boat showed no great evidence of mishap, apart from a few scratch marks and streaks of blood that were later taken for analysis and found to belong to the family.

Then the owners were identified through relatives and friends reporting the disappearance of the family. Experts took a closer look at the boat, and certain oily deposits were identified on the gunnel of the boat. How had they occurred? Could the occupants have bumped into something floating in the bay, which caused the boat to tip over?

The newspaper reporters had a fine time of it with their speculations, but no one came forward with a clear-cut idea. There was a mounting wave of public uneasiness about the number of incidents that had taken place in the area lately, which could all be connected with the sea or its environs.

Jason read the reports with great interest and wondered to himself. A germ of an idea was forming in his mind, too vague, as yet, for him to put a name to it. In fact, if he had to utter it out aloud, it sounded like the ranting of an imbecile. It would be better to keep it to himself for the present, subject to further investigation.

Yet there was a mounting wave of public uneasiness about the number of incidents that had taken place in the area lately, which could all be connected with the sea or its environs.

***

Carlos and Freddie were old friends who had gone fishing together for years. They used a really battered old dinghy with oars out of the Ark, that they used to propel themselves to just outside the breakers on their catching expeditions. They didn't particularly love the sea. They used it merely to catch fish with which they augmented their income as retired and pensioned grocery packers at a local store.

The two men were fond of most types of fish, for meat was largely out of their price bracket. And what they caught was free, including exclusion from income and sales taxes. That already improved the taste of the fish they caught, and it was definitely dead fresh — they could vouch for that.

Their fresh catch had a sweeter smell to it than some of the tired-looking seafood lying limply on ice in the heat of the shop counters, with an occasional blowfly to keep them company.

What they could spare from their own requirements was sold to the local fish shop, the small amounts of cash being most useful for other budget items.

It was a weekday morning. Both of them had earned time off for working over the weekend to spell the regular staff.

They never went far out to sea. They were both fearful of its immensity and quickly changing temper. Within hours, it could change from a benign surface to a raging sea. They had seen this happen with their own eyes and had had a few narrow escapes. It was not easy to row a stubborn old boat wearing a life jacket, which they couldn't afford anyway, so they didn't bother with them.

They both knew that it took time to row a boat ashore should the weather change suddenly, particularly if the wind was blowing offshore and picking up the swells and breaking waves. So their experience had taught them to stay well inshore if they were in any doubt as to a possible change in sea conditions.

This day they were keeping to their basic rules, There was a gentle swell but nothing that they couldn't manage. After all, they were tough old birds with a lot of experience behind their grey beards, and they could both row with a steady rhythm that was deceptive in its efficiency.

That was why they were so startled when two huge humps bore down on them at frightening speed. Until then, the easy swell had given them no trouble, but the bow waves that the two killer whales generated were problems in themselves. The beasts swept right up to them without their being able to do anything about it and virtually climbed into the shallow craft.

Their massive weight submerged the vessel and its occupants, who didn't even have time to defend themselves with their oars, not that their weak swipes at the orcas were going to stop these determined beasts in their tracks. The two men yelled out in their fear, but their voices were drowned as the force of the sea, and then the attacking leviathans, engulfed them with ease.

The combined weight of the giant dolphins had broken the boat's back. There was not much left to identify the onslaught after the attackers had swum away, barring some torn pieces of clothing, broken oars and pieces of wood remaining from the wreckage of the old boat.

There was nobody to mourn the passing of the two old men. They had lived together in an ancient hut and were little trouble to anybody, and they kept to themselves. There was nothing much to salvage from their lives, apart from a heap of old clothing and a pile of empty bottles.

They did like to warm their bodies after a cold day on the sea. The liquor was probably their only pleasure, but they were canny enough to keep the empties out of sight from prying neighbours. They were given a paupers' funeral, with only Jason Malvy in attendance. And he really did grieve for the two men. He had read all about their broken old dinghy floating ashore in pieces, and their mysterious disappearance. It appeared to be yet another piece in the puzzle that was forming in front of him.

He had spoken to the reporters who had done the minimum effort necessary to provide a few lines on the deaths of the two fishermen, stuck somewhere on the inner pages of the competing local newspapers.

To the young man, this was the last straw. He felt that the public and the press were getting too blasé about the occasional deaths which were increasing with steady regularity along the local shoreline.

He went to the police and asked to speak to someone in authority. 'I'd like to report my findings and suspicions regarding the spate of deaths that have occurred in the area of late, which seem to be connected with the sea in some way or the other.'

It took some persuasion for him to get through to someone who wasn't merely a desk sergeant appointed to steer publicity-seeking crackpots away from those higher up the seniority ladder. And this was only achieved by his tenacity and threats of going to the newspapers and the government on a national scale.

Eventually he was allowed to speak to Vincent Labor, a liaison officer for the upper crust of the local constabulary.

This gentleman was none too enthusiastic about having to handle this young hothead who had a case of murder and/or rape and/or kidnapping logged against him, which was in the process of being investigated. He left instructions that the young man was to be frisked and accompanied by an armed and uniformed officer while in his presence. Who knew what the man was up to?

When Jason was eventually led into his office, the high and mighty officer made no effort to offer a hand, merely gazing at his own fingernails to confirm that they were in perfectly good order. Barely inside the office door, with the policeman at his side, Jason stood patiently waiting for some recognition.

Eventually the pompous officer, who obviously was on a fast track to an eventual position of great importance, thanks to good connections in the right places, lifted up his head and deigned to pay his visitor some attention.

'So, what can we do for you?'

Jason didn't waste any words of civility on this ass. 'You're probably aware that there have been a number of deaths associated with our local shores...' he began.

'Oh, I wouldn't say so,' interrupted Vincent Labor, busy once more with his fingernails, which seemed to take up a lot of his time. 'The death of your lady friend has not been slotted into any category as yet, and it's not unusual for a few persons to have accidents at sea, if one thinks of some of the mad risks they take. Personally, I think that they're out of their minds, putting to sea in some of those nasty little tubs they use.'

'But some people were taken while they were bathing along the shoreline!' Jason exclaimed.

'Oh, nobody can say what two oversexed people will do while prancing about in the waves on a dark night. I'm afraid there are no trends that one can identify from a hotchpotch of incidents like those.'

Jason stared at the man in surprise. 'So you're not even prepared to listen to my theory I have to offer?'

He couldn't believe it when the man yawned and didn't even manage to get his hand in front of his face in time.

'If I had to pay attention to every mad... er... member of the public who comes in here with novel ideas, I'd have nightmares every night.'

'Well, this is not a mad idea. This concerns a group of orcas who, I suspect, have turned away from their normal behaviour of tolerance to man. There has been a fairly recent escape, or unauthorized release, of some of these creatures from a local theme park. I suspect that something has stirred them up and allowed them to run wild, putting mankind at risk.'

Labor's mouth hung open at the speed that his visitor was rattling off his information. Jason did not normally talk at that rate, but he wanted to get the gist of his argument into the open before this yawning berk with the closed mind shut down his attention span completely.

'These things — these conkers - that you're talking about —what on earth are they? Anyway, what can a few fish do to mankind? It all sounds far too preposterous to me, to be a believable story.'

Jason explained patiently: 'The word is "orcas", or killer whales, to use a common term. And they're not just a few fish, as you put it. An orca is one of the largest creatures in the world and can snap a man in half, without really trying. In fact, it can kill the largest of whales. It can rip the tongue and the cheeks out of the biggest of whales when it can corner them, which is often enough.'

'This all sounds more than a little farfetched to me.' At least Labor had stopped fiddling with his nails for now.

Jason continued: 'If you need confirmation, then I suggest you do a little research to verify some of the facts I've given you. But I'm not here to impress you with facts and figures. It appears that both the police and the press haven't any idea why these deaths and disappearances have been occurring. I believe that I've come up with the answer to the mystery of the disappearing beachgoers.'

'Well, that's easy for you to say, but this information needs to be carefully analysed before we go off half-cocked and make fools of ourselves,' replied Labor.

'I assure you that you'll be making bigger fools of yourselves if you don't do something pretty soon. I may as well tell you that my next stop will be the newspapers. Even if they only sneer at my thoughts, at least they'll put it in print — to amuse their readers, if for no other reason.'

'Listen, you can't go and do that…' said Labor.

'What, are you going to arrest me for disclosing state secrets, when you don't seem to be taking me seriously in the first place?' asked Jason.

'Wait a minute, you can't come in here and threaten us like that. There are laws about threatening the police…'

Jason interrupted: 'Who's threatening? I'm simply telling you what I plan to do next. Now that's not a threat, that's a fact.'

With that, Jason turned on his heel, opened the door of Labor's office and walked out. He left the door standing wide open. That room could do with a little fresh air.

***

Jason was not one to make idle promises. His next stop was at the offices of the newspaper, where he asked to speak to one of the reporters who had interviewed him after Tilly had disappeared. He decided on this approach because the man had at least been attentive to him and had written a fair report.

The alternative would have been trying out a fresh and unknown reporter. Well, at least he knew where he was with this one. Luckily the man was available and also prepared to see him.

'Hello, Jason, thanks for asking for me. Most people never want to see me again, after they've read my reports.'

Jason shook hands with Terence Pollard, the reporter who had handled his interview.

The younger man grinned. 'No, you weren't too libellous. But actually, I've come to speak to you about something else entirely. You must know that there've been more than a few unexplained deaths along the shoreline lately. I've become interested because I'm a diver, and I'm naturally more than merely curious regarding my girlfriend's disappearance. And I couldn't have done them all in, could I?'

'You're not going to expect me to back you up regarding your lady friend, are you? Tell our readers what a nice guy you are?' asked Pollard.

'No. All I want to do is to present you with an idea that I've had. You can make of it what you wish.'

'Fine. Tell me what you've got in mind.'

Jason presented his exposition on what was causing the disappearances in the area. At least Terence Pollard knew all about orcas, which was a good start. He listened attentively.

'Apart from publishing your theory to a wide audience of our readers, what do you want me to do with it?'

Jason replied: 'I don't have the resources to delve into all the facts and reasons behind research on orcas. Maybe your paper can do a little scratching about for me.'

'I'll enter into a bargain with you: I'll do what I can to back you up and dig out facts for you, if you keep this whole story with our paper, so that I can get a jump on our opposition. I don't relish having a war over this kind of thing, where we'll spend more time tramping on each other's toes and arguing about what are facts and what are hearsay, instead of getting on with the job.'

'That's a deal for me.' Jason stretched across the desk, and they shook hands on it in the way that gentlemen do.

Chapter Ten

It was a hot and sunny Sunday, and the beaches were crowded. There were two types of sand and water lovers: those who went to church early and then felt entitled to go and enjoy the rest of the day at the beach; the others went directly to the beach and called this communing with nature or being directly in the presence of their particular God, in whichever direction their beliefs lay.

Whatever the reason for their being on the sand and in the water, almost all of them were having a wonderful time at Safehaven Beach. At least until a large group of huge creatures hove into sight. After gawping at them for some valuable seconds, the lifeguards weren't exactly sure what they were, but they decided to play it safe and get the swimmers out of the water.

One of the lifeguards, with the clearest voice, was elected to call everyone back onto the beach by loudhailer:

'Looks like we've got company, folks. They must be one of the biggest whale groupies in town. Everybody out of the water immediately, if you please. This isn't Sea World, and we don't know how friendly these critters are or what they're looking for. From here they look ginormous, and we'd like you to keep completely out of their way, until they decide to move off and play somewhere else.'

Perhaps the announcer was too chatty. He didn't want to alarm the bathers, but his calm approach led many of them to believe that this was no real threat to them. Sea creatures of this tremendous size only attacked people in story books and certainly not in modern times.

Whatever the reason, a number of swimmers stayed in the water, half hoping that they would be lucky to have a close encounter with these smiling sea monsters. A few daring ones even swam out to meet them. They were the first to die.

As the killer whales closed in, people who loved to count everything established that there were at least twenty orcas headed for the beach, and they meant business. They weren't coming ashore to make friends. In fact, a couple of them used handy gullies to get in really close and drag sunbathers into the water, who thought that because they were situated on dry land, they were completely out of danger from being attacked by creatures of the sea.

Mayhem reigned as people were snatched while playing in the water and devoured right in front of horrified spectators, some of whom were friends and family of those being split apart before their startled eyes.

A red tinge began colouring the foaming breakers as legs were ripped off bodies and bodies were ripped in half. Screams of agony changed to gurgles as gasping heads were consumed and crunched to death.

Little children were not spared from a terrible destruction. While mothers and fathers ran wildly across the beach, calling on their young ones to get out of the water, the children were pulled apart, limb from limb, right before their unbelieving eyes. They couldn't believe that these smiling black and white creatures, straight out of story books, could do anything nasty to them.

One little boy, braver or more stupid than some, put out a hand to pet a killer whale that had swum right up to him. The creature accepted the child's hand, as well as his arm up to the shoulder, before devouring him with a loud clap of its jaws. The watching mother could do nothing but scream in utter agony as she saw her beloved little son disappear into the creature's maw.

Where they couldn't get close enough to the shore, with all the bathers and their own orca companions in the way, the great black and white creatures cruised through the mass of humanity like oversized trash bins, their mouths snapping open as they swept up the terrified paddlers and their detached limbs and tore them to pieces in great gulps before changing direction, ready to devour the next treat.

A few women and children in the waves even tried to seek protection from equally terrified men standing in front of them, but it was purely the luck of the draw. The sheer mass of the killer whales buffeted the human objects out of their way, while seeking more interesting prey in the background.

Blood and body parts swirled about the scene of gore as the ravenous sea creatures swam into the trapped humans, diving around and between them like youngsters at a funfair picking apples out of a barrel. Some bathers were so blown out of their minds by the mayhem around them that they stood hopelessly, like ninepins in a bowling alley, shivering in fear while waiting for their turn to be executed.

A young woman was dozing on her stomach, with her baby playing at her side. Unfortunately for her, she was too close to the breakers. An adventurous orca bellied up to her by using a nearby channel and grabbed her feet, pulling her down to the water. Her baby clutched at its mother and slid down by her side, screaming in fear as it clung to her arm.

A really brave middle-aged woman jumped up from where she was sitting to grab the baby and pull it to safety. It was a courageous thing to do, but she was a little too late. The killer whale's mouth closed on her wrist as she stretched forward to pull the child clear of the killer whale, and she was dragged down towards her death along with the baby and its mother.

It was terrible for the bystanders to watch the orca reach the water and swallow the two women and the child; and it was not an instantaneous death for them. They were crunched and ripped apart as the helpless crowd watched, many of the spectators screaming and crying out in their anguish.

The killer whales were in no hurry to complete the mayhem they had created. There were half-eaten bodies floating about in the breakers, and the killer whales did a good job of cleaning up the bits and pieces of human remains before they retreated into deeper waters and left the spectators to count the cost of their horrific time at the beach, which had occurred in a matter of minutes.

They stood and stared at the bloodied water and were too shocked to say much, with the exception of the parents and partners who had witnessed their loved ones torn to pieces in front of their eyes. They wailed and beat the sand and were inconsolable. How had the authorities allowed this to happen? But nobody could give them an answer, simply because there wasn't one to give.

Others lay with their faces buried in the sand, not willing to own up to reality. Maybe when they sat up and brushed the sand from their eyes, they would find that it had all been a terrible dream, or even their worst nightmare. They would see their loved ones rushing up from the breakers with arms outstretched, wanting to be cuddled and cosseted, whether young or old. They would have shared a hug or kiss, as was their habit, before shaking the sand out of their clothing and going home together.

In fact, there was very little that anyone could tell the grieving next of kin about what had gone wrong. Even Jason, when the news broke, could hardly put this happening at the feet of the police or anyone else, when the attack had been so unexpected. This was not something that had merely gone wrong. It was a calamity of the worst kind and hardly a situation that the human psyche was designed to handle.

In fact, this was not the only drama that unfolded that Sunday. Someone had seen a lone fisherman being washed off a rock where he was fishing. A wave had come up out of nowhere and he had been swept into the sea, where he was picked up and devoured by the orca that had cunningly created the wave that had washed him off his rocky perch in the first place.

Even so, there was not much space in the weekend and daily papers to report this lone event. There were such a lot of terrifying items to report that the media were nearly swamped by all the reports that came flooding into their offices. Everybody had video footage and mobile phone snapshots to offer.

Of course, there were many who wanted to make a fast buck out of what they had captured of the ghastly happenings. Editors were on a knife edge, having to decide what brilliantly gruesome footage should be published and how much of it should regretfully be destined for the cutting room floor.

In the meantime, the nation was astounded by the mobile phone photos that had recorded the events of that Sunday at the beach. Many of the slides could not be shown in an untouched form, due to their being too disgusting or brutal for the public to handle. If they weren't regretfully discarded by hardened and scoop-oriented editors, they were skilfully touched up to lessen their gruesome impact.

Not only the American public was shocked by the news. The reports were spread across the world for the public to scrutinize, some with shock and horror but others with spite and satisfaction in their hearts. The world was agog at the news that humans on southern and western American shores were being attacked by killer whales, and many people, particularly from the East, got great pleasure out of the news regarding a Western calamity that they could gloat over.

It wasn't only swimmers who felt insecure. Anglers positioned at their favourite point on the shoreline or on rocky outcrops, minding their own business, appeared to be targets for orcas that had mischief in mind. One moment they would be standing in the hope of catching something worthwhile, and in the next instant, a black and white colossus would unexpectedly rear out of the sea in front of their target, mouth wide open and ready to engulf them.

This was when having a rod and reel in one's hand was a handicap rather than a weapon. The angler would instinctively hold onto his beloved rod and reel while trying to stumble backwards. It was traditional for him to be standing right on the edge of a jagged rock or with water lapping at his feet, or even at his knees. The deeper in, the nearer the angler would be to the fish, was the thinking.

But it was also the nearer to one's gruesome end when an orca put in an appearance. Most anglers slipped and fell when facing their death by a killer whale gobbler. That reduced their chances of escape to nil. The big creature didn't mind grazing its chin on the roughness of a rock when attacking a fisherman. It usually didn't feel a thing. And the grit and gumboots were usually shaken off while positioning the catch for its final descent into the hunter's belly.

Divers were also put into untenable positions when meeting an orca somewhere out in the bay. A sports diver, using nothing more than a pair of flippers, snorkel and face mask, could well lift his head up out of the water to face an incredible creature with evil intent in its heart.

There was no way out for the sports diver. He couldn't outswim it, dive away to safety or even use his diving knife as a defensive weapon. A stabbing with such a thing would be like a scratch on the nose of the monster.

Then there were the divers tethered to a boat overhead, by means of a lifeline of oxygen. They were in double jeopardy. They could be attacked while underwater, by a monster appearing out of the gloom, without being able to abandon their air supply. Or their boat and its crew could be wrecked by a killer whale, with dire consequences for the poor diver trying to suck air from an untended pipe.

Strangely enough, there were still those bathers who ventured into the water after it became clear that the great attack had not been a random one. There were other attacks on shores, where it was as if the killer whales had gathered together and decided to terrorize humans.

It was hard to believe that this sort of combined decision had been reached by a group of stupid fish, the public decided. Orcas had always been so tame. Maybe they could be trained to shoot out of the water the way they did it in Sea World and other amusement parks. They could leap for food or toys after months of training, but they surely didn't have enough brain matter to come to a mutual decision.

No — something else had disturbed them. Or someone. What about those Mideastern hotheads who had it in for the West? Or Russia, or China, or North Korea? Afghanistan? Iran? It seemed like the western nations were most unpopular in every country where they wanted to make friends.

These nations all had oil or spices or something else that the West could make urgent use of. It wasn't easy to take the advice of fireside experts and simply withdraw all troops, embassies and military hardware and pull the anti-nuke defence cover over one's head, while waiting for something to happen.

There were even nationals on holiday in foreign countries to think of. The government couldn't merely abandon them because the leaders of that holiday destination had their knives into wherever they came from.

The summer tourist season had been brought to a sudden standstill within a matter of days, at least for those who wanted to wallow on a beach in the sun, with an occasional dip in the sea thrown in to cool off a little. It was no use reporting that killer whales didn't crawl for great distances across the sand to drag their victims into the sea.

Even a quick swim in the sea could be classed as comparatively safe if one kept an eye on the breakers to avoid surprises. But it was understandable that a degree of overcompensation would take place.

One learned researcher, when asked whether he would venture into the sea that summer, replied: 'Why should I? I have a perfectly good pool to relax in at home.'

But it was not only bathers who could be classed as being at risk during that time. After reading about an interview with an ex-navy diver who had lost his own girlfriend and had had a murder charge thrown at him because of her disappearance, there were quite a few people, particularly in the police force, left with egg on their faces.

Readers did start wanting more advice from this young Jason Malvy, who seemed to know what he was talking about. He had tried to alert the police to the dangers of rogue killer whales, only to have been laughed out of their offices. It had taken a newspaper reporter to publicise his ideas and theories.

Jason Malvy was invited to give interviews at the local radio station and was even invited to a TV talk show, where he was feted as the man who had almost averted a catastrophe. As is the case with sudden celebrity, he was now the flavour of the month. Everybody wanted a piece of Jason Malvy.

The day came when Jason received a phone call from someone who identified herself as a publicist and image shaper. He was intrigued and arranged a meeting with the woman — Janine Whitlock. They met, by appointment, in a coffee shop, "to get to know each other", as Janine put it.

She was well groomed and self-assured, and Jason estimated that the attractive woman was about his age, although he found out later that she was a good few years older than what she appeared to be. She was tall, fairly good-looking, had a slinky figure and knew how to make the best of herself. Jason could see that she had a forceful personality, but she knew where to take a more relaxed and attentive attitude when the occasion suited her.

Janine could talk a blue streak when she was selling an idea, and she pulled out all the stops at that first meeting.

'Jason, what I would like to do is to market you in such a way that you realise your maximum potential. The people you're dealing with right now are using you to further their careers. Once they have sucked you dry, or the public's attention begins to focus on another newsworthy item, you'll be left high and dry.

'My object is twofold: firstly to get fair compensation for your time and your expertise. Everybody but you is being paid healthy fees or salaries for the job they do. Why shouldn't you be paid accordingly? I'm willing to bet that all the participants in the radio show you were involved in yesterday were well reimbursed for their time and knowledge. All except you, that is.

'My second target would be to set you up in a line which would be self-sustaining. By that, I mean that you will build up a career or a business, based on your expertise or know-how, which will provide a steady income for you in the future. It doesn't have to be present expertise. You could acquire it along the way, or through self-study, if you felt so inclined.'

He studied her with a twitch at the corners of his mouth. 'This all sounds most exciting, but I'm a straight talker, if you don't mind. I'm not one to pussyfoot about. What would you get out of the deal?'

'I'm glad you asked that. If you didn't, I'd feel that I was dealing with an idiot. I'll ask for twenty percent of all your gross earnings after your initial five thousand dollars a month, which means that I won't steal bread out of a baby's mouth.'

He thought about it for a few moments. 'So, you'll do quite well out of the deal, if I strike it lucky and start earning big time.'

'That's right. You've hit the nail on the head. If you earn a pittance, I get nothing out of the deal. But if I'm worth my salt, I'll make you a pile of money and you'll become a multi-millionaire. And I'll be a fifth of a multi-millionaire.'

Jason laughed. 'It all sounds so reasonable. And do we keep in regular touch with each other?'

'Virtually daily, and we'll often travel together on lecture trips and so forth.'

He grinned in his mischievous way. 'Then you'll be spending more time with me than in the company of your boyfriend. Do you have one, by the way?'

'Not at present. Boyfriends don't like their girls to travel around the country with good-looking and successful men.'

'Thanks for the compliment, but you need to look at my bank balance. Neither would I, to be honest. So, there's an immediate reason for me to take you on. I'll be the lucky one, spending so much time in your company.'

Janine's smile had faded away. 'There's just one thing that we need to get out of the way before we get to the contract-signing stage. I'll always be my own boss, and I won't kowtow to you merely because you pay me a commission. That includes the prospect of your claiming bed rights and other personal services.

'If you needed a back rub, for instance, one of us could find a masseur who would do it for you. But maybe I'd be in the mood to do it myself. I generally like to please people, but then you would have been fortunate enough to pick a good day to develop a sore back.'

Jason nodded. 'The message that I'm getting, loud and clear, is that I pay you for your expertise, but I don't own you?'

'That's it, in a nutshell,' she agreed.

While they had been talking, Jason was studying Janine carefully, not that she wasn't aware of it. What he saw made him wonder why some man, or men, didn't have the balls to hang onto this woman, who was well-proportioned and rather attractive, at least as far as he was concerned. *I wouldn't mind travelling with this good-looking girl just for the pleasure of her company, even if she doesn't achieve half of the successes she hints on arriving at for me.*

Then he realized that he'd gone quiet, and she seemed to be aware of what was going through his mind right then. So he shook his thoughts straight and concentrated on the next situation he had in mind.

After making arrangements for a contract to be drawn up, Janine had a proposal to make: 'How about my riding shotgun for you over the next week or two? We can size each other up on the next trip you're due to make. Then we can both get a feel as to how this is going to work out.

'Personal and travelling expenses to be met by ourselves, of course, unless the sponsors are generous enough to pay for both of us, which I think they will be in most cases. This usually works, especially if I go and have a good chat with them. Mostly they are aware that I can get an additional mile of publicity for their cause, whether it's cleaning up the shoreline or selling more toothpaste, if I can go along for the ride.'

***

Danny Foulkes phoned to congratulate Jason on his recent fame. 'I hear that the prosecution has put your case on ice. After a time to save their faces, I'm sure that it'll be finally chucked out. They just don't have the guts to do it right away. How about a beer or two with the guys and me at Sandy's Pub and Dance, one of these days, when you can find the time?'

'I'd like to, Danny, but I don't have the space on my itinerary right now. I'm off to Los Angeles with my PR in a couple of days' time, and I need to do a lot of preparation before we leave.'

'PR? That sounds interesting. What does that stand for? Personal Rent-girl?'

Jason sighed. These guys would never think above their navels. 'Don't be disgusting, Danny. She's my public relations woman, and I can tell you that she doesn't come cheaply.'

'Oh, so now you're such a hotshot, who can do what you like in the open, like carting a fancy woman about the country? All you have to do is to give her a title, like your public relations woman.'

'Cut it out, Danny. Everybody wants a chunk of me at the moment, most of them for free. Janine is a highly successful organizer, who is going to make me lots of lolly, I hope. Now there's one thing that's even better than sex.'

'What's that, Jason? More sex? Well, enjoy what you're not going to get, Jason, my mate. Just think of me over the weekend when I'm busy on the job and you're sipping cocktails with a bunch of prune-faced professors, with their dried-out old wives on one hand and their sexy PR's waiting to service them on the other. If their old and dried-out hearts can take it, that is.'

'Don't worry about me, Danny. I can survive without hugging a bimbo at a bar for a night or two, if it means building a future career. I've got to grab my chances while I'm still young. There's no telling where a push here and a shove there will get me. Those in the know tell me that there's big money waiting out there for those who are willing to lock onto the opportunity when it comes past.

'I'll come and give you a ride in my Cadillac one day. I'll need a car as big as that to fit in your wheelchair after you've buggered yourself up with all the STD's you'll have picked up from the bars where you hang out.'

The two men liked to rib each other when they got half a chance. They laughed and shared a few more digs before ringing off, one feeling rosy with pride and the other one green with male competitive jealousy. Danny Foulkes didn't like to make an issue of it, but he still needed to find a job, and he didn't have the faintest idea where to start looking for something worthwhile.

Ah well, he was meeting up with the guys today, but he would definitely start job-hunting seriously from tomorrow.

Chapter Eleven

They caught the connecting flight to Los Angeles. Jason had attended a real estate seminar the previous evening, before returning to the office to complete some paperwork. He was keeping up his career as a realtor. Joe Caldecott, who ran the agency, had advised him to carry on his plans as an active agent after his meteoric rise to prominence as a diver and an orca aficionado.

He smiled to himself. Neither title was technically true, but what the public saw, they believed in.

Joe had been right. 'You say that you're no expert as a diver or a killer whale know-all, yet you did spend a lot of time in training orcas at places like Sea World. You must have learned quite a lot in your time there.

'But most important of all, the public has faith in your knowledge regarding these subjects, of which most people know absolutely nothing. Do yourself a favour and study up like mad on orca data, so that you can cope when asked basic questions on killer whales and associated subjects. Surely you must know quite a bit about diving by now. You were with the Navy Seals for five years, not so? Aren't they all diving experts? Or is it about time for me to change my country?

'Getting back to your career in real estate — everybody wants to either buy or sell their property through their local hero, Jason Malvy. When we tell them that you're not available, they get cheesed off and accuse us of stalling them. The other agents are complaining that I'm not giving them a square deal, even though we advertise almost all our properties in their names and not yours.

'When you get half a chance in your busy schedule, contact at least some of your fan club, and you'll begin to make yourself a packet of commission. I know all about Janine Whitlock. She's a smart cookie who knows how to operate. I've heard about a couple of guys who've been promoted by her, and they've gone far.' Joe paused for a few seconds.

'Look, this is none of my business, but one of the guys who used her service thought that he owned her. He got hold of her one night and came close to raping her. He thought that she had become his property, lock, stock and barrel. But Janine can look after herself, all right. She hit him in the eye with the heel of her stiletto shoe. He ended up blind in one eye, but Janine wasn't taking any chances. She drove after the ambulance that she called to pick him up, and she had herself tested. He had treated her badly before she let loose on him, and there was semen everywhere.

'There was no way that he could put up any defence in court against her, and the matter didn't go any further. Just remember to have respect for the woman, that's all I have to say. Now, getting back to your situation, keep in touch and we'll keep you up to scratch. Handle as much of the current workflow as you can but make this a decent career for yourself once your popularity cools off, and believe me, it will. I've been around long enough to see this trend happen over and over again. One day the public makes you their hero, and the next day you're last week's stale bread.'

***

He could hardly believe that he was flying to Los Angeles with such an attractive woman sitting next to him, but he honestly felt a bit smashed after his hectic previous evening, rounded off by a few stiff whiskies to see him off to sleep.

Janine turned to Jason and studied him speculatively. 'You look sort of thrashed, my friend. Were you partying last night?'

'I wish I was,' replied her companion. 'I had a seminar to attend to, and then there was a mound of clerical work to finish off. I must confess that I couldn't sleep, so I downed a few whiskies to help me on my way.'

'All right, you're probably not going to like what I'm about to say, but your image means everything in this world of public debate that you're entering into. You can do a reasonable amount of drinking at the event itself, or better still, at the bar afterwards while you connect with important people, but please not on your own. A man who drinks alone will develop problems if he hasn't got them already.'

'Right, I get the message loud and clear.'

She patted him on the arm. 'Thanks for not showing resentment at your first lecture from me.'

He grinned. 'As long as you're doing it for my good, I don't mind. Just don't develop into a nag. Now, have you got something to soothe a heavy head?'

'You're in luck. Your companion is a walking chemist that everybody sneers at until they need some medication or other. Let me see what I have for you in my box of tricks.'

What Jason admired about his new adviser was that she seemed to know a little bit about most things, or else she took the trouble to inform herself in preparation should the subject come up the next time. She was also interested in other people and their lifestyles, offering little of her own opinions unless asked for them.

Jason had to smile when he found out that Janine had registered the two of them as Mr and Mrs Jason Malvy, wherever their personal details were required. She was sharp, all right. His eyebrow lifted when he saw the travel and hotel documents for the first time.

'Don't look so surprised,' she said. 'I'm not trying to pair us off or anything like that. In the first place, we need connecting rooms in hotels for when we have to put our heads together over some problem or other. If we register under separate surnames, many people will think that you've brought your dolly bird along for the ride.

'Our luggage will tend to go down the same chute at the airport, and seating arrangements are less likely to get messed up. Finally, it will also help to keep the man-hunting tigresses at bay that are always on the lookout for a good-looking sugar-daddy.'

'Wow, you've sure sewn up the loose edges,' he commented.

'That's part of the job,' she acknowledged with a pleased smile.

He took the tablets that she gave him, after a thorough scratch through a bag that would make a good defensive weapon in a mugging. But then, she had confessed to being a travelling pharmacy, and the pills actually put him out of his buzz-headed misery.

In fact, they bombed him out completely. The last thing he remembered was looking at her beautiful smile before everything faded into a gentle blackness. Then he felt her shaking him awake.

'You'll have to return to the real world,' she said. 'We're about to land.'

Jason was suddenly aware that his head was nestling on Janine's shoulder, and he didn't want to move it. That delicious aroma had to be her heady perfume that made him want to lick her creamy neck to see if it tasted as good as it smelled. Luckily, he resisted the temptation and sat up straight.

'Sorry about using you as a pillow,' he mumbled.

'That's what a travelling companion is there for,' she smiled. She took a small hairbrush out of her bag of endless tricks. 'But please let me persuade your hair back into shape. You look like a porcupine on a bad hair day.'

As she bent forward to brush his hair back into place, he couldn't keep his eyes off her neck. He really wanted to look down her front, but he knew that it wasn't the decent thing to do when she was taking the trouble to smarten him up.

Janine was well aware that her lacy blouse gaped a little to show off her cleavage, as it was designed to do, especially as she leant forward to tidy Jason up. She knew that males got a thrill out of such peep shows. Smiling to herself, she hoped that he was enjoying the view, if that was where he was gazing.

They were met at the arrivals reception area by a uniformed chauffeur carrying a name board. It was a cool, overcast day with heavily laden clouds warning that an attempt to brave the weather was not a bright thing to do.

On arrival at the hotel, Janine booked them both in at the arrivals desk, and they followed the bellhop into the elevator. When they arrived at their suite, Janine had a fair tip ready for the young man to smile at, as he showed them around their temporary home for the next six days. Everything looked comfortable and in its place.

Jason lay back on the pillows in his room with a satisfied sigh. 'This is the life,' he murmured, his eyes closed.

Janine walked through the connecting door, where she had been putting toiletries away in her room. 'Come on,' she said. 'You've had your snooze for the day. What preparation do you have to get together for this afternoon's opening session?'

'Nothing really. It's all up here,' he said, tapping his head.

'Then you're even cleverer than I thought you were. *Orcinus Orca* is such a flavour of the month that I would have thought everybody would need to brush up on their resources before jumping into the pool with the rest of the sharks.'

Jason grinned guiltily. 'Yes, I suppose I'd better go over my notes once more.'

'If you would like me to, I'll sit in on it with you. I'd like to sharpen up what I know on the subject. It all looks so interesting. I've only been able to delve into the topic on a skin-deep basis, so boning up on it will do me a world of good.'

Jason was surprised to hear that Janine took matters all that seriously. 'I must admit, I didn't think that you'd be so interested in the nitty-gritty of the subject,' he remarked. 'Most of the data would bore the average person out of his, or her, mind.'

'I'm sorry if I surprise you. I have a curious mind, and this killer whale story is a tremendous one. What little that science has discovered about them is threadbare in its coverage.'

'You're right. The average person in the street is not even aware that they are actually dolphins and not whales at all. But the biggest mystery is what has turned them from relatively mild-mannered sea creatures who have virtually no reputation for attacking mankind, into ravening beasts who are now seeking out man in particular.' He stopped. 'I'm sorry. You wound me up. I'm giving you my speech long before I'm due to present it.'

Janine grinned. 'Don't feel bad about it. I was enjoying the intensity of your delivery, but it might be better if I get a fresh version of it when you're ready and willing to give your speech.'

Jason nodded. 'Yes, you're probably right. There's still plenty for me to refer to, but don't let me get carried away and start lecturing before the time. Whenever I deliver a speech, I tend to lose my enthusiasm, and then I present the facts in a monotonous way if I become too slick in what I have to say.'

After a whip through Jason's notes, they went down to a fairly light buffet lunch before the opening ceremony, which had been delayed until the last of the delegates had arrived from their far-flung outposts of civilization. There was a conglomeration of delegates, assistants and interpreters present. Other than when someone was officially introduced from the rostrum, with his or her interpreter by their side, it was hard to know who was who.

What did help was that everybody bore descriptive name badges that pinpointed their names, titles and countries of origin. This did help in personal identification but only where close contact was possible. What did secretly amuse Jason and Janine was that many of those attending the conference couldn't easily be identified from a country of origin point of view, as far as looks were concerned.

There were Asiatics and Indians from England, and East Europeans from the United States, having hopped from country to country in search of grants in aid and better living conditions, including freedom of expression.

Brilliant Israelis and Germans and French scientists intermingled with one another, a healthy sign of future collaboration to come. Now, apart from a few seedy-looking characters directly out of a James Bond movie scenario, most of the delegates looked genuine in their thirst for knowledge and willingness to share information with others in their field.

There was a break of two hours between the afternoon session and the evening meal. Some of the scientists used this time to share information, while others took a nap or followed divers interests. Jason spent most of the time resting, while Janine spent a lot of her off-duty period making herself look glamorous.

Jason's eyes nearly popped out on stalks when he saw how lovely Janine looked in an evening dress that one would expect to see at an Academy Awards presentation. When she pirouetted in front of him, he could only let out a "Wow" of appreciation, which said it all. Her cheeks glowed with pleasure when she saw how genuinely appreciative Jason was of her ensemble. He gave his partner a spontaneous hug and a kiss on the cheek, which slightly embarrassed both of them.

He stepped back with a blush that he seldom displayed. 'I'm sorry if I overstepped the mark, but that was purely instinctive. In fact, if you were a male, I would have done the same thing.'

They both laughed, and he felt more at ease. Janine said nothing, but she secretly enjoyed Jason's reaction to the effort she had put into beautifying herself — largely for his sake, if for no other reason.

This special moment spurred Jason on to making himself as smart-looking as possible. He also looked rather handsome, in the end, but he had to admit that a lot of it was due to the individual attention he received from Janine, who acted as his personal manservant and chambermaid rolled into one.

They attracted a lot of attention as they entered the banqueting chamber, and they mingled with the other guests before sitting down to a splendid meal. Jason was pleased that the dinner suit he had hired was large enough to allow a little leeway about the midriff section, as he had dined more than a little too well.

Sometime during the evening session, it was his time to present a paper on "Possible Reasons for Changes in the Mentality of the *Orcinus Orca.*"

He didn't try to be flowery and showman-like in company with others in his peer group. When called and introduced to the audience, he marched straight up to the rostrum after being introduced by the Master of Ceremonies, and he began his speech without making any dramatic opening.

After outlining his practical experience with the training of killer whales at oceanariums and his diving experience, he explained how killer whales were captured with ridiculous ease, being too tame to put up much of a struggle to escape the nets that encircled them when they were being trapped.

They were kept in confinement for many a year, limited regarding "elbow room", and they were supplied with only a small variety of foods, when they were used to a selection of the contents of the ocean as their choice. It had been observed that orcas sometimes refused the food that they had been supplied with over lengthy periods, much the same as humans vary their diets out of boredom, changed circumstances or when moving to different countries.

The orcas were also known to stick to one life partner, but this could change from time to time, when they mated with others in their pod. Possibly for that reason, they often mixed with small and large pods of their own species, from which they could pick playmates, sexual partners and a nursery for their own offspring.

But the most important disadvantage the poor animals faced in a dolphinarium was the noise factor, with crowds of spectators yelling their heads off day after day, session after session, while their trainers expected perfection from them in their acrobatic stunts. In the wild and open seas, however, they could roam where they wanted, eat what they liked and be as free as the ocean was immense.

There were no boundaries out in the seas, no humans screaming at them, no stress causing a build-up of tension until the final breaking point was reached, which few humans had given a thought to.

'What happened to Samson, the huge killer whale that escaped from his confines? An anonymous tipoff recently reported that his life partner and their baby were killed by a cruel act of pure bloody murder. Where is Samson now? Is he inciting revenge for all the terrible deeds committed against him and his kind?

'The day that these giant creatures can be regularly trained up to attack the warships of opposing navies, a disaster will develop, bigger than what the world has ever known. But following that line of thought, it is on record that dolphins have been trained by both the American and Russian Navies, since the late 1950s, to locate electronic equipment from the seabed.

'Apart from their sensitive ultrasonic abilities, dolphins are being armed with explosives, including mines, to be directed at enemy ships and mines, in order to destroy them. One can imagine where all this is going. In the future, no ship, or port, will be safe from attack at any time.

'It is a well-kept secret — at least from the public — that efforts have been made, using these animals, to guard sensitive key points, such as nuclear submarines and their bases. To date, these methods have proved to be unreliable, because there are methods available to distract these animals. One can never be sure if defences such as these can remain watertight. Truthfully, we don't know, for sure, enough about what makes them tick.

'Let us all keep a sharp eye on any developments designed to train these magnificent beasts of the sea into becoming death-dealing monsters, like the human bomb-carriers of today, as well as seals that have been trained to carry explosives in warfare, apart from the human SEALs who were named after them.'

Jason gave a formal bow and went back to his seat. There was a stunned silence, until a slow wave of applause erupted and reached tremendous proportions. Virtually everyone stood up in respect for both the speech and the concept that this young man had introduced.

Janine stood with the rest of the audience and clapped vigorously until her hands were sore. At that moment, she would have done anything for

Jason. She was normally a well-controlled and balanced individual who would never put herself too far out on a limb for anyone else. However, unknown to Jason, he had entered the realm of super heroes in her estimation.

***

There were other people, many of them internationally respected, who had points of views to present. Some of these statements were quite radical. Jason could begin to see that Russia, China and the Middle East had completely different points of view from that of the West, which they ground out with a lot of poisonous intent. Of course, they pleaded innocence in the use of seals and other creatures for the purposes of warfare.

Japan was particularly vociferous in this regard, as well as the butchering of orcas and whales for their flesh. According to them, they only killed orcas for research purposes. This was the same sort of yarn they had been spinning forever and a day, regarding the killing of whales and seals of various types.

They argued that the orca was an international creature found worldwide and not confined to the West. Each country should manage its local populations, because the overstocking of these creatures would cause a depletion of the fish stocks required for human consumption.

There were many other arguments put forward, but most of them were obstructionist and anti-West in nature. The young diver didn't think that much new information was being added to the stockpile.

Janine couldn't wait for Jason to take his seat next to her, after all the papers had been presented and all the speeches made that had been on the day's agenda. The dignitaries and the speechmakers left the podium to mingle with the general audience. She turned to her companion with pride, as he approached. She did surprise him — as well as herself — by planting a full-blooded kiss on his lips.

'Don't get any ideas, buster,' she whispered in his ear. 'This is a special award which you've earned with a brilliant speech about a heart-breaking subject.'

Now was the time for the symposium members to circulate and to pat each other on the back while muttering all sorts of things, whether insults or compliments, in a variety of languages.

Jason, who had a wicked sense of humour, took Janine on a tour of the minute dance area set aside for those who needed the exercise, wanted to get a firm grip on a member of the opposite sex or hungered after sharing a juicy piece of gossip at close quarters.

'I must tell you,' he muttered, while enjoying the occasional bump as less talented dancers cannoned into them, 'that some of these people are spies and madmen who have had themselves invited here under false pretences.'

He gestured towards a man who had given a speech in Russian, suitably translated for the gathering.

'That is Pucharov, who is not really interested in killer whales, so I've been told. They say that the man is a crackpot who wants to lay mines right along the coast of the United States, or so it's been rumoured, but he would have to get everyone out of the water to accomplish it. Americans are not going to stand by and allow that to happen, unless Russia is looking for World War III.

'You'll notice that he's dancing with a Chinese lady, who is not really the wife of the Chinese Foreign Minister. She is a spy who has been assigned to team up with the Russkies to bankrupt the United States by losing them all their tourist trade, as well as their fishing income. Other shipping will come to a sticky end after all the mines have been laid. Nobody will be able to disarm the mines because they'll be too scared to go into the water, for fear of meeting up with a killer whale. They will also have to abandon their nuclear subs, because nobody will be able to effect entry and exit manoeuvres while practising for deep-sea catastrophes.'

Janine was giggling so much that she could hardly dance any more. 'What other intrigues are happening at this time?'

'Well, over there is the Egyptian Foreign Minister, who thinks he's easily as good an actor as Omar Sharif. He's looking for somebody to round off his training by teaching him poker. The trouble is that he hasn't learned to count yet, except in Arabic, and they don't have a Joker in their card games. He's employed as their prime minister.'

Janine couldn't keep in step any more. 'I give up. I'll be having bad dreams tonight.' She didn't realize the truth of her prediction.

They took a break and sat down, but other men had noticed Janine and wanted to swing around the floor with her in their arms. She could hardly refuse them, although she would have preferred to dance with Jason.

If she had been better informed regarding the position of all the spies at the conference, she would have been amazed at the activity that was going on around her. More than one silky-smooth dancer whispered sweet propositions in her ear, which were carefully worded to establish where her interests lay in the scheme of things.

They had done their research very well and were aware that Janine was not married to Jason Malvy. Then why was there the subterfuge of their signing in as a married couple? Was Malvy up to something more than exchanging facts and ideas at a conference of this sort?

The Chinese were particularly interested in what the Russians were up to. They had come to a secret agreement to pool any information they could glean about the movements of the West, but the Russians, whom they hated fiercely, appeared to be withholding everything worthwhile to their cause.

The avaricious Chinese would keep a sharp eye on the Janine woman and turn her by using a gadget that they had recently perfected.

Jason decided to be noble and do his duty for the sake of his sponsors. He drifted about, chatting with some of the people he recognized as knowing their expert way around the subject of orcas.

There were eyes centred on him that he wasn't aware of. Heads bent towards one another, and a few words were exchanged now and again. It was a pity that he didn't understand what was being said. Jason would have been shocked had he understood a few of the terse messages that were passed from mouth to mouth.

Janine had worn herself out with all the dancing that she was doing. She excused herself from her admirers and landed up at the bar, in the company of men who were enjoying her presence. Jason was keeping an occasional eye on her as any well-mannered escort would.

He had met up with an elegant woman who was a good few years older than he, but she was most attractive and very well groomed. She was Professor Cora Nugent, who had read a paper on sea creatures in confinement and how their natures were altered by their circumstances.

When he came to think about it, almost everyone at the conference was older than he. Jason felt like a gate crasher at a senior's party.

The woman was tremendously interesting, and he was fascinated by her. Jason became absorbed in every word she uttered, drinking in her knowledge like a treasured wine. He couldn't seem to get enough of her melodious voice as it smoothly covered new ground on her pet subject.

Then he snapped out of his near trance to take another cursory glance in Janine's direction and was worried to see her wobbling on her seat and gesturing towards him with an outstretched hand. She was on her own, for once. Jason felt guilty about forgetting all about her while he had been absorbed in the company of the fascinating Cora Nugent.

She looked to be in trouble. Jason hurriedly excused himself from the presence of his current font of knowledge that he was conversing with and moved smartly over to where his companion was sitting.

'Are you all right?' he wanted to know.

She clutched at him desperately. 'Help!' she slurred. 'Been drugged. And my ear aches like hell.'

He looked about, but she was surprisingly alone. All the men who had gathered around her, like bees taking pollen from a flower, had drifted off to other sources of honey. It was as if her vibrations of distress had sent out a signal about which they didn't want to be involved.

Jason didn't waste any time in arguing with her. He fetched her wrap and took her purse from fingers that were too weak to grasp it properly. He put an arm around her waist and eased her off the stool in a smooth movement.

He tried to make it look as if Janine was only slightly wobbly on her feet, but he carried most of her weight in one arm, making her look a lot less paralytic than what she actually was.

After getting her out through the hall exit, that was luckily nearby, Jason practically carried Janine to the elevator. Janine leant on his arm, and he felt as if it was ready to break off under the strain of keeping his partner reasonably upright.

At their floor, the resolute young man dragged his partner out of the elevator and towed her down the passage, her high heels leaving twin tracks in the thick-pile carpet. He still had his key in his pocket, so he propped the limp woman against the wall and quickly unlocked the door of their suite, but he was not fast enough.

Janine slid down the wall and landed on her rump with her elegant dress crumpled about her upper thighs, before Jason could catch her. Once more, a mighty heave managed to land her on her rubbery feet, her stiletto heels buckling under her. He flung the door open with one hand while his other arm took the strain of holding her, and then they were inside their suite.

Luckily they had left the lights on while making their earlier exit. Jason was a strong young man, but from then on, he would never accept the casual handling of unconscious women as portrayed in films. He managed, with some final burst of energy, to get her onto her bed.

He went through for an urgent pee after recovering his breath. Being well raised by a penny-pincher father, he turned off the lights and then wondered if Janine was not in a worse condition than he had originally thought she was.

Back to her bedroom he went, turning on a light or two on the way. He'd never get any sleep if this care-giving stunt didn't come to an end, sooner rather than later. She was still out like a light, flat out on her back. To his imaginative mind, she resembled a sack of discarded potatoes.

Jason surveyed the scene dispassionately. There was this beautiful young woman, lying in an equally beautiful evening gown that was already getting rumpled under her splayed out limbs. Surely she wouldn't think much of him if he didn't take steps to preserve it for her.

The trouble was that he didn't know where to start getting the damned thing off her. He shrugged. Better to have tried and failed than not having tried at all. Jason was sure that he'd read this homily somewhere, written by some or other poor bastard who'd needed to strip a woman, also having only the best of intentions. Supposedly there was some truth in the quotation.

It was like disarming a landmine. A hook here, a zip there, a few extra buttons. And while all this was being disconnected, his sack of potatoes fell about without rendering the slightest help, apart from an occasional groan which seemed to signify that his not summoning the house doctor hadn't been such a massive mistake after all. At least she did not appear to be dying, or her condition even worsening.

Not that his own condition was improving at all. He thought that he could identify at least three ligaments and four muscles that required urgent medical attention, and he still had a long way to go before his toils would come to an end.

Now came the tricky part, where the dress had to be slid off the patient, who was so out of this world that her jaw was sagging. Staring at her beautiful features, Jason couldn't leave her to gape like that.

He found a piece of ribbon on her dressing table and bound it around her head and her jaw to give it some support. She looked much like a spoiled baby at a birthday party. He giggled inanely to himself. Now he was probably really deep in the shit.

No matter. Life went on. He wiggled and jiggled, and her dress slowly came off her curvaceous frame like the skin off an emerging chrysalis. Tipsy and tired as he was, he had to stop for a minute and gaze with reverence at the sight below him. Then he shrugged his shoulders and took the dress away to the cupboard, where he found a coat hanger for it.

He was surprised to see a commode at the bottom of the cupboard. He hadn't seen those things in a long while. But the sight of it made him wonder if Janine needed a pee. After all, she had apparently been putting it away more than he, and he had needed to go more than once. If he allowed her to wet herself, and even her bed, he could be in deep trouble on both counts.

Better to play it safe. He picked up the commode and took it to her bedside. Maybe she could comprehend what he was suggesting for her.

'Want to pee, Janine?' he asked, in the politest voice that he could muster, while swinging the potty nonchalantly by its handle, after removing it from its frame.

He took a step backwards in surprise when he heard her mumble "pee". Or that's what he thought she said. It was actually "tea", but he would pay dearly for that misunderstanding later.

In the meantime, he breathed a sigh of relief. Not only was she coming around, but she tacitly approved of the very personal service he was providing. He carried on with a new sense of purpose. They were getting somewhere at last, although the next bit might turn out to be the trickiest operation of all.

Then he thought about his own expensive dress suit. Any miscalculation now made could prove both costly and messy. Without a second thought, he stripped off his jacket and trousers before shrugging and adding his bow tie and dress shirt to the pile. He kicked off his shoes and socks next. Who wanted to walk about in a wet sock due to somebody's poorly aimed delivery?

Tired of being tidy, he kicked all his castoffs into a heap and turned to his partner's needs. Maybe her needs were getting more than merely urgent, seeing that she could find the strength to mumble "pee" from the depths of her misery.

Heaving her to a sitting position, he swung the comatose woman's legs over the side of the bed and put her arms around his neck. 'Now hang on, sister,' he ordered.

Surprisingly enough, she obeyed him, although her grip was pretty slack.

He didn't mess about. He slipped off her lacy panties, like a magician pulling a coloured scarf out of a hat and flung them over his shoulder. Next he picked up the potty, got Janine into position and urged her to let rip. After a lengthy pause, a trickle started up, that developed into a waterfall. *The poor woman must have been near bursting,* Jason thought.

But his sympathy turned to mounting terror as the cascade kept on and on coming. *What happens if the damned thing is not big enough to hold it all and I can't get her to stop?* Jason had a vivid imagination, and he was in a mood that was almost stretched to sane limits. He had a vision of a stream of Janine's pee running out of the hotel room, down the passage and out of the main hotel entrance.

The tired nursemaid caught hold of his sanity just in time. He was on the point of falling asleep due to sheer exhaustion. Janine's grip around his neck had given way and she had fallen backwards onto the bed, luckily without spilling the impressive reservoir of urine that she had voided.

The container went into a sort of speed wobble but did not tip over, although the worn-out man had nearly let his drooping face fall into it. That did shock him into wakefulness. He managed to get the heavy container onto the carpet, with a wrist that felt like breaking under the strain of supporting it.

Another horrible thought of either of them kicking over the commode accidentally, made him push it well out of the way, where no damage could be done by clumsy feet in the middle of the night, not that there was that much left of it.

Staring at Janine from a position that only a senior midwife would normally be in, he decided to finish his labours with a flourish. He found a wet facecloth and wiped the helpless woman off, using toilet paper to dry the area up. As a parting gesture, he pulled up her panties and finally inserted a large wad of toilet tissue in case an emergency might occur later on. He stood back, dazed with exhaustion, but generally quite proud of his work.

She still looked most beautiful to him, in spite of the visual and physical performance that even a husband is not normally put through. He swung her into a sleeping position and pulled the rolled-up top coverlet over her. Jason was still not all that happy about her state of health, and he was really too tired to go to his own bed.

He simply pulled the coverlet over himself as well, planning to hop out of bed early in the morning and sort things out before having to face the music. He suspected that he would have to bear the brunt of explaining the reasons for his actions when she eventually woke up. Having woken up next to other women who had regrets and concerns about what had transpired the previous evening, he had an inkling of what to expect.

Then a black curtain dropped over his eyes, and he was gone to a distant land where he fought with land-going killer whales and was chased by wild women who wanted to tie him up and torture him by stomping on his head, while peeing all over him at the same time. He didn't even have the satisfaction of finding out what it was that he'd done wrong. All the same, a bad dream is a bad dream.

Chapter Twelve

Jason was a restless sleeper at the best of times. He also dragged Janine out of her sleep in the worst possible way. When a woman has woken up with the most terrible headache ever — partly hangover and partly drug induced — and has a severe pain in her left ear, accompanied by a faint buzzing, and then has a heavy hand slapped across her breast, with her nipple casually squeezed between a finger and a thumb through the delicate material of her bra, it will not be remembered by her as a pleasant interlude.

Janine gave out a yelp of distress, initially putting it all down to a bad dream. Even the yelp sounded foreign to her, until she realized that she could hardly open her mouth at all. Maybe her jaw was dislocated. Janine put up a shaky hand and found that her jaw was tied up with a large ribbon.

What the hell! She followed the binding and found that it was tied firmly around her head. The irritated woman whipped it off her chin and yanked the ribbon off her face, flinging it to the floor. By then she had woken up properly, to find the situation hadn't changed a bit during the last several seconds.

In fact it was worse, because her nipple was getting more painful and she was beginning to realize that she was wearing nothing but her scanty bra, along with her panties padded by a vast lump of tissue down below. This looked much like a topknot worn by a Hindu, who would never be given the pleasure of getting his head down there in the first place.

And Jason, Hindu or not, was lying next to her, his morning glory proudly raising the roof of the coverlet, like the supporting centre pole of an army tent during a wartime air raid.

The swine! This was her thanks for all the trouble she had gone through to help him and get him sorted out. The old trick: get a girl drunk and then abuse her sexually. Yet the strange thing was that she had no recollection of anything untoward happening, apart from the presence of that huge ball of toilet paper in her panties.

The more she thought about the injustice of it all and her misplaced faith in him, the angrier she became. And Janine could get angry, all right. She had a vicious temper that even she was frightened of. Like many pretty women, she tried to be nice for so much of her wakeful time in order to live up to her image, but it was a magnificent release, on the odd occasion, to let go totally and become the queen bitch of the civilized world. The secret was in the ability to choose when to be an alluring princess and when to let go and be a total harridan.

Jason woke up from a complicated dream to receive a sock on the nose and one in the mouth. They were full-blown punches thrown with the power of justice and righteousness behind them. The instant pain made him cry out and bleed at the same time. His nose gushed, and his lip oozed. He shot upright with his hand to his face.

'Ow! What the hell was that for?' he cried out.

'You dirty bastard! What did you do to me last night?' she replied angrily.

'Nothing, you stupid bag,' he mumbled, through a blocked nose and a dribbling lip. 'Except save you from disgracing both of us when you passed out, and having to drag you here like the ton of bricks you weigh, and saving your dress from the way you were ruining it, and helping you with the potty when you were about to pee in the bed…'

'What rubbish are you talking about now? I would never pee in my bed. And here's a bundle of tissue paper. Wipe your nose and your lip with it before you do your own damage to the furnishings. And by the way, what the hell were you doing, binding up my face with a ribbon? Is that another thing that turns you on?'

She watched Jason wipe the blood off his face and then put a hand to her mouth. She had suddenly recalled where the tissue had come from. Wisely she kept quiet about her temporary error.

'Well, you came damned close to doing it in the bed this time,' he mumbled through the tissue paper. 'If you look somewhere on that side of the room, you'll find a bucketful of urine. Mind you don't trip over it — you may drown. For your information, I bound up your jaw with that ribbon because you were snoring so much that I thought you could dislocate it.'

Suddenly a vision came to Janine of Jason helping her with the potty. He must have taken her panties down and held the potty for her while she hung onto him and peed into it. Then the lump of toilet tissue… It was all too horrible to contemplate. But she had to admit that it had not been a standard date-rape scenario. Nobody could be that quirky, could they?

'Wait a minute: why did you take your clothing off and lie down next to me?'

'For a start, I was protecting my suit against your peeing all over it, and I meant to lie down next to you only for a few minutes, because I was worried about the state you were in. At one time, I'd even thought you'd stopped breathing. I must have fallen asleep without meaning to, but you don't have to worry. You must have started up again, without any help from me. You were quite safe from a sexual attack, by the way. Nobody would want you in that condition.'

Janine had to admit to herself that she had swung at Jason before hearing the full story, but she was a long way from admitting to her mistake.

'You've got to admit that it would look highly suspicious for me to pass out suddenly and then wake up next to you, both of us being nearly naked.'

'I don't know,' Jason replied. 'I was too tired to care, at that stage. Personally, I don't get sexually attracted to drunken women who pee into potties that I hold for them. Besides, it was no different from falling asleep on the beach and waking up with a helluva headache and an extremely sore face.'

His companion supposed that he had a point there. But one didn't usually see a man's digit standing up like that at the beach.

'Then do you always raise a flagpole when falling asleep on the beach, or is it an S.O.S. you're sending out, or maybe you're merely trying to make a point?'

With that clever remark, she swung her legs out from under the coverlet, to realize that she was dressed only in her panties and bra. What the hell. He had ogled more of her when he'd been busy seeing to her than the average gynaecologist would be able to take in. Another little peek at her, this time with her panties on, was hardly going to change his opinion of her.

'I'm going to fetch the emergency medical kit that I always carry with me. You need a little damage control.'

She bit the bullet. 'I'm sorry that I punched you so hard, after you probably meant well last night. I must admit that I got a tremendous shock when I woke up to find us both almost nude in bed together. And it didn't help to wake up with your trying to crush the life out of my nipple. What made you do that, anyway?'

'I dunno. I was having a rough dream about being stomped on by vicious women. One leant over me to see if I was still alive, so I grabbed her tit in self-defence and hung on for dear life. Or maybe I just liked the feel of yours.'

'Now you're being rude, but I'm still sorry for roughing you up a little.'

'Roughing me up? I feel as if I've run into a cement-mixer.'

'I did say I was sorry, and I really am. I'm sorry for spoiling your looks, which aren't half bad for a man.'

That little speech was her way of abjectly apologizing for changing the shape of her companion's face to some degree. Now she began to wonder if there wasn't something about her that put him off a little. Janine wasn't used to being turned down when she was dressed in nothing but her undies. He couldn't be a poof, could he? After all, he did wake up with a hard-on, didn't he?

She thought a little longer. 'I'd like to know who the devil was who laced my drink. I only had a couple of them, you know. I always take it easy at these conferences, if only to keep up appearances for the sake of my client. I can remember talking trash with some Oriental man while he fiddled with my ear. This out-of-control performance was definitely not my style, Jason.'

Jason had his own ideas. He happened to agree that Janine was too level-headed to make an ass of herself at a public function, when her career was at stake. These affairs were always well covered by closed circuit television, for a number of good reasons. One camera was usually focused on the bar counter.

He would visit the hotel security manager a little later on. A look through last night's tapes should reveal some interesting viewing. He wouldn't be at all surprised if somebody had laced Janine's drink. Seeing that it was an event by invitation only, it should be easy enough to identify the culprit — or culprits.

While Janine did the hundred and one things that women do to themselves when they've woken up in the morning with the feeling that the skin is falling off their faces and their bodies have drooped out of shape in sympathy, Jason had a quick shave and shower. He tried to preserve his clothes for the next outing, with the assistance of a chambermaid, before mentally sifting through the happenings of the previous day.

There had been quite a few speakers doing a lot of talking, but not much that was really worthwhile had been said. For all the wisecracks he had made when dancing with his personal assistant, some of his wisecracking about the foreign delegates must have been reclining somewhere in his subconscious thoughts.

Most of what he had said seemed to be too crazy to be taken seriously, but modern technology was laced with way-out ideas that started from somewhere, some of which actually worked.

For instance, the orcas had suddenly turned against man, particularly along the west coast of the United States. Why there and not elsewhere? Killer whales were generally known not to be overly aggressive to mankind, yet this lot was going out of its way to target people and not so much any of the other creatures that they would normally be expected to prey on.

In spite of all his joking while dancing with Janine, what would be the outcome if an aggressive nation found a way of setting orcas up against the West? Could the huge mammals be trained or programmed to react to their handlers and other humans sharing the oceans with them?

He sat down at the writing desk and made a list of the zany ideas that he had come up with during the previous evening. He would like to run some of these ideas past one or two of the knowledgeable orca experts that he had met at this conference, who would have Western interests at heart, together with vivid imaginations.

Naturally, some of these daydreams would need to be modified at first, if he were to be taken seriously. But they were no more insane than other brainwaves that were being passed around for the approval of the scientific gathering.

When they were ready to face the world again, the couple went down for a delayed buffet breakfast during a morning that had been left clear of official meetings and presentations. Janine and Jason had agreed to split their forces to cover more ground in the limited time available to them.

Between linking up with people that Jason had selected to be useful to his cause, he arranged to view tapes with Laurie Bridewell, the hotel's head of security. He reported that his partner had almost certainly had at least one of her drinks doctored by a person — or persons — unknown.

'Is it possible to run the tape or tapes focused on the bar about the time that my wife's drink was possibly tampered with?' he asked.

Bridewell wasn't entirely convinced that Janine had not merely reacted to a drink too many. 'It's a pity that you didn't call the house doctor in to make a separate assessment and to do any tests on her that he deemed to be necessary.'

'You needed to see the condition she was in at the time, Mr Bridewell. My initial reaction was to get her out of the limelight to avoid embarrassment to her and also to our dear old sponsors. After I managed to clean her up and calm her down enough to get her to bed, there was a steady improvement in her condition, so my decision was to keep the doctor out of it.'

Bridewell came to a decision that his duty was to protect the hotel guests rather than keeping his department's nose clean. Perhaps he should go through the motions in a neutral fashion.

'If you're so sure that your wife has been "got at", why don't we ask the doctor if there's any benefit in doing tests at this late stage? There might still be traces of a foreign substance, which would indicate that somebody has been up to no good. At the same time, I'm quite prepared to let your wife go through the tapes in order to identify somebody who was acting suspiciously. Let's call in both your wife and our doctor, and we'll see what can be arranged. In the meantime, what happened to that lip of yours? And it looks as if your nose took a punch, as well. Not a good evening for the Malvy family, was it?'

Jason gave a wry smile. 'My wife is usually in control of her emotions, but last night was the exception. She put up a hell of a fight while I tried to calm her down and get her to sleep off whatever was bugging her. A couple of wild swings did the damage when I least expected it.'

While Bridewell rounded up Dr Gresham, Jason called Janine and asked her to make herself available to the doctor for blood tests, and also to view the tapes with him once the relevant segments had been isolated for viewing, based on the approximate time she had spent at the bar.

The young woman was not all that happy that Jason had taken the previous evening's events further without discussing them with her and getting her support for his action. Janine was embarrassed that she had passed out at an important function. For a woman who needed to be in control at all times, this was not the way that she wanted to be assessed by the circles in which she would like to operate.

Not only was there little hope of pinning down who had done this to her — if her drink had been tampered with in the first place — but what would she gain out of it? Having a good understanding of what motivated men, she guessed that this event would be a turn-on for many. They would presume that she had done at least something to encourage the dirty deed and would imagine her as the focal point of a long line of admirers.

She was keen to build up her reputation as a facilitator for important men who needed her special type of logistic and personal support. There was no need, in her mind, to gather a reputation for outrageous happenings and public displays of the wrong sort. There was also the question of her temper that needed to be kept in check.

The hot-blooded young woman still cringed inwardly at what she had done to Jason's face. She had done her best to repair the damage to his lip and his slightly swollen nose, but it was clear that he would have to spin a story about walking into a wall, falling down the stairs or something a little less tried, as an excuse for allowing oneself to be beaten up by one's partner. How many times had those weak excuses been used by battered partners in the past?

She was quite surprised that she wouldn't have minded getting at least a fat slap in return for her mindless attack on Jason. There was no masochistic need for pain on her part; it was simply that the episode had made him look like a hopeless wimp, when she sincerely hoped he was nothing of the sort.

A naughty thought came into her mind as she wondered what would have happened if her bedfellow had simply rolled over on top of her and taken what he had been presented with. Would she have gone all hysterical, or would she have given in and resigned herself to her fate — and also maybe to her pleasure?

Janine cast the idea out of her mind and tried to concentrate on the long tale of woe that a delegate's wife was pouring into her overheated ear. It had something to do with her bastard of a husband who had suffered a mild heart attack while romping in bed with a colleague's wife.

She gathered, idly, that secret liaisons would be par for the course at these dried-out functions. The various disinterested partners would have nothing better to do than to jump into bed with a suave foreigner while their partner was trying to impress his or her peers.

She resisted peeping at her watch, while waiting for a break in the diatribe so that she could excuse herself and dash off to the hotel medical centre. In a funny way, she now hoped that they would find some unusual element in her blood to prove that she had been "got at", and was not merely "stagger" drunk.

Chapter Thirteen

Samson, the orca, didn't have the ability to converse in human terms, but he could communicate much better than mankind, by using other means. He could whistle and grunt in a wide variety of ways that other sea creatures of the more advanced kind could understand quite clearly, and they would also be able to respond to his various calls, at tremendous distances if necessary.

He had also learned to respond to various noises and sounds made by humans, and even certain key descriptive words, in the New World Aquarama where he had been held captive for so long.

It was hard for people to credit that his brain had developed along lines that were completely different to that of mankind, because of the different substance of the element the killer whales and other sea animals lived in. Vibrations and echoes and whistles were the newspapers of his undersea world. There was never any problem with communication between Samson and his peers.

What Samson did know was that he had lived too long in an isolated environment, which frustrated and created neuroses in him. Messages sent and received by him bounced off the cemented walls of his boringly confined living space and were distorted out of all understanding.

Then there was the daily grind of a routine which bored him infinitely, along with a limited food source that he had no choice in selecting for himself, together with constant spectator rowdiness and impure water.

His keepers had no real conception of how clean and limitless the ocean was in the circulation and never-ending flow of its waters. If the liquid mix in an elemental area became tainted with red tide or some man-made poison, or he was unhappy with the salt content or something else that caused him to be uncomfortable, he could simply move away to a healthier place.

The killer whale was also conscious of the moods of his handlers. On a bad day, they brought their own irritations and bad vibrations to the poolside, along with their headaches and bad breath, taking out their sourness and their personal boredom on the sea creatures that could never escape for a few hours and take a break the way the usually immature keepers could do on a day-to-day basis.

There was also meanness, where they snatched food away for the fun of it or yelled unnecessarily at their charges when suffering from a hangover or some other bad attitude, or even a personal crisis that had nothing to do with the animals in their care but was nevertheless allowed to interfere with the daily routine.

The huge creature, larger than any that the New World Aquarama had known, finally came to a day that he had decided was more than enough for one immense creature to handle. He was ready to do some act of defiance because of the way that he was treated by the aquarium staff, in general, with the exception of one trainer called Bessie Middleton.

And yet he was bound to the side of his partner, Delilah, of course, who was much bigger than the average female orca and the love of Samson's life. And there was another problem. They were separated more than they were together, the keepers deciding that they didn't concentrate on their tricks all that well when they were in each other's company.

It was more by good fortune than careful planning that the two creatures found it possible to mate when they were accidentally left together. Well, not entirely by luck. There was one female handler with an understanding and a heart larger than her spare frame, who understood the pair of orcas better than other keepers working at the aquarium in a job that held no future for them.

It was Bessie Middleton who had "accidentally" allowed them to mate, which brought almost as much joy to her as they did to each other.

The management was most unhappy when it found that Delilah was pregnant, reasoning that the forthcoming birth would cause an interruption in the routine performances both orcas were involved in, but there really wasn't much they could do to prevent the joyful event.

They would simply have to go to the trouble of restructuring their show around other orcas until the female was free of her nursing duties and able to concentrate on her performance again.

The young Bessie Middleton, who loved them wholeheartedly, happened to get the most cooperation out of the orcas. They made a special effort for the keeper because she had an infinitely better understanding of their needs, so the management reluctantly let her continue with her work, even though she didn't appear to show an awful amount of remorse for what she had done.

She knew that any promotions or special trips were not going to come her way, but she didn't need the income or the job. Her father was wealthy and didn't mind spreading some of it around for his young Bessie.

'Let them keep their lousy job,' he advised his daughter. 'They don't want a trainer. They're just treating you as a janitor, who is prepared to do all their grinding and dirty work with a glad heart.'

Bessie thought about what her father had said, but she wasn't going to leave her beloved orcas in the hands of others who had no feeling for them. So, she had a quiet chat with her oversized pets one night, before letting them out of their prison and allowing them to go free.

That action also released the young woman from her guilt-ridden conscience, for she was deeply entangled with Samson on an emotional level. To the rather plain woman, who had never had a serious relationship in her life, he was both her beloved child and her friend, even as far as having possession of her aching heart.

'Whoops!' she cried out the next morning. 'I must have pressed the wrong button. Well, you won't want me around after this, so I'll just clear out my locker, pick up my outstanding wages and be off.'

There was no way that the directors could prove that Bessie's actions were anything but accidental. After all, she'd lost not only her job but also her career, when word got out about what she'd done.

Some months later, a baby orca had appeared at mother and father's side in the bay. And not too long after that came the news that both mother and baby had been wiped out by a joyrider with precious little feeling for animal life.

When Bessie Middleton heard about the tragedy, she took it as a personal injury to herself, after all her years of love and care ministered to the orca couple. So, she took her daddy's sea cruiser into the bay, staffed with its full crew of course. They cruised about for hours, until they came across the broken-hearted killer whale, now a lonely widower. This was shortly before he shook the misery off his shoulders and rejoined the company of others of his kind.

Somehow the impressionable spinster with a big heart would have liked to wear a wedding dress on her reunion with Samson. She felt like a bride going to meet her man, to ease his heartbreak and to offer herself to him. But she knew that swimming in a flowing wedding dress was not safe and could also upset the giant groom, never mind her father when the captain reported her antics, as he was sure to do.

Another idea had been to approach her lover completely in the nude, but this might upset her lover, as well as the boat's crew. He was also a creature of habit and was used to the wetsuit she always wore in her work with the orcas. When the captain had told her that they'd located the orca, identified by its individual markings, Bessie was overjoyed beyond her expectations.

Now she could commiserate with her big baby that she'd cared for over so many years. She put on her wetsuit and entered the water with joy in her heart. Knowing the killer whale's proven habit of having an excellent memory, the wound-up Bessie couldn't wait to get up close to her beloved Samson.

There was hardly any chop or swell in the water that day. In fact, the conditions were almost perfect for a reunion between killer whale and caring woman. The young woman took her time in approaching the giant creature. She didn't want to rush her arrival and possibly spoil their meeting by frightening him off. She had even elected not to use a snorkel and swim fins so as not to interfere with the sea creature's recognition of her.

And there he was — magnificent in his size and bearing. By then she was sure that he was aware of her presence. She took her time in getting closer, already thrilled with being so near to him, the way they used to be in the various aquaria pools.

Then another thought entered her jumbled brain. She would go to him in the most natural way she could. Careless of being watched from the boat, she stripped off her wetsuit and let it float away.

He was virtually motionless now, clearly waiting for her next move. It was time for her to get in closer to her great animal. She moved up against him, held onto his side and pointed downwards with her free thumb, a signal to be carried downwards.

The orca obeyed her instruction and towed her for a short distance under the surface of the water. Bessie moved forward and put out a tentative hand to touch his mighty jaw. Samson opened his mouth and gently but firmly closed it over the woman's wrist.

This was not usual, but Bessie remained as calm as she could. She was taken down many metres underwater until she began to feel the pressure building up in her chest, due to the increased depth as well as her lack of fresh oxygen.

But then he let her go free, and she felt intense relief. It had either been a misunderstanding, or Samson was merely being playful. However, her release had been a temporary one. The huge killer whale firmly turned her pale body so that Bessie's head was facing him. Then he opened his cavern of a mouth and delicately swallowed her upper torso.

It was pitch black inside his maw, and the young woman felt a sudden onrush of abject terror. But her fear didn't last for more than a couple of seconds. Was this not what she wanted, to become a part of him? Then she felt a tearing pain as Samson bit her body in half and proceeded to rip it up with his dozens of needle-sharp teeth.

***

The captain of the leisure cruiser waited and waited, but nothing more was seen of his owner's daughter. He was a worried man. He was going to get the chop over this. How could he let a young woman swim away from the boat he controlled, in nothing more than a wetsuit and not even a snorkel?

And was that not her wetsuit floating away over there? As he watched through the binoculars, Samson, clear from his markings, came up out of the water to grab the wetsuit and tow it away until he was out of sight.

The captain sensed that something strange had taken place under the water but decided that he would keep quiet about this. He had been using the binoculars and was surprised to see her strip off her suit. He had wondered what she was doing. Now he had a glimmer of understanding, being, himself, a lover of the sea and its marvellous creatures.

Where was her armed escort, or any other protection that could be offered to the defenceless young woman? Had he tried to talk her out of her foolish quest? If not, where was his sense of responsibility towards his owner?

They scoured the area for hours after the captain had reported the disappearance of Bessie Middleton. There was no sign of her or her body, apart from a torn scrap of material that might have been part of her wetsuit. Nobody actually saw the orca devour its ex-minder, but there was plenty of speculation regarding what had happened to the brave but impetuous young woman.

Unfortunately, apart from her immediate family and friends, few people would remember the sad mystery of what had happened to Bessie Middleton, probably because of the future spate of deaths involving the sea.

***

Samson had now rid himself of all connections with his past, including the one human who had been really kind to him. But what had been the purpose behind her kindness? When would she have begun to display the insidious evil that was inherent in Man? Now there was no possibility of even that young human turning against him.

He swam away, ready to start a new chapter in his life — a future that he would use to eliminate as many of his human enemies as possible.

Chapter Fourteen

Jason and Dr Gresham were waiting for Janine when she arrived at the Medical Centre, a grand title for a waiting room, an examination room consisting of a gurney behind a curtain, and the doctor's office with a plaque on the door reading "Consultation Room".

'So, what happened to you, Mr Malvy? It looks as if you ran into a wall or fell down the stairs. Are you sure that you're all right? He must have been a real brute.'

'Wait until you see him. A beautiful face and a dreamy figure…'

Dr Gresham laughed. 'No! Are you trying to tell me that your wife did this to you? You really must have said the wrong thing.'

Jason grinned sheepishly. 'Actually, I was asleep at the time, and it was all a mistake.'

'Then I'll be careful not to make mistakes around your wife, because that little error must have been a damned painful one.'

He fiddled with Jason's nose and pronounced that it didn't appear to be more broken than it had been on a couple of occasions in the past.

'Your cut lip is another matter, but it seems that someone, hopefully your wife, has been attending to it, with some success.'

Jason gave a lopsided, painful grin. 'Yes, my wife has a mobile dispensary that should really be licenced to make it legal.'

The doctor was one of those easy-going medical men who don't like working hard for a living, preferring to apply the occasional plaster to a cut finger or suntan cream to a nasty burn. He also had a sharp eye tuned for the admiration of the female figure.

When he saw Janine stride into his offices, he was almost sorry that he hadn't recommended a thorough physical examination of her, to ensure that no nefarious handling had taken place by persons unknown.

To take a few phials of blood out of her arm, Dr Gresham ran his hands up and down the well-shaped limb, like a cellist tuning his instrument. He found a vein easily enough, although Janine was pleased that she didn't require more medical attention than what she was receiving. The way his fingers were twitching, she felt as if he were tuning her up instead of a stringed instrument.

'I'll send off the blood samples at once, and they should have a verdict by tomorrow,' Dr Gresham announced. 'From what your husband has told me, it does sound as if you were dosed up with something that was meant to put you under.' He continued. 'How are you feeling now? Would you like me to give you a thorough going-over, just to be on the safe side? The usual, you know. Checking your lungs and your heart and feeling your stomach for any internal swelling? A knee tap to assess your reactions?'

Janine was fairly sure that her shortish skirt had something to do with the proposed knee tap and one or two of the other procedures. With a coquettish smile, she declined the offer.

'I'll be in contact with you or your husband as soon as the blood tests have been completed,' the doctor promised.

Then he phoned Laurie Bridewell to let him know that the Malvys were ready to view the tapes and were on their way to his office.

They immediately knew that they'd come to the right place and were speaking to the right man. Laurie Bridewell was one of those people who regularly look over their shoulders, even when they're sitting with their backs to the wall. That was exactly the position this man liked to be in.

He was a tough-looking, burly character with a heavy beard and moustache. He also had plenty of extra hair sprouting from out of the neck of his shirt and his cuffs, like an overgrown weed garden. He was definitely not the sort of guy you'd like to meet in an alley on a dark night, Jason decided, particularly if you'd been rude to his mother or punched his father when the man wasn't expecting it.

'So do you have an idea what the man we're looking for looks like, Mrs Malvy?'

'I've got a pretty shrewd idea who it could have been. There were a few men at the bar counter but not that many. Someone bought me a drink, but I'd only had a couple of mouthfuls before I needed to go to the loo. Up to that point, I felt fine. When I returned, this man cornered me with a few long stories and silly quips.

'Soon after, I felt my head starting to spin, and I could feel that something was going horribly wrong. I turned around to look for Jason, and luckily, I caught his eye and beckoned him over. By the time he got to me, I was losing consciousness fast, with my head against somebody's shoulder, but I don't think that it was the man who was keeping me company. There seemed to be more than one man paying me attention at that point.

'My bar counter companion had disappeared by then. Somewhere between the two of them, it felt as if fingers had been fiddling with my ear, but I checked later and both my earrings were intact.'

There were tears in Janine's eyes as she relived her experience and realized how close she had come to being overwhelmed by the men at the bar.

'Cheer up, Mrs Malvy, we're on your side. Let's see if we can identify the swine that did this to you.'

Bridewell had been convinced by Janine's straightforward statement that she had been got at. He felt quite purposeful in tracking down the culprit who had probably wanted to spirit her away, unobtrusively, through the "exit" door that Jason had later used to get her out of the room.

Janine had given him the approximate time of the attempt to possibly kidnap her. While closely examining the second tape, she gripped his arm tightly and blurted out: 'That was the man! He was the one who bought me a drink and kept paying attention to me.'

Bridewell nodded his head. 'I'm not at all surprised. Before this sort of large-scale event, we try to vet those guests who have a reputation for being troublemakers and dubious types that need to be watched carefully. That is Alexei Kilmanov, a member of the Russian Defence Minister, Pucharov's, shady-looking bunch.' He rubbed a hand across his chin. 'I wonder what he was up to. From a sexual point of view, you were safe, Mrs Malvy. Alexei Kilmanov is one of the biggest queers in town. You were more at risk if he was after you, Jason.' He continued, 'So there must have been some other motive. Something either of you were doing or saying that caught their attention. Cast your mind back, Jason. Was there anything that you've said in public lately that could have lit the fuse of the Russian secret service?'

'The only things I've uttered in public were included in the speech I gave yesterday, but it was all fairly general. Mine was one of the opening addresses, and I only touched on the use of orcas to attack warships belonging to foreign navies.'

'Then you don't understand the mindset of the Russian, or the Chinese, for that matter. If they get a bee in their bonnet that you, or the USA, are planning or preparing something important, they will go flat out to find out what it is all about. Perhaps one of their countries is busy right now with exercises or plans, along the same lines as those pointed out in your address. Have you got a copy of your speech with you, by any chance?'

Jason grinned. 'Unfortunately I don't operate like that. What I said was very much off the cuff, but I do recall the gist of it.'

'Well, getting a copy of your speech is easy, because these bureaucrats record everything at these functions. All the verbal dissertations would have been carefully placed on tape, for purposes of copyright or merely for future reference, but it may take a little time for me to get a copy of your address in hand. I'll call for it to be provided as soon as possible, and it will be supplied to me, but I was hoping that we could have something, in the interim, to get our teeth into.'

Jason nodded. 'All right, do you still want me to go through it now?'

'Yes, please, if you will.'

Bridewell switched on a small tape recorder, and Jason went through what he had covered in his speech. Nothing much attracted Laurie Bridewell's attention until Jason began talking about the use of offensive weapons in relation to the training of killer whales and other dolphins, including what had already been achieved in this field. Jason stopped his recollection soon after that.

'That's it!' Bridewell enthused. 'I presume that you know nothing specifically about possible present plans to arm orcas or to train them in the use of offensive weapons against the Western forces?'

'No, not at all. The scenario I presented goes way back to the time of the Vietnam war in the 1950s.'

'But Pucharov and Kilmanov don't know that. For all they know, you've tripped over something which they are engaged in right now, or maybe some new strategy allied to, or improving on, the old ideas. By the way, they sound like really tough guys, but they're the biggest poufs in Russia, and they live in neighbouring apartments but only use one of them for general purposes. The other one is permanently empty except when they entertain guests.

'Anyway, they have been messing about with training different animals that they could use to cripple the West. My contacts tell me that they've even got together with the Chinese on this one, although they can't stand each other. China hungers after becoming the country with the largest economy in the world, apart from wanting to take over everything they can lay their hands on.

'Russia, on the other hand, wants to have the biggest military force, in order to overpower the West. Heaven knows what this poor world of ours would be like if both of these countries got their way. But it's no use being morbid and crying about what could happen if they both pulled off something big between them. We've got to get in there and somehow stop them in their tracks.

'So, what do we do about it? I, for one, am going to do my damndest to upset their plans, and if enough of us use our brains and our efforts, we'll win through in the end. But we can't do it all on our own. We need people like the two of you to stand against the monster nations.

'Anyway, to get back to your spiked drink, Janine, there are a few options that they might have in mind. Either they want to find out what Jason knows about their plans — if anything — or they are trying to find out if Jason has knowledge of any specific procedures that the West could be working on.

'This might sound funny, but they either suspect that our scientists are getting somewhere with our own procedures and are way ahead of them, or else they would like to kill any successes we are on the point of achieving.

'From the tapes we've been viewing, it wasn't only the Russians who were getting at you, Janine. There was more than one Chinese gentleman who was hanging about the bar counter with you. In fact, you may notice a break in the tape that someone has expertly spliced. But there is a clock above the bar that reports a gap of four minutes.' He cleared his throat. 'A lot can happen in four minutes, or even less. Dr Gresham was not examining you for the pleasure it gave him. He was on the lookout for places where probes could be implanted to keep track of or control you.

'You'll be relieved to know that nothing like this was found, although that's not to say that they haven't been successful. I wouldn't put it past the

Chinese to have had success with this, so I advise both of you to keep an eye open for any strange patterns that you might follow from now on.'

Jason was listening to all of this in some sort of a daze. 'Where are you getting all this information from, and how accurate is it? It sounds as if scientists on both sides are running about wildly, like hens with their heads cut off.'

'All right, I admit that a lot of this information is based on supposition and hearsay, but now I'm going to take you deeper into the underworld that we spies move in daily. However, before we go any further, I must warn you that everything you hear or see from this point forward will be strictly denied, if necessary. There will also be no backup if you get yourselves into trouble. Do I have your agreement to this?'

Both visitors nodded their heads in unison.

'Right. Firstly, you do know that the performing orca and his mate Delilah were released by Bessie Middleton, their keeper and trainer? Everybody believes that Bessie released the orcas out of love for them. But the actual reason is that, although the young woman truly loved both of her charges, she was hypnotized by a Russian mind-bender, before allowing a Chinese scientist to implant a special transmitter/receiver into Delilah and then, later on, letting him implant another one into Samson, once it was established that the idea and the methodology was feasible.

'The first transmitter worked well enough, with some minor glitches, but Samson's gadget, although performing more or less as intended, could not fully overcome his emotional feelings for his trainer, Bessie Middleton, who had become a sort of mother figure to him.'

'This is all very interesting,' interrupted Janine, 'but what I can't understand is the type of instructions that were being fed to the orcas by the Russians and the Chinese?'

'A good question. Although the transmitter/receivers had other functions, their main purpose was to kill off as many people as possible in our coastal waters and to produce chaotic shipping conditions at the same time. Mining ships, damaging nets, terrorizing fishermen and tourists; there is a long list of activities planned by our enemies, much the same as you extemporized in your speech, Jason.'

Jason was eager to hear how the spy story was unfolding. 'What happened between Samson and Bessie Middleton?' he wanted to know.

'Right. At the cost of her job and her career, Bessie Middleton released the orcas, but she didn't do this willingly. She was troubled by the implants that she had been party to. She instinctively knew that these operations were wrong, but she didn't have the power to stop herself.

'Then Delilah's implant began to go haywire, but there was no way to rectify the machine, with the creatures out in the bay. So the Russians sent out a boat to eliminate Delilah, which was achieved. But the baby got in the way and was also killed.

'After that, they had a battle to control Samson, who went berserk after his mate and her baby were killed, but they managed to stabilize his machine in the end. The technical adjustments they made from their side finally sorted out their problem.

'But Bessie Middleton was now an unnecessary thorn in the plotters' sides, so they arranged for her to go out to Samson and virtually commit suicide by swimming up to the giant in an act of pathetic devotion, although the poor, demented woman didn't see it that way.

'The end result is that they now have a killing machine swimming about off the western seaboard, with both a controlling machine in its brain and hatred for man in its heart. It has been programmed to join up with as many pods of killer whales as possible, to train them and to influence them along the same thought patterns that it is directed to follow.' He leaned forward and laid his hands on the desk in front of him, continuing earnestly: 'If we allow this killing machine to go on its own sweet way, it will cause mayhem along our coastline, including innumerable deaths and disasters. The longer we take to find a solution to the problem, the more Samson will influence other orcas to follow suit, and between them, cause irreparable damage to our shipping and our fishing, let alone to our warships, one of their prime targets.'

'I don't envy you your job,' remarked Jason.

Bridewell put up a hand. 'Wait a minute, my friend, it's not as easy as that. We need your help, along with everybody who is able to lend a hand.'

'But I'm just one guy and his sweet helper,' the young diver protested, as he put an arm around Janine.

Bridewell smiled mirthlessly. 'We know all about you, Jason. You're not married to this woman standing beside you, the knowledge of which will do irreparable damage to your present image as a sort of local hero.

Secondly, you have had no murder docket legally withdrawn by the prosecutor in your case. We merely asked for the heat to be removed in order to get you on our side.

'If you elect to step out of line and turn us down, I can assure you that a whole heap of evidence, that you're not even aware of, will pile up against you. There's every chance that you will receive a heavy sentence once we get the right prosecution to manage your case, let alone having the authorities appointing a "hanging" judge and jury to ensure your conviction. That bloodstained towel found in your car is like a dripping sword hanging over your head. The evidence is incontrovertible as they say, let alone all the circumstantial evidence that's piling up around you.'

He sat back and waited for Jason's response.

'But a lot of it is sheer nonsense,' complained Jason, in a shocked voice. 'For instance, somebody has said that Tilly and I had a serious argument at the bar, even before we went to the beach together. That's a load of hogwash. What was there to fight about? 'We'd only just met each other that afternoon, and she was happy enough to go to the beach in my shorts, my car and with me, after all.'

'That's the whole point of it,' replied Bridewell. 'We can produce witness after witness to incriminate you if you won't step up to the plate.'

Jason began to see what was facing him if he didn't agree to join the Anti-Terrorist, or A team. He felt anxious and unsure of himself.

'I suppose I'll have to agree to go along with you. You sure know how to play hardball, don't you?'

'When you sit down and think about how many lives are likely to be lost and what our economies will look like if our antagonists have their way, then it's the only way to play our hand, folks.'

Bridewell sat back in his chair with a satisfied smirk. Before they left his rooms, he had one last matter to discuss.

'Do both, or either of you, have a gun licence?'

When he heard that there was no restriction to their handling weapons, he went to his safe and produced two automatic pistols that were much the same, except that the one he presented to Janine was a little smaller than the one he handed over to Jason. He passed on a generous supply of ammunition as well.

He turned to Janine. 'Yours is a little lighter, so it won't feel like a ten-tonne weight in your purse, but it will probably do the same damage as the heavier one. They are to be returned to me at the end of the conference.'

Jason held his weapon up in the air. 'I don't know if this is such a good idea, Laurie, if I may call you that.'

The familiarity sailed over the spy's head without being noticed. 'Why?'

'Well, I've been used to lugging weapons about for years, and I've fired them a lot in practice, but I've never had to use them in battle conditions. Why should Janine and I need them now?'

Bridewell shook his head sadly. 'This is not a healthy exercise session. Ask the woman who ended up in an orca's gut if she enjoyed the game. Speak to the bathers who were murdered, or the families torn out of their boats. These people, who want to reduce our economies to chaos and frighten our folk, feel nothing about our attitudes towards weaponry.

'A couple of airliners have been blasted out of the air during recent times by the psycho Russians, and North Korea and China are also quick on the trigger, never mind the extremist Arabs who are fond of beheading people or blowing them up. It's about time that we started realizing what sort of fanatics we're up against. Honestly, I wouldn't feel happy letting you walk away from this office without lending you some lifesaving protection.'

Jason and Janine walked out of Bridewell's office feeling as if they'd come out of some sort of spy film, not having much to say to each other at that point.

Chapter Fifteen

Both Jason and Janine were feeling fragile. They had been sitting through one more session of speeches — luckily fairly short this time — and a luncheon where they sat and cracked polite faces at a Scandinavian couple who obviously had not been paying attention when they were taught English at school.

After lunch, there was another afternoon cocktail meet-and-greet. Although they separated to cover more ground, both of them were on the lookout for the Russians or other unfriendly faces, only paying distant attention to the delegates they met up with. Time passed slowly, and they were relieved to see that the evening would be free of formalities. They could do as they wished.

'Are you carrying your hardware?' Jason asked, when they got back to their room and threw themselves on Janine's bed, without any protest on her part.

'Don't worry,' replied Janine. 'I've heard what Bridewell had to say, and it all made good sense to me. From now on, if anybody tries any nonsense with me, they're going to get a bullet in the balls before he or she messes about with my body or my drink.'

'Wow, that there's fightin' talk, woman.'

She stared at him through half-closed eyes. 'Obviously you've never felt the vulnerability that we women do when men are around. If you go too far with a woman, she can't do much more than slap your dial or simply turn away…'

'Or punch him in the face a couple of times, while he's got his eyes closed.'

She grinned with embarrassment. 'Okay, okay, message received and understood. But the point I'm trying to make is that women need a pistol in the purse much more than men do. I didn't see that Russian in the cocktail patrol today, but I'm not really surprised that he didn't pitch up. He should know that I'm waiting for him.'

Then she heard a snigger coming from alongside her.

Janine glared at Jason as if he were the spokesman for the entire male gender. 'If he shows his face again and tries another move on me, he'll get a bullet where his mammy hasn't washed him for a long time.'

Jason put up both hands. 'Right, I hear you. Peace in our time, and all that jazz.' He looked at his watch. 'It's still early, but I don't feel like hanging around this hotel any longer, meeting earnest academic faces around every corner. I'm also tired of five-star bland cooking. Let's find a little place that serves a hot curry, or something Mexican and wild. If you're still in the mood for action, we could take in a show, if there's anything worthwhile playing.'

'Sounds good to me. And if you see me putting a hand in my purse while we're out and about, don't go and dive into the nearest skip. I'll probably only be reaching for my lipstick or a tissue.'

He grinned. 'I'll bear that in mind when I see flames coming out of your purse as you trigger the wrong cigarette lighter.'

'I'll try to remember to point the muzzle in another direction, should I ever be about to make that mistake. "Friendly fire" must definitely be the biggest misnomer in the English language.'

Jason hesitated. 'I don't know whether I should ask this without your having a cadenza, but have you had much experience of firearms, Janine? I mean, Bridewell simply slammed a weapon into your fist and never once asked if you'd ever used one of the damned things before.'

'I suppose he merely presumed that I could use it efficiently. After all, did he ask you for any qualifications?'

He lifted his head off the pillow and stared at her with one eye closed. 'Are you being funny now? You must know that I was a Navy SEAL up to a short while ago. We were trained to use all sorts of weapons. But you're ducking the question. Can you handle a firearm or not?'

'Maybe Bridewell assessed me as being a capable sort of woman when he saw the damage I did to a tough Navy SEAL's face after he grabbed my tit while pretending to be asleep. But if you must know, I had an uncle who had a ranch not too far from here, where we kids did plenty of shooting and fast drawing. When the family went there for a holiday, he would get us on horseback and make us ride past cans and bottles on fence posts, which we shot at with great glee. Have a go, sometime, at shooting at a can and hitting it while cantering past it at a rate of knots.' She gave him a wide and challenging smile. 'If you want to try me out, let's find somewhere where we can shoot at targets from the back of a horse. If you want to go against me for a decent wager, I'll be willing to take you on right now.'

Jason put up a defensive hand. 'All right, all right, I just wanted to make sure that you could handle yourself in a firefight. It would be too late to ask the question and find out that you didn't know how to handle it, if we got caught in an alley with a bunch of thugs charging towards us.'

'Well, I know how to handle a gun. Maybe you should get in a little practice at handling your own weapon. Don't you navy guys use spear guns or torpedoes or something? A spear gun is not going to be much use in a street fight.'

'Very funny. I always wanted to spend a whole lot of my time with a woman having a weird sense of humour.'

'And I always wanted to hang about with a man who likes to undress women and wash them down but doesn't go any further with the story.'

'Now, what's that supposed to mean? Don't you want to acknowledge when a fellow's being decent and showing some respect for you because you're so drunk that you can't stand up straight?'

'That's really a shitty, below the belt thing to say. Have you somehow forgotten that I was drugged when I wasn't looking?' Janine's face was red with anger as she turned to the man lying next to her.

Jason glared right back at her. 'You were hanging around at the bar with the weirdo foreigners long before they fiddled with your drink. What sort of vibes were you sending out? What's the word for a "come on" in Russian? You can count your lucky stars that I was there to save your bacon, otherwise you would have become their handmaiden. "Hand her over here when you're finished with her, Boris. Then I'll hand her back again."'

That was enough for Janine. She swung the back of her hand at Jason's face, catching him on the cheek with a ringed finger. Then she completed the movement by rolling over onto her companion and head-butting him fiercely. She was not exactly an expert at head-butting. Both of them suffered from the impact, but neither of them would let on that they were hurting.

Janine's terrible temper had caught fire. She kneed him repeatedly in the area of his groin, with varied success. A groan from him encouraged the enraged woman further. He couldn't believe how vicious her attack was becoming. His body was throbbing from her constant blows to his loins.

Jason had given up the thought of being a gentleman, with this wild bitch trying to permanently damage him. He grabbed her wrists and heaved her body off his, before rolling onto her in turn. He held Janine down on the bed, crushing her with his full weight upon her.

'Now we'll see how dirty you can fight, you slut.'

In answer, she sent a gob of spit flying into his face. He was disgusted. He ducked his face against her cheek and wiped away what he could onto her skin, before spitting a gob of phlegm back at her, aiming for her mouth and getting a bullseye.

'See what mine tastes like, you filthy witch!'

Her eyes were burning orbs of hatred. She lifted her head, opened her dripping wet mouth and bit him on the nose, holding on with all her force and sinking in her sharp little teeth as much as she possibly could.

Jason let go of her wrists and gave out muffled squeals of pain as Janine refused to let go of his nose, hanging on like a tigress protecting her cubs. He had to get free of her. The injured man rolled off and tore himself loose from her grip. They were both breathing heavily, and he held his bloodied nose in both hands, sobbing in pain.

'Ow, ow, ow, ow,' he cried, his eyes closed and his hands dripping with blood.

'Shut up, you ninny, or I'll beat you up again.' She sat up and stared at him in disgust. 'You know how to give pain and to spit out hurtful words, along with filthy lumps of gob, at the weaker sex, but you're not so good at taking it on the nose, are you, my tough navy man?'

He groaned once more.

'Are you going deaf? Can't you hear me speaking to you? Or do you want some more rough treatment?'

'No, please don't hurt me. My face and my balls are on fire. Please cut it out now. I'm sorry. I'm sorry.'

Strangely enough, Janine had calmed down a little. Looking down on Jason's battered face, she was a little sorry that she had done that damage to his looks that were so manly and strong, if not all that evenly proportioned. She also felt bad about his throwing in the towel and giving in to her the way he had done. Men were not supposed to do that. Her heart churned with pity when he apologized like a beaten little boy. She wanted to put her arms around him and mother him, but first he needed some repair work done to that poor bleeding face.

Out came her repair kit. She was running low on certain stocks and would have to get some more bandages, adhesive tape and antiseptic salve if they kept on squabbling like this. She shook her head when she examined the damage she had done this time. Damned if she hadn't let her vile temper run wild once more. When was she going to be able to control that devil inside her that always needed to prove a point and to win an argument? She'd be surprised if Jason still found it worthwhile to ogle her the way he did.

He must have gone through a self-controlled hell when he undressed her, cleaned her up and got her into bed last night, without pouncing onto her and making wild love. Now he probably wouldn't be keen to come near her with a ten-foot barge pole. But maybe there was still a chance that she could bring out his feelings for her.

She would have to bury her devil and show Jason how gentle and loving she could be. It shouldn't be too difficult to manage, for it had been a long time since she had made love to a man of her choice, and she was about ready for him.

***

The nurse in her took a long time about repairing the damage she had done to her companion. Janine cleaned out blood clots from the inside of his nose and used ice from the courtesy icebox to reduce the swelling. The exterior bite marks were something else. She had really done some damage there.

Not only did they look painfully deep, but they had been lacerated badly as the two of them had fought each other. The bite marks were probably infected as well. It was common medical knowledge that human bite wounds were among the most infectious of them all.

Then there was the cut mark on his cheek, where her ring had torn open the flesh. It was an ugly wound, but her skilful fingers repaired the damage as best she could, making the scars less noticeable to a casual glance.

Last but not least were the powerful kicks she had administered to his groin area. Jason had dropped off to sleep during his lengthy repair job, but now he woke up groggily as Janine gently removed his trousers and underpants to find out what damage had been done around his genitals.

He made to stop her at the critical stage of his undress, but Janine was a forceful woman, as he had found out earlier. Finally he lay on the bed, fully exposed and not really caring. The sedative that he had been earlier given by his amateur nurse had a lot to do with his calm state.

She was impressed with his statistics, but his was not the biggest that she had ever seen. Janine believed strongly in the adage that it was not the size of the equipment that was so important, but how the man used it when making love.

Janine bathed his bruises in a healing balm and smeared on a cream that would aid the healing process. She was pleasantly surprised to see how her patient's penis reacted when she handled it in an almost purely professional manner. There was still plenty of vibrant life evident down there. A few hours' rest and he would be ready and willing to romp in the rain.

The tireless caregiver dressed her patient in a pair of his sleeping shorts and spread a coverlet over him. He was soon out like a light, thanks to the short-acting sedative Janine had given him earlier. He looked as peaceful as a baby.

She kissed him carefully on the forehead, to avoid the spot where she had head-butted him and treated with a soothing cream. Hell, but there wasn't such a lot of him that wasn't newly out of a war zone. It was probably just as well that his mother couldn't see him now, she thought.

She was covered in pastes and creams and blood spots. Janine phoned for a room-service meal and a couple of bottles of chilled wine to be left just inside of the door of their suite, before going to have a slow and luxuriating shower. She was in no hurry at all. Jason was fast asleep and would stay that way for a while.

When she heard the meal arrive at the door of their suite, she judged it to be the right time to get out of her comforting shower, mainly because her skin was starting to wrinkle like an albino prune. In no particular hustle to finish her toilette, Janine dried herself off carefully in front of the mirror, while examining her well-shaped figure of which she was inordinately proud.

For no special reason, the fully relaxed and deeply cleansed woman chose her sexiest nightie to wear, because a girl never knew, did she? The snores coming from within the suite suggested that she had a long innings of adult babysitting ahead of her that night. The way she was feeling right then, she was almost ready to invite the bellhop in for a taste of honey.

Janine sat down to a hot and fairly tasty meal, along with some of the chilled wine. She was one of those lucky ones who enjoy their own company most of the time. Talk shows and sitcoms were also up her street.

So, she switched on the telly when she'd finished most of her meal, after saving some of it to have with her patient if he should wake up hungry within the next hour or two. She sat happily watching what was available over a broad range of channels, having missed a lot of the action lately.

Later on she woke up with a start, surprised to hear an annoying buzz that signified that the channel she'd been watching had closed down for the night. She sleepily switched off the box and went to the toilet before going to see how her patient was doing. Surprisingly, he showed some signs of emerging from his fog when she clicked on the bedside light.

Janine sat on the side of the bed, studying him. Then she saw his eyes open, and recognition come into them.

'Hello, old thing,' she softly hailed him. 'How are all your aches and pains coming along?'

'My face and nose are sore, along with my head, and I have a few aches and pains downstairs. What the hell happened to me? Did I get run over by a bus, or did the sky fall down on me, or what?'

'Nothing like that. I just gave you a beating because you were giving me a hard time, that's all.'

'C'mon, seriously. What's been going on?'

'Don't you remember anything?'

'All I can remember is you sitting on top of me and trying your best to bite my nose off. And you bloody well wouldn't let go at all! You hung on like a tigress. And that's why it's so damned sore!'

'So you do remember some of it. What actually happened was that we started arguing over rubbish, like, could I handle a firearm or what...'

'And can you?'

141

She sniffed. 'If you want to start that up again, I suggest you feel your head, your cheek, your nose and your balls, before we go any further.'

'Oh, it's like that, is it?'

'Only if you make it so. I'm sorry I beat you up. You're far too handsome to deserve that, but you were really asking for it.'

He was staring at the front of her nightie that was displaying more than a little cleavage, as she leant forward at the side of the bed. In fact, one breast was easing itself out of its confinement, and she absently popped it back into place. Jason got a big shock when he stared at the shapely breast and didn't feel a thing. He couldn't remember that ever happening before.

She paused. 'I ordered a meal for us because you were going to take me out before we began our little argument. I couldn't wait any longer, so I've had the major portion of my share, but I'll heat your steak and mushrooms up for you, if you're ready for it. There's a very pleasant wine to go with it, if you're interested, with an extra bottle just in case you want to party. I'll join you if you like.'

Considering how his partner was dressed, or undressed, there still remained some promise in the evening, he decided. 'Right, as long as you're dressing for dinner exactly like you are, then I'm game for anything.'

She raised an eyebrow. One couldn't keep this tough cookie down for long.

'Well, it's all there for the taking, if you make the right moves, of course. I'll lean forward a lot, if that helps.'

He slipped on a sports shirt, because it didn't seem right sitting bare-chested at the small dining table opposite a woman in a cross between an elegant evening gown and a sexy nightie. Janine kept an eye on Jason, who was still a little wobbly after his drug-induced sleep. But she could see that he was coming out of his daze, even to the extent of getting some of his appetite back.

Jason was thirsty. He poured wine for both of them, with a hand that was more than a little shaky, and drank deeply from his glass.

'How are you feeling now?' his dining partner asked him.

'Slightly smashed,' he replied, underlining his statement by missing the rim of his glass with his still-healing lip. He clumsily wiped away the dribble off his chin.

Janine studied him objectively. He still had a battered look about him, but his wounds looked a little less raw than they had only a few hours before. She felt quite proud of her repair work.

But he was starting to droop again, and he'd only eaten half of his food. She leant forward and rescued the half-full glass of wine as he was about to knock it over. Quick as she was, she was too late to prevent his face from landing in his salad. Luckily the lettuce, cucumber and tomato would do little damage to her repair work on his facial damage.

She moved smartly around the table and caught him as he began to lean sideways. 'Right, buster, I'm going to return the compliment of last night and take you to the toilet before you let go of all that wine you've just drunk. Unfortunately, I can't support you the way you did for me. You're going to need to cooperate to some degree if this is going to turn out to be a successful move.'

He was heaved onto his unsteady feet and helped on his way to the toilet, leaning against his concentrating helper like a drunk being supported by a mobile lamppost that staggered now and then.

When she had placed him in position and remembered to lift up the seat lid, Janine pulled down his shorts and took his large and floppy penis in hand, pointing it in what she hoped was the right direction. Nothing happened. Obviously, he needed a little encouragement.

'C'mon, do a little pee-pee for Mommy,' she encouraged.

Still nothing.

'Hurry up, Jason, you're getting bloody heavy to hold up with one arm. And in case you're getting inflated ideas, I'm referring to your body, not your penis.'

Suddenly she saw the funny side of the situation and started giggling. The jerking of her hand woke up the digit, and it started moving about like a blind worm in the light and enlarging all the time.

'Well, now, that's why men like dirty jokes. They get the old dingdong going. There's something new to be learnt every day.'

At last, a small dribble appeared, followed by the satisfactory stream that she had been trying to encourage. When it eventually trickled to a stop, Janine gave it a firm shake to get rid of the drops, as she had seen it done in bawdy films.

'Now I've got a problem. I don't need to wash your hands because you've done damn-all to help out, but I wouldn't mind washing mine. But what do I do with you, dummy, while my hands are full? Of course.'

She sat him down on the toilet seat after putting it down and pulling up Jason's shorts. Then she had a quick wash while keeping an eye on him as he threatened to tip over against the washbasin. But it all turned out well in the end.

Before long, he was back in bed. He was already out like a light. She leant over him like a mother should and kissed him on the top of his head, one of the few unmarked places remaining above his neck. As she stretched over him, a boob popped out again and nestled in one of his eye sockets. She retrieved it as she stood up.

'See what you've been missing, you silly man. In future you might remember not to mess with me. Think of all the fun you've had to go without.' She added, 'And me too, I suppose.'

Chapter Sixteen

Samson had met up with a small pod of orcas that were peaceful in their demeanour, as were almost all of their kind. There was nothing in the ocean that they were frightened of, ready to take on the biggest whale and tear its tongue and cheeks out of its mouth when on the hunt. Humans were the only threat to them, with their superior weapons, but the orcas were largely unaware of this.

There was no battle for supremacy between the males, although that may have had something to do with the fact that Samson was much, much larger and heavier than any of the males in the pod. This was also underscored by the females who acknowledged that Samson was their leader, and they were all more than willing to mate with him.

Although there were orcas that mated for life, there were many females who would accept any male at certain times. In fact, some males joined forces in order to pressure a female into mating with them, taking this procedure in turns if this was the only way that they could succeed. They would gather around a female and attempt to turn her over if she avoided intercourse by lying on her back, thus avoiding penetration by these undesirable males.

Samson didn't take long to establish his supremacy as the pod's leader. None of the others, whether male or female, were prepared to argue about the situation. They were easy-going followers of his ways, although their new leader had to make serious efforts to stir up some aggression towards humans, something that they had not thought about previously.

The followers sensed that the pace had stepped up since Samson had joined their pod, but it didn't matter much. He seemed to know where to find good pickings and they all ate well, although food had been short in the area, of late. In fact, he was introducing them to a new diet — a human diet — that they hadn't tried before.

Then their new leader led then towards another group of orcas. This made them nervous, because the numerical size of the new group was larger than their total number. But Samson calmed them down and made peace between the two pods.

Once again Samson selected the females that were to his liking, without any opposition from the males in his enlarged pod.

Now there were thirty-five orcas cruising the ocean together. Samson thought that it was a good start. He was, slowly but surely, stirring up a sense of aggression towards humans in his new fleet of destroyer orcas. Because of the size of the pod, he needed to find a larger source of food for his pack, which included his prime target.

The time had arrived for them to pull off their first attack as a group. There was a yacht race scheduled to start in the bay, and Samson could see them gathering for the race. What a beautiful situation in which to create havoc.

His fleet of orcas had been directed to upset as many yachts as possible and devour every yachtsman they came across. He didn't know how he knew of the race, but something in his brain told him that the regatta would take place.

Eating humans was not their form of lifestyle, but Samson's followers liked their new leadership and the plentiful food that it provided. If their leader wanted them to have a meal of yachtsmen, that was not a great sacrifice to make for all the food and other benefits they were receiving since the advent of their great leader.

In accordance with the plan that their brainy leader had developed, the killer whales started off cruising in small groups, completely out of the way of the yachtsmen. They were spotted and their position noted, but they were not anticipated as having any effect on the race, so the yachts were sent on their way. It was a decision that the organizers would come to regret.

The orcas waited until the yachts were well offshore and about halfway through the race, before closing in on them.

'Hey, those massive whales are coming closer!' yelled a crewman on one of the leading yachts.

'Stick to your job, man!' called out the skipper. 'We'll not win this race if we start losing focus now.'

'I'm doing my job, but I'm not blind, you know,' called out the crewman, shuddering as a capricious wind sent a spray of icy spume down his neck.

'He's right, you know,' shouted the only woman on the team. She had been chosen because she looked like a carthorse, but more importantly, worked like one.

'Sure, and they're coming right this way, Skipper.'

It seemed as if the whole crew was choosing this critical moment to rebel, when the race lead was almost in their hands. What were they going on about? He looked over his shoulder to see four killer whales bearing down on them from an angle which looked much like a collision course to him.

'What the hell! You know, you're right. Take avoiding action. Drop the sails. Do something, quickly!'

It was a little too late for that. They were heeling over at a dramatic angle, and the huge shapes were almost on them. Geoffrey Crancutt was a fairly good skipper when it came to choosing the right sails for the wind conditions and making the most of a fair wind to squeeze a few more knots out of it, but he was useless in a tight situation. And that was where they were right then.

Riding High was the name of the sailboat, and it lived up to its name when the orcas hit it broadside on and flipped the crew out of it. The boat shot up into the air, and five surprised crew members were catapulted out of their craft before landing in the boiling sea.

The killer whales were not interested in the boat. They were after the people struggling in the water. They picked four of them up like cherries out of a pudding, leaving the spare one as a reward for Samson, their leader.

He had earned the bonus, due to his organizational skill. The only problem they had was about having to get through all the waterproof wrappings as they chewed on their catch. Luckily, their razor-sharp teeth could rip through almost anything that stood in the way when they fed.

But their day of feasting was far from over. Other boat crews had seen the attack on *Riding High.* Some veered towards the stricken vessel to render sportsmanlike assistance, but others got the hell out of the area when they saw how their competitors and mostly friends were being cut to pieces on the sharp teeth of the hunting orcas, which were purposeful in their attack.

Some sailors tried to clear out of the area. There were no power brakes on a yacht. To change direction was quite a performance. While they were adjusting the sails to put their craft about, a second line of vicious-looking predators was bearing down on them. They didn't stand a chance, stalled as they were, in the water, with their sails flapping pathetically.

It was almost too easy. Another five heavily clothed humans were floundering about in the water, helpless in the path of five eating machines. These hunters didn't mess about. They had much work to do. The rest of the fleet was dispersing in different directions, unaware that there were more killer whales waiting under the surface of the water for them to pass by.

The organizers on shore didn't have much of a clue as to what was happening. Through their binoculars, it appeared that the competing vessels had come to a standstill or were scattering to the winds. Here and there a garbled radio call came through, which was not easy to comprehend. Something about "being put under attack by whales" was probably the most lucid message of all, but where were the whales coming from? They had been miles away when the regatta had started off. Why should they get in the way now? Anyway, what could those on shore do about it?

They did have a couple of powerboats on hand, in case of tragedies and general emergencies. These were sent out to aid the competitors, while radio contact was being established with those yachts that were not directly involved in whatever calamity that was happening out there.

There was a lot of confusion and even chaos occurring in the middle of the bay. Crews were landing in the water, and other good-spirited sportsmen were trying to rescue them out of the swells. The killer whales were quite happy to pick up as many as they could get into their busy maws.

More and more of the attacking orcas were putting in an appearance, wanting to join in the meal, while others began to chase after the yachts that were trying to beat a hasty retreat over the horizon. Those desperate escapees had to put their foot on the gas to get away from the hungry beasts trailing them.

The powerboats arrived in the middle of this mess. Nobody carried firearms, so there was not much they could do to defend the yachtsmen, or even themselves. The two powerboats buzzed about and did drag a few flailing bodies out of the water. But then the killer whales caught the crews of the powerboats stationary in the water as they tried to pull frightened people out of the sea.

The orcas were on hand to make life miserable for the newcomers as well. They only needed to try the old trick of scrambling onto the boats and tipping the humans off them. This was one meal they needed to hurry along, because they instinctively knew that the humans on land would be likely to come to the rescue of their own kind as soon as they were able to.

In the end, the powerboat crews were added to the tally that the killer whales were building up, along with the yachtsmen left struggling in the water. Recreational sailors were not even waiting to fall off their boats now. Their eyes were riveted so much on the mayhem about them that they collided with unmanned boats drifting about in the water, along with others that were yawing out of control, their helmsmen gawping at the chaos in front of them.

One yachtsman was not going to be taken that easily. Seeing a now-familiar bow wave approaching his boat, with a killer whale pushing in behind it, he leaped at the mast and wound himself determinedly about it with both arms.

The move might have worked, but the giant dolphin moved in close and bit off both of his legs with its razor-sharp teeth. The legless thighs were the next to go. In terrible agony, the yachtsman lost his grip and slid away from the mast, and the orca took what was left of him.

The powerboats added to the flavour of the day for the attackers because their occupants were not as heavily suited as were the competitors. An orca lifted a squirming woman out of a boat and spun her into the air. As she came down again, it bit into her buxom body which collapsed like that of a rag doll, as the fierce creature's many razor-sharp teeth ripped into her.

She screamed terribly until her head was mercifully torn off at the neck by the creature's myriad teeth, which could take a hefty chunk out of the largest whale if necessary, ripping out its tongue if it could be reached.

What the rest of her felt inside the crunching creature's maw, nobody could say. There weren't many sailors who escaped the carnage that afternoon. For once, the advantage was in favour of those competitors who had been trailing behind the rest of the fleet when this feast of the great fish was in progress.

The sailors turned about and made for home, their heads swivelling about every few seconds to stare behind them, judging whether they were remaining in the clear. Maybe they were also registering the great satisfaction in feeling that their necks were still able to rotate freely.

Seaplanes were called out to see what could be done, but it was all too late. The killer whales submerged after a good meal had been eaten by all, and they wisely swam away from any retribution that could be thought up by the authorities. No sailing cups were presented that afternoon because there were no finishers.

In fact, there were hardly any entrants left to report their shock and horror at seeing their competitors — many of them good friends — being expertly ingested after a few casual tosses into the air and then being caught and swallowed on the way down; sometimes in a ball, but often with arms and legs sticking out for a second gulp. The few who escaped being eaten alive were taken to a nearby mental institution for some much-needed therapy.

Life being what it is, they were sedated and put into a communal ward for the sake of company. The television was switched on and Jaws 2 was shown to the shivering audience.

'Are they bloody mad!' someone shouted out. 'They're killing us all over again, the miserable bastards.'

Luckily their ward was well insulated, for there were some terrifying screams that drowned out the dramatic background music to the film. A couple of inmates simply solved their problem by ducking their heads under the pillows and trying to think of cool streams and lakes, with no orcas in them.

***

The shambles that the orcas turned the yacht regatta into was televised and broadcast worldwide. There were many deaths, all of them most gruesome. Low-flying planes covered the area, looking for survivors, but there were none to be seen at that late hour. From what had been reported regarding the latest orca attacks, none were, in fact, expected.

There was not much the rescue seaplanes and helicopters could do to help, unless the pilots wanted to offer themselves to the orcas by landing on the sea and being overwhelmed by the hungry giants. The only upside of it was that tremendous sequences of humans being devoured by killer whales were captured on film. Most film and newspaper editors could never print these without some serious editing, but some of this did get published, with many of the gruesome bits being blurred out.

Broken boats and scattered possessions littered the area. There was absolutely no sign of life. About two hundred sailing enthusiasts had lost their lives, and the yachting fraternity was in turmoil as the nation mourned their loss. The problem of the marauding killer whales was discussed in the highest circles, with experts in this field being consulted, but solutions were slow in coming forth.

The only positive offering was that all orcas off the western seaboard of the United States should be eliminated, with this extreme method being extended further afield if this effort did not achieve its purpose. Of course, there were "tree huggers" who thought that this was a terrible way to handle the problem. They were then asked, in public, if they had any better suggestions to offer. Was the sea around the United States to be surrendered to these killers?

In the meantime, other methods were being studied continuously, in search of a better solution. Until then, the public was advised to keep away from the sea, by all means, unless proper safety measures were to be carried out.

The atmosphere in the country was a morbid one. It was bad enough to have to put up with the threat of a number of extremist Muslim movements and their various hate campaigns, leading up to a major outflow of emigrants spreading into Europe and other countries; Russia with its military aggression; China with its financial muscle; and now this latest attack on the western seaboard of America.

In its usual way of throwing cash at a problem, the Government was in the process of releasing large sums of money to finance seminars and working committees of all kinds to come up with a solution to the orca threat.

Knowing that there would be a backlash of protests from the public, the US Navy was quietly sent into action.

A senior officer made an announcement to his sea captains: 'We must certainly clear the surrounding sea areas of orcas by attacking them with powerful ships and arms that they can't withstand. But this must all be done completely in secret, otherwise we will have trouble on our hands from every old lady who can still hold a protest flag.

'There's an election coming up fairly soon. If we don't control the orca problem, we'll be out on our ears; and if the public learns about the methods we're using, the same outcome will develop in the other direction. So do your job well; and do it silently.'

Warships of an intermediate size drifted unobtrusively out of various harbours in a quest to eliminate the local killer whale population. It was a drastic measure, but it was the only one that came to mind until a better solution would turn up.

Of course, major shipping movements of this kind could not be kept secret for long. Although the crews were sworn to secrecy, the nosey press had ways and means of finding out what the navy was hiding right then. And money always opened tight lips, if enough of it was splashed about.

The first ships had hardly eased out of harbour before someone bought somebody a drink, with plenty of money changing hands for the information given.

Somebody had a contact who was a reporter with one of the local newspapers. He had a gabby brother who was on the clerical staff of the local shipyard. His information, mostly gleaned during a family barbecue, had unwittingly bought many a drink, or a few bucks, for his brother-in-law.

The informant was not at all unpatriotic in his own mind. After all, there were others in the know who could also have passed on valuable information to the press. What difference would it make to pass on an extra little bit of information now and again?

So, what that he had sworn an oath under the Official Secrets Act? They'd never be able to pin it on him. Anyway, most of the stuff he passed on was not going to be the cause of starting World War III. A few ship movements here; a couple of patrols there; the big shots liked to make a mystery of the war games they played, although he couldn't see what difference a little whisper in his brother-in-law's ear could make.

Chapter Seventeen

Jason woke up feeling stiff and sore. He heard a snore coming from next to him and carefully turned his head to see Janine lying by his side. He unglued his eyes slowly and had a careful look at her. They were obviously in his bedroom, and she'd changed into a nightie even more enticing than her dinner gown, judging from the fact that her nipples were visible, and their skin tones were discernible.

Her mouth was hanging open, and he thought that he could see her epiglottis waving like a fan in a limpid breeze. Not a pleasant sight. He closed his eyes again. He didn't want to be caught staring at her. He'd seen enough anyway.

It was strange that men hankered after seeing breasts, nipples, and other intimate parts, until these were dangled under their noses day after day. Then the thrill soon wore off. Too much of it could be like watching a woman brushing her teeth and seeing her foaming at the mouth like a rabid dog.

Maybe it was due to waking up out of a deep sleep to too much nudity, but he was feeling slightly queasy right then. Jason hoped sincerely that this woman was not going to want sex. He honestly was just not up to the thought of bouncing about on top of a woman until he worked himself up to a ball-breaking climax. It was quite a strange sensation, feeling the way he did. He would never admit to any of his pals quite how he felt about it right then.

Maybe the shine had worn off because Janine had beaten on him a couple of times. He'd never had a woman panel-beat his face the way this woman had done. It didn't feel all that good for the ego. And yet, there was his morning glory standing up and staring at him. He would have to go and pee, but he needed to ease out of the bed carefully so as not to disturb this virago.

It was damned difficult to slide out from under the covers smoothly when his bladder was saying: "C'mon, c'mon, I'm ready to burst." His stiffness didn't help him to flow like a ballet dancer, especially when he got his big toe stuck in the coverlet just as he thought he was in the clear.

The bed jerked. Jason cursed silently and turned to look at Janine. Her eyelids were moving. Time to get out in a hurry. He was starting to lose control. He could feel the first drops of urine sliding down the inside of his penis.

'Where going?' his bed partner mumbled, as he took off for the bathroom.

'Gotta pee,' he mumbled, not in a condition to stop for anyone.

He hung about in the bathroom for as long as was indecently reasonable. He sat on the can for a fair time and was just going to move off when he had to lighten his load anyway.

While he was there, he had a shower, giving Janine time to drop off again. It was quite tricky to avoid getting his healing places wet under the bandages and plasters. Finding no further reason to stall any longer, he dried himself and came through to the bedroom with a bath towel wrapped around his middle.

Janine was sitting up in bed, her hands supporting her head as it rested against the headboard. She was staring into space when he came into the room.

'Morning, sunshine,' she greeted. 'I thought you'd got lost down the plughole. What's with all the early morning energy?'

'Hi there,' he responded, bending forward as he dried his hair, his damaged face away from his towel.

Janine stared at his patched-up face. 'It looks like it's healing up quite well.' She patted the bed. 'Come sit here next to me and let me have a good look at it.'

He didn't know how to refuse a reasonable request like that. He sat down, and Janine pulled his head slightly forward to look at some of the patched areas. She had leant forward herself, causing a curious breast to investigate what its mistress was doing with a handsome man on her bed and his head in her hands.

It squirmed forward, and its sensitive and friendly nipple stood erect and announced itself to the young man, whose face was not that far away

154

from it by now. His bilious feeling of disinterest had become a thing of the past. Being a healthy organ, his penis felt the tension growing in his master's body and began striving to find its way out from under the towel.

Janine's eye caught a pronounced movement under the towel, and her nipples swelled up even more. She couldn't resist the urge to put down a hand to feel the growing swelling between Jason's legs. She was pleased to see this reaction from him, because she had sensed some off-handedness in him when he'd sped off to the bathroom earlier on.

She tapped the bulge gently, and there was a responsive twitch in reply.

The interested woman gave a little giggle. 'It looks like you're feeling a lot better now. Would you like to feel a little more? If we go slowly, we can avoid doing any damage to your poor body.'

And that killed the urge for sex in Jason. It wasn't so much what Janine said to him; it was the patronizing way in which she said it, as if she was going to feed a nice bowl of ice cream to her little boy in compensation for the two beatings she had given him. The more Jason stared at her body, the more he was put off having sex with her.

Janine sensed that something was going wrong. She slipped out of her nightie and pulled off Jason's towel. Then she took his penis — by then buckled and bent — in her hand and gave it a friendly wiggle or two. Then she tried to push it into her vagina, but it didn't want to do anything but go to sleep.

'What the hell's wrong with you?' Janine complained. 'You get an opportunity to make love to me and you go as soft as a rubber duck in a bathtub. Can't you see that I'm ready for you now? I've never been treated like this before. Maybe you're a queer or something. Do you want me to go down on my knees in front of you? Forget it, buster. That's one service this girl won't perform.'

She swung out of the bed as she began crying, but she did not neglect to give a spiteful chop to Jason's groin as she grabbed her nightie and parted from him. He buckled in agony and held his hands to the injured area, but he was secretly pleased that Janine had taken out her spite on him in this way. This low blow underlined the mean streak that was never far from the surface.

It seemed that here was one woman who had a permanent problem with her temper and her self-control. He was glad, now, that they'd not had sex together. At least she had no hold over him. Once a bitch, always a bitch. Jason sensed that he would have had to pay for any intimacy, somewhere along the line.

***

Neither of them referred to the morning's fiasco, as they readied themselves for another gathering. They spoke to each other as if nothing unusual had happened before breakfast, but there was no camaraderie between them. Something had definitely forced them subtly, but permanently, apart.

Anyway, there were plenty of women out there. Jason was not too worried that his current liaison — for it could hardly be called a love affair — was not really working out. It was better to sort this out now, before they became too involved with each other. At the same time, he didn't want to rock the boat before this current seminar was over.

He couldn't really judge Janine's feelings for him at all. With her quick temper, she could cause trouble for him by throwing a tantrum at the wrong time. Better to say goodbye to each other at the end of this seminar on reasonably good terms.

Before the start of proceedings, Jason phoned Terence Pollard, the newspaper reporter who had shared a special arrangement with him regarding the sharing of information. He brought Terence up to speed regarding the latest news coming out of the seminar, most of which he'd covered with a special cell phone link they'd agreed to use.

'So, have you got anything interesting for me?' Jason asked, more as a formality than anything else.

'As a matter of fact, I have. Word has it that the dolly bird you've appointed as your PR woman has been got at by either the Russians or the Chinese, or both. She's been placed there more to keep an eye on you and to pass along any information you dig up, than to facilitate your efforts, particularly if it has anything to do with their involvement in the orca issue.

'This is all very unofficial and extremely fresh info, so don't place any bets on the veracity of this news. In fact, my editor is still trying to check out the information before he's prepared to print it. Please keep it to yourself, or my neck is on the line.'

Suddenly Jason felt the need for a friend that he could trust; someone to cover his back if necessary. And the only one he could think of, who would fit in with his needs, was Danny Foulkes, his Navy SEAL buddy. He rang him up at once.

'Hi, Danny, it's Jason Malvy. I hope it's going well with you.'

'Hi, Jason. Well, I still haven't got a girlfriend or a job yet. Maybe I'm not washing behind my ears or something.'

'Maybe you're boozing too much.'

'Not really. It was only my freedom from the navy that I was celebrating. But that's come to a stop because my funds are running low.'

Jason was relieved that his man was available and in need of funds.

'Danny, don't go around shouting about this, but I could use you right now, if you feel free to join me. All expenses will be paid, and there'll be something extra in it for you, if you want a little adventure in your life.'

'Sounds good, Jason. Tell me more.'

'I can't really, Danny. It's a little hush-hush right now. You'll have to trust me on this one.'

Danny Foulkes was never one to think too much about a decision that needed to be made. 'Right, send me the plane ticket, and I'll be there ASAP.'

'Sorry, Danny. I can't even do that. I'll wire you the money and book you into a nearby hotel. We don't know each other from there on, Danny.'

'Sounds mysterious. All right, I'll start packing and wait for your instructions.'

They said goodbye and hung up. Jason felt a big sense of relief. At least he had somebody on his side, for a change.

He phoned Terence Pollard again. 'Terence, I'm afraid I'm going to need your help. I've got someone — and don't ask me who it is — who will be covering for me, now that my PR is no longer of any real use to me. But I can't just dump her because she'll know that her cover's blown. So, I've now got two mouths to feed, apart from my own. Is there any chance that your newspaper can start funding me?'

'I must say that your timing is good, Jason. My editor is over the moon with the inside info you've given us. He asked me if there's any help you require, particularly financially. So, this all slots in nicely with your needs. Give me your account number, and you'll be in for a pleasant surprise. Just keep all your vouchers and receipts if you please. But if you decide to take clients out for the night, preferably not to places that blatantly call themselves whorehouses.'

Jason laughed, and they rang off on that note.

***

The Russians and the Chinese were trying to take over the seminar, with North Korea trying to push its weight about under the rickety and aggressive leadership of Kim Jung-Un. As usual, Putin disavowed knowledge of any troop and ship movements being made by Russia off the western seaboard of the United States.

China was funding massive manoeuvres by North Korean troops and armament, because most of the North Korean people were starving to death and their leader needed some brash activity to keep them occupied. But they stuck to stirring up the soup off their own coastline, largely because they didn't have the funds to go global.

China didn't want to go to war, which was going to appear too bad for their smiley global image and the value of their exports to other nations. They would rather secretly fund North Korea to do their dirty work for them. China had plenty of money hoarded away, including vast investments in the American economy, holding billions of the American national debt in their sticky fingers. Even the Chinese banks were owned by the state. They would never let go of any form of power, if they could help it.

Instead of being an open sharing of knowledge about how to handle the orca situation, delegates were stalking about with their papers pressed against their bodies, while they gazed apprehensively over their shoulders. The initial sense of working together, with which the seminar had begun, was now a thing of the past.

Jason and Janine joined the throng. There was a sort of unofficial armed truce between the two of them now. They had retreated to their own bedrooms after hours and were operating more as a brother and sister team rather than in the steamy situation that they had created for themselves previously, although Jason couldn't help but notice that there was precious little information coming in to him from his assistant, regarding the movements and plans of the Asian bloc.

Now that they had cooled off towards each other, the J twins had more time to circulate and less reason to keep tabs on their partners. Janine had the most conflicting of interests. On the one hand, she was contracted to ferret out information for Jason, but the deep-seated plug in her ear made her the handmaiden of the Chinese.

She compromised by sharing fairly innocuous gleaned information with Jason, but the really hot stuff was relayed to her Chinese contact man, who had suddenly put in an appearance. She knew who he was, because she was told who to look out for. A daily code word was all that was needed to share gleaned facts and figures.

The Russian pansies, Dmitri Pucharov and Alexei Kilmanov, were the most neglected operators within the diplomatic and the scientific circles, mainly because everybody expected them to be constantly digging for information, which was largely what was happening.

To a large extent this was true, but the two Russians had built up such a powerful and detailed establishment over an extensive period of time, that the show virtually ran itself, and they could afford to swan about quite happily without getting too involved in their team's day-to-day activities.

At the moment, the two men had cornered Janine at the bar and were pumping her for information, when she would rather have preferred to pass on certain titbits to her Chinese masters. She was also being pretty careful about watching the drink that she was toying with. No more knock-out drops for her.

Jason had gravitated to Professor Cora Nugent, who received him with unfeigned pleasure.

'I've got a map that my department has drawn up regarding the historical movements of orcas. I suppose you know that they are classed as the most widely distributed mammals in the world. It's too large to carry about with me, but it's in my suite if you'd like to have a look at it sometime.'

Jason nodded enthusiastically. 'I'd like that very much, Professor Nugent.'

She gave him a broad smile. 'Please call me Cora. I'd like that. And you are Jason, I believe. Would you like to see it now?'

He beamed at her. 'Yes, I really would, but won't your partner object to our meeting in your suite?'

She turned on a sad little smile. 'Jason, ten years ago my husband would have killed anyone getting up to nonsense in my rooms, but these days we keep the connecting door to our rooms locked. He drifts about like a minesweeper looking for female bombshells to trap in his net.' She grinned. 'I also need company at times, but I'm a little more discreet about how I go about it.' She gave a bigger smile. 'But my spies tell me that you're at this conference with your young and attractive wife.'

'Your spies are not fully informed, I'm afraid. The dear lady is my public relations person. We refer to her as my wife for ease of booking arrangements, general communications and so on, but I'm not particularly interested in getting too personal with her. If you examine my face, you'll see why I don't need to turn her into my personal relations partner.'

Cora had a good look at his upturned face that he was showing her. 'What on earth has she done to you? You really seem to have a wild time together. What makes her so vicious in her onslaughts?'

'The last attack came after a heated discussion on who was more skilled at using a weapon.'

'If by that she's referring to her fists and fingernails — and are those teeth marks on your nose? — then she certainly knows how to handle herself, doesn't she?'

'Yes, there's no room in my life for a romance with a tigress.'

'Then it looks as if we're safe together. I promise you that I'm a non-aggressive sort of woman.'

'Thank heavens for that,' he sighed, as they moved towards the hall exit.

***

Before long, they were bent over a coffee table in Cora's lounge, surrounded by reference books. Then they found it more comfortable to kneel on the lounge carpet, but that became hard on their knees.

'Cora sat up after some minutes. 'This is silly, as well as awkward. We are adults, after all. Nothing's going to bite us in the bedroom. Let's spread out all this stuff on the bed where we can be comfortable. If I carry all this paperwork through, would you pour us a whiskey from the cabinet over there, please? You may as well bring the bottle. I never seem to be able to stop at one.'

It was more comfortable poring over maps and reference books that were spread out over the coverlet of Cora's bed. With their jackets draped over a chair and having kicked off their shoes, they both felt like a couple of old friends playing an involved board game on a rainy Sunday afternoon. The whiskies also went a long way towards relaxing them both, more than they realized.

The two companions became so interested in their subject that their heads inadvertently touched from time to time, creating a personal and homely atmosphere on the bed. But perhaps the drinks unwound them a little more than they might have done under other circumstances.

After a while, Cora had had enough of bending over maps and statistics. 'C'mon, I'm getting tired of bending over like this, something like an arse... ostrich with its seed in the hand... I mean head in the sand. Boy, this whiskey's gob... gone to my head. Let's clear all this paperwork off the bed and just talk for a while.'

Her method of clearing the bed was to imperiously sweep everything onto the carpet and stretch out her legs, with her head against the backboard.

She patted the place next to her. 'Come sit here nex to me. An' take off that silly tie. It's choking you.'

She grabbed Jason by the tie and pulled him closer to her. She skilfully removed the tie and undid his collar button, throwing the tie onto the carpet.

'Might as well be comfy,' she said, undoing most of Jason's shirt buttons. 'Mine too,' she ordered, thrusting out her chest proudly.

Jason got the message and undid his companion's blouse buttons.

'Now unclip my bra. S'like a straitjacked.'

Now Jason was starting to fumble. This was starting to get serious.

'C'mon, just hooks in front. Simple.'

She grabbed Jason's fingers, and they unclipped her bra together.

Cora giggled. 'Now you can't say you took off m'bra.'

She pulled her front wide open, and Jason had a good view of her breasts as she exposed them for her new friend.

'Pour more whiskey for li'l Cora,' she asked, holding out her empty glass. 'An a big one for you.'

Jason bent over to fetch the whiskey bottle from the side of the bed and rescued his glass from the top surface of the headboard. Cora was feeling playful now. He tried to pour reasonable tots for both of them, but his giggling companion put her hand under the bottle and tipped it up until there were extra-large tots in their glasses.

'Now there's a decent tot,' she boasted, clinking glasses with her visitor. 'Somping to get our teeth into.'

He put down the bottle, which was feeling a lot lighter. They clinked glasses again, linked arms and drank showily, with only a little of the drink spilled onto the coverlet.

Cora seemed to have found her second wind. She pulled Jason's face towards her. 'Let's see that poor nose of yours.'

Jason moved closer to her, and she closely examined the damage. Then she pouted her lips and gave the tip of his nose the gentlest of kisses. Meanwhile, Jason studied her fully exposed boobs and decided that they were every bit as beautiful as Janine's full breasts.

'Like the look of my boobs?' She knew where he would be staring. 'You can kiss them if you want.'

She lifted a breast and offered it to her friend, who bent his head and took the nipple into his mouth, suckling like a baby, until she pulled his mouth away and put him on the other one.

After a while, she lifted his head and gave him an open-mouthed, wet-lipped kiss that he would never forget in its intensity. Her tongue went deep into his mouth and stroked him as gently as velvet covered with cream. Cora undid the last of Jason's shirt buttons and pulled the shirt out of his trousers.

She pulled his body to her breasts and rubbed herself against his chest. He felt as if he were exploding inside his torso. Their tongues were still flicking together when Cora brought up her knees and parted her legs, wrapping them around Jason's waist.

Cora moaned gently as she took his hands and ran them up her thighs, writhing with delight as he began fondling her silky panties. The squirming woman lifted her buttocks and Jason pulled down her wet panties, stroking her tenderly between her legs. She undid her lover's trousers and pulled them down as far as she could reach.

'I want you badly,' he whispered.

'Then take me,' she sobbed. 'I need you deep inside me, right now.'

Cora opened her legs as far as they would go and started groaning in anticipation of being entered.

He took off his trousers and underpants and pressed himself against her wetness. His penis was hard and twitching as she ran it through her labia. She raised her buttocks to meet his swollen digit and pushed herself against him. He slid into her warm flesh, and they both moaned with pleasure.

Cora felt as if she had been filled to near bursting as his body rubbed inside her. As he moved deeply into her, she raised her pelvis to meet him. They moved slowly at first, until they could both feel the urge to speed up their motion.

Faster and faster they went, until they were bouncing against each other with animal force. Then the lusting woman began turning her head from side to side as she felt his thrusts building up into a crescendo of effort. Finally Jason's body began jerking as his semen shot into her.

It may have been her fancy, but she could feel the warm force of his sperm as he drove it into her, their pelvises bouncing together in their ecstasy. Jason derived even more enjoyment out of spending himself inside Cora instead of the woman who had given him such a rough time.

Then their passion slowly subsided, and he took some of his weight off her but still remained inside her body. They lay together with their eyes closed, completely spent, in a world of their own.

But that world exploded when Jason began to get hit across his head, back and buttocks with the heel of his discarded shoe. Janine had gone looking for him to discuss some technical point or other, and someone with more than a little spiteful intention had told her that Jason was probably with Professor Cora Nugent, who was well informed on killer whales.

Janine had enough of a devious mind to imagine what kind of research Cora Nugent and Jason Malvy could be engaged in. She had listened to Professor Nugent's presentation while summing her up as a woman who knew what she wanted and would not hesitate to go after it when she was in the mood.

So she talked the male receptionist into handing her the Nugent suite key and had happily been the only one in the elevator that took her to the correct floor. Janine was building up an increased head of steam as she came up to the door number she was looking for, expecting the worst.

Using her key, Janine pushed out the one in the lock. It dropped soundlessly onto the thick carpet. Unlocking the door, she quietly let herself in after she had put her ear to the door and heard faint squeals coming from inside the suite. She moved in carefully and crept up on the mating couple lying together with closed eyes, as they recovered from their strenuous bout of lovemaking.

She was positively boiling with rage. The dirty bastard had rejected her after crawling all over her body and playing with it as he pleased. Then he'd spurned her obvious offer of sex out of sympathy for him, only to jump on top of this older bitch, like a slavering dog. What proper sods men were.

Seeing his bare bum on top of that woman made her want to do something outrageous. His own shoe was the weapon her eyes lit upon. She picked up the heavy chunk of leather and bashed him wherever she could find a bare place.

When her own hand began hurting, Janine put her hand in the heavy shoe and began poking and digging into the man she hated more than anything else at that moment. The more Janine hurt him, the better she felt.

'You filthy, low-down, dirty, rotten swine! I've been doing all your work for you while you've been screwing this old hag. If you'd wanted sex that badly, I could've given it to you, but I don't appear to be good enough. Well, you can stick your PR business where the monkey put his peanuts, for all I care.' She continued to rage. 'That's right, cover your head, in case I knock your stupid brains out. You should see how beautiful your back is looking at the moment. Tell that bitch, lying under you with her eyes closed, that she can consider herself lucky that I can't get to her right now, apart from those white sticks she uses for arms, but she hasn't heard the last of me, either. Yes, you can take that, and that, you prune-faced man snatcher.'

By now Janine had worked herself into a screaming, snarling and spitting virago. Jason had to lie spread-eagled on top of his lover and take most of the punishment, because he reasoned that Cora could face a terrible beating if he got off her at that moment. For all he knew, Janine had that firearm in her purse, and she was quite possibly riled enough to use it on the woman that she considered to be her competitor.

He put his head on Cora's breast and waited patiently for the pounding to stop.

Chapter Eighteen

They heard the door slam shut, and Janine was finally gone at last. They were still pressed together, but his penis had turned into a little worm and had crept out of Cora, going into fearful hiding.

They opened their eyes simultaneously and stared at each other. Then they began laughing self-consciously. Jason was not too sure what he was laughing about, because his back, his head and his bum felt as if they were on fire. But he laughed anyway, feeling the belly laughs coming from Cora underneath him.

'My poor man, you took a pounding for me, and I do appreciate it, although I've never needed to be protected in this way.'

She pulled his head towards her, and they kissed tenderly.

'Now do me a favour and get off me before that virago of yours comes back with a firearm or a baseball bat. I wouldn't put anything past her. She was completely out of her mind. As it was, she tried to break one or two of my arms, but she didn't do much damage, apart from flattening my torso with all your weight on me. Can I do anything for your back?'

'I don't know yet. I think I'll survive.' He rolled carefully off her and heaved himself to his feet with a groan.

Cora got up as well and examined the bruises and blood marks on her lover's rear. 'You've got some terrible cuts and bruises right across your back and your bum. Lie flat on your stomach on the bed, and I'll massage some soothing cream into you, to get the healing process going as soon as possible.'

She was back before long, with a tube of cream, headache tablets — which he really needed — and a glass of water. Cora rubbed the cream gently into his skin and then dressed quickly, while Jason swallowed his tablets and water. Then he staggered through to the bathroom and washed himself as far as he could reach, with the cloth his hostess had given him to use.

Jason returned to the bedroom, and Cora had to help him to dress, for he was as stiff as a board. She offered her breasts to him for a last kiss before she put on her bra and blouse and went through to the bathroom to rid herself of the evidence of their lovemaking.

When she returned, Jason was still staggering about, trying to put on his trousers. Cora smiled to herself, remembering how agile he had been during their lovemaking. Now she had to do up his trousers, put on his socks and shoes and straighten his clothes up before he was presentable again.

She'd run a brush through her hair and looked as good as new, after putting on a little lipstick and makeup. One would never have said that she had been wildly writhing under her lover a short while before.

Cora saw Jason to the door. 'I'd like some more of that, my dear, but you'd better sort out the situation between Janine and you before she catches us with our pants down and locked together again.'

He bent stiffly and kissed her. At least the hiding they'd both received had knocked the effects of the alcohol out of their systems.

'Try to keep me away,' he smiled. 'I'll be in touch, you lovely woman.'

***

He made his way slowly back to his suite, not sure about what he would find when he got there. Janine was nowhere in sight, and her door was unlocked. He had a look around her room. Everything seemed to be in its usual place. Maybe she had cooled down to some degree, although he wouldn't have minded at all if she had stalked out of the seminar in the midst of her rage.

Then he remembered that she was low on funds and maybe couldn't afford to give up her free meals and boarding, let alone her return flight home. He would play it by ear, he decided. In the meantime, although he was still in pain, he was hungry. Lunch would be served soon.

After that, he needed to pick up Danny at the airport and get him settled in at his hotel, which was just around the corner. He tried some mild stretching exercises, which hurt like hell, but they seemed to do some good. Another medicating whiskey didn't do any harm to him, either.

On entering the dining room, he kept an eye open for both Janine and Cora. He saw his lover across the room, and they exchanged secret smiles before passing on their separate ways. Her plate was well loaded for a woman with a slender to medium build.

Jason stared at her food and raised an eyebrow, which brought on a smile of pure sunshine. Obviously their recent gymnastics had done nothing but good for her appetite. His continued secret communication brought out an even bigger smile from her, but they chose to ignore each other, keeping their recent violent antics a very personal matter between themselves.

There was just enough time for Jason to finish his lunch comfortably and take an easy ride to the airport to meet Danny. He was glad that he didn't have to hurry, because he felt too fragile to go rushing about. He didn't notice Cora's husband, who was glaring at him from the other side of the room.

Janine had not wasted any time in stirring things up for Jason and his lover. It had not taken long for her to locate and inform Cora's husband, in graphic detail, about what the couple had been up to.

He had his own mistress in the vicinity, and he was more or less openly sleeping with her. There was also an elastic arrangement between Cora and him, regarding the taking of an occasional lover.

However, an airy arrangement between them didn't include getting a full report — with all the lurid details thrown in — on what was happening on the other side of the locked door of the suite that his wife and he were sharing for the sake of appearances.

He didn't need to know the gory details, but he got them anyway, true or made up. By the time Janine was finished, he was in a controlled rage. But he was a devious man, who would pick the right time to get his revenge.

Janine was pleased with herself. She had stormed out of Cora's suite in a blind rage, ready to pack up and get out of the hotel and the seminar. Then she went to her room and sat on the bed, assessing her position. She had very little cash, as Jason had little spending money to hand out.

There seemed to be little point in being dramatic and leaving the hotel because she had caught her so-called companion in bed with another woman, when they had never even had sex themselves.

'Take it slowly, Janine,' she muttered to herself. 'Punish the bugger, but do it at your pace and in comfort.'

All she had to do now was to wait for the explosion to go off. And the fun part was that she would be around to witness it. She chuckled. It would be fun to watch the outcome of the hornet's nest she had kicked over. This was much better than running away from it all.

***

Danny's plane was on time, and Jason and he spotted each other quite quickly. The two men were pleased to meet up again. They chatted casually as they ambled along to collect Danny's luggage. What Danny didn't notice, at first, was that he was doing the ambling and his friend could hardly keep pace with him.

'Have you had lunch?' asked Jason. 'We could stop for a bite, if you're hungry.'

'No, thanks, they served lunch, if one could call it that. There was more than enough available, because half the passengers were smart enough to turn down the food. But you'll recall that we ate anything in the SEALs. There never seemed to be enough grub, so I ate plenty, if not well.'

They moved along in companionable silence for a short distance.

'Why are you walking so slowly, bro?' Danny asked. 'There's usually a spring in your step, but it looks as if you've broken it somewhere, or it fell out of your body.'

Jason grinned self-consciously. 'Luckily we've got lots of time, because I've got a story and a half to tell you.'

His strange relationship with Janine came out into the open. Danny's eyes were wide open by the time that Jason came to the end of his story. They were sitting at the airport bar having a beer, while Jason tried to get his injured body into a comfortable position.

'So, does this affect me in any way?' Danny wanted to know.

'Look, the main reason why you're here is to find out what the Russians and the Chinese are up to. But for the record, you're here as a newspaper investigator, as far as the organizers of this seminar are concerned, and answerable to Terence Pollard of the San Diego Advertiser. We should possibly meet casually and appear to start up a friendship together. After that, we'll probably have to play it by ear.'

They emptied their glasses and drove to the place where Danny would be staying during his time at the seminar. After booking Danny into his neighbouring hotel, on a daily-rate basis, they separated but arranged to meet up as old friends at the conference room bar at a specific time.

After a big show of welcome, they stood with drinks in front of them, but Jason used the opportunity to point out key people to Danny, thus saving him a lot of time in not having to pick up the pieces on his own.

Then Jason left Danny to work the hall himself, so as to not make their relationship too obvious. Moving off to do his own circulating, he didn't particularly observe Cora's husband's eagle eye on him. He may have felt less positive if he had noticed the attention he was getting.

What he did observe was that Janine was still there, circulating with a frozen smile on her face. So, she hadn't upped and left, as he had half expected that she would do. Well, there was something else that needed to be stared down and sorted out.

He didn't see the point of housing and funding a woman who made a habit of giving him a beating whenever she was given half a chance. What transpired between Cora and him had nothing to do with Janine. In Jason's eyes, the woman was heading for a mental breakdown in the not-too-distant future.

Jason noticed that Cora was keeping well clear of both Janine and her husband, probably a wise thing to do in the circumstances. It appeared that she was involved in a learned conversation with some moon-faced delegates that Jason had done his best to avoid during the seminar. *Rather her than me,* he thought.

He caught her husband glaring at him. He wondered if the man had any idea that he had slept with Cora.

A new set of presentations started up, and everybody stopped circulating and pretended to be interested. There was nothing much new to be disseminated, but at least one could remain in one position, preferably in a seat, with a drink to sip and showing a neutral face.

After an hour and a half of boring repetition, the audience was released to do its own thing again, and Janine and Danny found themselves seated together at the bar. Perhaps she had seen Jason talking to Danny and was curious.

Jason hoped that Danny would not go and reveal their relationship. On the other hand, the man was a master at picking up women at bar counters.

Jason left them to it but was soon anxious to know what they were talking about so animatedly, like long-lost friends.

**

Perhaps this was a good time for Jason to make some phone calls, seeing that he was doing more ducking and diving at the moment than anything else. He supposed that he needed to contact his parents, because his mother, at least, would be worrying about him.

'This is the Malvy residence. To whom am I speaking, please?'

'Hello, Mom. It's Jason. How are things at home?'

'Jason! My son! We're fine. The important thing is: how are you?'

'I'm fine. Weathering the storm and all that.'

'Your father's not here at the moment, son. He went out to do something, but he didn't tell me what it was or where he was going. He never does, you know. He always says it's none of my business when I ask him. But that's not important now. I hope you're not in any trouble with the police, or anything like that.'

'My dear mom, I'm not really as reckless as Dad makes out. You know that the prosecution have temporally withdrawn the kidnap and murder case against me. They did that not because they were being kind, but because they were saving face. There was no evidence to call on and thus no case to prosecute. So you see, you were worrying for nothing.'

Mathilda Malvy answered quietly: 'Jason, that dear girl must have been ripped to pieces, and she was in your company and your care at the time. If that poor girl hadn't asked you to fetch something from the car, there would have been the two of you taken together. You should be on your knees, thanking the good Lord that you were spared, as I do at least once a day.'

For a change, Jason was speechless. He'd never looked at the tragedy from that angle before. There was a cold shiver of recognition going up his back. Tilly had been taken, but he had been saved. What for?

'Are you still there, Jason?'

'Mom, I was taken aback a little. I've never thought about it that way at all.'

'Good for you, dear. We all overlook the obvious, at times. Now, is there anything in particular that you wanted to discuss with your father?'

'Not really, Mom. Is he still giving you such a hard time?'

'Your father is what he is, Jason. I can't see that he'll ever really change. I have learned to live one day at a time and to not let him — or anyone, for that matter — get under my skin, if I can help it. There are times when he treats me inconsiderately, but I've learned how to keep the peace in this house.'

Now there was a big-hearted approach to life, thought Jason. His mother didn't have to do great deeds to be good. He felt a deep sense of pride in her at that moment.

'I'll pass on your good wishes to him, Jason. I'm sure you want me to do that?'

'Yes, Mom. Deep inside, I do care for him, but I can never put that feeling into words when we talk to each other.'

'Two hard-headed men…'

'What was that, Mom?'

'Nothing, dear. Now look after yourself, and don't do anything rash. I'm convinced that you will, one day, save your life or avoid serious damage, by a second or two of deep thought and contemplation.'

'You should compile a book of wise sayings, Mom.'

'And where do you think I get all the wise sayings from, my dear Jason?'

He said goodbye and rang off, staring at the instrument for a short while. He should phone his mother more often. He was usually left with something to think about when he did find the time to give her a ring.

He decided to contact Greyton Elliott, his attorney, to find out if there was any matter arising out of his court case. The last he'd heard from Elliott had been a brief message to report that the case had been temporarily withdrawn, along with the conditions of bail.

He didn't get much sense out of the man, who hardly seemed to remember who he was.

Then, at last, the penny dropped: 'Oh, Jason, didn't you get my message?'

'Yes, I did, but it was pretty vague.'

'Vague? What part of "withdrawn" didn't you understand?'

'Well, what about the bail bond that my father had to raise?'

'Didn't your father discuss that with you? That's all been settled and refunded.'

'Certainly, between you and my father. Very little is discussed with me. But thanks for letting me know, anyway.' He put down the phone, resisting the urge to smash it into the cradle. Obviously, his money was not as important as his father's.

The next one on Jason's list was Joe Caldecott, his father's property agency partner.

'Hello, Joe, Jason Malvy here. Are you well?'

'Right as rain. How's the conference going?'

'The way all conferences go. How do they manage to make it all so boring? They take a serious subject and strangle it in no time at all.'

'They get it right because some people fall into the category of caged animals, pacing up and down their self-made prisons to attack one another, and so prove their worth to humanity. Be patient. How long has it still to go?'

Jason told him that it didn't have long to last, as far as he could tell. It was open-ended, like someone with gyppo guts. There was really not much more to share, and all that was happening was that various delegations were using the opportunity of sniping at one another. 'I guess that it is likely to be all over by tomorrow, or the day after, at the latest.'

'Why, that's nothing. When you see all the messages you have piled up for your personal attention, you'll look around for another conference to attend. Have patience. Your job awaits you.'

They rang off, and Jason smiled to himself. That man would see the bright side of a black hole. If he had to suffer being mugged, he would class it as a toughening-up process and think of himself as a better man for undergoing it.

Jason put his list away. He'd made enough duty calls for one day. At that moment, he was more interested in finding out whether Danny and Janine were still talking and what Danny had learned from her, if anything at all.

He rang his friend on his cell phone. It was switched off. That was strange for Danny. He had a curious nature, and the only time he switched it off was when he was with a woman. Intimately with a woman... oh no!

Jason went to the interconnecting door and tried the handle gently. It was locked. It hadn't been locked when he'd been into Janine's room to find out whether she'd packed up and left the hotel. So, she'd returned to the room, after which she'd locked the door. That was the sort of message that he would expect her to send to him, but was there more to read into it than that?

Curiosity got the better of him, so Jason went to the door and put an ear against it. He could hear faint sounds of grunts and groans, with an occasional wail or squeal thrown in. It sounded very much as if Janine wanted the world to know — and more particularly, Jason — that she was having the time of her life and that sex with any virile man was good enough for her.

Did she already have her claws into Danny? That didn't surprise Jason in the slightest. Apart from her finding out what Danny was really doing at the conference, it would be her way of thumbing her nose at her now ex-colleague, as well as showing him how desirable she was to other men.

Chapter Nineteen

The press and other media had requested full details of killer whale sizes, weights and other dimensions earlier on, but there were differences in the reports published, due to carelessness by the reporters, so a venerated professor gave a lecture primarily based on known statistics, as well as a rehash of well-known facts:

'The orca, or *Orcinus orca,* to give it the correct scientific name, can, in males, grow to thirty-one feet — or nine and a half meters in length — and weigh up to eight thousand kilograms, or seventeen thousand six hundred pounds.

'We suspect, however, that our chief attacker, an orca named Samson, who was released by a keeper at one of the dolphinariums, together with his mate, was substantially larger than the maximum measurements given for males. A creature of this size is not put on the scales every day, you'll understand.

'Killer whale females are somewhat smaller, measuring a maximum of twenty-three feet in length — or seven meters — with a maximum weight of four thousand kilograms, or eight thousand eight hundred pounds. Both sexes have large flippers that are paddle-shaped, and they have ten to twelve sets of large, conical teeth in their mouths. Their markings are invariably black and white, with certain subspecies showing different arrangements of their colouration.

'The dorsal fin of a male is usually upright in younger males and can reach heights of six feet in the older males. On the other hand, the females have dorsal fins that are shorter and curved.

'They have a broad spectrum diet, eating almost anything available, but only a few attacks on humans have been noted, until now. Almost all the known attacks have been on keepers in various dolphinariums, which have been put down to boredom or frustration. Possibly stress disorder and crowd noise has something to do with this, interfering with their fine-tuned echo-sounding system.

'There is also the difficulty of echolocation. The high-pitched whistles the creatures generate, bounce off objects in their path, guiding the animals into discerning what lies in front of or around them. The concrete or plastic surrounds of their confinement areas serve to distort these signals. This can cause the creature to misjudge distances when, for instance, retrieving an object from a keeper's hand.

'Of course, there are arguments for overly restricted living circumstances and relatively poor water conditions, allied to possible tormenting by keepers and unhappiness with the food varieties they are given. As far as water temperatures are concerned, the killer whale is widely spread throughout the world. Warm and cold waters don't seem to affect it in any way, although slight variations in species have been noted, particularly in the polar regions.

'Certain subspecies, particularly the young, don't take too happily to being transferred directly from the warmer seas to sub-zero conditions, but their thick layer of blubber protects them from an extreme climate, in most cases.

'The killer whale, to give it its better-known name, has no known enemies other than humans and is normally fairly docile, and it is easily trapped and caught. There have been many examples of killer whales actually assisting whalers in trapping whales and other large sea creatures by herding them towards the whale boats.

'Yet they can also be killing machines. They definitely have a superior level of intelligence, which has never been accurately measured. They regularly herd the fish they intend as their food supply, with the help of others within their group. Working in groups, they often attack the biggest whale species, ripping out tongues and the linings of their mouths. The younger whales are most targeted by killer whales.

'Their intelligence has been widely reported. For instance, killer whales, working together, dislodge seals from ice floes by tipping the floes, using a group's combined body weight or by creating an overlarge bow wave that washes the seal off the ice. They seem to operate together in a predetermined pattern to bring them maximum success. Then they share out the spoils of their hunt, without fighting over the outcome.

'Killer whales mate belly to belly. The male usually slips in underneath the female when mating takes place. If a female killer whale does not choose to mate at any time, she rolls onto her back to prevent males from impregnating her.

'On their part, a few males will gather around the female at such a time and do their best to turn her over. She will need to turn onto her stomach at some stage to inhale air through her blowhole, as it is underwater when she lies on her back. So, there is quite a battle of strong wills going on in a situation like this.

'The question is: Have killer whales, which are normally calm and purposeful, suddenly become more aggressive, or are they being subjected to some outside influence? Remember that there are not many paired orcas that have been known to have previously been in captivity that could easily be manipulated by humans.

'This doesn't help us to understand the reason for the massing of pods of these creatures that have gathered together in order to create mayhem along the western seaboard of America.

'It would be most difficult to establish the cause of any change in their nature, due to outside influences, as these attacking orcas appear to be far more aggressive than they were in the past. We need to find some way of examining one or more of these mammals in order to establish why such a marked change in their natures has taken place, and so suddenly.'

Jason had heard this all before, and there was nothing new for him to absorb. Instead, he spent the time in keeping an eye on the Russian contingent that looked most unhappy with the way this data was being presented. This was seen particularly when the lecturers mentioned that Russian whaling ships and fishermen had molested orcas in the past. The Chinese, on the other hand, were keeping their usual inscrutable image during this open discussion.

Yes, you buggers, Jason thought, as he gazed at the Chinese contingent. *You're not batting an eyelid while the possibility of outside interference is being discussed, but how much of all this trouble has been caused by you and the Russians?*

The professor went on to give a great deal of data regarding details of populations of killer whales, gestation periods and their life expectancy, and where the majority of them were situated. He then presented a map which

177

compared the situations where the latest number of recorded attacks had taken place.

It was clear that a locality on the western coast of America, somewhere in the region of San Diego, was the starting point of the problem, but there was a tendency for the attacks to spread out on either side of that defined area.

***

The way that the professor had presented the facts made it seem obvious that some outside influence was responsible for the sudden aggression of the orcas.

We've got to catch them at it, thought Jason. *And we've got a pretty shrewd idea who's causing all the trouble.*

The Russians, Pucharov and Kilmanov, had lost interest in this lecture. Along with the Chinese contingent, they had moved out of the conference hall and were clearly up to no good somewhere else. And Danny and Janine were also missing from the conference hall. Jason was curious as to whether they were still having a heated time of sex in Janine's room.

Danny liked to brag about his staying power, and Jason wanted to put his ear to the interconnecting door again, to establish what was going on in Janine's room, even if he missed the data being handed out on killer whale statistics.

He'd heard all that many times before, so there was nothing more for him to learn. He slipped away from the conference and returned to his room. Jason didn't waste time. He went to the interconnecting door and held his ear to it. There were still the grunts and groans of excessive lovemaking going on.

There was no doubt in his mind as to what he was hearing, but he couldn't clearly identify what was going on in there. He was getting quite horny, when there was a sudden explosion that came from the other side of the door. He sprang back, his eyes round with shock. His head was ringing with the force of the blast.

Jason stumbled back from the door. He stood there, not knowing what to do next, when a naked Danny turned the key to the door and opened it wide. The room was filled with smoke, and Danny was wearing a dazed look on his face.

'What the hell happened in there, Danny?' Jason asked, still trembling from the effects of the explosion.

A circle of hair had been burned off the back of his confederate's head. There was a spatter of blood in his hair, and he seemed confused. He wobbled back to the side of the bed and sagged onto it. Jason could now see what was left of what he presumed to be Janine's head and face, as she lay in the nude with her legs apart, on a pillow that was covered in blood and brain matter.

Sickened as he was, by the sight of the gory remains, Jason gritted his teeth and approached the messy remains of a body that had registered at the hotel as his wife only a few days previously. It was obvious that there was nothing in this world that could be done for her.

He went to the drinks tray and poured whiskey for both Danny and himself. He handed a drink to his friend, who took it automatically. He sat down next to his friend, whose head was hanging like that of a condemned prisoner.

'Now tell me. What the hell happened in here?'

'Jason, we were having a great time together. I don't know who was doing the most digging for information, but I think that Janine wanted to have sex with me to get back at you for your perceived lack of loyalty to her — the way she saw it.

'She got the message across to me that she caught you in bed with another woman and was as mad as hell about it, seeing that you and she were sharing this suite and were on the way to permanently sharing only one of the beds. I didn't mind being used as her sex toy, so I was busy giving her the full works.

'I played with her in so many ways that she squealed and squirmed as if she'd never had sex before. Somehow I found this hard to believe, seeing that she knew her way around the sexual romping delights and thrashing legs performance in such detail. We kept this up for ages.

'She didn't really appeal to me that much, because I sized her up as being as hard as nails, but I acted the part of a great Romeo to charm her totally, which wasn't all that hard for me to manage, seeing that I consider it my hobby and my specialty.

'Then I started fondling her inner thighs and kissing her between her legs — the whole porn scene. Now began the finishing touches of the show she was obviously putting on for your benefit, probably because she suspected you'd be listening at the door. She started jerking and jiving and after that, she went beyond ballistic.

Danny paused to swig at his whiskey.

'She seemed to enjoy what I was doing to her, with fingers, lips and tongue, to such an extent that she wrapped her bloody solid thighs about my neck like a vice and started throttling me. Although my ears were being blocked by her legs, I heard her hit a really high note.

'I had just started battling for air and was trying to pull her legs apart, when there was this explosion, after which the woman went limp. There was this flash of heat where the top of my head was exposed. It's still burning like hell.

'Then I dragged myself out from between her legs and looked at her face; or where her face should have been. It was a total mess. Something has blown the woman's head apart. I don't want to look at it again, but tell me what you think.'

Jason gulped down the rest of his whiskey for courage, before standing up and approaching the corpse again. It appeared that half of Janine's face had been blown away, together with half of her skull and brain, but mainly on one side.

There were the remains of a wire protruding from the most damaged part of her face, with a jagged hole where her ear had been. Jason felt bile rising in his throat as he bent over the unsightly remains of what had once been an attractive person. A frayed piece of wire dangled from the void. Was that a wisp of smoke or steam that came out with it?

Taking a toilet tissue in his hand, he delicately pulled out the wire from the gaping hole. At the end of it was the melted remnant of some device that looked like a complicated electronic earphone.

He shuddered and dropped it back into the void, discarding the tissue into a small waste bin at the side of the bed. Then he backed away from the bloody mess, turned and made for the hand basin where he threw up the bilious sourness that had been sitting uncomfortably inside him ever since he had ventured into the room.

'We need to report this,' he told Danny, who had also visited the hand basin before he got there.

'Can't we just bugger off?' asked his friend.

'Not a chance. Everybody knows that you and Janine were hanging about together. They'll be after you like a shot, trying to pin a rap on you. I've had a taste of this, remember?'

Then he recalled the name of Laurie Bridewell. He was the right person to contact. If anybody could sort this mess out, he was the one. He told Danny what he intended doing, got a nod of agreement and then phoned Bridewell.

'You've caught me at a rather busy time, Jason,' said the head of hotel security, when he answered his phone. He sounded rattier than he'd been earlier on when they had last spoken. 'I'm standing amongst a group of foreign VIPs, all with blown-out brains and any one of whom could cause an international scene of tremendous proportions if this is not handled diplomatically.'

'Well, Laurie, my friend, Daniel Foulkes is sitting with a corpse on his hands, having had half of her head blown away as well. Is that important enough, or can we just wander down to the bar and have a few toots and a game of poker while we're waiting for someone to have a look at the body? Oh, and by the way: do any of your corpses have strange wires sticking out of their ears, or where their ears once were? If so, then I suspect that our corpse has caught the same disease as your corpses, or she's had it electronically communicated to her.'

'What?' Bridewell gasped. 'Hold on. What's your suite number again? I'll be there shortly.'

Jason put down the phone, wondering why his hand was shaking so much. After all, he had nothing to do with this latest mess — or had he?

'Right, Danny, the posse is on the way and will be here at any moment. May I suggest that you put on a shirt and a pair of shorts, which I'll lend you, so that they can examine your gear — clothing and all?'

'But I first need to shower, in order to get some of this shit out of my hair and off my head.'

'Be patient, Danny. You look most attractive at the moment, but I'm suggesting at least a pair of my shorts, or you'll put the cops right off their work for lack of ability to concentrate.' He handed his empty whiskey glass to his friend. 'Now, I've poured the whiskey for us. Please wash the glasses, dry them and put them away, before the cops begin to wonder why two men sat drinking whiskey and having a friendly chat after coming across a tragic scene like this.'

Jason avoided staring at Janine, with her parted legs, on the way out. Some memories were better left intact.

***

Laurie Bridewell was far more than merely the hotel security head. He had been secretly moved in by the FBI, because they had come to the same conclusion as Jason Malvy that the Russians and the Chinese were up to no good. Then again, whenever these two nations became involved in world affairs, dramatic action tended to follow.

The FBI had the advantage of being a large organization that had built up a base of information; and a group of agents that could achieve far more than one man could be expected to handle.

Soon after Samson, the killer whale, had been given his freedom by Bessie Middleton, some solid citizen had been out in his boat, doing some night fishing with his teenaged son. He had heard the sound of a fast helicopter clattering towards him so, being a cautious man with an outdated boat licence, he doused his boat light, which was pretty dim anyway.

Not only cautious but also curious, he took up his night glasses and trained them on the unmarked helicopter. It had now stopped its forward progress and was rotating in circles around some large object in the sea.

'Take some photos of that blob in the sea, together with the helicopter, John,' he told his son.

He switched off the boat engine, and the two fishermen thought they heard a "plop" sound, before the bulky object in the sea disappeared from their sight. The helicopter hovered for a short while longer before returning along the path it had come.

'Now that's strange,' he commented.

His son agreed with him. 'You should report that to the FBI, Dad. Something funny happened out there tonight.'

The fisherman was in no hurry to go to the authorities with his photos, which were pretty indistinct anyway, but his son egged him on, until he handed in his photos and his story to the FBI. He was quite surprised at the interest they took in what he had to tell them. They enlarged the photos and clarified them. Then they took the shots to an expert analyst who had a vivid imagination.

After establishing that there were no official helicopters flying over the bay area during the night in question, he sat down with his group of peers, and they began brainstorming some ideas about.

'A fancy modern helicopter with no markings, moving swiftly.'

'That's a marksman. There's the barrel of his weapon, protruding from the helicopter hatchway.'

'Then he shoots, and the big blob vanishes. Looks like a whale to me.'

'But who would shoot a whale in the middle of the night?'

'It's sure a big one. See the black and white markings.'

'Black and white? That's an orca! Wasn't there one released with its mate a few days before this all happened?'

'So, you think they were hunting down Samson, the killer whale that was allowed to escape?'

'What else would make one take the trouble to go hunting it in the middle of the night?'

'But why shoot it?'

'Maybe they weren't shooting it but only darting it.'

'Now this is getting interesting. It sounds like the sort of deal that the Russians would get into.'

'Maybe this is starting to explain the peculiar behaviour of that killer whale. If the Russians, or maybe the Chinese with all their fancy gadgets, could influence large creatures like killer whales to obey their commands, then we have a king-sized problem on our hands.'

'But it seems to me that it's exactly what the devils are doing. They're creating enough problems along our coastline, but I suspect that this is only the beginning of the mess that we're going to have to sort out.'

Chapter Twenty

There was a peremptory rapping at the door, and Jason hurried to open it.

Laurie Bridewell bulldozed his way past the diver. 'Right, tell me where's the damage,' he instructed.

Jason indicated the interconnecting door.

Bridewell put up a hand. 'I want to inspect it first, along with this guy and his camera, before everything gets tramped flat.'

Using a glove, he pushed the door open, but even he came to a sudden stop. A nude woman, with a large piece of her head missing and blood and brain matter spattered everywhere, was not an artwork that a viewer would want to admire.

After a short while, Bridewell called out from the death scene: 'Malvy, come in and tell me what happened here.'

'Actually, you'll have to ask Danny Foulkes here. He was busy in there when it happened.'

' Okay, the Toni twins. Bring your friend in here, and let's get to the bottom of this mess. Please remember that I'm in a hurry. There are foreign bodies all over the place upstairs, and I want to get the general picture in my mind, before the cops start kicking any clues about and bury vital evidence. So,' Bridewell pointed at Danny, 'it looks as if you were on the job here when it happened? Give me the gory details.'

'That's right, sir. Luckily for me, I was kneeling between the deceased's legs, and she was really getting excited at what I was doing with fingers, tongue, the works. The woman was crying out aloud and yelping like a pack of wild dogs on a kill. She hit a really high note as she came, and then there was this explosion immediately after. I felt a wave of heat rush over my head — it actually burned my scalp — along with a shower of blood and bits of brain, I gather.'

'You don't sound too broken-hearted about her sudden demise. Don't you normally feel things like that?'

'If I were in love with the woman, probably yes, but this was purely a first-time pleasure bang.'

'Some pleasure this poor woman got out of it,' Bridewell grunted. He turned to Jason: 'Were you the next one in the queue?'

'No, thanks. I wasn't interested in her. She wasn't my type.'

'Yet you were registered as a married couple.'

'That was Janine's idea. She thought that it would be more convenient for us to register as man and wife, for the sake of efficient communication.'

'So, you say that you felt nothing for her? Poor girl. You hung about while these two were having it off together. Two men in her suite, one on the job and one not interested, and then she gets her head blown off. Talk about bad luck. Now, what do you know about this thing dangling out of her ear?'

'Nothing really, but I can't imagine that anyone would choose it as an ornament. Seeing that she came here to be acting on my side, I'd say that she knew nothing about that gadget. I'd guess that somebody inserted it while she was unconscious at some stage or other. Although how they managed to do that, I don't know. Perhaps it all ties in with her experience at the seminar, when they gave her a knock-out drink.'

'Sounds like good reasoning. And who would do a thing like that? Do you think that this whole business had anything to do with our little chat in my office about her date rape experience?'

'My money's on the Russians or the Chinese.'

'That's not a bad bet. As a matter of fact, I've got two Russians and a Chinese with holes in their heads, much the same as this young woman. This is not funny, but I'll hazard a guess that they were all involved with one another, in some way. In fact, if I had to stick my neck out a bit further, I'd say that she wasn't aware that she was wearing a modern sort of wire, and that her hitting a climax in her sex life caused her to squeal so loudly that she blew the works for the three stooges, as well as for herself. Talk about going out on a high!' He gave a cursory glance to Danny's head. 'You'd better get that seen to. I can imagine your writing a book in the near future: "I nearly fried when she died." The trouble is that the FBI would never let you publish it.'

Danny went up to Dr Gresham's offices to get treatment for the burn on his scalp.

'This is highly irregular,' said Bridewell, 'but neither the local cops nor the FBI have pitched up yet. Come along with me, if your stomach can take it, and see if you can find anything interesting about the three goons with holes in their heads. Just don't touch anything, for Pete's sake.'

When Jason entered the room where the three corpses were lolling around a table with their heads down on it, the atmosphere was still smoky. The furniture and walls were sprayed with a mixture of blood and brain matter. The scene looked like something out of an ultra-modern painting by an artist that one would be nervous to befriend because of his deranged thinking.

'Look on the table,' said Bridewell, wrinkling up his nose at the smell of the place.

There, in front of the three corpses, was an accurate drawing of an orca with a dart sticking out of its body where Jason would expect the brain of the creature to be situated. Underneath it was a detailed line drawing of an electronic device, which was too complicated for Jason to interpret. But he had a guess that it would be put there to gain control of the orca, in order to direct it in a certain way. What had orcas been doing out of the ordinary, lately? The diagram, together with where it was found, told Jason more than many pages of a report could relate. He shared his feelings with this security man who appeared to have a strong position in the FBI.

Bridewell had been studying his reaction to the diagram. 'Right, that's really what I brought you here to see. Now, let's get out of here before the boys in blue arrive. I've already recorded this business, photos and all. I think that we've just discovered what made probably only one orca so angry with the world that he's busily going around forming gangs of killer whales to help him.'

***

When he returned to his suite, there was a madhouse of investigation going on in the bedroom next door. Luckily the investigating officers had decided that Jason's bedroom was not part of the crime scene, so they left him in peace, of a sort.

He decided to update Terence Pollard regarding what was going on, both at the conference as well as in general. The man had been patient with him until now, supplying all sorts of information without getting much in return.

Using a text message on his cell phone, because he didn't trust the local landline facilities, what with international spies drifting about, he brought the newspaper reporter into line with current issues. The cherry on the cake was when he decided to spill the beans about the explosive earpieces. He reckoned that word was going to leak out any minute and that Pollard deserved a real scoop, ahead of all the national newspapers.

Pollard hit the roof at this latest information, coming right back to Jason with a long list of questions, most of which he could answer.

'Better get someone out here pretty soon,' Jason advised. 'This business is due to break out into the open at any minute now.'

If Jason thought that he could remain in the background, he was mistaken. Within a couple of hours, he was being inundated with phone calls, telexes and personal visits, as well as newscasters who were shoving microphones in front of his face. They were all desperate reporters wanting to get a jump on the news. He put up with a lot of their rudeness because he felt sorry for them.

In the middle of all this commotion, there was a small break in the frenetic activity. Jason decided to phone his parents, partly to keep the baying bloodhounds away. He knew that his mother would be avidly studying the news reports.

She was aware of where her son was now, and she would be devouring every bit of information that she thought had anything to do with him. It would be a good time to tell them that he was safe and happy and that the situation was fairly good for him at the moment.

And yet he was aware that his position was not really all that great. Janine would be the second woman to have died a violent death virtually within his presence. It was the sort of coincidence that the newspapers would pick up and run with, while creating all sorts of innuendoes that could harm his image in the long run.

His father, however, didn't want to discuss anything to do with Jason. The old man buried himself in his study and asked to be left alone. Mathilda Malvy suspected that he was keeping himself updated with what was happening at the conference and what was going on in general, specifically regarding killer whales.

It was as if she had been waiting at the phone.

'Hello, this is the Malvy residence. Who's speaking please?'

'It's me, Mom. How are things going with you?'

'I'm fine, son. I've just been wondering what's been happening to you. Are you well? Are they feeding you properly?'

'Yes, Mom. I really phoned just to say hello. How's grumpy?'

'He's fine, Jason. He pretends that he's not interested in your affairs, but he's buying lots of newspapers lately, and he watches the TV news channels like a hawk, flicking from one to the other to reel in different viewpoints.'

'Is he there now? I'd better say hello to him.'

'Right, son, I'll put you through to him. Look after yourself, and don't drink too much.'

'Yes, Mom. I'll be a good boy.'

There was a pause. 'Who's this? Is that you, Mathilda?'

'Jason on the line, Charles.'

'Well, put him through, woman! Hello! Hello! Is that you, Jason? Speak up, I can hardly hear you.' Which was not surprising seeing that Jason hadn't yet been given the chance to get a word in edgewise.

'Yes, it's me, Dad.'

'It is I. It is I. When are you young people going to learn to speak properly?'

'Yes, it's still me,' replied Jason, his blood pressure already beginning to rise. 'Are you keeping well?'

'As well as can be expected, considering the mess that this world is in. I've been meaning to ask you: I received a thousand dollars in my personal banking account a few days ago, referenced to you. What's that all about?'

'Well, the other day you were going on about my not repaying you for board and lodging and study fees and things like that. It's clear to me that it's troubling you, so I paid across a first instalment of the debt I owe you. There's no real hurry, Father, but I'd like a detailed statement, when it suits you, of what is still outstanding, so that I can plan my finances and clear away my debts to you. By the way, my bail bond should be refunded to you now that the police have withdrawn my case.'

'Yes, yes. I don't doubt that you'll pay me back eventually, but there's no desperate hurry about it. I'm not a poor man, you know. Actually, I'm quite well off, by modern standards. Very well off. Where does the money that you deposited in my account come from, anyway?'

'Legitimate sources, Father. Fees, sponsorships, and commissions — things like that. Everything is above board. Nothing untoward, I assure you.'

Charles Malvy huffed and balled his fist in his inability to get down to a personal level with his son. 'I didn't think so, for a moment.'

'Right, Father. Look after yourself. I'll keep in touch. Goodbye.'

Jason heard a grunt on the other end of the line as he put down the phone. Why did he always end up feeling irritated when he'd been speaking to the old man? It was like having sandpaper rubbed across his face.

There were a few things he would have liked to have shared with his dear old mom, but his father never gave a thought to putting his wife back on the line. It was as if he lived in a world of his own, where other people were of lesser importance to him.

The young man sighed pensively. Perhaps fathers were there not only to teach their sons what to do and how to behave, but also what they should not do. His father had taught him to be upright in business and in his dealings with others, but he had noted his father's lack of communication skills and promised himself that he would never be as cold and unfeeling as his father was to him and others, like his mother, whom he pitied in her lonely life.

***

The newspapers were full of reports of attacks by killer whales on beaches and against small boats, but Adrian Dewey was a stubborn man who mostly did things his way.

'It's so hot today. Let's take Ann for a romp on the beach,' he suggested to his wife, Laura.

'But Adrian, there have been countless warnings about killer whales attacking people. The tourist numbers have dropped off, and very few visitors go to the beach these days.'

'Well, then they're damned stupid. The killer whale is a huge creature that can't get very far up a beach, with all its bulk. All one has to do is to keep one's eyes open, especially when playing about in the breakers.'

'I don't know. I wouldn't like to risk Ann's life for a few hours at the beach, when there are so many other things we can do.'

'Laura, how many times were you taken to the beach as a kid? I can remember all the fun I had in the sand, as if it happened yesterday. Are you going to prevent our little girl from having all that pleasure in her life, just because other stupid people have scared one another's pants off due to their inability to figure things out for themselves?'

'Well, if you must go, for heaven's sake stay clear of the water, and keep your eyes peeled in case that horrible beast makes an appearance.'

'No, Laura, I think that you should come with us. You'd be most unhappy to have me looking after our little girl when you know that you're the only one capable of caring for her. At least you could sit on a rug so that it doesn't blow away, and keep a lookout for roving sea monsters.'

'Now you're just mocking me. I'm only voicing my concern for the safety of our little girl.'

'Yes, you're right. I shouldn't tease you. But let's get going before the afternoon wind comes up and blows sand all over us.'

So, they were soon packed and off to the beach, with Ann jumping up and down on the back seat of the car in her excitement.

Her father watched her antics in the rearview mirror. 'If you're so concerned about your daughter's safety, why don't you get a car seat for her, or at least see to it that she's strapped in properly?'

Now Laura had something else to worry about. 'You're right. I don't know why I've never thought of that before. I'll do something about it tomorrow. Will the car be available?'

'Tomorrow's Sunday, but maybe it'll be a good day to get a seat or belts, because I won't be needing the car for business.'

They parked the car and were soon making sandcastles with their daughter, but these kept on collapsing.

'The sand's too dry,' Adrian decided. 'Let's move down to near the water's edge, where the sand is damp, and we can build with it.'

'Yes, Daddy. Let's make big, big ones.'

'Adrian, you promised that you wouldn't go too near the water's edge,' scolded his wife, as her husband prepared to move.

He shook his head in answer to her negativity. 'Honey, look out there. The sea's as flat as a pancake today. There are hardly any waves to speak of. Where do you think a huge killer whale could be hiding? Be reasonable. It just can't happen to us — or anybody else, for that matter. Not on this beach, anyway.'

'Then where are all the other people? There are only a few bathers sharing this big area with us, and they're all keeping well clear of the water.'

'Oh, don't worry about them. They're all chicken-hearted. If you feel so worried, then stay where you are and keep a good lookout for us.'

After a while, Ann got bored with the half-hearted company of her father. 'Daddy, why doesn't Mommy come down and make sandcastles with us? There are two buckets, and we can build much faster if she comes and helps us.'

'You're right. C'mon, Laura, Ann wants to know why you're acting so otherwise today. Nothing's eaten us yet, you know.'

His wife did feel a little silly, as if she were going out of her way to make a point. She moved down to join her family. Now they really got busy in building a little palace, with Ann getting more excited as the turrets went up. Sometimes they had to be rebuilt, however, as the tide edged in and washed them down.

Time passed by, and the sun began dipping in the sky.

'I think it's time to pack in our castle building,' said Laura.

'Oh, Mommy!'

'Don't be difficult now, Ann. We can always come back another time, even tomorrow after church, if the weather holds.'

'That sounds good, Ann,' her father said, supporting his wife, for a change. 'C'mon, my cute little daughter, let's wash the sand off our legs, while Mommy shakes off our towels for us.'

Laura's mouth opened to warn her husband off going into the water, but he had already grabbed is daughter's hand and was charging off into the surf, which was admittedly light. There were only occasional waves that lapped against the shore.

With his daughter giggling at his side as she tried to keep pace with his long strides, Adrian Dewey charged into the water. There was a dip off the beach, and father and daughter tumbled into it, getting soaked in the process.

Laura tut-tutted. Now they would have to be dried off, and she would have to change Ann before they could get into the car and drive home.

But where had they got to? They'd simply disappeared into the breakers. The white foam had enveloped them, and they had been swept under the waves. They were gone, without a trace. Then the anxious woman noticed a hump in the small breakers that were building up near the water's edge.

The bulge in the water retreated, and then there was nothing out there that seemed strange or out of the ordinary. The only odd thing was that her husband and her little girl had disappeared.

It couldn't be. Laura ran into the water, where she had seen them last. She tripped and fell into the same hole that they had fallen into. Then she clambered onto her feet and stood, up to her waist in the water, screaming for them to come back. She looked down and there, floating about her knees, was the leg of a doll. The frantic woman bent to pick it up. It was not a doll's leg. It was the severed limb of her daughter.

Laura kept hold of the limb and beat about in the breakers, not willing to give up her family. But the pathetically torn, little leg was all she would ever have left to show of her sweet, little girl.

Chapter Twenty-One

Anybody who could be classed as an American electronics expert, with a class A rating for secrecy and loyalty, was sought out by the investigators headed by Laurie Bridewell, who had cast off his cover as head of hotel security. They were delegated to examining, analysing and interpreting what the detonated earpieces were all about.

What was their use? Fortunately, one of the gadgets had not totally disintegrated. So the analysts were left with two problems to solve: why had all four devices detonated at the same time, and what was their purpose?

One or two of the analysts were hazy about electronic gadgetry but full of common sense. Because three of the dead had been having a presumably quiet meeting, and the fourth one — the woman — was being sexually blasted out of Earth's orbit, she was pinpointed as the likely cause of the connected explosions.

What was left of the only partially intact gadget had a Chinese look about it. But the rest of the world knew that sometimes their Oriental urgency in stretching their electronic horizons led the Chinese into taking shortcuts in the material and the workmanship that they provided.

They reasoned that the woman had simply put too much pressure on her device, and it had blown a portion of her head apart when it exploded, in true Chinese fireworks tradition. By extrapolation, it could be further argued that the three other devices had exploded in conjunction with one another, due to a major power fluctuation.

Maybe the pitch of the woman's squeal had gone off the measured scale, like a top C breaking a fine-blown and delicate wine glass.

Were there other gadgets, also connected in a chain? It was unlikely that the Chinese would ever disclose their further limitations in gadget design and devious spycraft. It was recommended that the local Chinese community and diplomatic establishments be secretly put under surveillance for reported staffing reductions and movements, as well as the transfer of bulky packages, particularly at night.

They came to the simple conclusion that the earpieces were simply a method of monitoring one another, and also for having quick communications between themselves. The experts also felt that the woman's earpiece had been installed in a limited timeframe, possibly while she was temporally unconscious, while the other three gadgets had been more precisely put into place. That may have been the reason for the one failure when put under extreme pressure.

What interested the scientists far more than the earpiece fiasco were the drawings that had been under discussion when the Russians and the Chinese had holes blown in their heads. They gave an accurate picture of a much larger electronic device that was seemingly intended for insertion in a killer whale's brain. The diagram was in much more detail and gave a clearer picture to the scientists who studied it.

This one wasn't a twisted fragment of material, glued together in little, partially melted lumps. The heading over the detailed line drawing was in Russian, but it had been translated into describing "Control and Manipulation of Orca Brain."

The jigsaw puzzle was falling into place. It was fairly obvious why the killer whales, led by Samson, already bearing a grudge or two and probably the biggest of his species, were going on the rampage. This all tied in with the fisherman's report of a while back, together with enclosed photos, of a helicopter crew darting a killer whale, presumably Samson.

They were using the orcas to terrorize the inhabitants of the west coast of America, with the view of extension of this onslaught right around the USA, ruining the commercial marine cargo business and the fishing and tourist trade; but what else would the unholy Chinese and Russian alliance have up their sleeves to threaten America?

If the orcas, led by Samson, could be trained to plant mines on warships in and around San Diego, and other naval targets, it would give America more than something to think about. If more killer whales could be successfully trained, this could be extended to cargo ships. Following this tactic up right around the nation could seriously cripple America's might in the world leadership stakes.

Now came the tricky part that the American diplomatic corps had been dreading: the simultaneous dealing with the Russians and the Chinese officials, while the world looked on.

It didn't much matter what the American scientists had figured out or what the Secret Service had found out; the more obviously guilty the two delegations were found to be, the more they would kick up diplomatic dust in order to cover up their tracks, as they had so often done in the past.

It worked most of the time for the officials of the two countries. Neither of them allowed their people access to international opinion. Their whole population was heavily censored, and they were only told what their leaders wanted them to hear. So some judicious twisting of the facts had led the public to believe that it was the evil West at fault all the time.

In the meantime, the Russian and Chinese leaders kept up a constant barrage of accusations and denials that sometimes even confused their own officials into putting their feet in their mouths, excusing what had already been flatly denied by their hard-pressed colleagues.

The furore ended up at the United Nations, on the opposite coast from where the action was taking place. That was the forum where nations sought a peaceful means of war, by ganging up against one another. Usually Russia and China took turns in vetoing anything that the West put up for resolution, with some Middle Eastern nation like Iran throwing in their support, but now Russia and China were standing shoulder to shoulder in their putting up a smokescreen to cover their tracks.

'Where's the proof?' they argued. 'Executing two Russians and a Chinese diplomat, who are having a pleasant chat together, hardly gives grounds for all this talk of electronic gadgets. Aren't diplomats from neighbouring countries expected to have discussions now and then? Isn't that what diplomacy is all about?

'As far as who caused the deaths is concerned, security in the hotel was under the control of the Americans. If they weren't liable for the deaths of the murdered diplomats, then who is prepared to take the blame for these evil deeds that lost Russia and China these brilliant officers?

'The woman who is accused of setting off the ear devices in the first place was busy having sexual intercourse with a young man who had been co-opted onto the hotel security staff. On what grounds he was appointed remains a mystery. He was, at the time of these terrible deaths, a member of the American SEALs, an arm of the American Defence Force.

'What the woman was doing at the conference was debatable, but it has been suggested that a great deal of her involvement has taken place while she has been lying on her back, in the style of many female American spies. This style of information gathering goes completely against the Russian and Chinese principles of good international relations. It may be a reason why the females in the West get cocky so easily during their conferences.

'Slipping some plans in front of three corpses is hardly proof of any wrongdoing on the part of the Russian and the Chinese diplomatic staff. It would be far more interesting to know who set up the diagrams post-mortem and what the reasons were for doing this.

'This is obviously a set-up by the capitalist system, and the Russian and Chinese embassies are not prepared to stand for this corrupt and blatant use of guile and manipulation.

'To sum this all up, it may look as if our heroic countrymen were stirring up mischief, but it's all a dirty plot engineered by the West, as it always is. Their underhand tactics have gone horribly wrong, and our innocent and hardworking officials are doing their best to provide worldwide peace, as we so often do in countries like Afghanistan, Syria and Yemen, to name but a few.'

'Maybe we didn't get a confession out of any of the Russkies or the Chinks,' said Laurie Bridewell, 'but they never admit to anything. What is important is that we've solved what's been going wrong with the orcas, even if we haven't found a way to eliminate the problem yet. We've also got rid of some nasty foreign agents, by some good luck. Maybe a great deal of all this drama will settle down now, and we can get down to winning tennis and creating track records, never mind basketball and athletics trophies. You know, all the important stuff that we do so well. And we'll do even better, now that the sporting world is beginning to crack down on Russia and China because of all the doping tricks they've been getting up to.'

***

Danny Foulkes had gone back to the Navy SEALs after his vacation, pleased to get out of the unfavourable limelight that he found himself in. There was still a ring on top of his head that made him look like a friar without a robe. It made him the butt of his friends' rude remarks, but they secretly envied his few days of notoriety.

'Hey, Danny, what was it like having sex with a woman carrying a bomb in her head?'

'Now we believe you when you say that you can make a woman explode with pleasure.'

There was much laughter.

'Hey, Danny, did you blow her up by mouth like a party balloon? You must have a hefty pair of lungs on you, making her pop like that,' quirked another bright spark.

Danny Foulkes was hauled over the coals for his moonlighting activities while supposedly on leave, but he was lucky that Laurie Bridewell protected him when he found out that Danny was in trouble.

'This man took on a dangerous operation, even though he didn't have to do it. He received precious little reward for his efforts, yet he carried on in spite of the risks involved. He was injured in the service of his country and has still not fully recovered from the shock and injuries that he received. The man deserves a medal for his efforts, but he will probably never receive one due to the nature of his services that he provided. We should all be proud of him, and I wish him well in his continued career in the navy.'

'Danny,' his mates chaffed, 'thanks for taking on the enemy on our behalf, but let us know if we can relieve you at any stage, if they call on you again.'

'Were you laying depth charges at the time, Danny?'

He was allocated to a destroyer armed with depth charges, and the ship was sent out on fast patrol in the bay area. The navy didn't intend having one of their ships blown out of the water by orcas creeping up to it and planting mines on its hull. At the same time, they had instructions to blow any orcas they came across, out of the water, by gunfire or depth charges. Samson and his mates had to be stopped.

***

With all the drama that had happened at the conference, the wheels had come off to a large extent. Whatever the Russians and the Chinese had to say on the matter, it became fairly clear how the intrigue had developed and who was to blame for it.

At least the problem of the attacking orcas was now localized and not yet widespread, as it had been feared to be. The general consensus was that it was indeed one killer whale that had been equipped with a device and that it was influencing others to join it in its attacks.

The question of how to eliminate the problem was now largely in the hands of the United States Navy. It would have to isolate the orca and its infected — or influenced — pod and then unfortunately eliminate them before the campaign of hate was extended right around the world. The navy would also need to patrol the coastline to identify any ships — particularly foreign ones — that might be arming other orcas.

Now that there was a firm resolve regarding how to finalize the problem, with the exception of Russia and China with their minority vote, it was resolved to dissolve the conference by the close of the following day.

There were final meetings and contacts to be made, together with a few closing speeches and a cocktail party, but Jason now found himself with some time on his hands.

He first phoned his mother to tell her of his plans, because she liked to get his room ready for him if he planned to come home, as well as laying in some of his favourite foods, much to the disgust of her husband. Mathilda Malvy had not had a happy time of it since her previous chat with her son.

'Son, I think you know me as a reasonable person; a bit fluttery and vague at times, yet mostly having all my buttons in a row. But the situation with your father has steadily worsened since you left home to become a navy diver.' She continued, 'I don't know whether it's the onset of Alzheimer's Disease or something else, because he refuses to visit a doctor or a hospital. He says that they're only after his money, and you must know that he's got more than enough of that.

'He sits in his office all day, doing whatever it is that he does in there. I've yet to discover what that is, although I've found lists of figures and projects that never seem to be fulfilled. Half the time he wants his dinner served in his office, and when he emerges for a meal, he's morose and negative about his food, the economy and the state of the world.

'His feelings for you are mixed, I would say. On one hand, he listens in on the radio and watches TV news channels, mainly to keep informed on the orca situation, particularly as it affects you. So there seems to be an amount of pride and fatherly interest there. Yet he can't seem to resist badmouthing you — hopefully only to me, seeing that he never leaves the house these days.'

His mother sounded worn out. Jason wished that he could do more for her.

'I do know that he's found out that you've picked up your old career as a realtor again. The other day I was walking past his office, and I heard him shouting to someone. You can call me nosey, but I had to stop and listen in. Your father was talking to Joe Caldecott, if you could call that talking. He was going on about Joe pandering to you by giving your old job back to you. It sounded as if Joe was asking him to keep out of it, as he had always done. Joe has always had a soft spot for you, but then the firm has made a lot of money out of your deals. So I rushed to my extension in the kitchen and listened in. This is my affair as much as that of your dad's, after all.

'So now I could pick up both sides of the conversation, if one could call it that. They were still arguing when I started listening in. Joe was saying that you were a hard worker and that you had a flair for the property business, but your dear father wouldn't listen.

'"Look Joe," he said, "I'm the majority shareholder in the business. I demand that you get that boy out of there."

'Now even I know that one doesn't treat Joe that way. He's a fair man, but he's as hard as nails when he wants to be.

'"Charles, old man," — a phrase which your father hates — "You were once as sharp as a pin, but now you seem to be slowing up, or even grinding to a stop. I've been ploughing the bulk of my share of the profits back into the business, as per our original agreement. If you'd care to shift your butt out of your house sometime and come to study the books, you'd find that I am the majority shareholder at this time," emphasized Joe. "You don't know whether you're Arthur or Martha, regarding the business right now, so if I decide to stay, you'll have to put up with both your son and me. If I decide to leave, on the other hand, Jason will probably come with me, and you'll be sitting with a heap of debts and no cash flow. Oh, and I'll take your best clients and contacts with me. Now do me a favour. Sit and sulk in your office while I make us a heap of money with the help of your smart son, Jason, or phone your twisted attorney, who has you by your shirttails. Either way, I'm ready for you, buster."

'So, your father slammed down the phone, and he hid himself away for a while, but now I was really steaming. You want to see me when I'm truly mad. That's not often, but boy, I can really let rip when I'm in the mood for it.'

He didn't like to hear about his parents' squabbles, but his father's difficult and authoritarian ways had to put someone's back up sooner or later. It was like enjoying a movie. 'So, tell me more, Mom.'

'Well, I quietly simmered for a while, but then I had to let out some of my steam. Your father was sitting quietly in his office, no doubt brooding about life being against him. So I went to his office and knocked on the door.

'"Go away!" he said. "I don't want to speak to you."

'"You'll speak to me now," I said. "I'm your wife, not your servant."

'"I said, go away!" he barked.

'"I want to speak to you now!" I repeated.

'"You can't. The door's locked, and the key's in the slot."

'By now it felt as if fire was coming out of me. I went to fetch a chopper and started hacking at the door panels.

'"Stop that! You can't do that! You're damaging the door," he screamed at me.

'"Well, it's my door because this house is in my name, together with a number of other important assets that you want to keep out of your portfolio, for tax reasons," I shouted at him.

'"But you know that it was done purely as a book entry."

'"Tough luck, Charlie," I said, because he hates that shortening of his name. "It's all properly registered, as you well know. So, I'll chop up the office door in my house if I want to. And now it appears that I've broken through. Mind your fingers don't get chopped as well, if you get them in the way. Wouldn't it have been simpler if you'd just let me enter in the first place? Now that I've managed to break into your inner sanctum, I have something important that I want to discuss."

'"So it seems that I can't avoid you today. Discuss away."

'"Charles, I've had enough of your bullying, and I'm leaving you. Although I've tried to get you to a doctor, you are showing all the symptoms of Alzheimer's Disease. I'd be prepared to stay with you and to nurse you for the rest of your life, but I'm not prepared to throw away my future by looking after the bully that you've become."

'Jason, he stared at me for a few moments, probably not believing what he was hearing. Then he asked: "Where will you go, or are you planning to eject me from my own home?"

'"I'm not like that, Charles, and you should know it. My sister, Johanna, has been living in Vancouver, Canada, since her husband died. She's aware of the trouble I've been having with you, so she asked me to spend our last years together as friends, as well as sisters."

'"Wonderful!" he said. "And what about your blue-eyed boy? You're not going to abandon your son, are you?"

'I told him: "I don't think Jason would want to stay under the same roof as you. Now that he can afford it, he'll probably set himself up in a nice apartment where he is free to come and go without being picked on by you all the time; and we'll keep in touch, he and I. We get on well together, mainly because we understand each other."'

Mathilda Malvy paused while she gathered her thoughts. 'Your father still had the cheek to ask me whether I was going through the change of life or something, because he had never known me to be so aggressive. That was my fault, I suppose. I put up with a lot of his bullying because of his unfairness towards you, but now you're your own man and you are more than able to look after yourself. This is my chance to get my own life back again. I think that Johanna and I can be happy together. Just keep in touch with me now and then because I'll miss you terribly.'

It was with mixed feelings that Jason wished his mother well and said goodbye to her. 'Tell me when you're ready to leave, and I'll take you to lunch before dropping you off at the airport.'

'That sounds like a great idea, Jason.'

***

201

'I'm going to miss you, Jason,' Mathilda Malvy said, when she eventually met her son for lunch on the day that he had arranged to take her to the airport. 'But it's high time that you built up a life for yourself, away from your father. He's an evil old man who tends to bring out the worst in those around him. As it is, there's a little devil wandering around inside you, that you fortunately keep well under control most of the time. You're the type who takes a lot of provoking before breaking out and doing something regrettable.

'How did you manage to put up with the old man for so long, Mom?' Jason asked. 'Maybe it would have been a good thing if you had broken out now and again.'

'Well, at first, it was to keep the family together while you were growing up and in your teens. Then, when you were old enough for me to not use you as an excuse, I seemed to slip into a comfort zone where it was just too much trouble to uproot myself and start a new life from scratch. I would have to give up my home that I had made comfortable for myself. But now he's getting out of hand. He's far worse than he was before. It's as if he has a cancer that's growing in his brain and taking over all his reasoning powers. I find no pleasure in life any more, living with that tyrant. There's not a day that passes when that man doesn't go out of his way to make my life unpleasant for me, sometimes without meaning to, but wilfully at other moments, often when I least expect his bitterness.' Sadly, she continued: 'In some strange way, I pity him and wonder what's going to happen to him after I've left him on his own, but that's for him to figure out. Honestly, Jason, the man is stifling me. No, even worse, he's throttling the joy of life out of me.'

'So where do we go from here?' Jason asked. 'I promised to take you to the airport. Are your cases still at home? How did you get here, anyhow?'

'I came in a taxi, because my sister, your Aunt Johanna, went to hospital yesterday for a few tests, and they've kept her there indefinitely because they're not happy with the results. She'll have to stay in hospital for a day or two, at least. In the meantime, I've had to postpone my flight until we have more certainty regarding her condition. So, I'm afraid you may have to take your nuisance of a mother to the airport on another occasion, if you don't mind.'

Chapter Twenty-Two

Samson was intuitively conscious of the fact that fewer humans were making themselves available for slaughter by his kind, of late. They were clearly wary of meeting up with him and his followers. He would have to use better planning to catch them in shallow water but catch them he would.

It seemed that humans loved to be in, or on, the water, just as he and his kind did. Maybe, long, long ago, they used to frolic in the sea together. But now humans had turned against orcas, and in their turn, the sea creatures were beginning to get their revenge after all those years of torment by mankind.

And then the super-intelligent killer whale found what he was looking for. It was a sound, running parallel to the sea, where a large and slow-moving river ran inshore, parallel with the coastline, until it found a final exit into the blue waters of the Pacific Ocean, depending on the rhythmical patterns of periodical tidal movement.

There were plenty of fish in the sound, where breeding fish came for sanctuary from rough seas, sharks and other carnivores. A plethora of small creatures provided food for young fish, encouraging them to roam within the calmer stretch of water. The fishermen knew this too. It was a favourite place to angle from the banks, or in small boats, on a peaceful afternoon.

Dolphins, of which the orcas were family, always seemed to have a permanent grin on their faces, giving them the appearance of forever being in good temper, even when things weren't going well for them. But this afternoon had every reason to put a smile on Samson's face, if he ever felt inclined to wear one.

Now the tide was coming in, and eight black and white shadows were making their way through the gentle breakers that led them into the calmer waters of the peaceful river. Strangely enough, they didn't attract much attention, at first. Everyone was doing his or her own thing, checking their rods and reels and replenishing bait, while their little ones collected shells or dabbled after tiny fingerlings in the pools near the banks, using butterfly nets to catch them and then running back to their families with their prize.

One or two people did notice a swirl of water, but they didn't want to comment on what they saw. Fishermen have a habit of telling tall tales, so nobody tends to take their stories all that seriously. Therefore, they kept quiet, not wanting to be laughed at, when everybody knew that the fish in the sound were sometimes on the large side but not big enough to create a bow wave. It must only be the tide nudging the water over the bar to push upstream.

The intruders cruised at their ease through the low-running waters of the sound. The slightly warmer water caressed their flanks with gentle fingers, and there was an air of contentment about them.

And then there were eight horrendous humps surfacing out of the relatively shallow water. They seemed to be everywhere one looked. People stopped chatting or calling to their kids. There was a deathly silence as the onlookers began to realize that something strange was happening. Then a great number of them began screaming and shouting and waving their arms at the same time.

A couple of boat fishermen made it easy pickings for the orcas, by swaying in their shock where they stood and falling out of their boats as they lost their balance. The killer whales had been well schooled by their tutor, Samson, sweeping over to the men where they struggled in the water, trapped by their fishermen's gear and still instinctively clinging to their rods.

At last, the sight of two fellow fishermen being bitten in half and swallowed by hungry orcas woke the rest of the sportsmen out of their trance. They threw their rods to one side and grabbed their oars, only to wonder why they weren't making any headway, until they remembered that they were still anchored in position.

Orcas put them out of their dilemma by leaning on their boats and tipping out the occupants. These fearful souls started a frantic and panicky sort of crawl before the efficient orcas closed in and took them with more grace and skill than their little ones were using on the fingerlings they were trying to catch in their butterfly nets.

But the young ones were not interested in watching their fathers being swallowed by the orcas. For once they comprehended what danger they were in, choosing to run to their mothers on the river bank where they sat reading, knitting or simply dozing in the sunshine.

The trouble was that panic had set in, particularly amongst the little ones. They were knee-deep in muddy pools or struggling against slippery banks that appeared to maliciously push them back into the water, to face an implacable driving force with a gaping mouth that showed its clear intent as it moved in for the kill.

They panicked and cried out and tripped and stumbled, until the orcas scooped them up like fruits that had fallen from a tree, while their desperate mothers watched in mind-blowing agony. Then they disappeared in a trice, as if they had never been there in the first place.

The children might as well have never been there, right from the start. They might as well never have stretched their mothers' bodies to the limit during their birthing pains, or kept both parents awake at night with a raging fever that no antibiotic could tame; or never have been the cause of birthday parties when they put a careless little hand in the icing and painted a crusty old aunt's face with it. No snatching at a favourite ornament and breaking it; no swallowing of a button, causing a hurried trip to the casualty ward. All these adventures and misadventures had been for naught, for the little boy or girl was gone, never to be seen again. And now the mother had to fend for herself, for she had rushed into the mud and was stuck, long enough for the marauder to lunge forward and grab her as well.

Stuck there in the mud and watching the huge mouth open to receive them, some women simply blew their minds as they watched the sharp teeth ready to rip them apart. Something burst in their brains and they went into a state of shock, thankfully spared the agony of feeling themselves ripped apart, flesh from bone, as those teeth masticated them in the dark cavern where they had landed on the wet tongues of their black and white ravagers.

Maybe there were a few especially hardy women who remained conscious, with undamaged brains and their hearts still beating, while their pink, sun-protected and delicate bodies were torn to pieces. They watched in agonized horror until their minds went blank like the screen of a switched-off TV set.

The orcas couldn't devour everyone at the same time. As if they realized that there were plenty of targets to choose from, more orcas came surging into the sound to take their pick of the humans who were milling about like a herd of wounded buffalo, not knowing which way to turn.

There was hardly anywhere to go on the narrow spit of land that the sunseekers and sports fishermen found themselves. The sea was on one side, and a line of grisly monsters lunged at them from the river. And the killer whales took the muddy shallows in their stride, paddling in inches of water or skating on the slippery surface, as if they had been doing this all their lives.

Some sportsmen, not fully committed to fishing when the orcas arrived, were more ready to make their escape than were some. Those in sailboats had less hassles in getting a clean start, but the trouble was that their attackers caught up with them in no time at all. They capsized the light boats and took their pickings from the desperate sailors left floundering in the water.

Those with powered boats had things to do before they could get going. They had to cut the anchor rope and get the engine swinging over before starting on their way; provided the engine didn't flood or stall, which often happened in panic situations. If the killer whales had much of a sense of humour, which hungry beasts don't usually have, they would have been amused at the clumsy efforts some people used to attempt an escape from their clutches.

Then there were people who stayed calm enough to get their boats across the river and beach them, before running like hell to avoid the monstrous sea creatures that had to give up on them and turn their attention to victims on the other side of the river within their easy reach.

The men swung around to watch the orcas retreat, before they began to realize that their wives and families were still running about like crazed deer, trying to escape the huge creatures while their menfolk stood and watched from their safe positions on the other side of the river. Some brave men couldn't take the thought of standing by and doing nothing but watch in dismay as their loved ones got swallowed up and eaten right before their eyes. Sure, that they were going to their deaths, like riflemen charging up an unprotected hillside in the face of machine gun fire during wartime, they turned their boats about and went out into the jaws of death. And that was what happened. At least they offered up their gallant lives, while their wives and children jumped into the sea and tried to swim to a place of safety that wasn't really there waiting for them right then. Most of the women drowned in the rock-strewn surf that day, with their children at their sides.

There weren't many souls who got away with their lives that afternoon. Of the one hundred and fifty adults and children enjoying the sunshine that day, few more than about thirty individuals would survive the massacre. They were picked off like cherries from a tree.

The only resistance put up was that of a few sportsmen who had brought their handguns with them, what with the alarm bells ringing out about all sorts of attacks by denizens of the deep.

Those were brought out from under cover and used to shoot wildly into the river, until all the ammunition was used up. Nobody had told them that shooting into water only works in Hollywood films. The force of a bullet is quickly spent after just a short penetration into liquid. Only a direct hit would mostly be effective, and the shooters were too pumped up to get their aim right.

As if they had received a command, the killer whales stopped their slaughter, which was virtually complete at that stage, and turned around to find their way out of the sound. The orcas could be heard whistling, so they were certainly communicating with one another. Maybe it was Samson issuing instructions, or maybe they felt too confined where they were. Whatever the reason, the orcas backed off and swung about in formation before making their way out through the bar into the open sea.

It was a wise move on their part. A couple of people had been sensible enough to use their cell phones to send out distress messages. The Civil Defence Force was on its toes after all the recent challenges it had experienced. Heavily armed helicopters were sent out, backed up by armed men in speedboats, to counteract the latest attack by the killer whales.

Unfortunately, they were too late to do much good, except to try to clear up the mess and to take the few injured people and survivors to hospital. Fishing, boating and picnicking along the south-western seaboard of the United States was turning out to be not that much fun any more.

The rescuers were shocked at the chaos they found when they arrived at the scene of the latest attack. There were broken boats bumping aimlessly about on the water, and torn scraps of clothing littered the scene. A few anxious survivors staggered about, waving their hands to get some attention.

Once the helicopters had found a place to land, they discovered that there were not that many people remaining to care for.

***

After all the dust had settled, there was not a lot that the authorities could do but to tidy up the disaster scene and clear the scraps of clothing and remainders of bodies away. Of course they sent out a team of investigators to the scene of the carnage, but there was really nothing new to report, except to underscore the advice of being extremely vigilant near or on the sea.

There was not much that could be done but to assist the next of kin regarding funeral arrangements and financial help for those who needed it. Psychological help was offered to those who had survived the trauma of that time of horror, but it was understood that, for most survivors, these nightmare images had been locked into their memory and would not fade away that easily, if at all.

Jason had been loosely included in an investigative team that went out to interview the survivors of these events. It was not a pleasant job, but it did serve to fill in the occasional gap regarding orca behaviour, particularly where Samson's marauding pod was concerned. But any additional knowledge only served to underscore the superior intellect of the *Orcinus orca* species, putting it on a virtual par with that of mankind, considering the advantages that humans enjoyed.

Although Jason was not a killer by nature, he had come to accept that Samson had too much of a track record to be left to roam the seas, doing what he was doing. He had to be done away with as soon as possible, before every orca in the sea was infected with his programme of hate.

It would also be a good idea to find a way to retrieve the electronic implant that was strongly suspected to have been fired into Samson by the Chinese and the Russians, working in concert with one another. Without the allies analysing the weapon and finding an antidote for it, the enemies of the West would set about replacing it with others of its kind.

If a counter was developed to the gadget, this success could well be the key to the calling off of the Eastern bloc's efforts to wreak havoc amongst its perceived enemies in the Free World.

As it was, all that could be achieved would be the hunting down and killing of the rogue orca, and that effort was to be undertaken as soon as possible.

Chapter Twenty-Three

When Jason returned to the hotel where the conference was being held, he found that he had not really missed anything, as he had suspected. There were a number of messages — most of which were routine advisories or personal invitations — which he chose to ignore. Only one of these interested him.

It was a call from Cora Nugent. At least she still wanted to communicate with him. He rang her number with some interest. Her melodious voice answered.

'It's Jason. Jason Malvy. Are you well, Cora?'

'I know which Jason it is, you know. I don't have that many Jasons in my address book that I'm likely to mix you up with anybody else. And I'm fine. I've simply been missing you. I hope that you're healed up by now.'

He chuckled. 'Fortunately, I'm a quick healer.'

'Healed enough to come and have a farewell drink with me, seeing that we're all leaving this evening?'

Jason hesitated. 'That depends. I caught your husband glaring at me after our last little romp in your room. I'm sure that dear, departed Janine spilled the beans about us when she left off beating me up and stomped away.'

'Oh, no doubt she had a lot to tell him. He came in here ranting and raving sometime later.'

Jason's eyes widened. 'What did you say to him?'

'My dear man, my husband and I have a clear understanding about our relationship. We are free to go to bed with whom we please, as long as we keep our liaisons as private as possible. He can't have his cake and eat it, and he knows it. The first thing I asked was how things were getting on with his own lady friend that he brought to the conference and shacked up somewhere. That calmed him down a little.'

'But I suppose that Janine presented him with a "worst case" scenario?'

'Certainly, she did. What he accused me of doing made my hair stand up on end.' She gave a little giggle. 'In fact, she's handed me a few good ideas for the future. But seriously, I calmed him down and tried to explain that the woman was off her trolley to some extent, that she was jealous of you and that she was merely gunning for you out of sheer spite.' Cora paused. 'I know that one shouldn't speak ill of the dead, but her death in the middle of a sex act actually confirmed what I said to my husband, that she was an oversexed mischief maker.

'Anyway, the net result is that the heat is off, as far as we're concerned. So do come up to my room to say goodbye properly, without worrying about jealous husbands safely packed away on the other sides of locked doors.'

***

After arranging to visit Cora in half an hour, Jason had a leisurely shower and took a box of chocolates, a packet of crisps and a bottle of whisky from his courtesy bar, in order to sweeten up proceedings. Although Cora had not said anything outright, he could be in for a reasonably hectic time of it.

Now that Janine was not a factor in his relationship with Cora, he was looking forward to a really good time with her. He was feeling quite excited to find out what was in store for him this time.

She was waiting for him when he arrived. His hostess looked stunning in a powder-blue peignoir. She had obviously done her hair, and her make-up had been carefully applied but not overdone. In fact, she looked years younger than her visitor suspected that she was, although she was one of those women who can manage to look classy and feminine at any age.

'Come in, handsome,' she said, holding the door open to let him pass through.

He was no sooner inside her suite than she closed the door and locked it firmly, making sure that the security bolt was in place this time. Then Cora took her lover by the hand and led him to her bedroom. She turned towards Jason, and they hugged each other warmly, before Cora pulled his head down to her shorter level and gave him a deep kiss. Their tongues thrashed at each other in a wet and wonderful way.

'I've missed you,' she breathed, as they came up for air.

He stared deeply into her liquid brown eyes. 'And I've missed you too. Strange that it was only a couple of days ago that we became so close, as we sat on your coverlet and studied maps together.'

She smiled. 'You men don't ever see the wood for the trees. I had those maps especially delivered so that I would have a reason to entice you onto my bed.'

He stared at her with his mouth open. 'Go on, I don't believe you!'

'But it's true. I've already returned them to the friend from whom I borrowed them.'

'You didn't tell her why you wanted them, did you?'

'Of course, I did. We girls share things like that — if we're good friends, that is. In fact, she wanted to know all the details when I returned them to her.'

'You didn't tell her how that virago gave me a hiding with my own shoe, did you?'

'Of course, I did. In fact, that was the best part of the story. She laughed so much that I had to bang her on the back to stop her choking on her drink.'

'How can I ever look her in the face?'

'You don't have to, my young lover. You might recall that I live in Oklahoma City, and I don't intend flying halfway across the country to carry on our glorious romp after we part company tomorrow.

'And if you're ever silly enough to follow me to my hometown, I'll have to fight off my daughter — who's about your age, I would guess, or maybe a couple of years younger. If you met her, I wouldn't stand a chance of competing with her for your attention. So, this is the last kiss and cuddle we're going to have, sweetie pie.'

Cora stepped back and undid her sash, letting her gown swing open to display her still-trim body in its glorious nakedness. 'I'm really burning for you. So, kiss me all over and then pour me a whisky. But don't hurry and spill anything too soon, there's still plenty of time for us to enjoy each other.'

'I don't usually spill things.'

'Well, you may get a little over-anxious this time.'

***

He was still on his knees, his face pressed between her legs and one of her hands holding his head tightly against her, while the other held a glass of whisky, when there was a tremendous crash at the interconnecting door. It swung open with its lock blown away. A drunken husband stood with gun in hand, wearing a really mean look on his bloated and sagging face.

Jason only had a glimpse of his wrath when the terrified Cora remembered to let go of his head. She stood riveted to the spot before bending over and grabbing for her gown on the carpet next to her, in order to conceal her nudity, but she didn't get any further with her efforts to cover herself.

The door hung askew, with fragments of the woodwork scattered on the carpet. Byron Nugent seemed to be dazed by the intensity of the noise of his own gunshots, as much as the others were shocked. But he was also very drunk.

The chances were that he'd been listening and waiting for Jason to arrive at Cora's door. He'd had a well-used bottle of whisky in his left hand, with his pistol tightly gripped in the other. He'd been getting steadily drunk as he waited for his opportunity to break into his wife's bedroom.

Then he heard his wife's groans of ecstasy as Jason caressed her with his tongue. Byron's imagination did the rest. He roughly aimed his weapon at the door lock and pressed the trigger three times, blowing it to pieces. The door swung open, and the drunken man stood there, stunned by the sound and not sure what his next move should be.

And there stood his wife, with her legs apart and her gown spread out on the carpet, in front of a man — presumably Jason — whose face was still buried in her groin. With a shaking hand he pulled the trigger twice more, aiming it unsteadily at what he could see of the fellow's chest, seen through Cora's legs, from behind.

But his unsteady aim had been too high. Cora fell forward to land on top of her lover, who was pinned underneath her. Byron had clearly shot her by mistake. There were two ominous holes in her back, pumping out copious amounts of blood.

Jason heard the two shots moments before Cora collapsed onto him; and then he was trapped under her weight. Panic now set in. The husband, Byron, was going to drill him next, but he could hardly move under the

213

wounded woman's mass. Using all his strength, he wormed his way out from underneath her and made for the broken door, without looking back.

Byron Nugent had been shocked when his wife collapsed on her lover, with blood streaming out of her back. The shooter dropped the pistol onto the carpet and instinctively went to help her. In the meantime, the trapped Romeo had managed to drag himself free from his burden, got to his feet and ran for it.

All he wanted to do was to get the hell out of there before the husband did a better job of shooting him. He was sure that the bullets hitting Cora had been aimed at him. Another few inches, aimed lower down, and he would have got it in the head.

Luckily for Jason, seeing his wife go down because of his shooting had side-tracked her husband. Now he was filled with remorse and wanted to hold her tightly in his arms, as if that was suddenly going to make her feel better.

She was lying sprawled out on her face. He turned her over and began crooning whisky-laden fumes over her face, until an innocent passer-by saw a bloodstained man charging out of the Nugent suite as if the hounds of hell were after him. That was Jason, putting space between him and the maddened Byron.

The new witness was in for a rough time. Cora Nugent was covered in blood, which was pouring out of the holes in her back, her chest and out of her mouth. She looked like someone who had been caught in a bomb blast.

'What the hell has been going on here? Are you people mad? This person is dying on us. We must get help fast!'

Fortunately — or unfortunately — the young man didn't notice the pistol still lying unattended on the carpet.

He was a sensible fellow who quickly took in the situation that Byron Nugent was not much use to anyone right then. He immediately took control. He used the injured woman's gown to stanch as much of the blood as he could, while the husband mooned away alongside him.

Then he dashed to the telephone and reported the shooting to security. Meanwhile, the trauma of shooting his wife had sobered up the drunken Byron to some extent. He had moved out of the way when the passer-by had taken over the care of the now unconscious Cora. He was standing in an alcoholic daze, prepared to let the stranger handle the situation, until the cause of it all presented itself to his befuddled mind.

Jason Malvy. The young bastard. He was the root of all this trouble. Where had he let that gun fall? He still had a score to settle with that young wife-snatcher. While the good Samaritan was busy on the phone, he found his gun and waddled out of the suite, past the stranger, with it comfortably in his hand, ready for the committing of murder of the first degree.

The man looked up to see Nugent disappearing out of the room. He dropped the instrument and went after the drunk. 'Hey! You can't just walk off like that! You've got a badly wounded woman in there — your wife, I reckon. You can't just leave her like that!'

Then he saw the drunken man entering the elevator with a pistol in his hand. That made him stop his shouting and let the fellow go to wherever he was headed. It was one thing to help a badly wounded woman, but he didn't want to end up like that lady who was lying on the carpet in the suite that he'd run out of.

Elevators make it easy for one to move about in a building, if everybody stays out of the way and allows one person freedom of movement. Byron Nugent was fortunate to pick a quiet time in the hotel, or maybe the other residents were the lucky ones.

He clambered out at Jason's floor, but he didn't know the suite number. Some people, however, have all the luck. While he stood uncertainly outside the elevator, someone walked past him.

'Jason Malvy?' he mumbled, trying his luck.

'Next suite but one,' called out the man, without breaking stride.

You're a dead man, Malvy, he thought to himself. Then he limped on, heading towards the Malvy suite, gun in hand for instant use.

***

When Anthony Beecham, to give the Samaritan his correct name, rang security to report a life and death shooting, one of Laurie Bridewell's staff took the call. The security head had a vivid imagination. When he heard his man repeating everything that he was being told, he strongly suspected who was involved. That silly, young Jason Maltby ended up in the middle of everything.

Bridewell then heard that the husband had left the suite with a gun in his hand. The secret agent knew very well where Byron Nugent was headed. The man was hell-bent on revenge. The lunatic needed to be stopped. And fast.

He picked up another phone and rang the suite number. It was engaged. He was right. The nutter was on the loose. Slamming down the instrument, he used his walkie-talkie to summon support and medical assistance as he collected his handgun and charged out of the office.

No time to wait for the elevator. Running for the stairs, he stumbled down them, flight after flight, while issuing staccato commands to his staff, and anyone else he could think of, on his walkie-talkie. He slung himself around the short flights and hammered down the stairs. If he didn't stop Nugent quickly, there would be another murder in the hotel at any moment.

***

Meanwhile, Anthony Beecham had put down the phone and had trotted back to the woman who was now lying on her back, with more blood pouring out of her. The anxious helper had never thought that one body could contain so much blood. Surely, she couldn't last much longer with that sort of outflow.

Then he remembered reading somewhere that an injured person could easily choke on their own blood if they were left lying on their backs. He didn't want that to happen on his watch. He carefully positioned the inert figure by bending her right knee under her and turning her onto her right side.

Pulling a bleeding woman about in all her nudity, with all her feminine parts displayed, was not an easy exercise for a lone male to perform. But somebody had to do it. He fervently regretted that he had chosen that moment to walk past this gruesome event.

However, the upside of it was that he could be saving a life, whereas this poor woman may have been left in the care of that drunken idiot who had gone off carrying a gun.

He grabbed a sheet and covered her. That cheered him up a little. At least he was being useful. He busied himself in looking for toilet tissues and handkerchiefs to use for plugging the awful holes that were still oozing blood.

Please come quickly and give me a hand, somebody. I don't want this woman to die on me because of my ignorance of how to save her life.

Was she still breathing? He put a tentative hand on her neck to feel for a pulse. There was something there, yet it seemed very thready. He slapped her face gently. 'Come on, old dear, hang in there. Help is on the way — I hope.'

Then there was a racket as the rescue team first tried to enter the locked door before going to the next entrance and finding their way in.

'Mind out of the way, please,' somebody called out.

Anthony Beecham was only too happy to slide out of the way and leave the medical squad to do their job. There were six of them, and a couple of them looked at him askance.

He put up his hands. 'I don't know her from a bar of soap,' he called out. 'I was merely trying to keep her alive until you people arrived, which, thankfully, you did.'

They were friendlier to him after that. After all, when you're a medical person, dedicated to saving lives, and you arrive at a shooting to find a man covered in blood, with his arms around a badly wounded victim who just happens to be stark naked, you are likely to come up with a first impression or two.

The team was really there to prolong Cora's chances of making it to the hospital before she died, for she was in a really bad way. While they waited for an ambulance to arrive, they did what they could by giving her injections to keep her system going. They also gave her blood plasma to replace some of the volume of blood that she had lost.

The woman was battling for her life when the ambulance arrived, and the attendants hurriedly made her comfortable before they drove her off to the nearest trauma unit.

Meanwhile, Laurie Bridewell and Jason Malvy had problems of their own that they needed to take care of.

***

Jason Malvy struck a new low when he escaped from Cora and Byron Nugent's joint suite. Firstly, he ran out on his naked lover without even looking back. Now that might sound like a stunt that a real low-lifer would pull, but the weapon in Byron's hand cancelled out the seriousness of his misdemeanour almost totally.

Where Jason really acted despicably was to leave Cora in the hands of a drunken husband who had already shot her twice in the back, no matter whom he was aiming for. The least he should have done was to get help fast — medical help as well as security in the form of Bridewell's department.

To be fair to the man, being squashed against a woman's loins, only to hear three, followed by two, shots ring out, and then have one's mistress pour a nearly full glass of whisky over one's head and down one's back before collapsing over one's body, while gushing spouts of blood in different directions, is not conducive to the best of clear thinking.

Frankly speaking, he should have picked up the phone and rung for help, at least, when he unlocked his suite door and blundered inside. But he didn't. He was a nervous wreck by then. All he wanted to do was to wash some of Cora's blood and whisky off his body and try to stop his uncontrollable shivering.

Jason made directly for the bathroom and stepped out of his bloodstained clothing, as if in a trance. He cleaned his teeth to get the taste of blood and of Cora out of it. Then he ran the shower at the highest temperature he could bear, before getting into it.

He suffered the heat determinedly, shocked to see the amount of blood that was running off his body. It seemed to keep on coming. How much of it was there? How much could a human body hold? Had this all come out of Cora? She had bathed him in her blood, and he had run away from her! What kind of man was he?

Reaction was starting to set in, along with the beginning of an awesome feeling of guilt. What kind of man was he, to run away from a man with a gun when this injured woman needed him so much? Then he could feel bile rising into his throat. It was unstoppable. He bent forward, and a stream of vomit shot out of him in a stinking torrent, spattering on the shower floor.

Jason felt better when it was gone. He held up his mouth to the shower rose and washed out his mouth, his eyes closed. Then he opened them to stare into the bloodshot glare of Byron Nugent. The man had pulled apart the shower curtain with the barrel of his pistol, assured that he had this young punk at his mercy.

It had been so easy to find his wife's lover. The first door of the suite had been locked by Jason, but the second door was unlocked. Byron had simply walked in and followed the noise of the shower until he'd come across his quarry, casually showering with closed eyes. What a stupid fool.

The young man was no punk. He was strong and wiry. Instinctively he grabbed at Nugent's gun hand and pulled him into the shower, with all his force. The bigger man stumbled forward, tripped over the lip of the shower, and fell onto the slippery tiles, letting go of his weapon as he did so.

The younger man wasted no time in scrabbling for the gun that had landed somewhere under his adversary. He jumped out of the shower and ran out of the bathroom. In a blind panic, he ran to his clothes closet, not thinking of anywhere else to go. He opened the door and stepped inside, trying to bury himself amongst his sports jackets and suits.

But the closet was not really deep enough for him to lose himself amongst his clothing. Well, he'd given it a try. His life was now in the hands of fate and a maddened husband. He wouldn't bet on his chances right then.

Then the closet door was opened, and his enemy was facing him again but keeping his gun hand out of reach this time.

'You'll not grab my gun this time, you little bastard.' He pointed his weapon at Jason's head. 'Now you'll end up in hell, you wife-snatching creep.'

'Hold your fire, or you're a dead man!'

The loudness of the voice was enough to make Byron Nugent turn his head at the biting command. Laurie Bridewell stood behind him, with his drawn weapon aimed at his head. Jason wasn't going to mess about any longer. He grabbed Nugent's gun arm and pushed it out of the line of fire.

But his attacker kept on turning, and Jason lost his grip on the man's arm. Laurie Bridewell kept a bead on his target, but he was loath to pull the trigger, especially with Jason Malvy in the way and Nugent no longer a definite threat to anyone.

Nugent solved the problem for him. Realizing that he was cornered and outgunned, he made a snap decision. He had a splitting headache. His life was in a mess. Cora must be dead, and he had really loved her more than anyone could ever know. It was time to end it all.

If he had been sober, maybe he would have thought twice about his next action. But his brain was befuddled. He slowly lifted his arm, pointed the gun to his head and pulled the trigger. Jason was covered in another spatter of blood mixed with brains, as the shooter slumped to the floor, but it was worthwhile to see the end of this irrational man, who was clearly stone-cold dead.

There was silence for a while as the echo of the shot reverberated through the suite. The noise rang in their ears, and they stared at each other in stunned silence for some time. Bridewell was the first one to return to the reality of the situation.

'Well, that was lucky for you, young man. He's done us all a favour. You came close to getting the chop then. I must say that you're always involved in some intrigue or the other. And here I was, thinking that I'd been given an easy beat, taking care of a bunch of doddering scientists discussing ways of controlling whales and dolphins.'

He stopped and took a deep breath. The two men stared at each other, both secretly rattled by their recent close encounter with death.

'Shit! I'm tired of the messes that you get me involved in, Jason. And you're covered in blood again. Have another shower and then get dressed. Make sure that you've done your pants up tight, so that nothing obscene is sticking out of them, anywhere. Then get the hell out of my hotel before I help you on your way with a bullet up your backside.' He continued: 'D'you know how much trouble you've caused me with your twitching loins? Find a decent girl and marry her, for Pete's sake. Go after someone who's pretty enough but not beautiful. They're usually a handful, because there are other guys like you who can't keep their hands off good-looking women. Just try to be faithful to her, if that's at all possible.'

Jason couldn't believe that his life had been spared, although he wasn't too crazy about the lecture that he'd just received from Laurie Bridewell, a man he admired. But he had to know how Cora was doing.

'Have you heard any news about Cora's condition, Laurie?'

Bridewell sighed heavily. 'I've just been notified on my walkie-talkie that the medical team has managed to keep her going until the ambulance arrived and took her to the local emergency hospital. They just got her there in time to put her on full-time life support. She's in a bad way, and they don't know if she's going to make it, Jason.'

'Thanks, Laurie, you've saved my life today. I'm sorry about all the grief I've caused you, but I assure you that I'm going to try to keep my pants buttoned up, at least for a long while. I've actually had a gutful of women for a long, long time.

'But now I've got a problem. I've already disgraced myself by running for my life when Cora Nugent really needed me. I feel bad enough about that, believe me. However, I can't run out on her a second time. I must hang around until she is stabilized or not. With her husband out of the picture, I understand that she only has her daughter left as a dependant and next of kin. The young woman is still living at home, and somebody will have to contact her about her mother and father. I'd appreciate it if I could be included in the loop.'

Bridewell stared at Jason, speculatively. 'As a courtesy, I would normally see to it that the hotel would look after the daughter while she's visiting her mother in hospital, at least for a few days. This would be a gratis gesture on our part. If you want to stay here as well, I could organize a single room for you, but you will have to foot the bill for it. Hopefully your sponsors are still up for supporting you.

'I trust that you're not going to pull out anything smart if we include you in the welcoming committee. I'm doing this against my better judgement, you know. This young woman will be in an extremely sensitive state and doesn't need a young and horny buck pestering her right now.'

Jason put up a protesting hand. 'I'm really not as lascivious as you seem to think I am. If you must know, without wanting to speak ill of a very sick woman, Cora was the one who enticed me to her room in the first place. She even confessed, later, that she borrowed certain maps that she knew I would be interested in, and we ended up on her bed, drinking her whisky, with the maps spread out in front of us. One could hardly call that making a move on her.'

'Okay, I don't want to know the intimate details. All I ask is that the girl, whose name is Peggy, by the way, will be treated with decorum and respect while she's staying with us.'

***

After the body of Byron Nugent was removed from Jason's suite, he had another shower — his fourth for the day — which took another solid scrubbing to get rid of the blood and soft brain tissue. A lot of this procedure involved the psychological attitude of anyone towards being sprayed with the spongy material from a gaping head wound.

It was the last act he performed in that particular suite. By the time he finished his shower, the police had arrived and wanted to cordon off his room as a crime scene. Luckily, the friendly cop in charge allowed Jason to pack up his things, under strict police supervision, and moved him to a nearby room on a temporary basis.

Then he drove to the emergency trauma unit that was caring for Cora Nugent. He tried various ploys to get into her ward, but the nursing staff was adamant that she was critically ill and not in any condition to receive visitors.

Even the terms "colleague" and "close personal friend" didn't cut any ice for Jason. The best the staff would do for him was to allow him to view the patient through a window, not that this was much use to him.

'Ms. Nugent is asleep right now, which we are encouraging, to keep down her stress levels so that the body can get an optimum chance to repair itself,' explained the nurse who accompanied Jason. 'I should really let the surgeon tell this to you himself, but the patient's heart and lungs have been traumatized by two separate wounds, and she has also lost a lot of blood. Quite frankly, her condition is in a touch-and-go condition at the present.'

What he could see of Cora was hidden by an oxygen mask and tubes, although the rest of her face looked pitifully drawn. He sadly turned away from the window after handing over a bunch of flowers to the nurse.

'Look, she's not going to see these. Please take them home with you, rather than letting them go to waste.'

He got a sunny smile from the pretty nurse as he walked away. *Here you go, Jason. Can't resist them, can you?* Maybe Laurie Bridewell was right. He drew pretty women to him with his "come on" charm. Well, he'd better learn to cut it out, before he landed up with more tragedy on his plate.

Thinking black thoughts, he walked along the clinically clean, tiled passage leading to the exit. He wondered if he would ever see Cora alive again. Remembering the wizened arm protruding from the crispy, white hospital sheets, with needles and pipes pumping fluids into it, he recalled the fairly plump arm he had stroked and kissed that very morning, before he went down on his knees in front of her.

Would she ever return to being the vibrant woman he had known before? How was her daughter going to accept the critical condition of her mother, as well as her father's death? She would have questions that needed answering. How could he explain to her his part in the drama that might be ending Cora's life?

In fact, what was he supposed to say when she wanted to know his involvement in what had happened? Could he find the courage to tell her of his intimacy with her mother? Would she have any respect for him after that?

Jason climbed into his hired car and drove back to the hotel to find out when Peggy Nugent's flight was due to land, for he'd learned that she had bought an immediate plane ticket to see her mom, after being advised of her life-threatening status.

Chapter Twenty-Four

There was quite a reception committee waiting for Peggy Nugent on her arrival at the airport. Laurie Bridewell was there, of course, flanked by one of his agents, although why two security men were required to escort a young woman to the hotel mystified Jason. Would the Chinese or the Russians find anything sinister in a daughter visiting her near terminally ill mother in hospital?

There was also a young hotel receptionist there, holding flowers as a welcoming tribute. She was frequently commissioned to greet important guests in this way. There was also a nurse present, in case the moment became too overwhelming for the nerves of the incoming passenger.

The driver of the hotel limousine was also available, in his smart uniform, holding up a company welcoming board with the name of the guest prominently displayed, in case the new arrival got lost along the way or forgot her name.

Jason Malvy had been around the block a few times in his relatively short life, yet his jaw dropped open when he saw the young woman coming out of the Customs Clearance section towards them. She was a much younger and prettier version of her mother. There was no need to wave a board about to attract her attention. Both Bridewell and Malvy knew exactly who she was from the moment that the curvaceous woman swept through the exit door.

He remembered that his mouth was hanging open when Bridewell turned to glance at him in a threatening way. No words were required, nor exchanged between the two men. The head of security had successfully handed his message to the young man alongside him, loud and clear.

The newly minted orca expert felt an electric tingle run up his spine. All he wanted to do was to remove her from this group and take her far, far away, where he could get to know her and watch her lips and eyes and jawline moving, as she responded to his senseless chatter. Because he didn't know what to say to her. He simply wanted to be with her. Maybe forever, even if that was looking just a little too far into the future.

The eerie part of it was that he could see her mother hovering in the background. It was downright creepy, in a way. Would the spirit of her mother always be there, if their relationship could — Heaven be praised! — develop in the way that he would like it to go?

And here he wasn't, for one moment, thinking of what her mother and he had got up to together. She was too pure and precious to be approached in such an earthy, physical sense. Then he sensed that Laurie was staring at him again and that his jaw had dropped open once more.

He had come in his hired car, so he had to drive back to the hotel on his own. In some way that suited him, chasing the feathers from between his ears along the way. It was just as well that he was carrying no passengers on his return journey, for his driving was as erratic as hell.

It was hard to imagine that he considered himself to be something of a skilled driver behind the wheel of a car. He certainly didn't fall into that category on this day, if the glares of other drivers were anything to go by.

**

Earlier that day, Jason had become aware that even large and efficient organizations make outrageous cock-ups. And now he was involved with one of those problems. There was a completely new seminar due to begin on the morrow, and the hotel had overbooked its rooms.

To be fair to the hotel management, Jason was part — if not all — of the dilemma. His earlier performance with Cora Nugent, and her subsequent shooting, had caused her and her husband's suite to be closed down as a crime scene and scheduled for a major clean-up, including a fixed carpet removal for the eradication of bloodstains, the repair of a doorjamb and other chips and scrapes involving flying bullets and blood.

His suite, where Janine had blown herself up, was only now being finished off, due to his unwillingness to vacate the suite during renovations. His most recent confrontation with Byron Nugent had resulted in further damage to furniture and fittings, this time on Jason's side of the suite. Only now was his side of the double suite also designated as a crime scene.

Then there was the room where the three foreign dignitaries had come to a sticky end, with their heads being blown apart. The hotel was under distinct pressure, for which it could hardly be blamed.

Of course Jason was not keen to vacate his suite that day, because of his desire to visit Cora Nugent in hospital until her situation presented a definite outcome. However, he felt somewhat better when the accommodation manager told him that they were moving him just a few doors down the passage.

There was a solution of a sort, but Laurie Bridewell had shuddered inwardly when the idea was originally put forward.

The guest room in Jason Malvy's suite would be completely renovated by lunchtime, and the police had cleared it. Why not put the additional guest, Peggy Nugent, in there?

'Are you mad?' stormed Bridewell. 'What about that crazy young Malvy living in the next room? That's really asking for trouble, with a capital T.'

'Relax, Laurie,' soothed the accommodation manager. 'His room is now classed as a crime scene, so he'll have to move out anyway. There's a single room, a few doors down, which is all we've got left. We can move him in there for the time being. 'We'll simply take the key to the interconnecting door away from him. Problem solved.'

But to the security manager, many problems were never solved; they were merely papered over, with the cracks expanding underneath.

In Jason's case, the older man's assessment was spot on. Ever a cautious man, Jason had foreseen possible problems when Janine, his wayward PR lady, was occupying the room next door. Purely as a precaution, he had taken her outer door key to a locksmith and had a duplicate key cut, in case she would ever lock him out of her room.

And nobody knew about it. He was quite prepared to hand over the original key when asked for it, with a completely deadpan face.

Now he chuckled when he heard of management's plans. He would never use the key for illicit reasons — or for what he considered illicit reasons, anyway — but he had hidden it away just in case the time came when he needed it in a hurry. Better the key you know than the lock you don't.

Once Peggy had registered at reception, she smartened herself up a little, before leaving for the hospital in Jason's car.

'Now remember, Jason,' lectured Bridewell, 'you drive her there, you wait around until visiting time is over, and then you bring her back to the hotel. No tricks, please. She will get a nice hot meal, no matter what time you arrive back, which you can share with her as arranged. During the meal, maybe a glass of wine or two, and then escort her directly to her room. Remember, not into her room, if you please. I saw the way you were gaping at her in the airport arrivals area. Won't you ever learn? The girl is grieving for probably both her parents. If you want to do something useful, sort out her funeral procedural preferences, if she's cheered up enough by then. If we try to get the info at the wrong time, it might be harder to get choices out of her.'

'How nice and clinical of you,' muttered Jason to himself. 'I'll play it by ear, old man, but I will be cautious, you can be sure of that.'

He drove more carefully than when he had returned to the hotel. They didn't have much to say to each other at first. Jason was aware that Peggy was psyching herself up for her visit to her mother.

'I don't want to interrupt your thoughts,' he murmured. 'But I want you to know that your mother is in a critical state. I wouldn't like you to expect too much from her on your first visit.'

'So, you've been to see her?'

'I was there this morning. Make no mistake, I'm very fond of your mom. We hit it off immediately at the conference, on all levels. It was distressing for me to see her through a small viewing window, with pipes and machines at all angles.'

'So, you didn't talk to her?'

'No, they wouldn't let me into the ward, mainly because I'm not an immediate relative. But she appeared to be unconscious, anyway. Still, it was hard looking at her in that condition.'

'Why, you're crying!'

'If you'd been standing next to me this morning, you'd probably be crying too.'

'Oh, I'm not a cry-baby.'

'Well, we'll see about that.'

Seeing Jason showing emotion appeared to soften up Peggy, who had shown a reserve up to then, probably a protective layer against what she would have to come up against when confronting her mother's condition.

'How well did you really get to know my mother?'

'Very well indeed. We came from different backgrounds, I'm sure, but there was always a solid level of understanding between us.'

'I can't say I'm too happy about your discussing my mother in the past tense. Do you know that you're doing it?'

'I'm sorry, I didn't realize that I was. Purely a slip, on my part. Seeing her in that state this morning really got to me.'

'I can see that, and you're crying again. Can you see to drive in that condition?'

Jason took out a handkerchief and mopped his eyes before blowing his nose. 'I'm sorry, I look like a proper ninny, but I'm actually a tough guy, you know.'

'I can see that. You're built like one, anyway. The men I know don't cry; they sniff. I prefer it when a tough guy cries now and then, as long as he doesn't make too much of a habit of it.'

'I'll try to control it from now on. Anyway, here we are at the hospital, and I must put on my brave face, for your mother's sake, if for no other reason.'

'Don't worry, my mother will still think of you as a good guy.'

'What makes you say that?'

'Because that's what she says when she talks to me over the phone.'

They were out of the car and walking along the trauma unit's corridor, headed for Cora Nugent's ward. Wheels of worry were whirring in his head.

'How often does that happen?' he asked.

'Does what happen?'

'The two of you talking over the phone.'

'Oh, at least a couple of times a day.'

'So, what do you talk about?'

'You, mostly. Look, we're like sisters — well, almost. Mom tells me nearly everything, and what she doesn't say, I can usually interpret by reading between the lines. For instance, I know that you've been quite naughty together.'

Jason went blood-red in the face. 'I don't know what to say.'

'Jackpot! You walked into that one, but let's leave it there until I've seen my mom.'

They were at the nurses' station by then. They introduced themselves, and a nurse escorted them into the ward where Cora Nugent lay, very much in distress. Her eyes were closed, but they flickered when she heard her daughter's voice.

'How's Mom doing, Nurse?' asked Peggy.

'She has her ups and downs,' said the nurse, rolling her eyes where Cora couldn't follow what she was doing. She got the message across that things were not all that good.

'Is she awake, Nurse? Can she hear us?'

'Let's try her out. Cora, your daughter is here, with your friend, Jason. Can you hear us? Can you say something to them?'

Cora picked up a hand with an IV line plugged into it. Jason shuddered inwardly at how her arm seemed to have withered from that very morning when they had been last together.

'Well, that's a good sign,' encouraged the nurse. 'Let me wet your lips, Cora. Try to say something to us.'

She took a dampened sponge and gently moistened her patient's lips. Cora used her raised hand to grope for that of her daughter, who took the hint and put out her hand for her mother to hold. Then the other hand was raised.

'She's looking for you now, Jason,' murmured Peggy.

Jason moved swiftly to the other side of the bed and gently grasped Cora's hand.

'Now my two loves together,' came a whisper from the stricken woman's lips.

Peggy and Jason glanced across the bed at each other. Now they were both crying unashamedly. It seemed clear that Cora didn't have much longer than a few more minutes to live.

'Must look after her, Jason. Care for her. Marry her.'

Jason stared at Peggy, who was looking as shocked as he. It was so easy to make such a promise when this young woman seemed so kind and gentle. A beautiful young copy of her mother. He actually wanted to hold her in his arms and comfort her, more than he had ever wanted to embrace someone else.

Now he felt Cora's feathery pressure on his hand. 'Promise me.'

The answer poured out of him like pure water from a mountain spring: 'Yes! Yes! I promise. I do.' He felt the pressure again. He looked directly into Peggy's eyes. 'And I mean that, I truly do.'

Peggy was staring at him with her mouth open, when they heard Cora's thready breath:

'My dear Pegs, love this man and be his wife. Promise me you will.'

'I will, Mama, you know I will.'

The pressure of the dying woman's hands fell away then. With all the tubes in their way, the two young people took her hands as if they had been told to. They kissed her cold fingers and then gently put them down again, at her side.

They stood there for a while, with their hands joined across the bedding. Then the alarm started beeping to indicate that Cora Nugent's heart had stopped.

'I'm afraid she's gone,' muttered the nurse. 'She virtually kept herself going until both of you were here. I've never heard a dying wish pronounced like that before. I hope you don't feel too pressured by what she asked of you.'

'Not only do I feel pressured, I feel committed,' answered Peggy.

Jason nodded. 'That was a serious vow that we've just made.'

He could feel Peggy's agreement in the firm grip of her hand, which drew an immediate response from him.

The nurse stood there, round-eyed. 'Well, then, I suggest that you kiss the bride.'

'With pleasure,' agreed Jason, who came around the bed and kissed Peggy, who lifted her face to meet his lips.

'I'm sorry to be nosey,' said the nurse, 'but how long have you known each other?'

'We've just met, an hour or two ago,' smiled Peggy, 'but I feel as if I've known Jason all my life.'

The nurse put an involuntary hand to her mouth. She had a conservative nature, and this unexpected news was a little too much for her to handle right then.

Peggy turned to her mother again. 'Thanks, Mom, for taking care of my happiness with your last living action.'

She put her arms about her mother's lifeless form and embraced her, before moving aside and allowing Jason to follow suit.

'Thank you, Cora, darling, for giving Peggy to me. May you rest in peace, you sweet woman.'

They walked out of the trauma unit, hand in hand, bearing a mixture of sorrow for the passing of Cora, together with a great joy in the knowledge that they had both found a life partner. This could appear to be a blind step of faith, but they had both assessed Cora as being someone with a deep understanding of the human psyche.

***

The couple spoke about the Cora they knew, on their way back to the hotel. Although they had known her from different points of view, there was a strong similarity in the way that they understood her nature. What Cora had made them promise lay between them as an unopened box. Neither of them felt ready to bring up the subject right then.

Jason parked the car, and they announced themselves at reception. The staff was ready for them and had set out a table for two in a secluded area of the dining room. It was to be a candlelit meal, and a complimentary bottle of wine was cooling in an ice bucket.

Once they had settled themselves and placed their orders, Peggy turned to her partner. 'Jason, we've got a tremendous amount to talk about.'

He smiled at her, but his heart was troubled. Was this girl going to be satisfied with some of the answers he was about to give her? There was little point in starting up a binding relationship built on a pack of lies, but certain aspects of his most recent times could sound off-putting, at best. Jason hoped that his recent actions, and obviously his relationship with Cora, would not prove to be dealbreakers.

'Fire away,' he invited, mentally crossing his fingers.

'Well, let's get the most troubling issue out of the way, first of all. This is going to be rather difficult to handle, because we've both made a serious commitment to a dying woman, who is my mother and whom you got to know on a personal level in the week that you were at the conference.'

He had poured the wine, and she took a sip from her glass.

'Jason, that promise I made to my mother was from my heart and in the form of a binding vow. There was an atmosphere in that ward that felt creepy in its intensity. My mother's words reached out to my soul and gripped it. I was permanently bound to my commitment right then.

'Now I've said that I know you through my mother's eyes, but do I? Can I possibly expect you to follow through, regarding your promise, with the same intensity that I've felt in my heart?'

'Yes, you can!' he said. 'I know that we'll be exploring motives and meanings when we get this off our plates, but I've had an upsetting time of it lately, with a pile of problems and unusual situations falling into my lap. Your mom had her problems, as well, and we both tried to settle them in an unusual way. Whatever the rights or wrongs of it, we achieved an instant fast track of understanding between ourselves.

'Getting back to my promise to her, the first reason for my commitment is that I was stricken when I met you at the airport. It was like a loud voice calling to me: "She's the one! Don't let her go!" Now that's never happened to me before, nor even come close to shouting out the score to me.

'The second reason is that I fell for your mother in a strange way. Although we were a generation apart, and she was married — albeit unhappily, according to her — I recognized that, if she were single, I'd pursue her with the intention of establishing a permanent relationship with her.

'I don't know how much you have stood back and examined yourselves standing together, but you are a younger version of your mother. Frankly, I'd be mad not to commit to the vow we made tonight.'

Peggy blushed with the intensity of his words, but she waited until their meal was served and they were alone again.

'What you've said a minute ago was like music to my ears, but there are some things that still trouble me.'

'Let's talk about them.'

'Right. The first thing that you must understand is that my mother and I, having no one else to confide in, were like best friends together. As between many close girlfriends, there were certain personal matters that we discussed, and maybe a few that we kept to ourselves.'

Jason rolled his eyes and took a big mouthful of wine. 'I can guess where this is going.'

Peggy nodded. 'I think you've got the message. As a daughter, as well as a best friend, I must ask you: What were you thinking?'

'You've got a good point there. I obviously wasn't firing on all cylinders. But to defend myself when the other party is not around, Cora told me afterwards that she had borrowed maps that she knew I'd be interested in, before spreading them over her bed. A few glasses of whisky later, we were getting ourselves into trouble.

'Then along came my jealous PR lady — annoyed because I'd spurned her advances — and knocked the hell out of me while your mom and I were lying together. She then rubbed salt into the wound by telling your father a highly coloured version of events. Now that's as straight as I can put it.'

'Why did your PR only give you a hiding? Why didn't she attack my mother?'

Jason shrugged. This was the tough part. 'Because I was lying on top of her at the time.'

Peggy didn't look too pleased at the mental pictures that Jason had created.

'Yes, I got a tamer, watered-down version of the story, although it was essentially the same. But honestly, Jason, how could you have had sex with a woman who was probably lonely and full of drink at the time?'

Jason hung his head. 'Putting it like that, I did turn out to be a cad, didn't I?'

'Yes, I think you did, if you ask me, which you've just done. But what happened this morning? Hadn't you learned your lesson by then?'

'I know now that I shouldn't have gone to her room but remember that I was smitten with her. When I got there, she was dressed in a hostess-type negligee, which turned me on and blew away my inhibitions. She opened it up, and I went down on my knees in front of her, while she held me against her body.' He paused and shuddered. 'It was then that your father blew the lock off the interconnecting door with his gun and came through, drunk and ready to kill. I believe that he meant to shoot me, seeing me on my knees in front of your mom, but he aimed too high and shot her instead. I got up and ran to my suite, but he came after me, determined to finish me off, but he ended up shooting himself in front of Laurie Bridewell, who followed us to my room.'

'And you left her all alone?'

'A passer-by came in, and he was trying to stop her bleeding when I left.'

233

Peggy was crying now, and she pushed her plate of food away. Jason stood up and came around to her side, putting his arm about her shoulder, but the tearful woman shrugged his arm off.

'I was hoping against hope that you came out of this better than you've just admitted you did. It was spineless of you to run away, leaving her to be cared for by a stranger, and leaving her to drown in her own blood like that, after behaving like a porn star in a low-grade movie. Were you not ashamed of yourself?'

Her mascara was smeared, her nose was running, and her eyes were streaming. He tried to help her repair some of the damage, but she brushed him off.

'Leave me alone! I suppose you'll want to comfort me next, by stripping me and having sex with me to make you feel at home and in control, just as you were with my mother. You're proud of your sexual achievements, aren't you? Well, try them on someone else, but leave me alone! I'm not that sort of girl.'

Peggy jumped up from the table without another word, and not even looking at Jason, grabbed her purse and her wrap and stormed out of the dining room. Then she made her way to reception to get the key to her room.

Jason sat at the table after Peggy had gone, picking disconsolately at his lukewarm food. The evening of getting to know each other had gone horribly wrong. Strangely enough, he'd felt a little flicker of self-doubt about his actions, which he had immediately cast away, but he'd not expected such a strong reaction from Peggy. And yet, he could see her point of view quite clearly, now that she'd stuffed it down his throat so forcefully.

He could see that his evening of pleasure, consisting of getting to know Peggy, had been blown apart. If only he had stayed in Cora's room and battled it out with her husband, when the man had stormed in, instead of running away like that. It did seem to be a cruel and thoughtless action, when he saw it through Peggy's eyes.

Now what would become of the solemn promises that the dying Cora had got them to make before she died? Would Peggy think of keeping to her vow? From the look on her face when she had left him at the dining table, he was lower than a leper, in her estimation. He would be prepared to stick to his word if needs be, but he knew that wouldn't be enough to keep their combined commitments alive.

Jason wanted to go to Peggy's room and try to talk to her, but he decided that she had run away to be on her own. It was obvious that she didn't want him hanging about just then. Although he desperately wanted to take the grieving daughter in his arms and comfort her, he decided that it would be better to leave her on her own for the time being.

He could always try to approach her the next morning, to attempt to mend their relationship. In the meantime, she would have had time to reassess her position, after a hopefully restful night. But for now, he would let her know that he was there for her if she needed him, and no more than that.

When he got back to his room, Jason decided to bite the bullet and phone Peggy. She answered with a weepy and throaty voice.

'I'm sorry to disturb you, Peggy. You probably know that I'm in the room two doors down the passage. I don't want to pester you, but I want you to know that I'm here for you if there's anything you might need, or if you want my shoulder to cry on.'

'Thanks,' she said, with a sniff.

'Then I'll say goodnight, and I pray that you'll sleep well. I'll leave you to contact me in the morning, by phoning me on the intercom or merely knocking on my door — number thirty-six — when and if you feel ready for it. For the record, I'm still here to care for you and to help you where I can. I'd love to assist you in any way possible. Now, goodnight and sleep tight.'

He heard a muffled "goodnight," and then there was a click as Peggy replaced her instrument. He put down the phone and shook his head sadly. There would have to be a major change of heart in Peggy's case if they could ever become friends, let alone soul mates, as Cora had wanted them to be.

The current situation saddened him, but there was not much that he could do to rectify the water that had flowed under the bridge. He didn't think that Peggy was the type of woman who would put up with undue pressure on his part. Jason resolved to keep himself available to her but to give her breathing space in the meantime.

Having decided that, the saddened young man went to a bed where he tossed and turned for a few hours before he eventually dropped off to sleep, feeling very alone and sorry for himself.

Chapter Twenty-Five

Jason woke up early the next morning, still feeling downhearted after the previous evening's fiasco, but he was determined not to get too negative. There were still things that needed doing.

Firstly, there was the question of breakfast. He hadn't eaten much the previous day, and he had hardly eaten any of the dinner he had shared with Peggy. But he had told the young woman next door that he would be there for her whenever she needed him. So, he rang room service and ordered a hearty breakfast for himself. That way, he would be on hand if needed.

He was surprised at how much he enjoyed the lavish meal that was delivered to him. The hungry, young man went through potted fruit, breakfast cereal, devilled kidneys and a hearty mixed grill, reinforced by toast and jelly. Then he finished off his meal with a few strong cups of coffee.

The meal seemed to clear his head as well as filling his stomach. He pushed the debris away and contemplated his next move. There was still silence from her. He wasn't altogether surprised by this. Peggy had been through the mill the previous day and had probably slept badly, if at all. So, he decided to make the phone calls that were piling up, while he waited to prove useful or otherwise.

One of the first calls he made was to his home. Luckily, his mother picked up the phone. He didn't feel in the mood to spar with his father right then.

'Malvy residence. How may I help you?'

'Hi, Mom. It's Jason, of course. How are things going? Are you well?'

'Hello, dear. As well as can be expected, being married to a spiteful tyrant. And are you well?'

'Physically I'm fine, Mom, although I'm knee-deep in problems that are mostly self-induced. But don't let that worry you. I'm digging my way out, as usual. So, let's start with your situation. How are you getting on with Dad? Is Aunt Johanna still in hospital?'

'As regards to Aunt Johanna, she's had some bad news. They've found a malignant tumour in her stomach, and they want to operate on her pretty much immediately.'

'That's a shock for anybody to bear. How are you taking the news? Will you still go and live with her?'

'Oh, we're all shocked, as you might expect, except for your big-hearted father, of course. He feels nothing for anybody. As regarding going to live with her is concerned, it might be just the thing she needs, having her sister living with her and doing the housekeeping while she's convalescing. By all accounts, she's going to need a great deal of rest and recuperation for at least a good while. I'm quite prepared to carry the can until she's back on her feet.'

'You've got a good heart, Mom.'

'Jason, we're sisters, and we've always been fond of each other. Johanna would be only too willing to do the same for me, if our roles were reversed.'

'So, what did Dad have to say?'

'Oh, something like I'm willing to play housekeeper for my sister but not for him. He's threatened to lock me in the house to prevent my leaving for Canada, which will be as soon as they are ready to release Johanna from hospital.'

'How nice of him. You know I'm there for you if you need someone to stand up to him when the time comes.'

'Thanks, son. I might have to take you up on that. But now it's your turn to offload some of your problems on a willing listener.'

Jason began to go red in the face. 'Mom, I really don't know where to begin. Before I go on, this is a sordid story that I don't come out of smelling like roses. Perhaps I can simply say that I misbehaved with an older woman who had a strained relationship with her husband. I should never have become involved, I know, but I did. Her husband burst in on us and shot her when the bullets were really meant for me. She was rushed to hospital where she subsequently died of her wounds.'

'Jason, how could you do such a thing?'

'The thing is — I did. But there's a further twist in the tale. Her daughter, who is the most beautiful, sweetest person you could imagine, flew in to see her mother. I took her to the hospital. Her mother's dying words were that I should look after her daughter and that we should marry. She made us hold hands and promise to be joined together.'

'I don't believe it!'

'The point is that I would marry her at the drop of a hat, if I only got half a chance. She really is my type of woman. I'm desperate for her. The problem is that she thinks that I abandoned her mother as she bled copiously, when I ran away from her husband who was waving his gun and wanted to get me.'

'Jason, this is like a Mills and Boone thriller! What has the husband got to say after he apparently killed his wife?'

'He died after putting a bullet to his head, when the hotel security man cornered him.'

'And now the daughter is pinning the blame on you?'

'That's right.'

'I can't say that I really blame her. You are the root cause of a young woman having lost both her parents in a day. I would watch out for her if I were you. She may decide to seek her own revenge from you or do something drastic to herself.'

'She's not like that, Mom.'

'Yes, I can hear that you're really smitten. So now I suppose I must give you some mother's advice? Be there for her, but don't pester her. If she turns her back fully on you right now, you will always remain part of the most tragic day in her life. I can't see her bouncing back from a situation like that.

'What you must do is to woo her slowly and steadily, from now on. Try to get her to understand that you made a couple of bad decisions, which you will always regret, but that you are not really like that. Let her see the better side of you, which I know and love, but which she has yet to discover.

'I really don't know if this will work but try to get the three of us around a table if you get half a chance. Not only will I be able to assess if there's any hope for either, or both, of you, but I can slip in a few subtle good words for you, although surely that won't have much influence on her, coming from your mother. But it's always worth a try.

'My last word of advice is: Keep out of her bed, for heaven's sake, unless she positively drags you into it. And then make sure the door is well and truly locked. And then say, "Thank you for the compliment, but I want to receive my grand prize on our wedding day." That should impress her if nothing else does.

'My very last word of advice is to get your friend Danny to get you what I think they call "Bluestone" in the navy, and chew on it constantly, to kill that urge of yours to bed every fair maiden you come across. Sex is fine, my son, but there are other pleasures in life. Sex is surely messing yours up at this time. Try some self-control, as millions of other good people do.'

***

By the time he said goodbye to his mother and put down the phone, Jason was still reeling from some of the advice that she had given him. Yet he could see the sense in her logic. The hardest thing to do would be to avoid hanging about Peggy like a sick puppy, yet not to avoid her totally.

He was still staring at the phone when it rang. It was Mike Creaser, his dive boat friend.

'Hi, don't have much time to talk. The navy has been tipped off that a pod of orcas is headed out towards one of their ships lying at anchor in the bay, which I understand is one of their latest cruisers. I would guess that your friend Samson is at the head of the pack. The point is that at least one of them is fitted with an explosive device, which is to be planted against the hull of the ship.

'Whenever the instigator can verify that the deed has been done and the device is in place, they will explode the mine, or whatever it is, and one beautiful navy ship goes to the bottom. I don't have experienced divers on board at the moment, so I contacted Danny Foulkes, and he suggested that I arrange for you to join us.'

'I'd love to come along, Mike, but I'm sitting in the Seaview Hotel in Los Angeles, and it'll be hours before I can join you.'

'Not if I can pull a few strings. If there's a base in your area, I'll ask the commander to get a whirlybird to pick you up and take you straight to our boat, even if we're on the way. I hope there's a nice landing patch in front of the hotel. After all, this is a national crisis looming right now. People who won't cooperate are likely to get mud on their faces at a later date.'

'I'll be waiting for you,' said Jason, and they ended their call. He felt the old excitement rising in his throat, at the venture that lay ahead.

Then he remembered the young woman down the hall and his resolve to be on hand for her. Oh, what the hell! This was a national crisis.

He phoned Peggy's room, with his heart in his mouth. A sleepy Peggy answered the phone. She sounded dopey, which was quite right, seeing that she'd swallowed a handful of pills in order to get some sleep.

'Shmatter?'

'Peggy, it's Jason. I need to talk to you.'

'Imina mess. Don'wan to see me likthis.'

'All right, I won't look at you. I'll just talk to you.'

'C'min, then.'

'The door's locked.'

'A tricky Dickie doesn't' have key? Don' b'lieve it.'

Maybe she knew more about him than he thought she might.

'Just be a dear and unlock the door.'

After a short wait, there was a clatter as the key was turned.

'Don' come in yet.'

He waited. 'Okay, now you c'n come in.'

Jason was in for a surprise when he eventually got into Peggy's room. If one looked carefully, one could still see that she was a very pretty woman, but that was only underneath the puffy eyes and blotchy cheeks. Stress didn't treat Peggy in a kindly way. And her carefully groomed hair looked like it had been pulled through a bush backwards.

She didn't help matters by tossing it back and running her hands through it. She plonked herself onto the side of her bed, forgetting to keep her legs together, under her short nightie and wrap. Jason tried hard not to peer, which wasn't easy.

Peggy stared at Jason dimly. He thought that he'd better say what he'd come to say, before she toppled over and went to sleep again.

'Morning, Peggy,' he began.

She vaguely raised a hand in reply.

'I genuinely meant to let you sleep in, and maybe also give you some peace, but something's come up. The navy has contacted me regarding a pod of killer whales headed for an American naval ship that our lovely friends, China and Russia, plan to blow up. They'll be sending a chopper to pick me up, but I don't have the foggiest notion as to when it will arrive.'

'In't there somebody else in the navy to take care o'that? You don't even work for them any more.' Peggy appeared to be coming out of her fog.

'You're right, but the leader of the killer whales is thought to be Samson, the one who's causing all the mayhem along the coast. The reason your mom and I gathered at this conference.'

'Oh, I thought it was to get to know each other more than a little well.'

'Not very funny, Peggy. But I don't want to spar with you. I meant to stay with you and to help you sort out your problems, but now I have to go. I don't want to tell you what to do, but there are various procedures to follow, particularly in the case of a violent death.

'You may as well stay in this room while you're here. I'll ask Laurie Bridewell to look after you, if that suits you, until I get back sometime tomorrow.'

She gave a little sniff. 'I'm not sure that I want to be looked after by you, after the way you looked after my mother.'

'Another low blow, Peggy. Now stop trying to hurt this ex-sailor boy and wish him a safe return by giving him a farewell hug.'

He took a chance and moved forward to give Peggy a quick embrace, to which she gave an automatic half-hearted response.

'Be careful,' she muttered, as he went back to his room.

At least she had held him for a few seconds. Could that be classed as progress?

He rang Laurie Bridewell and explained the position to him.

'Jason, I don't mind riding shotgun for a grieving daughter for a day or so, but don't expect me to sort out your love life for you while you're chasing after a fish or two.'

'Laurie, all I'm asking for is that you put in an occasional good word for me, if the situation comes up. And Laurie, you owe me one.'

'Where the hell do I owe you anything?'

'I'm sure you've heard that if you save a Chinaman's life, you have him around your neck for the rest of your days. Well, you saved my life

241

when the mad husband tried to shoot me, so here I put myself into your care.'

'Bloody chancer!' Laurie said, before he slammed the phone down, but he was smiling, not willing to admit that he had a soft spot for the young man.

***

In the end, the offload went off rather well, although there were moments when Jason had his chills, hovering over a speeding dive boat with no helicopter pad, while the chopper crew slung him over the side and dropped him safely onto the deck, with some good aiming, as the grapnel and basket swung from side to side.

'And they said that diving was dangerous!' he said, as the boat crew disconnected him — prior to a final wave — and brought him into the cabin.

After greetings all around, he put on the gear that had been brought along for him. Everything fitted, for he'd dived from this boat many times before. There was a lot of banter and swapping of news between men who shared a dangerous pastime and accepted one another as they were.

Soon they were approaching their target area, and all those on board began scanning the sea for any signs of a pod of orcas and a large warship. Which one would they locate first? Would they get there too late?

There was a low cloud cover that had developed in their area, which prevented helicopters from joining in the hunt. There was no way that the helicopters could be risked so far out to sea, without refuelling facilities available.

To make matters worse, a sea fog was drifting in, providing a pea-soup effect that made visual sightings from the air virtually useless. As it was, the dive boat crew were going to find it tough enough to identify a pod of killer whales in this sort of weather.

They had an approximate position for the warship, but it was not hanging about waiting to be nailed by an explosive device attached to a pod of orcas sent out by the enemy to destroy it. The captain wisely kept on the move, not wanting to become a sitting target for any group of killer orcas.

A radio signal could be just the marker that the enemy was looking for, as nobody was sure about the technology built into the explosive device they were intending to plant on the warship. So, there was no way that the warship and the dive boat could communicate. It was like two needles in a haystack, moving about while trying to locate each other.

But then, determination, experience and trained eyesight combined to pick out the shapes of the orca pod, as they vented not far away from the dive boat.

Once the group had been sighted, two marksmen brought out their high-powered rifles equipped with special sights designed for these conditions. From then on, they tried to take a bead on the leading orca, which was presumed to be the one carrying the explosive.

What with the distance involved, the swell factor and the combined movement of the orcas and the dive boat, it was an extremely difficult exercise to handle. Captain Mike Creaser dared not approach any closer, for fear of chasing the killer whales away.

'I know it's going to be a difficult shot, guys, but you have to at least make the effort.'

They nodded, sighted on their weapons. 'Right, give us a countdown, so that we can get two shots off each, before they dive.'

The shots went off as one. The orcas dived immediately, without apparently coming to any harm, but keen eyes were watching, using strong binoculars.

'There was a gadget strapped to the head of the one in front, and it seemed to come loose.'

'Yes, I saw it too. It sort of sprang into the air.'

'Me too. It definitely parted from the orca.'

'Well, if it's fallen off, the additional pressure may well explode the damn thing.'

'Let's wait and see.'

'And keep dead quiet.'

They waited for a minute or so before there was a dull boom that emanated through the sound system.

Mike Creaser turned the boat to where the orcas had last been spotted. They did wide sweeps of the area, but the killer whales had fled the scene.

'We're probably wasting our time,' observed Jason. 'If our rifle fire didn't chase them away, then the underwater explosion probably did the trick.'

Mike Creaser agreed with him. He called off the chase. 'I think we've completed the important half of the job, men. We can go home now.'

'What's the other half?' someone asked.

'To blow the brains out of that leading orca that's too smart for its own good,' said Creaser, turning the boat back to shore.

Chapter Twenty-Six

Samson was answerable to no man, or so he felt. He couldn't understand why he was called, without being able to resist the electronic command, to a secluded cove to have gadgets — like the previous explosive — strapped to his head, but once it was in place, he was free to wander where he wished, or so he thought.

When the explosive was dislodged from his head, he felt neither happy, nor unhappy, to lose it, except for the brief pain he'd had to endure when it was shot away from its perch on his body, followed by the pressure of its blast on his body. It was gone, and its weight had been next to nothing, so he went on with his plan of punishing mankind for its cruelty to creatures of the sea.

Then another opportunity was presented to him, along with his willing pod. The navy held an annual rowing regatta to amuse the residents of San Diego, which event it didn't, in its wisdom, see the purpose of stopping this year. After all, it was the navy that was saddled with the duty of keeping America's seas safe for all.

It was to be carried out near the sea wall, for everyone to watch and admire the rowing skills of the fit young men — and also women, of late — who competed for the large and shining trophy, along with a number of smaller ones donated by various sponsors looking for naval business.

How Samson and his ever-increasing orca pod came to be aware of the regatta was one of the mysteries of the sea that scientists were keen to solve. Yet they were a good distance along that route. It had long been established that orca whistles and other calls could be heard many, many miles away. And so it was, in this case. It was not long after the magnetic mine was shot away that Samson decided to visit the festivities.

Of course, nobody took the interest and intent of the Russians into account. It was they who directed the orcas to create mayhem right inside a major American dockyard.

It took only one porpoise or dolphin to pick up increased activity within the naval dockyard and then to relay the news that an event of importance was on the way. All the practice sessions and fitness trials pointed to something big on the horizon. One didn't have to be a naval torpedo scientist to figure that one out.

There were plenty of seamen, in all sorts of small boats and big ships, available to protect the rowers from any sort of attack by orcas or anything else out to prevent the naval competitors from having their fun, along with all the spectators there to cheer on their family and friends.

The problem was that radar and echo-sounding equipment didn't work too well in confined areas, with echoes bouncing off ships and dockworks, and other confusing manmade clutter.

Samson and his followers moved into position with clockwork timing. His mate was at his side, but she had left her baby in the care of his aunts. There was too much danger present to risk the little one, although both parents appreciated their closeness to each other. Occasionally Samson brushed gently against his mate, and the feathery contact was reciprocated.

The start of the regatta was an outstanding success, with fit young men from various naval vessels competing for the glory of their ships and their shipmates. They were extremely able sailors, and there were other categories to compete in, like sailboats and rowing boats and more fancy thin-shelled skiffs like those used by the university students.

Nobody noticed the underwater flurries of movement as the orcas slid along the bottom of the dockyard and positioned themselves for a major onslaught. The condition of the water was dirtier than they would have liked it to be, but they knew that they wouldn't be spending too much time in the position that they found themselves.

They slid along the depths like well-oiled silk, hardly causing a ripple as they moved into position. If some of the sharper-eyed spectators had looked more carefully, they may have discerned the well-disguised black and white shadows moving into position, but they were focused on the daring young men in their boats. So were the designated lookouts.

The sea giants moved in between the flimsy boats and waited for Samson, their respected leader, to give the signal to attack.

The crowd roared, and proud families bellowed their sons and brothers on. There was even a competition for all the female cadets who were becoming sailors, in competition with the men, which the men rather liked, except when they got beaten.

The females were rather good at instrumentation, calculation, map reading and similar courses, proving that women were not as stupid as men thought they were. In fact, maybe they were cleverer at letting the males gloat about how smart they were, while the fair sex was wielding the gentle reins of power.

The relatively shallow dock basin presented no obstacle to the large and shadowy shapes that drifted past the ships, large and small. If there was enough depth to safely dock a ship, then an orca would find more than enough water in which to move about.

However, nobody was paying the water around the ships any attention, although there was plenty of equipment available to scan the water underneath the important hulls of these mighty ships. Even so, no one expected it to be, nor was it meant to be, used in only a few feet of water.

The navy, in all its wisdom, had not thought it necessary to particularly secure the perimeter of the competition area. After all, it was within the dockland of the finest navy in the world, and no one would dare to show themselves in the middle of all these fighting ships. Anybody daring to intrude into these confines was really asking for trouble in a big way.

And the positive attitude was the right way to go. The show went on without any major interruptions, except when a skiff suddenly overturned and ejected all the competitors. And then another went the same way. And yet another one flipped over. What was going on? There were plenty of "oohs" and "ahs" from the crowd, when a few more turned turtle.

Was this a gimmick staged to shock and amuse the watching crowd? A few bystanders decided to let out a nervous titter, simply to show that they were not easily suckered into such gimmicks. But they stopped their laughter when they saw the sea being turned red near the overturned boats.

Sailors who landed in the water simply disappeared, as huge humps appeared from under their boats. Gigantic maws opened, and the unprepared sailors were swallowed or cut in half, without any grace being said. Now the crowd wasn't cheering; it was screaming for something to be done to stop the mayhem.

The only one armed was the starter, who held a pistol that fired blanks. He bravely aimed his weapon at the nearest orca and pulled the trigger. The huge creature was not to know whether the shot fired was dangerous or not, but he settled the matter by cruising over to the trembling starter, who was wobbling in his little rowboat at the sight of the oncoming killer whale.

The immense sea creature gave the craft a solid smack on the side, the force of which tipped the starter into the water and almost immediately into the sea creature's mouth. It soon foamed red. He wasn't going to fire off any pistols after that.

People were helpless, in spite of being in the middle of heavy armament. It takes time to issue instructions to the gun crew of a cruiser, after having them charge to battle stations and put on their anti-flash gear. All this while someone, or a whole team, for that matter, fall out of their bunks to load up the requisite shells and other ammunition of the right calibre.

Then the turret control centre must calculate distances and trajectories, if they are awake and at their posts, and give firing sequences, and then the order given to fire in a dockland full of warships.

The few unsung heroes, who leapt into the water to aid their fellow servicemen, were brave young men, but they were actually no loss to the navy, in the long run. For their idiocy regarding their usefulness under fire in battle conditions would have probably seen them rise in promotion to being in charge of another Pearl Harbour situation, while facing oncoming waves of Russian and Chinese attackers.

Getting back to the horrible conditions of the dockland naval area, most people were glued to their seats, other than mothers of participants, who were holding screaming infants who had been watching their daddies rowing in their boats.

"Look, Oliver. There's your daddy, number three in the second boat. Look, they're catching up to the leader. Wave at him, Oliver, his team is closing up on the boat in front. They could win this! Wave, Oliver! Wave!'

Most of the viewing public was not as chatty as this.

In fact, the newscasters had run out of words. Phrases like "dead heat" and "neck and neck" were becoming embarrassing to use in these circumstances. Even their cameras had mercifully been switched off, "due to technical problems".

Back at the Naval Regatta, where the competition was fast running out of competitors, there was no way to stop the sailors being eaten. The only way was to fish them out of the water before the orcas got hold of them.

Of course, that was easy to say but not that easy to do. In fact, it was later calculated that more would-be rescuers were devoured by the killer whales as they leant over the sides of ships and boats with long poles outstretched and sometimes forgot to let go when an orca started tugging at the body from the other end, than those who were actually pulled out of the water and saved.

And here we're talking about whole bodies — not half-bodies that were left behind after the orcas had removed the section from foot to chest, that was left dangling so invitingly half out of the water as the midshipman clung desperately to the pole or rope that was offered to him.

Some rescuers cheered for themselves and felt exceedingly proud of their accomplishment when they hauled a survivor aboard with only a foot or a leg missing, although two lost limbs sobered the deliverers and brought home the seriousness of the situation.

A loving mother, with her baby in her arms, vaulted over the fencing at the edge of the water, screaming that she had seen her husband eaten alive and that life wasn't worth living for her baby and her any more.

There was a big outcry from the adjacent crowd, but nobody put out a hand to stop her. It was just too damned dangerous. Then up popped an orca and chewed up mother and baby in one satisfying gulp.

Some enterprising camera buff took a couple of good shots covering the one-handed clambering over the fence, the leap, the splash and the swallow. He got extremely well paid by a foreign media group for the sequence. It was a Chinese organization.

One thing about the regatta was that it was self-advertising, as far as the next year's show was concerned. The ticket prices went up and the stands were packed, but then nothing happened of note. Some spectators even went as far as asking for their money back, being most disgruntled when their demands were refused.

A discreet advertisement was placed in the papers, soon after the regatta, calling for navy volunteers to enrol for duties in San Diego naval base. Apparently, many posts were available for those who liked adventure in the navy.

There was a massive outcry from the public when this latest disaster became known. Commands and threats flashed right down the naval chain of command about bringing the orca threat to a close.

Every effort was being made to kill off the local killer whales that were deemed to be the source of all the trouble the navy was having, apart from the usual drama with almost every other nation in the world. If the Russians weren't sending warplanes to overfly naval ships at insulting distances, Moslem terrorists were sending boats out to attack US ships which were packed with high explosives.

And so it boiled down to the president's most recent speech:

"This must stop immediately! I will not allow this mayhem to continue any further. These are our waters, along with the decent and honourable creatures of the sea; not fishy murderers sent out by our arch enemies to plunder our oceans and subjugate our people. This America of ours must remain free and unfettered. We will overcome them on the beaches and in the seas and so on. We will never surrender!"

Aside from what the president had to say for himself, the navy was grimly determined to get rid of the local orcas, once and for all. The naval authorities made plans to eliminate the threat by ship and by helicopter. The plan was to locate the orcas before sending out the helicopters to execute them, in particular the infamous Samson. This ringleader had to be exterminated, at all costs.

Chapter Twenty-Seven

True to his word, Jason was back at the hotel late in the afternoon of the same day that he had left to hunt for Samson and his pod. He first checked in with Laurie Bridewell, before even attempting to find out the score with Peggy. At least he would know where he stood if Laurie laid out the situation for him.

He went straight up to the security man's office.

'So, how did the nurse-maiding go?' he asked Laurie.

'Pretty well, considering. She's obviously pretty cut-up at losing both her parents, and particularly under those awful circumstances, but she made an effort to brighten up, and we got a lot done regarding the sorting out of her parents' estates, in between doing a lot of talking about the situation between the two of you — as well as her future — now that she's on her own. She's resting at the moment.'

'So, where do I stand, Laurie?'

'Just hold your horses. It's not as straightforward as that. You should rather ask where she stands. Forget about your position for a bit and look at it from her side. She's cried on my shoulder, sure, but I'm not going to form a conspiracy with you to get her into a corner and make use of her.'

'Laurie, I don't want to use her. You must know that I'm crazy about her. I only want to avoid shooting myself in the foot by not spoiling my chances totally. If I have to stay out of her way for a while, then I will. But I don't want to lose her because I'm stumbling about like a drunken dodo.'

'Fair enough. Well, if you want my off-the-cuff assessment of the situation, you're still in the dwang, but less so than when we started out this morning. Peggy is a super girl, but she was on the defensive at first, thinking that I was going to talk a hole in her head by telling her what a great guy you are. Which I didn't do, by the way. I'll leave that all to you.

'Anyway, we sparred about a bit before we started relaxing with each other. Then she actually cried on my shoulder, but I'll kill you — I really will — if you repeat half of what I'm telling you.'

Jason nodded his agreement. 'So, what does she think about me right now, then?'

'She was a bit cutting when she agreed to go out with me to sort out the funeral arrangements, which, by the way, are far from simple. We went to the firm of attorneys that the hotel always recommends if someone expires on the property or is asked for a reference. No problem there, but the authorities won't release a death certificate all that easily, because of all the shenanigans that took place on the deaths of both parents. An inquest, as well as an autopsy, will have to be held before a funeral can be held, for both of the deceased parents. That means that there won't be a quick fix regarding the eventual funeral. This, by the way, could act to your advantage, because there'll be plenty of time to heal Peggy's wounds. If you're a nice guy and behave yourself, you may be in with a chance, but only a slim one at this stage, mark you.

'One thing I will say: you'd be dead in the water if it hadn't been for that dramatic vow business that her mother got the two of you to agree to. I'm not a very religious person, but you can go down on your knees and thank Cora for what she did for you then. Every time Peggy feels the urge to shrug you off, that promise of hers to her mother comes back to haunt her.

'Anyway, we arranged the flowers, the preacher, the media announcements and the messages to family. She's opted to have the service in her home town, which is reasonable, considering that most of her family and friends are there. In the meantime, she'll have to decide where to stay while she's waiting for the autopsy and the inquest to take place.'

'Can't she stay here?'

'I suppose so, but it could work out rather expensive, because the hotel is coming to the end of its goodwill trip, so I understand. I don't think Peggy's hard-up financially, but any insurance on her parents' lives will also be held up until the underwriters are satisfied that no skulduggery has been going on.'

'Maybe I can have a chat to Peggy about this.'

'Not a bad idea. Just go easy on her and don't try to force the issue. Remember not to shoot your mouth off about our little chat, even if you have to hear it all again. That sort of discipline is good for all men who want to get involved in marriage, no matter how sweet the woman they choose.'

Jason stood up. 'Thanks for all the graft you put in today, Laurie.'

'It was nothing. Remember that you're my Chinaman, and I'll have you about my neck for the rest of my life, heaven forbid.' He stood up. 'Try to wake up your lady friend now but be gentle with her. And next time I see you, I want you to hand over that gun that I lent you, along with the key to Peggy's room, purely for the sake of decency.'

'I must have expected this from you.' Jason slipped a hand into an inside pocket. 'Here's the gun and the key. Thanks for your faith in me.'

He laughed as he put up a hand in farewell and walked out of the office.

***

Jason let himself into his room with his key. He remembered that he had a secret key to the outer door of Peggy's room, but he dared not use it; certainly not now at this delicate stage of his relationship with Peggy.

He tapped lightly at the door and was slightly surprised to hear a sleepy voice call out from inside Peggy's room.

'Is that Jason?'

'Yes, I've just got back.'

'Come in, then, I left the door unlocked for you.'

At least that showed some sort of trust on her part.

He opened the door and walked in. Peggy was lying on her bed, under a coverlet.

'Hi,' he said.

'Come, give me a hug and let's make peace.'

They embraced gingerly, and he brushed her cheek with his before going to sit in a visitor's chair.

'So, how are you? I hope you're feeling a little better.'

'A little,' she conceded.

'How did things go with Laurie?' he asked.

'Rather well. He's a good sort; slightly gruff at first, until one gets used to him. But underneath that, he's a honey.' She smiled for the first time.

'And he thinks a lot of you but is almost too scared to say it, in case I get the feeling that he's biased towards you.'

He returned the smile. 'You should have been a mind doctor.'

'Seriously, I've been thinking about it. I'm genuinely interested in how the human mind works.'

'What are you doing right now to keep yourself busy?'

'My mom financed me in having a gap year after I finished college. I've been looking around, but I haven't really come up with anything that interests me all that much, quite honestly.' She continued: 'But what have you been up to, Jason? Chatting to my mom on the phone, I learned that you've had a jam-packed career up to now.'

Jason answered: 'Well, for a start, I have a father who thinks that if a young man's not working himself to death, then he's not up to much. As a teenager, I started helping out at the local dolphinarium, and I used the money, that my dad allowed me to keep, to equip myself with diving equipment that, one could say, is my sport. Then my dad upped my board after a couple of years, so I started working for Joe Caldecott, who runs a realty agency. I've done quite well at that.'

'Doesn't one have to study to become a realtor?' asked Peggy.

'Oh, that wasn't a problem,' replied Jason. 'I crammed for that while I was studying at college. My boss, who is a real star, let me work for his firm while I was doing my degree in Business Economics. That put money in my pocket, after paying for my board. After college, I joined the Navy SEALs, just to round off my education.'

'I suppose I shouldn't ask this,' said Peggy tentatively, 'but is your father hard-up, that he tries to squeeze every last penny out of you?'

Jason laughed out aloud. 'The old geezer's stinking rich, and you can see why. It also doesn't help that he doesn't have much time for me. When I left the SEALs a month or so ago, I went back to Joe Caldecott to see if my position was still open. We get on well together, so he'll take me back as soon as the authorities have picked my brains regarding the orca situation. Now the powers that be want me to go on the lecture trail, although it's not really my scene. But when my dear dad heard about Joe offering me my job back, he told him to kick me out, because he had a majority shareholding and overall control of the business originally.

'But Joe had the last laugh. He informed my dad that he now owned control of the business, so it was for Joe to decide to let me stay or have me leave the firm. At the moment, I'm sliding into my old position by picking up all the loose ends and even running the letting of certain apartment blocks.'

'The miserable so and so!' Peggy blurted out. 'Oh, I'm sorry, Jason. He's your father, after all.'

'Don't worry, Peggy. My mom would welcome you with open arms. She's busy moving out of the house right now.'

'Oh, I'm sorry to hear that. What's she going to do?'

Jason grinned widely. 'Well, the joke of it is that the house and a lot of other assets are in her name, for tax purposes, so she's actually sitting pretty, from a financial point of view. She was going to live with my aunt in Canada, but now poor Aunt Johanna has been diagnosed with cancer. Mom's prepared to nurse her back to health, but she will have to sit here for a bit, until the doctors have sorted out my aunt's health.

'Joe Caldecott has found me a super apartment, so there's plenty of room for my mom to stay with me until she settles in Canada. I actually feel a little sorry for my old man in his dotage, but he did bring all this on himself.'

'Joe Caldecott must like you a lot, showing you all that patience while you sort yourself out,' remarked Peggy.

'He's a wonderful guy,' replied Jason. 'I consider him my mentor, along with the owner of the dive boat I went out on today, Mike Creaser. He taught me all I know about diving, and he wants me to get involved with his business; but I can't see myself swanning about at sea for the rest of my life. I think I'm ready to settle down, and being a realtor still gives me scope to enjoy my other interests, while making good money.'

'Wow! Talk about a complex character!' exclaimed Peggy.

Jason put a hand to his mouth. 'I'm sorry, Peggy, I got carried away. When you asked me how I was or something, it made me open the floodgates. The last thing I wanted to do was to overwhelm you with my involved story. Please forgive me. I'm an insensitive idiot.'

'Actually, I'm the insensitive one,' Peggy interrupted. 'I wasn't very kind to you this morning, even when you were trying to be thoughtful. I'm really sorry.'

He decided to take a chance while the going was good. 'Right, if you're really sorry, cheer me up — for some of the damage I've done — by slipping on something pretty and coming to dinner in the dining room with me. But if you don't want to go public, we can have a meal brought in here. Then you can tell me how your day went, because, in my blundering way, I haven't given you much of a chance to talk about your own progress.'

'I don't think that I'm ready to face the world just yet. I can imagine all the patrons and staff coming up to our table and offering their condolences. Let's have a private meal but give me ten minutes to get myself in order, while they prepare the food.'

Jason got the message and left Peggy in peace, while he left her room and ordered their food. He took a chance and ordered a couple of bottles of wine with the meal, because he thought that they both deserved a little unwinding after the tensions that they'd been through.

***

To give Peggy more time to freshen herself up, Jason had the meal served in his room. The timing was good, because she came through just after the meal was served. Jason had also smartened himself up, so they looked quite a presentable young couple when Jason poured the wine and they clinked glasses together.

He couldn't help staring at her. Apart from some dark rings under her eyes, she really looked attractive. In fact, more than attractive. Jason had to remember to close his mouth when staring at his companion, which he found hard to do.

'I'm sorry,' he said. 'I've been known to put my foot in my mouth too often, which is why I tend to gape so much, but you look positively beautiful tonight. I just had to say it, but please believe me when I tell you that I'm not trying to get fresh with you.'

Peggy laughed with a delicious ring in her voice. 'Even if you are, I forgive you. You've said it so beautifully that I must feel your sincerity, although it's a little over the top. If I hadn't seen you pull the cork on the wine bottle, I'd guess that you've had a head start on me. Thank you, anyway, and you look pretty smart yourself, so let's drink to what a pretty couple we are.'

She grinned as she said this, and they raised their glasses with smiles on their faces.

Some meals are better than others, simply because the ambience is good, the wine is fine and the company is heart-stopping. This was one of those evenings that drags one out of the blues if one started with them and lifts one up to the stars if one is already on a swing to pure happiness.

There was a lot for them to get to know about each other. They'd been dropped right into the deep end from the start and would probably have immediately drifted apart if it wasn't for the force of circumstances that had kept them together until then.

Perhaps they shouldn't have started on the second bottle of wine, but they did. They would have finished it too, if Peggy hadn't needed to go to the ladies' room at some point. On her way back to their table, she stumbled as her heel caught on something. She would have fallen if Jason hadn't sprung out of his chair and caught her before she hit the floor.

Then he had her in his arms and held her tightly. She lifted her head, and their lips met for the first time. He felt a thrill run up his spine as they kissed. Peggy responded at first, but then she pushed him away. The magic moment had come to an end. She had recognised that she was tipsy and was almost willing to invite him into her bed.

The wine had also had an effect on Jason. Their kiss had thrilled him, and now he wanted her badly. He looked into her dulled eyes and made the mistake of saying: 'I love you; I truly love you.'

He kissed her forehead, revelling in the very scent of her. He bent forward and kissed her again.

It was too much for her to handle. Thoughts of her dead mother and father came flying back into her mind. Was she that fickle, to already give herself to the man who had been responsible for her mother's dying in such a horrible way? What kind of daughter was she? What sort of hold did this young man have over her family?

Peggy wrenched herself away from Jason's arms and fled down the passage to her suite. He wanted to go to her, to follow her, but he knew that he was far from welcome in her bed, or even in her room, at that moment.

He turned from the table where they'd enjoyed such pleasure together that evening, of sharing and getting to know each other, and he went to his bed with a feeling of bitterness in his heart.

Chapter Twenty-Eight

Jason woke up the next morning, not feeling his best. But he had to get his life on an even keel, even if Peggy was not prepared to stay on board. He phoned Joe Caldecott and left a message on his phone:

'Joe, I'm working through my problems, and I should be signing on within two or three days, at the latest. I'm really keen, Joe.

'About that apartment you messaged to me — I'll definitely take it. It sounds like the sort of thing I'm looking for. You can sign for it on my behalf, if you'll be good enough. I'll take immediate occupation if it's still available.

'I'll be moving my mom into the apartment at first, if she agrees to stay with me for a couple of months. I suppose that you know she's moving out of my dad's house to live with my aunt in Canada, but there's a problem, because my aunt's in hospital at present, being treated for stomach cancer.

'Please leave the keys for the apartment and my car at reception. I'll be calling for them soon. Regards, Jason.'

Next on his call list was his mother. He hoped to avoid making contact with his father, but luckily his mother usually answered the phone.

'Malvy residence. How may I help you?'

Thank heavens she was still answering the phone. 'Hi, Mom, it's Jason, of course. What's the situation between you and Dad?'

'It's pretty grim, Jason. No talky-talky, and he has a bottle with him as a constant companion, which is not usually his style. I'm starting to get fearful of my life, the way the man is ranting and raving throughout the day.'

'Well, I may have a solution for you. Joe Caldecott has found a very reasonable apartment for me, with two bedrooms, and another one that I can use as a study. Please move in with me until your situation with Aunt Johanna has sorted itself out and you can transfer to Canada.'

'Oh, I don't know about that, Jason. I don't want to be any trouble to you.'

'Trouble? I'm banking on your help to sort out the place for me. It's no fresh news that I'm not the most domesticated guy in the world. Please don't let me down. You know I can't handle this without you.'

'Well, if you're sure I'll be no trouble…'

'I'll be collecting you about eleven o'clock tomorrow morning. Look out for me. I'm not scared of the old man, but I'd like to avoid a confrontation with him if I can help it.'

Now, if he could only sweet talk Peggy into cooperating with him…

Maybe he should try a little more devious angle this time. The soft and gentle and loving way didn't seem to work too well. Maybe he should try a little pushier approach.

He tapped on Peggy's door. No reply. He knocked harder. Still silence. He thumped on the door a few times.

'What on earth? Are you mad or something? It's still the middle of the night.'

He'd really taken enough shit from this woman, beautiful or not. 'If you had to open your bloody eyes, you'd see that it's actually morning, when normal people start their day.'

'All right! All right! Come inside and tell me what's bugging you, then.'

He opened the door to find Peggy still curled into a ball under her sheets.

Be bold, my friend, be bold. He lifted the lump where he thought her head should be, and he was right. He planted a kiss on top of the dark curls.

'Good morning, bright eyes. You're definitely not a morning person, that's for sure.'

'So, what's it got to do with you?' she grunted. 'You fed me with too much wine last night, and now I've got the mother of all headaches.'

'Shame. I didn't force it down your throat, did I?'

'Maybe not, but you kept on pouring.'

'How was I to know that you can't handle alcohol?'

'Well, you're finding out all right, aren't you?'

'I give up. And to think I had something serious to discuss with you.'

That brought out her head from under the sheets. 'Like what?'

'Are you sure that you're awake now? You still look bleary-eyed.'

'You want to see what my eyes look like from this side, buster.'

'Oh, bugger it. I give up.'

'Well, don't. That was only a little joke. Where's your sense of humour in the mornings?' She dragged herself upright. 'All right, now you've got me up. Tell me what's so important that I can't sleep for another ten minutes. And where's my morning kiss, anyway? Do you only do that sort of thing at night?'

He shrugged. *Never miss a good opportunity*. He leant forward and kissed her firmly. It was delicious, even though her winey breath was mixed with a heavy layer of onion. Guess who hadn't brushed her teeth before falling into bed the night before.

'I want another one,' he declared.

'Only if you let me sleep for another ten minutes... no, make it a quarter hour.' She puckered up her lips, waiting to keep her end of the bargain.

***

He gave her a full half hour, ordering breakfast for both of them and having a shower while he waited. The extra time didn't help that much. Jason still had to drag the sheets off Peggy to wake her up. The only advantage was that he did see a lot of beautiful breast when he pulled too much sheet off her.

She grabbed the sheet back to cover her partial nudity, and he pretended that he hadn't seen anything, but they both went red in the face before he announced that breakfast was ready and walked out of the room to give Peggy some privacy.

After a shower, and wearing clean clothing, the young woman looked sad-eyed but appealing. Jason thought that even if she was wearing old jeans and covered in a layer of dust, she would still look lovely. He was more than prepared to overlook her swollen eyes and drawn face.

When they sat down to their breakfast, he took the bull by the horns.

'I think you're looking beautiful, but then maybe I'm just biased. What are your plans for the day?'

'Nothing, really, and thanks for the compliment. You don't look all that bad yourself.'

He smiled in response. 'And thank you. Have you seen to everything that you wanted to do yesterday?'

She nodded as she buttered a piece of toast, tears forming in her eyes. 'I'm done here, but I may as well stay for the autopsy and the inquest, if it isn't too drawn out.'

Jason nodded. 'I'm in a similar position as a key witness, but I do have a problem.'

'What's that?'

'Actually, two problems. The first one concerns my mom. I told you that she and my dad are splitting up, after years of marriage. He's a proper ogre, and she was really waiting for me to find my feet before moving out. She's going to stay with my Aunt Johanna in Canada, but the poor woman first needs to undergo an op for stomach cancer. My mom will then be willing to look after her.'

'She sounds like a sweet lady.'

'Oh, she is.'

'But you told me most of this last night.'

'Sorry, I must have been tipsy. But I need to transfer my mom to my new apartment, where I want her to feel necessary and helpful. Would you come with me and help me to make her comfortable in my new pad?'

'I don't know. When would that be?'

'What about right now? She's actually expecting me at around eleven this morning.'

'You must be joking,' Peggy exclaimed.

'No, I'm not. It's not much more than a hundred miles from Los Angeles to San Diego. We could be there in a couple of hours if we hire a car that you can use to get about in. Or else we could fly, but I think that hiring a car for you is a good idea.'

'And what happens to me when I get to San Diego?'

'Hopefully you'll be able to help my mom move in with me temporarily. If you feel comfortable about it, you can move in as well. There are three bedrooms, and Mom will definitely play shotgun over me while you're with us, so there'll be no hanky-panky between us, if that concerns you.'

'Why can't I merely stay on my own somewhere?'

He stared at her with all the seriousness that he could muster. 'Because I promised your mother, on her deathbed, that I would look after you, even when she half expected me not to do that after letting her down so badly.'

'Don't bring that nightmare scene up again. I prefer to forget it.'

'That's your prerogative. But we did both make a pledge, even while we were holding hands.'

She shuddered at the memory of that emotional scene. 'Let's leave that for a moment. What about clearing up your other problem?'

He sighed then took a deep breath. 'I've told you more than once that I'm crazy about you. But I've decided to let you make up your own mind, regarding your feelings. The only thing is that I don't know where I am. Last night, as with the night before, you dropped on me like a ton of bricks. Yet, in the morning, we were back to a friendly basis. I don't know where I am with you, Peggy,' Jason explained.

Peggy shook her head. 'You're not seeing things from my point of view. Jason, I like you a lot, and I'd feel far more relaxed with you were I not thinking of my mother. Her experience with you was the root cause of her losing her life. How do you think that affects me? My parents are standing between us right now. Until their images fade into the background, you're going to have to put up with my on-off feelings.'

'All right. But does that mean you'll still help me out with my mom?'

'Yes, I suppose so, but the whole situation seems a little fishy to me. It sounds as if you're moving me into your apartment on the pretext of helping out your mother.'

'Peggy, other than a couple of kisses — which I quite frankly found irresistible — I've not laid a hand on you since we've first met, not so?'

In both their minds flitted the first kiss that had sealed their promise to her mother.

'You'll be quite safe under my roof, especially with my mom keeping an eye on me. She wouldn't allow me to take liberties with you while she's about.'

Peggy shrugged her shoulders. 'Okay, if your mother doesn't mind having me hanging about your apartment, I'll keep her company for a few days, if that suits you.'

'Well, then, don't come too close to me. I might kiss you by mistake.'

'Very funny.' But it did make her grin.

They settled their accounts and said their goodbyes to the hotel staff who had been especially kind to them. They made a special trip to Laurie Bridewell's office to thank him for his help. He was not too shy to give both Peggy and Jason a great big bear hug.

There were no specific lectures, but he raised his eyebrows when he heard that Peggy was going to stay in Jason's apartment for a while.

'Remember what I said to you,' he muttered to Jason, before the couple left the hotel.

Of course, they were hardly around the first corner when Peggy wanted to know what Laurie had said to Jason.

'Essentially, he knows my feelings for you, but he said that I should go very easy on you and let you take things at your own pace, no matter how long it takes. And I'm doing that, aren't I?'

'Apart from your peeking at my boobs this morning.'

'Peggy! You've got to know that was an accident.'

'Yes, I do. I'm just teasing you a little. But did you like the look of them?'

'You didn't need to ask, did you now?'

'Just checking, that's all.'

***

It was good to get away into the sunshine, away from the hotel that held so many memories for both of them. They slowly began to find out what their outside interests were and what opinions they held between women's fashions and the latest sports scores. It was if a cloud had lifted off Peggy's shoulders, as she left the place behind where both her parents had died or been mortally wounded.

They stopped for milkshakes, colas and burgers, being tired of the rich hotel food they had been living on. Grabbing on each other's straws and stealing mouthfuls of cola caused the drinks to foam up all over their clean shirts, making a mess of the pristine cleanliness of the hired vehicle they were travelling in.

'You're going to have to clean up this car before I'll drive it,' threatened Peggy.

Jason grabbed her and licked along her neckline. 'You've spilled some drink. I'd better clean it up first.'

She pulled away as the car swayed all over the road, causing a few road users to sit on their horns because of his erratic driving.

Peggy shuddered. 'Why did you lick my neck like that? Now you've made me all sticky.'

He grabbed her again. 'Then let me lick it clean.'

'Why, you dirty beast. You've got some on your face.' She leant across and ran a very wet tongue across his cheek. 'There. Does that feel better?'

He wiped at the smear with his free hand. 'Yegh! Your spit is slimier than that of a Boxer dog.'

'Well, you seem to enjoy it, because you like to kiss me, so here's some more.' She grabbed his chin with both hands and stuck her tongue into his mouth. 'There! Does that taste like a Boxer's kiss?'

Jason pretended to drool. 'Yes, give me more. It's so refreshing.'

'You're not supposed to like it, silly.'

'But I do, my cute little Boxer.'

'I think you're sick to want my spit in your mouth.'

'Just do it once more, for the last time.'

'Okay, but no more after this.'

'Then really make it a specially wet one.'

It all sounded a little sickening, but they actually enjoyed their horseplay while it lasted. Afterwards, they held hands and were dead quiet as they felt the increased beat of their hearts.

They first went to Jason's realty firm, where he picked up his apartment keys and his car keys at reception, remembering to get the address, as he'd never seen the place before. He drove to the apartment in his car, with Peggy following on behind. To make room for Mathilda's suitcases, they unpacked their belongings from Peggy's car and lugged them to the elevator.

'Luckily we don't have to heave these cases up the stairs, because we're on the eighth floor,' he mentioned to Peggy.

'You can say that again,' she remarked.

'Luckily we don't have to lug these cases up the stairs, because...'

'Oh, shut up, funny man.'

Peggy was quite impressed with the view over the leafy park across the way, when she stepped out onto the patio. 'This is a pretty fancy apartment block,' she said, coming inside and strolling through the place.

Jason went with her. It was all new to him as well.

'This must be costing you a fortune,' Peggy commented.

'Well, it's not cheap, but Joe Caldecott, my friendly boss, knows the owner of the block and got a special rental for me, seeing that we do lots of extras for him. And it's fully furnished, which saves me a lot of money at this stage, and a lot of time spent in running around, choosing new stuff. There's also a communal swimming pool and barbecue area, which I could really make use of when I get the chance.

'Then I'm also doing well lately, with my lecture fees and my realty commissions rolling in.'

'You're going to make some girl a lucky woman.'

He stared at her seriously. 'Yes, please,' he said.

She blushed and turned away, at a loss for words.

Before they left, they switched on the utilities and locked up, before driving off in Peggy's car to pick up Jason's mother.

When they were a few streets away from Jason's parents' house, he phoned home, switching on the loudspeaker system. His father answered, for a change.

'Hi, Dad, it's Jason. How are you?'

'It's for you, Mathilda!' the crusty old man called out, without any greeting.

Jason and Peggy looked at each other with open mouths.

'Now do you believe me?' asked Jason.

Peggy shook her head in wonder.

Mathilda Malvy picked up the phone. 'Sorry about that. Is that you, Jason?'

'Yes, Mom. We're about two blocks away from the house. I've brought Peggy with me.'

'Wonderful, son. I can't wait to meet her.'

'Well, don't let Dad get her on his own, if you can help it.'

'I'll do my best. I'll be waiting for you on the front step.'

When they pulled up outside the house, Mathilda was true to her word and was waiting for them. She looked forlorn, standing in front of the great front door in her grey and black outfit, like an overgrown mouse. Peggy obviously didn't know her, but she felt sympathy for her already.

Jason popped the lid of the trunk and jumped out to take his mother's cases. His father was nowhere to be seen, but Jason didn't want to hang about until he put in an appearance. He didn't trust the man, with all his mood swings.

He gave Mathilda a hug and a kiss before taking her cases from her. Peggy got out on the passenger side, leaving the door open. She met Mathilda as she came down the stairs.

'Hello, Mrs Malvy, I'm Jason's friend, Peggy.'

The two women clasped gentle hands while Jason packed away the cases in the trunk.

The older woman made for the rear seat of the car, but Peggy had the front door open for her.

'Come and sit here next to Jason,' she said.

'That's all right, my dear. It's very sweet of you to offer, but I'm quite happy in the back. I don't want to split up such a fine couple.'

For all her mousy image that she generated, Matilda Malvy was a woman who usually chose her words wisely. A lot of what she said had various nuances that could be interpreted as one who chose to follow them. She was adept at her verbal intrigues, that flowed from her like spring water from a fountain.

As they pulled away from the front steps, Mathilda could see an upstairs curtain move.

'There's your father, checking to see that I'm not absconding with too much of the family silverware. Let's all wave and give him a send-off.'

They all gave an exuberant wave, and the parted curtain dropped back into place.

'I know that was naughty of me, but I couldn't resist it,' declared Mathilda, as they sailed around the corner, losing sight of the imposing house. 'Peggy, that's the first black mark that you can chalk up against me. Everybody thinks that I'm so staid, but I have a wicked little monkey inside me that occasionally prods me into doing unbecoming things, for an old lady who is, most of the time, expected to be so stiff and correct.

'So, my first apology to you is on behalf of my son, who inherited the trait from me. His father wouldn't say "boo" to a goose, until he gets to know you. Then you'd better watch out for his forked tongue.

'By the way, maybe I shouldn't ask, but why are your faces so sticky? Don't tell me that you've been licking on each other? Jason and his little cousin both hated being licked, so they did it to each other more often than not. I used to make them mad by calling it their first kiss. By the way, she was a girl, last time I saw her. One can never tell, these days.'

Peggy was having quiet hysterics in the front seat, eventually choking on her own saliva.

'I thought so!' exclaimed Mathilda.

'Stop it, Mom, can't you see she's choking?' said Jason, bringing back an arm to thump Peggy on the back.

'I'd bang her back for her, but it won't be half as nice as coming from you.'

'Now you're really stirring, Mom,' admonished Jason, in a pseudo-stern voice.

'Sorry, Jason, sorry, Peggy,' but the giggle she gave spoiled the apology.

To change the subject, Jason suggested that they stop off at a supermarket and stock up on groceries. He had noticed that someone at his firm had bought basic provisions like milk, bread, spreads and jellies and dairy products, but there was much more that Jason needed to provide for.

They went shopping with a sense of glee that youngsters would display if they'd been given carte blanche to spend what they wished, on whatever they liked. By the time they returned to the car, with heaped trolleys, they had to squeeze the foodstuffs in between Mathilda's cases, leaving her bunched up on less than half of the car's rear seat.

There was a lot of carting and unpacking to do when they arrived at the apartment, although Peggy and Jason remembered to wash their faces first. Jason asked Mathilda to set out an alfresco lunch on the patio, seeing that it was such a beautiful, sunny day. When they had finished moving the cases and packages upstairs, Jason let his mother have first choice of bedrooms, followed by Peggy.

'Why should you be the last one to choose a room?' asked Peggy, trying to be fair regarding Jason's choices.

'There's actually not much difference in size. With my being here, next door to Mom, she can keep an eye on me, to make sure that I behave myself — at least some of the time — and don't lick your face too often,' replied Jason, with mock seriousness.

'At least you have a little patio,' observed Peggy, wanting to change the subject.

'That's the whole point,' retorted Jason. 'If I come home late without any good excuse, I can climb up here without using my key or needing an alibi.'

'Do you realize what floor you're on?' asked Peggy.

'Oh, thanks for telling me. I may have got hurt if I forgot my key.'

Chapter Twenty-Nine

Jason was positively drooling for a good old Irish stew, the way his mother used to make it. The hunger for a meal consisting of rich chunks of juicy lamb mixed with an assortment of vegetables and potatoes, all on a bed of steaming rice, must have been accumulating somewhere in his body, as an alternative to all the fancy meals that he had been fed of late.

The thought of it had caused him to ensure that their purchases included all the ingredients for such a meal. When he mentioned his crying need for this hearty plate of food, his mother immediately stepped up to the plate.

'Then I'll make it for us, dear,' she offered.

'No, no, Mom, you know that I love your cooking, but I want this to be the opening salvo of many great meals made in this apartment. Please, ladies, don't be offended, but find something to fix, or to do, while I carry out my labour of love. As some great man said the other day: "I have a dream."'

He was in the middle of cutting, chopping and scraping when his mobile phone rang.

Jason tucked it in under his ear while he peeled potatoes. 'Jason Malvy speaking.'

'Hi, Jason, it's Laurie Bridewell. Are things going well? Are you looking after your little Peggy?'

'Like the precious jewel that she is.'

'Ugh, young love can be sickening most of the time.'

'So, is that what you called me to find out?'

'No, actually it's quite important. Our computer boffins have managed to crack the code of the gizmo that's driving your orca, Samson, into the anti-human frenzy that he's in right now.'

'So?' queried Jason.

'Well, now they can pinpoint exactly where the beast is at any given time,' Laurie replied.

'But how does this affect me?'

'They want to put an end to all the drama that Samson's been creating. Questions in the house and all that, you know. So they want to send out a team to execute the bugger with a new gizmo carried by a helicopter, and they want you to be present, just in case.'

'Isn't that going to be simple enough?' asked Jason.

'In politics, nothing is simple. They want to retrieve the Chinese device that the Russians have planted in Samson's head, and they also want to examine the rest of him, including stomach contents, at the same time.'

'Only I can't help them there.' Jason continued preparing his meal as he spoke.

'They want you there more for insurance than anything else. You know, if something goes horribly wrong, they can blame you or someone standing next to you.'

'Okay, how do they intend keeping Samson afloat after they execute him?'

'There'll hopefully be a suitable boat standing by in the region. It will tow the orca back to harbour, where they can examine it thoroughly, after pumping it full of air to keep it afloat, as well as using airbags.'

'They'd better be prepared to deal with a counterattack by the rest of the orca pod,' said Jason.

'They'll be ready for that. Also, in defence of any creature trying to take bites, or equipment, out of Samson after he's dead.'

'Are we going to be armed, in case we need to get involved?' queried Jason.

'Oh yes, and suited up too, in case you've got to go in. The navy is not messing about with this one. By the way, you'll have company. Danny Foulkes will be there with you, so he can report any last words from you if you get creamed.'

'How charming.'

'You know the navy. Ready, down to the last man; and him too, if necessary. They'll be sending a car around to pick you up at four o'clock. At your new address. Not at some chick's place, where you were supposed to have landed up by mistake.'

'That wasn't my fault. I was on a leave break, and nobody notified me that I was on call. Anyway, that was years ago. I was only a little bit tired and fell asleep, that's all. How did you find out about it?'

'In her bed, wearing her panties? Come on. We know all about you, buddy. If you get an itch in your bum, it's because we're in there, keeping an eye on you,' exclaimed Bridewell.

They rang off, and Jason went through to the women, who were sitting on the balcony and taking a breather from chores, while they sipped sherries and watched the sunset.

'Ladies, I've got a spot of bad news for you. I've just had Laurie Bridewell on the phone, telling me that the navy wants me for an exercise tomorrow morning. They'll be picking me up at four bells, and I need to get my equipment together and get some sleep, if I'm not going to fall out of the helicopter I'll be sitting in. He shrugged his broad shoulders. 'I'm sorry to have to bail out like this, but I'd be grateful if somebody would take care of the half-made stew while I put my head down and get some sleep. I'm useless without it.'

'Don't you want to eat something?' asked his mother.

'No thanks, I wouldn't like to have it come up and say "hello" in a few hours' time. I'll be all right, I promise you.'

'Isn't it a little mean of the navy to drag you out whenever they feel like it?' asked Peggy.

'Pegs, I knew all about this when I enrolled in the SEALs. If they need you, they can make the call, even if you need a walking stick to get around. It's like wartime. If you're under attack, you'd better do something about defending yourself and your loved ones, whether you're off-duty or not. And you don't get paid for the overtime, either.'

'Well, go and have your sleep then. Luckily for me, I'm busy pumping all the information I can get about you out of Mathilda. I could write a book about what you got up to as a youngster, up to not so long ago. Sleep tight, and please wake me when you get back, no matter what time it is. And don't try to climb up onto your balcony from outside.'

Peggy raised her cheek in the obvious expectation of a goodnight kiss. He didn't waste time. First, he pecked at his mother's cheek, then he kissed Peggy's cheek, and then he finished off by turning her head and planting a loving kiss on her full lips. It was returned generously.

The watching Mathilda had to say something: 'At least it wasn't a wet lick this time.'

They all laughed as Jason bounced away happily.

After he'd assembled his gear, he climbed into bed and lay there for a few minutes, thinking about the past day. It had gone much better than he had expected it to go. It was clear that Peggy and his mom got on well together, which promised well for the future.

His relationship with Peggy had also gone well, although it was possibly more fragile than it appeared to be. At least there had been no unpleasantness between them, yet this could also be a sign of them getting to know each other and being more prepared to make allowances for each other, in the short time that they had been together.

It seemed that they were both forthright people who could be headstrong when they felt it was called for. He would go out of his way not to put her back up unnecessarily. She was irreplaceable. He couldn't lose her, whatever happened. Peggy wasn't merely a gorgeous woman; she was his life.

***

'How're things with your new chick?' bellowed Danny, above the ear-blasting whup-whupping of the rotor blades above their heads.

'Great,' shouted Jason, 'but don't refer to her as a chick. She doesn't like that sort of talk. Her name's Peggy, and hopefully, you'll watch us getting married one day.'

'And you've known her for how long? A week? Is she aware that you were screwing her ma? Even up to the time of her being shot? Is she happy with that?'

'Come on, Danny. She and I haven't used those terms.'

His friend grinned. 'Did you explain exactly where your head was when her old lady took a couple of bullets in the back by mistake?'

Jason shook his head in irritation. 'Now you're just trying to rile me. Peggy and I are still trying to find each other, even though we started off on the wrong foot.'

'If you only started off on the foot, you wouldn't have a problem.'

Jason had been irritated enough. 'Okay, buster, how's your head healing? Isn't the navy worried that your brain could have been infected? With that greyish ring around your head, you should have joined a monastery, but maybe they were scared that you'd go off half-cocked.'

Danny had stopped smiling by now. 'Okay, let's change the subject. I can see you're getting tetchy.'

Just then the pilot called out: 'Right, men, we're coming into range, according to this fancy direction finder. Take your positions.'

Although some of them were dressed in diving gear, they were all armed. The navy wasn't going to let this opportunity slide away if they could help it. The helicopter was tremendously fast and equipped with the new silent blades. The beeping indicator pinpointed the pod of orcas exactly.

The killer whales dove under the water when they eventually heard the racket above them. This had been anticipated. But their leader, with his homing signal buried inside his body, had to come up for air, sooner or later. The chopper simply cruised above the slowly moving signal until the orca was forced to come to the surface.

While they waited, two marksmen, each with a cumbersome-looking weapon that resembled a rocket launcher, aimed at the approximate position, and waited.

Then Samson and his group rose to the surface — more or less together — but the marksmen weren't interested in the others. They both fired their weapons at Samson, who took two tremendous blows from the rocket-propelled projectiles. He rolled over slowly in his death throes, and Jason was certain that the king of the seas stared straight at him with a look of deep sorrow, before his eyes closed forever.

Further missiles were fired at the stricken creature, shooting out a gas which rendered the carcass unsinkable, by inflating it greatly. The orca was dying, and nothing could save it. It rolled over as its life ebbed away. The rest of the pod could do nothing for their once-great leader. They scattered and went on their way, including the grieving mate and her baby.

The chopper hovered near the orca until a whale catcher appeared over the horizon, sent to bring the carcass back to shore for dissection and analysis. There was a strong interest in the device embedded deep in the killer whale's brain, which was obviously a new form of controlling device. The United States Navy would dearly like to examine it in great detail.

Both China and Russia had made half-hearted protests about America interfering in a scientific project of theirs, designed to improve fish-farming methods, not that anyone took much notice of them.

What did raise concern was the news that a Russian ship was steaming in their direction, in an attempt to pull off a cheeky retrieval of the carcass. But they were trumped, for once, when a nuclear sub rose out of the depths to protect American waters.

The standoff was carried off like clockwork, and the chopper was able to return to base after the killer whale was taken aboard the whale catcher. The ship was escorted back to shore with great ostentation.

The crew of the helicopter was pleased with the success of the mission, although Jason wondered whether his presence had been truly necessary. He was saddened to see the ignominious end of such a magnificent beast, but there really had been no future for Samson. He wondered what would become of Samson's little calf.

Danny and he parted as friends after their trip to sea. They had rubbed each other up the wrong way, but that's what mates do from time to time. All was forgiven, if not entirely forgotten. In fact, Danny suggested that they go for a celebratory drink with the rest of the crew, after which he would give his friend a lift home, but Jason declined.

He could picture himself rolling home, stinking of booze and with a skinful under his belt, on the first night that his mother and his lady spent under his roof. Maybe he was slowly learning relationship skills. He was not to know how soon this conservative approach would pay off.

After being dropped off at home by the official naval car, he let himself in quietly, using his door key. It was eleven in the morning, and he was surprised that neither his mother nor Peggy was up and about.

Maybe they had sat up late and got to know each other while he wasn't in the way, he reasoned. Yet his mother was one of the old-school type, who believed that it was slothful to be in bed after six or seven in the morning.

The place felt like a morgue. Keeping out of Peggy's room for the time being, he tapped on his mother's door and opened it when he got no response. It was empty. Surprised, he then went to Peggy's room, but she was not there either. They were both gone. He checked his cell phone for messages and then found that he'd missed an earlier one.

"Pse call me Json. Big trble. Peg."

Her cell phone number was on display. He rang immediately, fearing the worst, but not quite sure what it could be.

Peggy answered immediately. 'Jason, there's been some drama and your father had a fall, but your mom and I are all right. Please come over to your parents' house as soon as you can, and I'll fill in all the details. Hold the questions until then. Please don't speed to get here. Be safe on the road. I'll see you later. All my love.'

She clearly didn't feel like talking on the phone and wanted him to come over as soon as possible.

Jason took his car keys and drove to his parents' house. As he came down the street, he could see that there was activity in front of the place. An ambulance was parked on the pristine lawn in front of the main entrance, where no vehicles were normally allowed. Jason's father abhorred tyre tracks in the lush grass. That was a bad omen in itself.

In the driveway stood two police cruisers, with their warning lights still flashing. Now he was really anxious, and all his internal alarm bells were ringing in his head. He parked next to them. A uniformed police officer ran up to him with an authoritative hand in the air, but Jason wasn't easily put off by officious people.

He got out of his car and stared at the oncoming cop. 'You got a problem, Ossifer?'

'You can't park here. This is reserved for police vehicles only.'

'Well, don't tell that to my dad. He's been paying rates on it for years now.'

'I was instructed to keep this area open for official vehicles only.'

'They didn't say a word to me, I assure you. They must have forgotten to let me know.'

He used his remote to lock his car and moved towards the front door.

The cop ran after him. 'You can't go in there. It's an accident scene.'

'Come on, Officer, give me a break. It's my family home.'

Seeing that he'd met his match, the cop backed off, shaking his head wearily.

Jason opened the great front door and stood looking at the scene at the foot of the grand staircase. Everybody seemed to be there, including his mother, Peggy, and a few cops he recognized from his recent interrogation and incarceration.

'What's going on here, Mom?' he asked, not recognizing the well-wrapped figure on the gurney, lying centre stage in front of the onlookers.

But Mathilda was being interviewed by one of the detectives who had given him such a hard time some months before. Peggy took his arm and moved him to one side.

'Hi, sailor, glad to see you're home safely.'

They kissed, as if it were quite normal for them to meet in the middle of the morning at an accident scene at the foot of the stairs in his family home.

'What happened, Peggy?'

'We came back here to pick up a whole stack of things that your mother forgot first time around. She was hoping to use her key and take the stuff without any fuss, but your father was waiting for her. There were some sharp words passed, and your mother went on filling the bags she had brought along for her things, as if his ranting was like water off a duck's back.

'Getting no positive response from her made him angrier, and he threatened every legal penalty he could think of, for her unlawful removal of property. This being her own clothing, by the way. She also ignored this and made for the stairs. She was acting calmly, but I think that she was shaking inside. He really was acting like a wild man.

'Suddenly he picked up his walking stick and tried to stop her by taking a swing at her as she went down the stairs. His stick got jammed in between the banister rails, but he clung to it when he should have rather let go. He tripped and took a tremendous tumble down almost the full flight of stairs, bouncing down them like a rag doll.'

'Tell me, what are these detectives interrogating my mom about, then? Do they think that the two of you pushed him down the stairs, or what?'

'Something like that. They're probably bored, with nothing better to do with themselves.'

'Is my dad dead, then? He looks awfully still.'

'Well, he's stopped ranting and raving, so I would guess so.'

Jason's lip twitched at this dry-as-dust remark. She was a character, this one.

He came to a decision. 'This nonsense has got to stop,' he declared. He moved in between his mother and the detective taking her statement, and he put a protective arm about Mathilda, who was looking very worn. 'Right, Detective Robson, this has gone far enough, and that applies to you as well, Detective Pearson.

'It took my friend, Ms Nugent here, about two paragraphs to explain how my father came to fall down the stairs. She, by the way, was a witness at the time. If you really think that my elderly mother pushed her equally unsteady husband down the stairs, then you should wait for your date in court.

'Now please leave us alone, and if I find any chewing gum on the carpets or furniture after you've left, Detective Robson, I'll bring it to your office and stick it right up your nose. Come on, Mom, let's get back to the apartment, if we can get these goons out of here so that we can lock up after them.'

He followed the gurney, with his father's corpse, out of the door, as it was wheeled to the waiting ambulance.

'This may be a shock to your system, Mom,' he comforted, 'but it could turn out to be a blessing in disguise. Dad was always a difficult man to deal with, but he has got worse over the past couple of years. I'd say that he was suffering from hardening of the arteries or something like that, ending up in a stroke. This was never going to get any easier, living with him.'

Mathilda was still in shock. 'Yes, I realise that, Jason, but I'm really grieving for the good years we could have had together.'

'Yes, Mom, I understand,' he comforted, giving her a hug.

Peggy looked on, pleased at what she saw. He was a kind-hearted, gentle man, in spite of his unfortunate history of female mishaps. Mathilda and others had confided tales of his romantic interludes to her, but he wasn't such a Romeo as what people imagined him to be.

If she wanted to build a future with this personable man, she would have to keep an eye on him, not so much because of any flirtatiousness on his part, but because of the magnetism that he emitted.

Maybe she could begin to better understand what her own mother had seen in him, and what she had wanted to pass on to Peggy. Her mother's deathbed matchmaking began to carry more weight, now that she was getting to know Jason better.

Chapter Thirty

Life was getting a little complicated for the Malvy family. Aunt Johanna was recuperating at a slower rate than expected, up in Canada. Her doctors felt that she would be better off in taking up her sister's offer to share the large house in San Diego with her, but she was still too weak to make the move right then. They said that she should wait a few months before making such a bold step.

Mathilda was also not yet ready to move back into her own home right then. There were too many ghosts rattling about the place for her liking, although she'd already been living with Jason and Peggy for a couple of months. At the same time, she had assumed a mother-daughter relationship with Peggy.

She'd always wanted a daughter, and now she had one. What was more, she couldn't have wished for a daughter who fitted better into her design of what a special daughter should be.

Out of the blue, she turned to Jason when they were alone one evening, while Peggy was visiting a friend. 'If you mess this one up, I'll be back to haunt you one day.'

Jason stared at her, wide-eyed. It was not her normal way of talking, at all. 'Don't worry, Mom. I also have a strong interest in the outcome of our relationship.'

'Well, until you two settle down to a steady courtship, I'm going to stick around, if you don't mind. You youngsters are too volatile, by far. One good argument and Peggy will go stalking off, and you'll be too stupid and proud to stop her going.'

'How can you say that?'

'Jason, you know that I'm one of the original strait-laced types, but your relationship with Peggy borders on the unnatural. You've been cooped up in this apartment for a couple of months together, and yet there's been not the slightest sign of hanky-panky. Don't get me wrong, but you two kiss "goodnight" and "good morning" and "hello" and "goodbye", yet there's never any sitting on the couch together, swapping saliva, when you think that I'm fast asleep.'

'But Mom, you know that I've been on a sort of trial, after being caught out with her mother.'

'Jason, that was two months ago. Feelings and consciences quieten down in good time. For goodness' sake, slip your hand under her skirt when she comes home tonight and see what her reaction is. Your father was too correct, by far. I was hardly sure where you came from, although I'm pleased that you did. We must have been tiddly at the time.

'Another thing: The funerals and inquest will take place in a couple of days' time. For all you know, dredging all the old and shocking stuff up in court will put further strain on your relationship. Be sure to make some progress before then.'

***

The first inquest concerning Tilly Markchester turned out to be a fiasco, after the long delay in having it. Tilly's family were a lot more approachable than her mother and stepfather. They'd never given up hope of finding her somewhere in the Middle East, wandering through the bazaars as a sex slave, owned by an eastern potentate.

Of course, it was clear what had become of Tilly, when her toe ring, her nose ring and her earrings were found in the gut of Samson, the orca. As some sort of goodwill gesture, both Jason and Danny were invited to the memorial service to be held at Tilly's aunt's house.

The two men could hardly turn down the invitation. Although Jason was bored out of his mind with answering questions about orcas, Danny had a tremendous time at the service. He spent the better part of the eulogy with his thigh pressed against Freda's — Tilly's sister — shapely leg.

She was a younger and prettier version of her elder sister, and she knew it. They couldn't wait to get out of the house and drive off in Jason's car, to a quiet spot in a heavily wooded copse.

They returned full of smiles and plans for the future.

***

279

The Nugent double inquest was a lot more involved than that. The press had been waiting for this one. Headlines covering the more sordid side of the case were spread across every newsstand, with plenty of photos to help the sales of newsprint.

Jason didn't want Peggy to attend the inquest because of all the gory details, particularly where he had been involved, but there was no way that he could keep her from attending the proceedings.

'Jason, I know that you were a bad boy and did some awful things with a woman old enough to be your mother, but that's all water under the bridge now. I've forgiven you months ago, although I must say that your dear mothers had a lot to do with helping me to see your good side.'

Mathilda saw it differently. 'Watch her, Jason. She's on a knife edge right now. She's learning to love you, but this business with her mother goes far deeper than messing about with an older woman. There's pride, respect, and disappointment in her beloved mother, as well as in you. If you can get through this inquest, let alone the murder trial that will naturally follow, you'll be able to claim her as yours. She will have gone through the fires of hell for you.'

Jason watched Peggy gradually fall to pieces during the first days of the inquest, until she walked out one day and disappeared. Jason went frantic with anxiety, out until late that night, hunting for her.

Finally, he got a call from a friendly bartender.

'I found your number on her cell phone, mate. She's out like a light, and I want to close up and go home. You'd better get here fast. She's offering herself to anybody who'll buy her a drink or whatever. I'll have to toss her onto the street in ten minutes. Then the wolves will really be scrapping over her. She looks filthy right now, but I reckon she's quite pretty when she's cleaned up a bit. Good luck to you.'

He found her crawling on her hands and knees across the grime-coated and urine-soaked sidewalk, with a boozer leaning over her, his hand between her legs. Infuriated, Jason slammed the hobo out of the way and held her head while she vomited up the stinking mash inside her shivering body.

Not wanting to touch her if he could help it, he towed the once-proud Peggy into the elevator when they got home. She fought him every inch of the way, with nails like rapiers, where they weren't chipped and broken. He was covered in scratches and blood flecks by the time that he got his sack of misery upstairs.

His mother couldn't quite believe that Peggy could be in that state, when they got her inside the apartment. She was usually so well turned out. But she held back her recriminations, and mother and son stripped the now completely limp young woman out of her stinking clothes and dumped her under the shower.

'What a way to see my sweetheart naked for the first time,' moaned Jason, as they brushed off layers of filth.

'Just you hope that it won't be for the last time,' replied his mother, wiping the latest round of vomit off Peggy's lips.

Jason wondered how to interpret this, but he was too busy with cleaning Peggy up to analyse his mother's remark, at that point.

When they'd done what they could for Peggy, they dragged her out of the shower and dried her off in a rough and ready way.

'Now don't bother about a nightie for her, Jason. Take her to your bed and keep her warm with your own body heat. It might do both of you some good, heaven knows. We'll see how she's progressed tomorrow morning, which is not too far away, I would say, looking at the sun coming up.'

At least he felt some emotion returning when he felt the heat building up between Peggy and himself. Sometimes his mother surprised him, but he was aware that the disgust he had felt earlier on had lessened to some degree.

The softness he was holding in his arms brought out his sensation of tenderness. It had been hiding under the battered surface of his feelings for her.

***

Peggy hardly seemed appreciative of all their efforts, the next morning. She was her normal morning sunshine self as she snarled and muttered and scratched her way through the breakfast that Mathilda had prepared. She didn't feel hungry, which wasn't surprising considering the muck she had brought up only a few hours before.

'I'm not taking her to court in her condition,' Jason told his mother. 'This is where I'm so thankful to have you around to help me out. Actually, to save my bacon.'

Mathilda smiled thinly. 'It's funny how seldom one's best efforts go unappreciated. Now take this young woman, for instance. She's going to give me a hell of a time all day, and tomorrow she'll lecture me on how I don't clean the stovetop properly. Meanwhile, her stovetop of a backside was the hardest of all to handle.'

Jason was panicking about getting to court on time, but he had to grin at that. 'Better lock yourself in and hide the key in a safe place,' he advised. We don't want her to go walkabout again.'

Mathilda was ultra-cautious and locked Peggy in her bedroom, as well as locking the apartment and putting the keys in a safe place.

'So, I'm a prisoner now,' Peggy whined.

'Why did you do it, girl?' the older woman enquired.

'Because I was ashamed of my mother and my father and Jason, and now myself, for sticking to a man who could have way-out sex with my mother and then run away when she needed him.'

'Come on, be reasonable. What else was he supposed to do? Spread his body over your mother and get shot as well? Would you do that? And how on earth would he have been able to stop the blood, which was internal anyway? Even the doctors and the nurses at the trauma unit couldn't save her life.

'I can tell you what your problem is: you want Jason to love you, but you think that you're letting your mother down. Meanwhile, she got the two of you to promise yourselves to each other, even as she lay dying. But now you want to spurn that final effort on her part, to wrap yourself in some imagined guilt.

'Jason helped me wash the crud off you last night. He said: "What a way to see my sweetheart naked for the first time." That nearly broke my heart. Then he took you in his arms and held your nude body against his for the rest of the night.

'You woke up safe and unmolested, unlike the rest of your time away from Jason. Then you began complaining about the way that your eggs were cooked. Get that monkey off your back, girl. You have a man who adores you, yet you treat him like dirt. That disgusts me.'

She got up and unlocked the door, before passing through and locking it behind her.

The young woman was stunned by Mathilda's words. Jason's mother had been especially kind to her since they had moved into the apartment, but now she had shot her down with a fistful of harsh words. Maybe she had been asking for them.

Peggy slept most of the day away, giving Mathilda the chance to also have some shuteye, which she badly needed.

When Jason came home, it was with good news. The inquest had produced a verdict of murder in the first degree, followed by suicide committed under conditions of stress. There was no recommendation from the bench for the prosecution to take the matter further.

***

They were in Jason's bedroom, and Peggy was wearing a pair of his pyjamas.

'You look far cuter wearing them than I do,' he observed.

'Well, I'll look even better if you let me get a nightie from next door. By the way, thank you for looking after me last night, both before and after you brought me home. And here's your mom now. Thank you, Mathilda, for looking after me like a daughter, even if I was in a disgusting state.'

Jason grinned. 'I've seen you looking better.'

'I'm glad you're both here. Mathilda, if I may call you Mom? I got a few words straight from the shoulder today, Jason, and somehow a weight has been lifted off my back, maybe also by my first dear mom.

'Jason, I've been feeling sorry for myself, but now I realize that what happened before I arrived on the scene was water under the bridge and really didn't have anything to do with me. So, I'd like to stay in your bed tonight, if I may, wearing a pretty nightie, or maybe none at all. I want to fulfil the promise I made to my mother, to you and also to myself.'

By now she was crying, but then so were Jason and Mathilda.

'I'm sorry about offering myself to Jason,' she said to Mathilda, 'but I can't wait any longer.'

'You made that vow months ago, to your mother and Jason. Better that than a crusty, old marriage officer who doesn't know you from a bar of soap, my dear. And you have the blessing of me, your second mother, as well. Welcome to my family, my sweetheart.'

***

Samson the Second swam alongside his mother, proud that he was the biggest calf in the pod. His mother had found a way, in their mysterious system of communication, to let him know how special he was. It must have been locked somewhere into his genes that he should harbour a fierce dislike for humankind.

That wasn't to say that he would plot the death of mankind in a planned or deliberate sort of way; it was just that there was a wariness — a guarded suspicion — regarding the doings of man. But enough of that now. He wanted to play with the other youngsters and to dominate them if he could.

After all, was he not the prince of the seas, son of the strongest and most daring of them all? Wait until he had developed to his full potential. Then he would show them what dominance was all about. He missed his father dearly, but he could feel the strength and vitality of his father, coursing through his veins. Yet he was patient. The world would duly find out about him at the right time.

THE END